# REMEON'S LEGACY

## REALMS OF CHAOS

## J.W. GARRETT

ISBN-13: 978-1-7335628-0-5 (Paperback edition)

ISBN-13: 978-1-7335628-1-2 (Ebook edition)

*Dedicated to my three little ones, who aren't so little anymore. You are the inspiration for all my stories.*

"It was the season of light, it was the season of darkness."
— Charles Dickens, <u>A Tale of Two Cities</u>

# INTRODUCTION

## BOOKS IN THE REALMS OF CHAOS SERIES

### Suggested Reading Order

Remeon's Quest: Earth Year 1930
Remeon's Destiny
Remeon's Crusade
Remeon's Legacy

### Realms of Chaos Timeline

#### 1929

Jack and Sam meet. Jack begins work in coal mine

#### 1930

February, *Remeon's Quest: Earth Year 1930* opens
Jack and Harry held captive on Remeon

1931

Jack returns to Earth after short return visit to Remeon to see
Whisterly and Arista

1931 - 1945

Jack and Harry work on Hoover Dam project
Jack and Harry serve in WWII

1947

March, *Remeon's Destiny* opens
Thomas captured. Visits Remeon for the first time
July, Thomas returns to Earth
July, *Remeon's Crusade* opens

1948

Jack and Thomas return to Remeon
*Remeon's Legacy* opens

1958

Epilogue

**Definitions for Realms of Chaos series:**

**Main Characters:**

Jack – Worked in the coal mines of Utah before being transported to Remeon in 1930. Husband of Whisterly

Harry – Jack's best friend, transported to Remeon with Jack in 1930

Sam – Jack's mentor on Earth; died in a mine collapse in 1930

Whisterly – Head of the council on Remeon. Jack's wife

Thomas (called Stephen on Remeon) – Lives on family farm in Virginia. Transported to Remeon in 1947; Belle's brother

Belle – Thomas's sister. Lives on family farm in Virginia

Arista – Daughter of Jack and Whisterly, first in line for Head of Council of the Day Watchers

Simon – Son of Jack and Whisterly. Second in line for leadership of the Night Dwellers

Daniel – Son of Jack

Vinique – Sister of Whisterly, second in line for Head of Council of the Day Watchers

Janus – Leader of Night Dwellers

Mila – Left the compound to become a Night Dweller, former maid of Whisterly's

Great Grandmother Arista – Witch and grandmother to Whisterly, great-grandmother to Arista and Simon

Damond – former Council member; was betrothed to Whisterly; killed by Jack and Whisterly

Remeonites – People of Remeon. Procreated using a laboratory due to the effects of the virus PR 251 on reproduction.

**Common terms:**

PR 251 – The virus that has been infecting Remeonites for generations – the cure derived from human testing is now being disseminated.

Universal translator – Device which allows all races to communicate on Remeon

Telepathy – All Remeonites (and humans who've been on the planet) can communicate via telepathy and can prevent others from accessing their personal thoughts with barriers they construct in their minds. Invasive telepathy is considered a crime on Remeon.

True Name – Holds controlling power on Remeon. With the knowledge of another's true name one can read all thoughts and compel another to act as the instigator wishes.

Coven – Gathering of witches, housed in magical basement in the Compound

Grimoire – Magical tome filled with spells and passed down through the generations

Magical basement in the compound – Where the coven and grimoire reside. Ceremonies as well as lessons in magic take place here.

# 1

*1948, Remeon*

*A* rising fear choked Whisterly's thoughts. All of their years together, spanning two planets, the two children they shared, the life they'd built together born of their love—all of it gone in an instant...

No.

Whisterly hovered on the precipice, strongly considering going back on her word to Jack. Screams of terror, a fire, a rock-slide, rampant death...all filled her senses. Why did she agree to wait to send in help? Her family's lives were at stake. If she reneged, Jack would never forgive her. There was that... He saw this opportunity as a chance to right a wrong done to their son years ago, when he'd been stolen away from them at birth, Whisterly not even awake yet to know of her twins. For Jack, this rescue of his children—Arista, head of the Day Watchers, and Simon, head of the Night Dwellers—represented a chance for a new beginning as a family.

No, Whisterly couldn't take Jack's dream from him, no matter how unrealistic it was. In fact, more than anything, she wanted it to come true.

No matter that all their lives were at risk, even the coven, even the Day Watchers—all in an effort to convert Simon from evil to good with a magical memory wipe. However, no guarantee that would happen either.

After attempting another telepathic link with Jack and Stephen, Whisterly growled out a sigh. Still nothing. She checked the time, willing her thoughts not to go to the depths of darkness again where she envisioned Jack's bloody, agonizing demise. Beating her rising dread into submission, Whisterly tuned back into Vinique and their developing plan of attack.

A sliver of Whisterly's tension eased.

Magic pulsed in her veins. The battle accelerated. Their troops in place.

The command given.

No more waiting.

THE NOISE ECHOED in Stephen's head—his own amplified heaving breath. He stole a quick glance at Arista, and her pained expression said it all. Aiming and firing two shots in quick succession, Stephen took out the two closest Night Dwellers still on Jack's tail. Crouched low, Stephen scuttled to Jack, relieved to confirm his bullet had hit its mark—Simon's arm. "Jack? God, I hope you can walk... Hang on. Damn it!" Stephen aimed, fired. Another Night Dweller dropped in a tangle of arms and legs to the dirt.

Jack twisted from under Simon's weight, wiping his face and eyes. "Thanks. How did you know Simon had gotten in my head?"

Stephen held Jack's gaze for three long beats. "Come on, Jack. We need to move. They're still coming. Put Simon between us." The two shouldered Simon's limp body and set off at a walk-run.

"You did know, right?" Jack asked again, through a cough, his eyes bleary with smoke.

"I had a strong suspicion," Stephen said, his gaze focused on their target, the jeep and Arista. "When I tried to communicate with you, your thoughts were a jumbled mess."

"Simon's skills are getting stronger. He's injured, unconscious, and still managed to reach into my thoughts."

"You don't have to tell me that. I know from firsthand experience that he's a dangerous son of a bitch." Stephen scoffed, his breath heaving. "I came this close to ending him, and I'll probably regret for the rest of my life that I didn't exploit this opportunity to the fullest extent."

Simon groaned as the trio approached the vehicle. Stephen adjusted Simon's weight, the sticky wetness of his blood clinging to Stephen's shoulder. Arista stood in the jeep, her arms beckoning them forward while she murmured a chant, her eyes shut tight. Behind them a rush of wind enveloped the Night Dwellers closest in pursuit, holding them at bay, as the men collapsed under the powerful gusts.

"That's it, love."

The two men hoisted Simon in the jeep and shoved him in the back, then clambered in behind him. "Stephen, you drive," Jack instructed. "I'll stay back here with Simon and watch for any Night Dwellers who might have made it through."

Arista broke her concentration, reaching for Stephen, then crushed her lips to his. "Thank you."

Stephen rested his forehead on hers, lingering a few seconds, catching his breath, before stomping in the clutch and turning the key. The vehicle coughed and spit smoke, mirroring how conflicted his insides felt. Arista leaned into her father's embrace, her tearful words evidently not lost on Jack, who choked on his response and settled next to Simon in the back for the bumpy ride.

A cool wind dried the sweat from Stephen's forehead, and as the jeep rumbled farther from the cave, away from the deep crevices torn into the earth, his unease loosened. Jack tended to Simon's bullet wound with a practiced efficiency honed no doubt by the number of times he'd patched up men on the battlefield. While Arista's escape hadn't been easy by any means, something felt...off. Stephen couldn't shake it. He tossed a glance to Jack. "Okay if I stop for a few minutes for water?"

Nodding his silent agreement, taking a glimpse at the road, Jack added, "Sounds good."

As they lurched to a stop, bursts of increasing gunfire sounded from the direction they'd come. A smile inched up Arista's face. "Our troops are fully engaged with the Night Dwellers."

"Good to know. Let's stretch our legs and tend to our wounds." Jack's gaze scanned the gashes and oozing burns littering Simon's body before coming to a rest on Stephen. "We're not staying long. No telling when Simon will wake, and I think we can agree it's best for all involved if he arrives still unconscious."

Stephen stepped into the back of the jeep, gathered Simon's collar with one hand and threw a punch, connecting with the left side of Simon's jaw, then released him with a *thud* and jumped to the ground. "I think we can keep him that way. Don't you, Jack?" A slow burning anger vibrated between the two men who paced the space like caged animals.

Arista maneuvered between them and joined Jack at the water's edge. Dipping a clean cloth from their supplies into the water, she circled her fingers until ice crystals formed, then set to work cleaning Jack's cuts. "Papa," Arista began, not meeting his eyes, "this is hard for us, having Simon so close, sensing his evil. If my brother could have his way, both Stephen and I would be dead. Don't be too hard on Stephen. He's struggling too."

Jack's hand cupped Arista's cheek, the pad of his thumb softly caressing the skin under her eye. "I'll do everything within my power to keep us all safe, little one." Arista extended her hand toward Stephen as she pressed her head against Jack's chest. When Stephen grasped her hand in his, she eyed them both. "Thank you for rescuing me, both of you." Arista brushed a kiss against Stephen's lips, then backed away, leaving the two in stoic silence.

Stephen stared over the water's smooth surface, its effortless calm mocking the tsunami raging inside of him. "With the exception of marrying your daughter, there's not much I want more than to kill Simon."

"I suggest you hang on to that first part. Let me handle the rest."

Stephen turned and narrowed his gaze on Jack. "You should be the one person on the entire planet who gets me. But I guess you've forgotten how you felt when Damond was alive." Stephen sensed the tension rise in Jack before it reflected in his stature and his face. Had Stephen gone too far mentioning the one nemesis of Jack's who'd nearly killed him, Whisterly, and their unborn children?

"You're wrong, Stephen. As long as I live, I'll never forget the ending we all almost had that day. And later, with decades stretched between me and my family, I endured longer still, reliving the pain with each passing day."

An icy exterior glossed across Jack's face and settled in his eyes, sending a numbing chill through Stephen. The next second the hardened killer in Jack glared back at Stephen. The one he'd almost connected with in the holographic bay, before Jack had reined in that part of himself. Seconds later it was gone, replaced once again by the man Stephen knew.

Jack laid a hand on Stephen's shoulder. "I pray you don't have to live with the same lessons that I took too long to learn." Jack released a heavy breath. "Let's go."

Stephen tucked Arista next to him, and they followed Jack to the jeep. Arista skidded to a stop, lifting her gaze skyward. Ahead, Jack paused, combing the area around him. "I feel it too, love," Stephen said. "What is it?" A restless eeriness hung in the air as the light and dark patterns altered, then bled together, slowly taking shape.

"Simon!" Arista screamed.

Jack reached his son first, but he wasn't awake. Instead, he twisted and writhed in convulsions that rattled his body. Jack slapped Simon as more spasms claimed him; Stephen grabbed his gun, aimed, and stood ready to fire.

"Wait. Let me connect with him first. If you attack Simon, you might be his next target," Arista warned.

As pockets of air drifted together, Arista scrutinized the strange entities. "These are wraiths, manifested from Simon's unconscious mind. The power within him is seeking a direction. Neither of you move. Wraiths can steal your soul." Arista's countenance shifted as she breathed deeply and closed her eyes.

Stephen and Jack swapped a wide-eyed glance, horror hollowing their cheeks.

*You've brought Whisterly in on this?* Stephen communicated telepathically to Jack.

*Yeah. Sit tight.*

The wispy figures continued to multiply, flying through the air, their whispered moans picking a path toward a spectral predestined duty.

∼

SIMON SHIFTED SLIGHTLY, aware of a sudden movement and a piercing ache in his arm, overriding the throbbing raw oozing burns covering his leg. But his eyes wouldn't open, and his lips wouldn't move. Instead, lost in a miasma of telepathic thought, Simon floated above the action happening, as if a bystander.

His mind sharpened though, with the absence of his conscious presence, somehow allowing him to focus inward, homing in on the acts perpetrated against the Night Dwellers. Jack and Simon's pet Stephen—aka Thomas, to those in possession of his true name—singlehandedly attacked the faction, claiming Simon's prize, Arista. Oh...his plans. His spirits lifted just revisiting them. They weren't gone, only delayed for a time.

Strong capable hands, sure and adept at their task, cleaned and dressed the bullet wound in his arm. Sucking in a breath, Simon gagged, his throat full of dirt and smoke. Hands grabbed him, twisting him on his side, and with another try, he breathed in the air his lungs needed. Jack. Had to be Jack. After all these years, his biological father was here.

To be clear, dear dad hadn't come to see Simon but to rescue his daughter, Arista, the council chair of the Day Watchers. Just a little longer and Simon's plan would have been fully implemented. For now his plans for his sister could wait, temporarily, until he freed himself from his current predicament.

His father, Jack... Simon sensed his presence. Jack was close, barring his mind from outside influence, and damn good at it too. During their prior telepathic conversation, the ironclad control Jack had wielded over his thoughts was impressive, especially for a human, though he did have Whisterly as his teacher.

Pain seized him, reminding Simon of his wounds, and with that, his lack of awareness as to their severity. Would his father and sister let him die? If the tables were reversed, Simon sure as hell would. Any tool at his disposal to eradicate the enemy worked...pure and simple.

Except, now that he'd met Jack, face-to-face, Simon had an unnatural desire to talk with him, not just telepathically but in person. Was that what it meant to have a father? Today they'd fought—a language Simon understood and thrived within. He craved the submission of others, like a drug. The power and control gained when triumphant in influencing another's will couldn't be overestimated. He and Jack were alike in this; Simon intuitively knew it to be true. They just went about gaining that influence differently.

A spark flickered in his head, died, then hummed to life again. As they rumbled along, the fire inside intensified, tugging at the mysterious parts of him that defied control. Reaching toward the guiding power that drew Simon like a magnet, he came up short. Denied, as before, to the knowledge-bearing portal of his birthright—the coven. Darkly clad in long flowing robes, the hooded members didn't acknowledge Simon's presence.

In a show of power, they had crossed their arms before them while murmured chants left their lips. Due to Simon's induction to the craft, he understood bits and pieces of their words, hushed on their breath. The spell was meant solely for him, against his wickedness, designed to shred his fledgling magic and rip apart his skin, if he attempted passage.

One came to the forefront, edging her way through the small gathering, as the rest cleared a path for the old hag. *You'll not pass.*

*We meet again.*

*Not yet, but soon—at the appointed time.*

Her black gaze pinned him still, and in the expectancy of the moment, a cackle rose in the old witch's throat as the coven lowered to their knees. Then, as one accord, a fiery ball of light cascaded toward him, pounding his rib cage where it landed.

His breathing ticked up, his heart thumping a rhythm that threatened to burst from his chest. Floating in the chaos of his mind, thrust again from the one place he should truly belong, Simon found his simmering rage had returned. Never far from the surface, the tangle of emotion and loss surged, seeking an outlet.

Why did the hurt magnify when the old women cast him from this place, affecting him almost as if his insides had been cleaved in half? Unlike the last time his thoughts drove him here, he didn't enter. The witches' guard-like presence hadn't been on full alert then. An odd sensation swirled in his gut, twisting, writhing, begging to be set free. Wrath and disgust warred within him, eating a way out. A streaming hiss passed his lips. Through his exhale, dark forms took shape.

Coalescing into hideous ghastly shapes, the beings drifted toward the Night Dwellers, summoned by the magic of their master. Once unearthed, the process unleashed, Simon had no idea how to end the onslaught. Years of pent-up grief poured into the creations that appeared to glide so easily from him now. Escaping from a long-held prison, the vented hate manifesting as wraiths continued their march toward the Day Watchers, where they fought Simon's forces.

A sudden giddiness overcame Simon with the cathartic release, a silent smile lingering on his lips. Sending his life force to complete his bidding transcended all the forms of control he'd used to date. The act left him thrumming, yet chilled in its wake. Free—he felt free.

*Baby? Can you sense what's happening here?*

*Jack, I'm grateful you and Arista are okay. We knew this wouldn't be easy.*

*So far we're holding our own. But you're right, we've had some close calls. Your troops were taking care of the last of the Night Dwellers until this latest development.*

*On some level Simon realizes he's being attacked, and the warlock in him is fighting back. Don't engage the beings.*

*We're not, but I can hear the screams of the men who are, even from here.*

*I'm going to help Vinique neutralize this new threat. Gods, Jack, we've got a long way to go with Simon.*

*We do. Don't you see, baby? It's like he's been a prisoner of war for all these years. He may not make it back to us, but I've got to try.*

*Correction, we...we've got to try. Now get yourself and ours back here safe, Mr. Livingston. Mrs. Livingston is waiting for you.*

*Count on it, baby.*

Whisterly shuddered a breath, shielding her thoughts from Jack. He was so content, stuck in his element. Not only that but he'd finally rescued their son. She could sense the elation coursing through him, along with several other emotions. Some of those feelings she shared—having her daughter and Stephen back here, for instance. But as she let her thoughts roam to Simon, all the helplessness came rushing back again, and she found herself right back in the place and time when she'd found out Simon had been taken from her.

By then Jack had returned to Earth, Whisterly had already discovered she'd been infected with PR 251—her lowest point in life, ever. Isolated, with her daughter for company, she'd soldiered on, but only by letting this one piece of her soul go. Simon... If she hadn't, Whisterly couldn't focus on her craft, on improving her skills, on leading the council, all the while, paving the way for Jack to return, one day.

These steps had allowed her to put one foot in front of the other, eventually meaning days, months, then years passed, but she never allowed herself to feel the loss of her son. This way she'd kept the soul-crushing anguish at bay. Now her carefully constructed wall threatened to cave in on her.

Would it have been better, healthier, even with her disease looming, to experience all that sadness right there with Jack as he'd raged from Earth? Maybe so. But she'd functioned the only way she knew how, working toward the day to bring Jack home to her, Arista, and Simon, biding their time until she and Jack were stronger, older, wiser.

Now that the time had come, could she connect with her son, when she'd effectively severed those bonds in order to function? A cool distancing had been her friend then and still might work to her advantage. Many distasteful decisions awaited her and Jack. Her heart thudded in her chest, jolting her fully back into the nightmare currently unfolding in the forest.

"Whisterly?" Vinique commanded her attention in a rush of breath. "What is your guidance on dealing with Simon's unexpected offense? I've revisited the grimoire, but as the acting council chair in Arista's absence, I want additional options."

The light gave way to the darkness as it loomed over the advancing Day Watchers army. Shadows formed, morphing into ghostlike creatures who floated through the forest, cloaked by the smoke and debris from the crumbling earth, until it was too late for their prey to see them coming.

As the first of Simon's creatures clashed with their men, fully engaged with the Night Dwellers, Whisterly experienced the loss. The soldier's mouth formed an O, his eyes frozen in place, while the wraith yawned wide, sucking the man's life force from him in a slow streaming hiss. Men collapsed, slumping lifeless to their death, their bodies a mass of bones and flesh, no longer connected to their world.

The troop of undead soldiers marched on, their wrath unleashed only on the Day Watchers. Screams hurled across battle lines, heard in between the stutter of gunfire and the clash of weapons, for brief horrible seconds before coming to a sudden halt. Simon might not realize exactly what he was doing...accomplishing with his unskilled magic, but his spells were improving and the impact on his enemy, deadly.

The maniacal cries of a Day Watcher soldier demanded her attention. His mouth hung wide and his eyes rounded in horror, an unseen cord connecting him to the wraith. A mist floated from the doomed man's lips, hovering an instant before the wraith swallowed the essence he'd beckoned. Still seized, the man crumpled, his crazed eyes focused on what he'd lost, his dying moan echoing in his mouth.

A chill swept through Whisterly as she worked quickly, verifying Arista had already created a shielding presence for Jack, Stephen, and herself. *Attagirl.* Her daughter was in full-on protection mode. Arista inherited many of her father's admirable traits—this was a prominent one.

More of the dark things ate at the life within the Day Watchers, bleeding their souls like leeches, while the soldiers struggled to comprehend in the seconds before their deaths what kind of force had them in their steely grasp. They weren't accustomed to defeat and had never been conquered by an army such as this.

Panic raced up her spine as Whisterly internalized the doomed men's fear, and one by one, they succumbed. Then feeling the unwavering resolve of Vinique wrenching her back from the edge and Jack's loving presence, Whisterly yanked herself free. The malevolence and ill intent had almost taken her under. She sucked in heavy cleansing breaths.

"Whisterly, are you with me?"

"Vinique, what would I do without you?"

"You won't ever have to. I sense the direction you're taking here. I pray to the gods it works. I'll focus on Simon. Shut him down while you work on that army of his."

"Killing a wraith is difficult at best, and we don't have that kind of time or energy."

"Putting them to sleep is brilliant, Whisterly."

"Let's just hope it works. Grandmother?"

*Here, dear. The power of the coven is linking with you...now.*

"Join in our consciousnesses, Vinique. Hurry."

"I'm here."

Buoyed by the presence of her sisters and infused by their power, Whisterly's murmured chants crossed her lips as her spell unleashed, twisting and writhing with the wind she'd commandeered. The words she spoke carried on the breeze, sliding through the ranks of the ghost army, easing their madness, sorrow, and pain, gently lulling them into a peace like they'd never known. Their anger, the main force driving the beings, dissipated, and the evil creatures rested—a concept truly foreign to the undead things.

*That's it, Whisterly, Vinique. You've led them so far from their aim, they are driving themselves toward your force.*

Relief spilled into Whisterly's thoughts. *Thank you, Grandmother, my coven sisters. We couldn't stave them off without your help.* Whisterly, Vinique, and Arista joined in the call as the gathered swept together in a celebratory chant, before descending again, their duty clear as they prepared the way for Simon's arrival.

Whisterly allowed Vinique's brief embrace. *Jack, let me hear you.*

*Right here. Thanks to you, Arista, Vinique, and I'm sure my extended family, your coven.*

*Thank the gods. And Simon?*

*No longer spewing forth the soulless apparitions. I gotta admit. I'm way outta my league here. Whatever is going on within our son appears to be getting stronger.*

*I agree. The forces driving him must feel the pull of his origin. He's closer to the grimoire now, where he's bound and from which his powers are born. Even expelling him from the tome won't change the*

*fact of that truth, once initiated. Remember the four of us are bound
there.*

*Oh, I haven't forgotten. Thank God you're on my side, baby. We
might be a little battered, but I've never been happier to say we're
coming home as ordered, Mrs. Livingston.*

As QUICKLY AS the glee-filled malice had hit Simon, it fell away.
*Arista...* He'd not soon forget her touch. Simon hadn't recovered
from his sister's skilled display of power earlier, when she'd
brought the cave and the Night Dwellers crumbling to their
knees. Her magic blanketed him.

Working him masterfully, she drew him in, then cinched
tight, the demons dying on Simon's breath. With a whispered
word she tangled his thoughts and froze the action coursing
through his brain. Left with no recourse, his body stunned to
complete inactivity, complied.

The whoops and cries of elated Day Watchers rang in
Simon's ears. So damn close...Pulling on cords of thought,
Simon attempted to contact his sergeants, willing any kind of
communication to eke past, but Arista's hold on him was
complete. All his directed thoughts—silenced—under Arista's
control.

GREAT-GRANDMOTHER ARISTA LET the sigh of relief come. Once
more they'd fended off Simon's anger-filled fury. His temper
and exasperation expressed in the form of crude magic endan-
gered all. The coven awaited her wishes. None of them were
unaffected by the brush with Simon's magic. Meant to be one of
their own and now rising against Simon instead, took a
powerful toll when his craft fell under the same umbrella as

Whisterly's and Arista's. Bonds created such as these weren't supposed to be broken intentionally. The action cut at the heart of the coven.

The old witch isolated herself, preparing for the tasks which lay ahead. Whisterly, Jack, Arista, and Simon would soon be here—physically here, together for the first time since the two children were in their mother's womb. The connection with her craft rippled through Grandmother Arista's borrowed body.

Stretching to her full height, she called forth the tome and immersed her essence in its wisdom. For only steeped in its knowledge would a way forward emerge for all. Carefully, delicately, pieces of Simon would fall away, washed clean like a blank slate. But later, the life-giving essence found within his magic would need to fill him anew. To do that, his ban from the grimoire would need to end.

# 2

_____

*J*ack slumped down on the creek bank, grateful for a few minutes alone to shake loose the cries clamoring for space in his head. They were never too far from him, and while he was getting better, the memories stilled gnawed at him, like a festering wound. Since serving in the Pacific Theater in World War II, he'd been a changed man in several significant ways.

Leading men into battle who'd then died while under his command carried with it a responsibility that he'd own for the rest of his life. Still others lived through the war but remained a prisoner, locked away in the depths of their minds, their own personal horrors too much to bear. Jack felt the loss of each one.

He recalled the painful blur of memory that he preferred to keep locked down tight. Corporal Henry Johnson died in Guadalcanal while on a mission to save Jack and his best friend, Harry. After being pulled from their prison, they'd both survived the ensuing battle that came next, but Henry did not. As the corporal lay in Jack's arms, his life slowly draining from him due to multiple gunshot wounds, Jack and Harry both pledged that Henry's son, Daniel, would have a home with them.

The boy had been a lifesaver for Jack. In fact, days came and went when Jack wasn't sure who was caring for whom in their relationship. The eight-year-old kept Jack alive and fighting during the endless stretch of days he'd been away from Whisterly and his family. And, at a time when Jack had been so lost in grief over the lack of a relationship with his son born of his own flesh and blood, Daniel had helped to fill that empty chasm. Gave Jack a place to pour that love, begging to be set free.

Typically the pair of them were inseparable. The boy's infectious laughter...his unconditional love, kept Jack putting one boot in front of the other during the days when he'd rather shrivel up on the floor and called it quits.

With bright little eyes shining up at Jack each morning, the boy convinced Jack had hung the moon, little by little Jack had found his place, secure in the love of the one who called him *Papa*. Hunting, fishing, shooting, playing ball, the activities they enjoyed together had no end. At times, their lives were a giant playground.

These more recent memories of Daniel had Jack glancing at his daughter, Arista, and his chest puffed up. His prayers had been answered when she'd accepted him back into her life, becoming the second person to call him *Papa*. His gaze lifted to the still-unconscious Simon, Jack's son by blood, Arista's twin. But the two couldn't be more different.

During their confrontation in the Night Dwellers' cave, Jack took an up-close look at Simon. Since finding out he'd left a son on Remeon, stolen at birth, Jack had tortured himself, playing out endless scenarios of their first meeting. Even knowing the deep hatred Simon harbored for Jack, when their eyes met for the first time, the revulsion he'd glimpsed there sliced him to the core.

Evil had seeped from the pools of Simon's heated gaze, centered on Jack, just before he'd beaten Simon senseless, in an effort to take him with the least resistance. Jack sure as hell hoped their plan worked. Breaking down the barriers Simon had built around him seemed unlikely, unless helped along by magic. Truthfully Jack wanted to hammer through Simon's walls on his own, by showing the kid what the power of love could do. Jack was living proof of that technique.

"Papa?"

"Arista, you were incredible."

Arista wrapped her arms around Jack's waist. "Thanks. Just doing my job."

"You saved us all."

"Not just me. My mother and Vinique were right here too."

"True," he admitted, returning his attention to the calm of the water before them, "but I'm still damn proud of you."

"What is it? Anything wrong? Thought you were ready to go."

"I did too." Jack gave her a quick smile. "But I need to do something here first. Once we're back at the compound, I may not get another chance."

"What is it?"

"Something I did for you when you were a tiny baby."

Jack grabbed his canteen, refilled it with water, then carried it with him to the back of the jeep. Knelling by Simon's side, Jack bowed his head.

"Stephen? What's he doing?" Arista prodded.

Stephen grabbed Arista's hand and walked toward the vehicle. "Looks like he's praying."

"Ah. To his god? The same one you believe in?"

"Yes, love. I do."

"But—"

Stephen raised a finger to his lips and bowed his head, giving Arista's hand a squeeze.

*Is this supposed to help Simon in some way? Because we don't want him awake. Not now*, Arista continued telepathically.

*I think it could. I hope you don't take offense. I've seen you do some incredible stuff, but in my opinion, this is the only power stronger than your witchcraft.*

*Hmm. Think so?*

Stephen shrugged as the edges of his mouth ticked up.

*But—*

Stephen kissed her temple. *I can't pray with you talking in my head.*

*Oh...sorry.*

Jack poured a liberal amount of water into his fingers, and while they were still dripping, squeezed his forefinger and middle fingers together, then made the sign of the cross on Simon's forehead. "I baptize you in the name of the Father, the Son, and the Holy Spirit."

Stephen mimicked Jack's action, making the sign of the cross on his chest, then kissed his fingers while Jack prayed the Lord's Prayer.

When he finished, Jack lifted his chin and pulled a chain with stamped silver tags from around his neck. In a tender gesture, a reversal from the aggression, fighting, and death of the last hours, he slid his own dog tags around Simon's neck. Then Jack leaned down and kissed Simon's forehead.

*Your god can fix all this?*

*Amen, love.*

Jack exhaled a long sigh and jumped from the jeep. "Thanks, Stephen."

He nodded. "I still wanna kill him. So I added some prayers of my own."

"Can I talk now?" Arista asked.

Stephen smirked. "Of course."

"Tell me, Papa, about when you did that to me."

His daughter's eyes lit up her face. "I'd love to, after we get moving." A new peace worked its way into Jack's heart. A release. His son had a fighting chance, and that's all anyone could hope for, here or on Earth. As the jeep rumbled along, and Stephen shifted into third gear, the voice of Sam, Jack's mentor and father figure, dead now, whispered on the wind.

*Well done, son.*

*God, I miss you, Sam, each and every day.* Jack shook his head to gain back his focus. "Arista, you were about six weeks old, I think, when I came back from Earth to visit you and your mom."

"You stayed at the cabin by the waterfall?"

"We did. And as days go, it was almost complete perfection. You and I walked along the fall's edge together. I talked." He huffed a laugh. "Presumably you listened, or maybe you just fell asleep on my shoulder. But I remember thinking that I'd never been more in love than right at that second, with both of you." Jack's voice cracked, and he cleared his throat. "I was wrong."

Arista homed in on Jack, her blue eyes fiery when they met with his gaze. "When were you more in love than that?"

"Two times actually... When I returned to Remeon, connected with you again, and you called me *Papa* for the first time, and after your mother found her way back to us."

Arista threw her arms around Jack's neck. "Will you tell me now about my baptism?"

"Sure. It was the middle of the night. You were screaming at the top of your lungs. Your mom was exhausted." A smile slid to Jack's face, remembering why Whisterly was so tired. "So I picked you up, hoping to rock you back to sleep. After a few minutes you quieted in my arms while we swayed back forth. When you stared at me, studying me, like you could see right through me, I knew what I needed to do."

Stephen, listening this whole time, brought Arista's hand to his lips, kissed it.

"And that's when you baptized me?"

Jack bobbed his head. "That's right. Yes, and your mother too."

AFTER HER TELEPATHIC communication with Vinique, Arista braced herself for chaos upon her return. Their small band of fighters fit right in with the walking wounded returning to the compound, victorious over the Night Dwellers, although the mood wasn't jovial. As the men filed inside, snippets of their thoughts reached her from behind their vacant stares. Horror relived secondhand was no less terrifying. Chills invaded her body, experiencing the wraiths soul-sucking onslaught this time through personal eyewitness accounts while the attacks occupied the men's minds.

Arista added another barrier, sequestering outside thoughts from hers. Stunned to silence, they all remained seated, a small island of stillness in the sea of pandemonium around them. Arista nodded affirmation to her father's unspoken thought, then proceeded to file away the scenes from today to be dealt with later.

Mother dipped into her thoughts. *Arista, I'll meet you in a while. I'll leave Simon's transport to you. Likely, with all the turmoil, no one will notice the four of you, but proceed under cover of magic before descending to the basement.*

*Agreed.* Her gaze spanned the reaches of the compound. *We must take good care of our citizens who've fought hard to overcome the Night Dwellers and Simon's creations.*

Vinique reached for Arista and hugged her tight, whispering, "Above all else, grateful for your return to us. Any other loss is acceptable."

"Thank you, Vinique, but don't ever forget. You're in this for the long haul with me. I don't plan on ruling the council without you by my side."

A smile crinkled her eyes. "Where else would I be?" Vinique turned and immersed herself in the triage operations.

"Right behind you, Arista, with Simon stretchered between us," Jack called over the din.

*Follow me. I'll cloak us when we get closer.*

Arista smiled to those who recognized her and cleared a path through the crowded halls, relaying calming thoughts to those gathered. The crowds thinned as Arista homed in on their destination. Sinking her teeth into her lip, Arista cast the cloaking spell upon their approach to the hidden door and the passageway below. Luck had been on their side so far, but no telling how much longer it'd last. Her grip on Simon's consciousness slipped as his cognition normalized to her outside influence. More force would be necessary as he adapted to her mind control, unwittingly seeking paths to freedom.

Next steps loomed in her mind while she mindlessly unlocked the ancient door, and the four eased past and disappeared down the steps. The door groaned closed, the noise settling to Arista, in her element now, her mind working ahead to various scenarios playing out in her head. When the last of the cobblestone path disappeared underneath her feet, Arista darted toward the opening to her sanctuary, then scooted inside.

"Little one, I've been tracking your progress." Whisterly squeezed her hand, then pulled her in for a hug. "Thank the gods you're all here safe. Simon?"

"Right behind me."

Jack and Stephen maneuvered Simon inside and carried him to the same slab of rock Whisterly had occupied not too long ago.

"Jack!" Whisterly cried out and hugged her husband tightly to her.

"Great-grandmother," Arista spoke to the others gathered with them too, "we wouldn't be here right now without the help of you and our coven."

"Anything to get you back where you belong, Arista. Simon's malignant intentions were clear. Now we'll implement more permanent plans for his containment. You should never be at risk like that again."

Arista gave her attention to her parents, locked in an embrace beside their son, swaying slowly together, as murmured words passed between them. Stephen slipped an arm around Arista's waist. "I'm all for getting this wacko under control, but should I go or stay?"

"Stay, if you don't mind," the old witch encouraged. "We all might need your strength before this is over, especially the one who's been waiting for you down here for several hours now."

Stephen's brows arched upward, just before Belle plowed into him. "Of course, anything for you, little bit." He laughed, tousling Belle's curls.

A burst of pain shot through Arista's head as she maintained her magical hold on Simon, adjusting to keep up with his defenses. She locked gazes with her great-grandmother, struggling with deep breaths.

"It's all right, dear. Ease up a bit. We've got him secured here. Plus Whisterly and Jack need a few minutes to speak with their son—to hear the *real* Simon."

"Very well." Arista unleashed a sigh, taking a position in between her parents.

Simon growled a moan, contorting his mouth to match the inner workings of his heart, Arista imagined, watching her brother gather his wits about him. As Simon's eyes fluttered, she willed for Papa's true love to overtake the bitterness in her brother's heart, so they all might begin again. But she feared even the unfailing love Papa had for his family couldn't break through the evil she had encountered with her brother in the Night Dwellers' cave.

Simon blinked, momentary confusion stealing across his face. Arista's heart reached for his as Simon's features played with her head, lessening her fears because he favored his father.

Simon coughed and sputtered, then scanned his surroundings. "Well, Jack, seems you kept your word. Here I am." A maniacal grin eased up his lips. "I did want to work my way back here though, to the place I've visited so often in my dreams. So I'm not sure how this little side trip works in your favor."

"Soon you'll see," the old witch replied.

"Ah. I remember that voice too." Simon twisted and grunted at the invisible bonds that bound him to the rock formation underneath him.

"Just sit still. You can't get free at the moment," Jack explained.

"What do you want with me, Jack? I've already made it clear I want no contact with you. You broke up an important session with Arista, one that I went to great lengths to arrange."

"You'll be tried for kidnapping," Whisterly began, "or we could arrange alternate forms of punishment."

Simon burst out a laugh. "You think you can hold me? Even right now, stuck on this table, I can feel power flowing through my veins. Anytime now I'll break free and bust outta here."

"There's nothing left to return to, Simon, other than ruins and bodies."

"My future. I've still got that. In fact, your little interruption only postponed my plans. Didn't change them."

Arista strolled closer to her brother, locked eyes with him, then slid her gaze to the numerous wounds covering his body. Gathering her resolve, she snapped her fingers and arced the growing flame toward the angry burn covering one-third of her brother's leg. "I think it's time you shared those plans." Flicking her wrist closer, Arista allowed the flame to graze his newly formed blisters. At the same time, she plunged into his brain, not with the stabilizing control of before but with a localized shot of power.

Beads of sweat formed on Simon's forehead, and he gritted his teeth against the pain.

"Not quite the same fun and games when you're the one on the table, huh, brother?"

A sarcastic laugh left his throat. "I guess that's so. But I'll have my way soon enough. I always do."

Arista sensed her brother's thoughts brushing hers. Edging her fire along his raw skin, she burned a new path, his unbridled scream letting her know just how much the pain had hit home. "Now, what were those interrupted plans?"

"An heir," he panted, lost in his own agony.

"What? How?"

"You know how... Your egg, my contribution... A lab... Months later I have the pure offspring I need."

Arista's mouth gaped open.

"I know... Brilliant, right? The child would be a medical marvel. A powerful magical Remeonite with unimaginable capabilities, pure of blood, never to be tainted with PR 251. Perfection personified."

Arista didn't see Stephen until, from a full-on launch through the air, he landed on Simon, pelting his face with back-to-back punches, blood spewing from her brother's nose. Simon's eyes rolled back in his head; Jack pulled Stephen free. His gaze bounced from Simon back to his own bloodied hands, horror and yet hate consuming Stephen's face. "Jack," Stephen huffed out, exertion still working his chest, "there's never gonna be a day when I don't want him dead."

"I know, son. I know." Jack wrenched Stephen closer, until they fell into a hug.

Arista guided Stephen to the edge of the cave. Jack looked on while Arista whispered softly in Stephen's ear as she walked, reaching out to Belle to include her in Stephen's care.

WHISTERLY LEANED INTO JACK. "We're doing the right thing."

"They're good together," Jack said gruffly. Tears rimmed Jack's eyes. He blinked, trying to keep them at bay. All the people he loved in this room were hurting in one way or another.

Studying Jack, Whisterly could see the tension he held in his shoulders from the horror of the day, Arista's abduction, the encounter with the wraith army, the internal war with his own feelings for his son that Jack fought on an ongoing basis. "They are good together. She's strong and in love with Stephen, despite what she's been through."

"I can see that. A brother intending this type of harm to his sister is hard to stomach, especially from my son."

Whisterly nodded. "It's disgusting, but Arista has inherited your steel armor and a tiny bit of my tenaciousness. So she'll fight her way through this with support from those who love her."

A ghost of a grin fell to Jack's lips. "A tiny bit?"

"That's what I said."

"Thank God she did." Jack glanced away and squeezed Whisterly's hand.

"You can't really hide your feelings from me."

"I'm fully cognizant of that fact, baby."

"So tell me..."

"I baptized Simon today and spoke with Arista about the night I baptized her and you."

"I see. And you thought he might wake, and your God would have fixed our son?"

"No, not exactly. I'm not sure it works like that. The Spirit can work through him, but Simon will have to accept it on his own."

"*Hmm.*"

"I'm convinced, now more than ever, that our only chance is a clean slate."

"I love that part of you that you shared with me... Your faith in the unseen. It's so uniquely...human, although I think it's rubbing off on me too. I mean, look where we are because of our faith in our love. I could never have gotten here on my own."

"I'm happy to hear that, Mrs. Livingston. You and my faith are all I'm certain of." Jack pressed his lips against hers, reminding Whisterly with a kiss. With a nibble to her lower lip, he pulled away, cupping her cheek. "This is gonna be a long road."

"When have we ever had anything else?" Whisterly felt a nudge of her thoughts. She tossed a glance to her son. "He's coming around."

"He took a pretty good beating."

"You two are gross," Simon sputtered, coughing blood. "And *he* can hear everything you're saying."

"Glad you're back with us," Whisterly said drily.

His scowl twisted into a smirk. "Are you? Jack, why don't you just screw her out of your system and head on back to Earth? Nobody needs you here, especially not me."

Whisterly seized Jack's thoughts, urging him not to react. She watched while the veins in his neck pulsed and his jaw tightened, followed by his anger flowing back through her own head. For better or worse their telepathy worked this way— each hearing the other's thoughts as well as sensing the emotion behind them. Personally, Whisterly considered their connectivity a gift and treasured every moment.

"Big changes ahead for you, Simon," Jack announced, his tone even and strong. "As I told you before when we communicated, we can't undo the past, but we can affect the future. You need guidance for those powers inside you that you don't understand. The compound has resources to help you."

Simon arched a brow. "You haven't seen a recent display of my power. I'm handling damn well on my own. That applies to the past and especially to my future. I don't need you... I don't want you, either of you."

"Simon, you can't demonstrate anything down here. The coven has your abilities completely under their control." Whisterly sensed Simon pull at his essence, once, twice...

Gritting his teeth, he gasped. "Bitch."

Jack's fingers curled into fists, punctuating the anger he couldn't vent.

Whisterly gave an imperceptible shake of her head and laid a steadying hand on Jack's arm. "I never had the chance to see you when you were born, Simon, apart from the visions I had later, after I realized you'd been taken from us. Janus's and Damond's evil plans hurt a whole generation of people."

"You had more resources than anyone. You could have come for me," Simon hissed.

"I don't expect you to understand. But I did want you to hear from me, even though I was sick with PR 251, raising a child on my own, devastated from the loss of my parents and Jack, I mourned for you and believed that one day we'd be reconciled."

An angry silence filled the air before Simon broke in. "Save your sob story. That day will never come. Not while I'm alive anyway. Soon I'll take what's rightfully mine and expose you for the fraud you are."

"Not while I'm alive," Arista chimed in, moving across the floor toward Whisterly. "I'll fight you every step of the way."

"And I will as well." Whisterly dipped her chin to her grandmother. "There is no scenario under which you gain control."

The old witch aligned with Whisterly and Jack, lifting her head, acknowledging the movement above.

The coven began their quiet descent, and Simon's eyes widened, focused on the hooded beings' eerie glide, the silent swing of their garments, their putrid ruined flesh as they stole a passing glance at him, mustiness filtering through the room in their wake. The witches filled in the space around Simon.

Straining and pulling at invisible ties, he struggled to yank himself free.

"Not quite as fun when the tables are turned, brother?"

"Enjoy this while you can. You can't begin to imagine my plans for you. All of you. Things you don't have the stomach for. Things you'd never dream of."

"I think you're underestimating the strength, control, and magical ability right in front of you." Whisterly flicked her wrist, and Simon squirmed, mumbling curses.

His breath rasped, gurgling in his throat, and his muscles flexed with the effort to get free.

Jack leaned in whispering, "What's he seeing?"

"Nothing I would ever speak of out loud. Atrocities. Some of which you've probably experienced."

Jack's gaze zipped from Whisterly back to his son. "How long will you keep this up?"

"Not much longer now. Until I feel his surrender. In that state he'll be more amenable to our next steps."

Jack swallowed hard.

"Without breaking him this way, the warlock within him will be difficult to control. Do you need to leave, Jack?"

"No." Wiping sweat from his forehead, Jack planted his feet

and arranged his face to a stoic facade. "Just don't let this go too far."

A small tug parted a path through the gathered. Shorter than the rest, she was hard to spot. Whisterly tilted her head, trying to get a reading on Belle. Though she was effortless to penetrate, her thoughts weren't clear. Clumps of wet dirt and rock oozed through her fingers, and when Belle reached the slab where Simon was bound, she squished her hands together, making a sticky paste.

"Simon," she murmured low.

His maddened glare turned toward her, unfocused and wild.

Closing her eyes, Belle laid her hands on Simon's arm, then blew on the poultice.

The tension in Simon's face eased, and his breathing calmed.

"Not much longer, Vinique will be here soon," Belle told Simon. "Then we'll begin. This will help make those images in your head easier to bear."

Simon cocked his head, and Belle grimaced back. "Yes, I can see them too."

**3**

---

*V*inique rocked her foot back and forth, her legs crossed, not fully tuned in to the voice of the man beside her—the warlock beside her. The longer she sat idle, the more the to-do list mounted in her head. But the process gave her something to do. Kept her productive while she gave Kix the time he'd asked for. After all, he didn't have her full attention anyway—a win-win from her perspective.

"I understand you're distracted," Kix droned on. "We're waging war, for the gods' sake, but you did seek me out to start working through these terms. However, I have the distinct impression you're not here with me at all. Maybe engaged in more worthwhile telepathic communication, *hmm*?"

*Right on target...* "Rest assured I'm listening and also capable, by the way, of multitasking. As you know, I'm the acting council chair with Arista still away."

"Of course I, as a council member, realize that your load is heavy at present. Thank the gods Arista is safe, back in the compound, and those wretched Night Dwellers did no long-term damage to our council chair."

Vinique cleared her throat, giving the rage inside her time to settle, so she wouldn't spew it out, ruining the work she'd already done so far with the creature in front of her. "She's not been debriefed. The extent of her injuries, physical and mental, haven't been formally evaluated yet. But we'll know soon, and I'll update the council at that time. Probably by then we'll have an idea of the length of her extended absence as well."

Kix shot Vinique a piercing glare. "Maybe the balance of this discussion should wait until your plate clears a little."

The tendril of power he threw her way was meant to be subtle, no doubt, to ease its way into her thoughts, almost subconsciously, so his will would meld into hers, becoming one. Clearly he had no idea as to the depth of Vinique's training. Whisterly's and Vinique's ongoing exercises with the coven kept Vinique's skills honed and razor-sharp. Suppressing the laughter working up her throat, she continued. "No, Arista let me know these discussions were a priority. I'll follow her lead."

"I wouldn't want you to concede to anything rashly or to have any regret as to what was agreed upon."

"Kix," Vinique raised her brows in mock surprise, "have you ever known me to be rash in my decision-making?"

"No, *dear*, but we are discussing matters of the heart. Anything could happen, right?"

"Let me be frank."

He chuckled. "But we're having such fun."

"That's debatable. Your first choice in this blackmail attempt of yours was Arista. I've offered myself as a substitute, since there is no scenario in which the two of you will be mated."

"I take issue with your offensive word choice. This is, after all, a mutually beneficial arrangement, but continue."

"Your motives are clear."

"As are yours. See to it that I have cochair leadership, and we'll remain evenly matched, balancing out each other, while seeing to the needs of the council and the great people of Remeon."

"We will strictly hold you to the terms of our agreement. In exchange for our mating, you will agree to training sessions with Simon when arranged, and you'll release no more data from Remeon in any format to your contacts on Earth. Earth's development will proceed as it should, when their knowledge and know-how are in sync—not when pressed forward by an outside magical entity, skewing the forces of power in the universe. You'll need to find another avenue to assure your family's safety on Earth."

Kix nodded, paused, tilted his head, and nodded again, as if considering and giving his mutual assent, while Vinique spoke. "I'd like one additional consideration. After all, I'll be abandoning my family on Earth. The forces I've been allying with can no longer assure their safety, without the compensation I've been relaying."

"You're resourceful and a warlock. Surely you can come up with something."

"Well, yes"—a cocky grin slid to his lips—"but not along the same vein as you've suggested. You see, it's all about family, really, and a future."

"Spit it out then."

"Let me explain first." He sucked in a deep breath. His heartbeat increased, and his eyes shifted side to side. Kix started to speak, then stopped himself. Twice.

Vinique avoided the urge to delve into his brain and grab the words hanging on the edge of his tongue, floundering, waiting to be set free, but the man hadn't the nerve to turn loose. What was it that he wanted to sweeten this deal that had already taken the highest toll of all—her freedom? For a time anyway.

The look that crossed his face hid an emotion she couldn't reconcile.

"I'd planned to go to Earth one day and live with the band of warlocks and witches who I've supported and protected all these years. That dream dies a sure death with this deal we're making. Yet family is important to me, always has been. I've been committed to my Earthly relatives because of my long-term goals and the fact that I was helping the people there reach for so much more."

"Your point, Kix? The council will not take responsibility for your family's care, if that's the direction you're going with this."

"No, it's not. Not exactly. I do want to provide for a family however." Kix hesitated, as if waiting for the weight of his words to provide a warning for what was to come next. "Agree to procreate with me—through a laboratory, if you wish—so that I may have the opportunity, here on Remeon, to have my own family. One where the resulting child will undoubtedly possess the gifts of magic from both mother and father, skilled in the arts as we both are."

A shudder skittered up her spine, and she fought to push down her gag reflex. Someday Vinique wanted the kind of love Whisterly and Jack enjoyed. Privy to their love story and Arista's and Stephen's as well, their journeys, rough though they were, appeared well worth their ups and downs along the way. Both couples had found their soul mates, from across the galaxy no less. Vinique wanted a true love like that too—but most decidedly not with Kix, even the old-fashioned Remeon way.

The wild barbaric form of mating the people of Earth practiced was real and full of the love she wanted to experience with another one day. And now that a disease no longer kept their race confined to test tube babies, Vinique wanted the love of a man who desired her as a woman, not only for her magical prowess. "A child? I've given no thought to having a child," she stalled, her mind a whirlwind of speculation regarding her own little one who could brighten her life one day.

"No time like the present, and your acquiescence would close this deal. And we all want that, right?"

"I promise I will give your request the careful consideration it deserves."

"As long as you come back with a yes, then we're good. Otherwise, all bets are off. Keep in mind I've already made concessions. As you mentioned, Arista was my initial request, and I've agreed to settle for you instead. So it's your turn to give in return. Think of the potential of a child with the combined essence of you and me."

Vinique stood, slowly straightening, attempting to quell the anger that pulsed through her veins, before she reduced the warlock in front of her to a pile of smoking ash. "As I said, I'll take it under consideration. Remember. We need your contact included in this documentation, whoever you've been funneling information to on Earth, in order for these negotiations to culminate into a deal. Now I'm needed elsewhere, so if you'll excuse me?"

Kix flashed a smile. "I look forward to a long and happy partnership, like Remeonites have had for centuries. Our combined leadership will blaze a path into the future and provide for the next generation."

*Over my dead body.*

Simon gagged, his senses on overload from the smell of rotting flesh suffocating him, taking him right back to Janus's last days. PR 251 hadn't offered a graceful or kind death to his adoptive father. He'd died an oozing, stench-ridden, body-wasting painful demise, and Simon had witnessed each step as the man had fallen deeper into the clutches of the disease.

Not that Simon had minded finally being rid of the man who'd arranged Simon's abduction at birth. Janus's time was done—Simon was at the helm now. Of whatever remained of the Night Dwellers.

Under Janus's tutelage, Simon had gained a firsthand look at the inner workings of people...learned what made them tick. Once one ascertained that knowledge, well...controlling the individual became a simple matter. Subjugating another, bending them to his will, was like a drug. He needed the thrill it gave him as surely as food and water. Soon Whisterly, Jack, and especially Arista, would understand just how much Simon excelled at this particular skill. But first he had to get Janus, the dead Night Dwellers' leader, out of his head. Then Simon needed to get free from this place.

Belle's touch cooled his skin, at once easing the burning sensations along his leg and dimming Whisterly's horror show playing out in his head. Until now he hadn't given Stephen's little sister much thought, other than the fact that she was irritatingly talented for being in the right spot at the right time to assist those she loved.

From her single touch Simon verified that list included everyone in the room, coven witches aside, except for him. So why did she alleviate his pain, and what were these abilities of hers? He couldn't place the source or get a solid reading on her —something crucial when controlling the essence of another.

With the lessening of his pain, Simon's vision cleared, allowing his full attention to fall on Belle. His eyes narrowed. "Why are you helping me? Look around you. Nobody here gives a shit about me. Why do you?"

Her grimace gave way to a small smile, its effects doing something odd and uncomfortable to Simon's insides. What was that lurking behind her eyes? And why did he care? Belle did as he asked, doing a little turn as she took in the stares of her friends and family. "I felt your same pain, here and here," she said, gesturing to her head and heart. "I knew I could help, so I did. It doesn't change that you're sick inside or what we have to do now."

Simon's mouth twitched as he snarled out his next words. "I don't care about your opinions, disgusting little human, just how you did what you did."

"Your pain drew me to you. About the rest, I don't know, other than I have a connection with the power that lives inside the ground, binding all of us. It works through me somehow."

A sneer inched its way across his face. "You could be useful, indeed. Are you even human?"

"I'm—"

"Belle dear, you are quite the kind soul. I'm sorry those visions appeared to you," Whisterly interrupted.

Belle shrugged. "It happens a lot. I feel the pain of others. I think it's because I can help them. So when I can, I do."

Whisterly ran her fingertips over Belle's forehead. "There. That should take those images from you."

"Thank you, Miss Whisterly, but I'm used to the negative thoughts and feelings of others. Making them go away, when I can, makes me feel useful."

Simon sniffed at the drying mud on his arm.

"You'll find it's only dirt and rock you smell. Her ability can't be replicated, not by you anyway," Arista clarified.

"*Hmmph.*" Simon grunted. "We'll see about that." Simon extended his thoughts into Belle's. If he could get at her, harness the aptitude that worked through her, learn it, then maybe he could use it for his own advantage. If her ability could ease pain, could it also intensify the feeling? Just imagining the ways this skill could add to his arsenal almost made him forget his captive status.

Belle whipped her head around. "I may be a kid, but that

doesn't mean you can play in my head." Her kind little face scrunched into a scowl, and with her decided thrust, Simon was once again on the outside looking in.

The encounter reminded him of his brief glimpse into Arista's quarters not long ago. Belle had made quick work of him then too. That night he'd been exploring his newly gained powers—his mind had accessed the magical book and led him back here. Through some odd combination of telepathy, will, and his newly attained magical ability, he'd gotten to Stephen and Belle, almost as if his wish had made it so.

For a short time Simon had reasoned the strange circumstance could have been brought about by his knowledge of the siblings' true names. After all, having this information did grant him the ability to gain any truth within one's brain matter. But Belle had pushed him away. Clearly this child was no ordinary human.

That night Belle had joined Simon, on a level equal to his own. The fact didn't mesh in his head. She wasn't a witch. An awareness surrounded an individual, their aura, as with Whisterly and Arista and the coven that hovered close by. They were the same as Simon. But not Belle. Her aura was decidedly different.

Closing his eyes, Simon sensed Belle's nearness. The light that clung to her shone with a brilliance that made Simon wince, even with his eyes closed. His vision altered to include Whisterly and Arista, their auras similar, strong, with a signature he now identified as magical and intuitively...family. He swallowed down the lump in his throat, knowing that his aura would reveal his familial bond with the two women.

Lastly he sought Jack and Stephen. The two, unlike the other three, entirely human, but with auras which burned hot with strength—and something else... Love. The love they felt for another came first in their lives, and it showed here in the force that defined their being.

The field before him collapsed, then reformed behind his closed eyelids. The man he'd seen before in a vision, the man so like Simon that he'd sought in the midst of his magical foray almost consuming Simon in the process, whispered across the murky mass. Simon already knew it in his heart, the confirmation ringing true now. *You're a warlock, Simon, born the son of Jack and Whisterly.*

*Who are you?*

*Kix. Another uniquely of your kind. A warlock.*

The images fell away again, only to be invaded by the old hag in the room with him.

*Are you quite done, Simon?* She laid a hand on Simon's shoulder, and the cold hard surface of the rock underneath him made itself known with a jolt. *I'd say that little escapade means you're ready to proceed.*

Simon blinked, opening his eyes to the abrupt ending of his exploration and another woman joining with the others. Vinique. Instantly he distinguished her aura and identified her as associated with Whisterly.

*Excellent. We'll begin now. Vinique, take your place,* Arista announced.

Clad now in the same black robes of the coven, Whisterly, Arista, and Vinique blended in with the shadowy figures, Arista alongside the hag. The congregated now joined hands and levitated into the air.

"What will you do to me?" Simon asked no one in particular, his gaze seeking Jack's.

*I'll be here, waiting for you, son. You'll have a fighting chance. The rest is up to you,* Jack communicated.

Simon's heart thundered as individual tongues of illumination lit the hands of the witches, adding a chilling glow to the darkened space. At the head of her coven, Arista twisted a ball of fire that writhed like a live thing in her hands. After gathering the ribbons of flame, she released the unruly fire in a burst of energy that displayed the intricate markings on the ceiling as it soared above.

One of the witches scuttled to Simon's side, her hood drooping slightly, revealing a smile marred by one rotting tooth and a cheek partially eaten away, by time or vermin—there was no way to know. Focused on her appearance, Simon almost missed the gleam of silver as she brandished a knife. He flinched away, yanking and jerking his body, desperate to break free, his exertion ultimately proving futile. His eyes went feral, and fear sliced an icy finger through his chest. "Belle!"

"Here, Simon," she offered, appearing alongside the rock bed.

"Stay, Belle. Stay..." he begged.

～

A VISIBLE SHUDDER coursed through her brother as Arista nodded to her coven, and with her great-grandmother, mother, and aunt at her side, she set to work.

Tuning into Simon's bared thoughts, Arista paused, wrapped up in the moment right now. Cool steel cut a path across his palm, allowing for the collection of his blood needed for this complex spell. Tension and anxiety rolled off him in waves. Arista handed the blood to the waiting coven, who set to work on the concoction needed for the incantation. This must be a rare moment, indeed. When was the last time the infamous leader of the Night Dwellers was scared?

Dipping into Simon's thoughts, Arista merged their consciousnesses. Only for a few minutes. He'd had no barriers, and soon, even if only for a time, these memories would be buried deep, where no one could access them, not even via witchcraft, though witchcraft would be responsible for tucking them safely away. The agreed-upon avenue forward made sense. Gave Simon the opportunity to develop relationships with his family without the baggage that came from his years underground, where he'd honed his skills as a Night Dweller.

Arista looked on while a trembling young boy sank to his knees, his tearstained face arranged in a grimace; pain clearly etched there. Janus hovered over Simon, yelling obscenities, as a young woman cried in the corner. Mila... Simon's self-appointed mother and kidnapper. Sympathy was hard to dredge up for the woman, Whisterly's ex-maid, who'd helped engineer Simon's kidnapping. Bruises littered Mila's face, and each time she tried to reach out to her "son," Janus would beat her into submission once more.

Within the memories Arista witnessed, Simon clawed at his head, crying out a guttural wail. What a change to see him defenseless and small against the forces of Janus. In order to survive in this environment, Simon would have either had to adapt or die, and he'd chosen to adapt, learning mind-control techniques at Janus's bended knee. This unguarded glimpse into her brother's psyche was the first step in the purge to come.

More intense memories would rise to the surface as he lost the ability to access each one. First the major life-defining ones, like this one, all the way down to the seemingly insignificant; they would disappear, occupying space in his head like a fleeting goodbye, before surrendering to a temporary lockdown.

Here in the basement, Simon thrashed, the sounds coming from his lips more animal than Remeonite. A sliver of silver flashed through the air, snatching Arista's attention, her father's dog tags collateral damage to the spells in process.

Belle caught Arista's gaze, from her brief evaluation, Simon's raw pain instinctively tugging at Belle's heart.

*Yes, Belle, ease his transition.* Arista sensed Simon's body quiver as another excruciating memory left him, but with his exhale, followed by Belle's touch, the tight lines straining his face relaxed.

Steeling herself, Arista settled her gaze on her father. He swiped at the sprawled dog tags strewn on floor and shoved them into his pocket. Before giving her full attention to the coven, Arista leveled her gaze to his. *He'll make it through, Papa. Simon's survived all those years by drawing on the core strength you've already given him. It'll serve him now.*

Papa gave a tight nod, then leaned into Stephen's whispered words.

Smiling inwardly, Arista gave thanks for the two men who held a guiding force in her life. Even in this, somehow they came together. One would quite frankly rather see Simon dead than alive, the other seeking a rebirth for his son. Their common thread? They both loved Arista unconditionally.

Chanting from the coven hummed low in the background, pulling Arista into its rhythm and words.

*Now*, Great-Grandmother commanded.

The tome flew open, the pages swishing back and forth in their expected dance in anticipation of the work ahead. The pages fluttered to a stop, perched open, ready to fulfill the words Arista uttered. Born a powerful warlock, Simon had been joined, like Arista, through the immersion process, so he already possessed the knowledge within this book, even with his temporary ban by the coven, as they collectively struggled with Simon's ultimate fate.

Subduing his past thoughts and memories would allow others to impact Simon's journey, giving him a chance going forward to shake loose from prior bindings that held him, offering an opportunity instead to alter the circumstances that led him down his current path. But only if the spell worked. And then Simon must survive the recovery afterward.

Arista took the cup and slowly dripped the enchanted mixture into the creases of the book, closed her eyes, and whispered the spell on her lips while the pages beneath her fingers drank the crimson liquid, staining them a deep red. Whisterly's and Vinique's consciousnesses melded with Arista's own, then united with the spirit of her great-grandmother Arista and the power of the coven.

A chill swept through them as the contents of Simon's stored memories trickled through their bound thoughts, each one nestled into storage within the vast tome, until the time in the future when these remnants would be summoned again through a spell. Reunited at that point, restored to their owner, for better or worse.

*That's it, little one. Almost done.*

*Thank you, Mother. Without you, Vinique, Great-Grandmother, and the full coven's power, we couldn't carry through with this task on a warlock.*

*Don't underestimate yourself, dear. Banning Simon from the tome assisted in the effort as well, but through the combined skill of the three of you, we have reached a new pinnacle. First, with merging Whisterly's consciousness within a new body and now storing memories for later retrieval. Your skill is unmatched and stronger still when combined. The same is true for warlocks, however.*

*If Simon and Kix find each other and merge their powers, they will create a force difficult to overcome. Don't forget this fact. With the coven on your side, the scales would tip in our favor, but in a battle with magical powers, outcomes are never a certainty.*

Arista, Vinique, and Whisterly shared a glance. Kix had to be dealt with, and the ensuing fallout mitigated. Soon.

"We need to discuss our friend Kix." Vinique rolled her eyes. "We have a new agreement on the table. One I'm hoping not to honor."

"*Ugh.* Vinique, no. You didn't," Arista chided.

"If you mean, did I agree to a child—not yet. But he's made it clear his added condition will make or break our deal."

"Excuse me. Could I ask a question?"

"Of course, Belle. What is it?" Arista asked.

"How long should Simon be asleep from the spell?"

"That depends on his body's reaction. Right, Great-Grandmother?"

"Correct, dear. We'll care for him here. A coma is the likely result of the trauma to his brain. He'll emerge from it when his body is ready." Several coven members hovered near Simon, checking vital signs, assisted by various incantations.

"I'd like to help, Arista...with Simon."

The three silently communicated, considering Belle's request.

"If you're sure, I think that would be fine," Vinique answered. "I have a feeling Simon would want you here."

"He does. He told me so."

A sudden shudder raced up Arista's spine. *How is that possible?* "Did he? He hasn't communicated telepathically with any of us gathered here since the final spell was cast."

"Just now he told me so. I'll let him know he won't be alone."

Arista raised a brow and threw a nervous glance to Whisterly, Vinique, and her great grandmother.

"Child, anything is possible with little Belle. She's just beginning to blossom, and I can't wait to see what fruit she bears."

"Is that a yes?" Belle asked again.

"Yes, Belle. We'll work it out with the coven."

Six sets of eyes focused on Jack as he gently lifted Simon's head and replaced the wayward dog tags.

Jack murmured softly, but in the dead silence hanging between them, all could easily hear his words. "It's a fresh start for us, son. You'll see. With no more Night Dwellers maybe we could work toward a friendship." Jack's voice came out raspy and strained. "But let's take it one step at time, huh?"

Stephen ran a hand through his hair and took several steps back from the emotional scene.

*Love, I gotta get outta here. Want me to meet you later?*

*I think I'm done for a bit. Let's go.*

*Thank God. I'm suffocating this close to Simon. Coma or not, I still feel his presence... his control...*

## 4

_K_ ix let his thoughts drift while he perused the books in his chambers. With a flicker of his fingers, he amped up the light shining from the fireball in his hand, allowing for better illumination along the rows of books in front of him, his ongoing negotiations with Vinique—and intriguingly his most recent communication with Jack—competing for space in his head.

While the disappointment of losing Arista as a mating option still weighed heavily on him, Vinique wasn't a bad second choice. An accomplished witch from what Kix could tell, Vinique efficiently ran the council, being asked to step in for Whisterly on multiple occasions in the past, and more recently for Arista during her unfortunate abduction.

Maybe he'd given in too soon. Maybe Arista was still within his grasp. Maybe that was the reason for Jack's visit.

A mating with Arista, his original plan, would keep the bloodlines pure, the resulting offspring the cream of the crop for leading the council into the future. _Damn... Should have stuck to my guns._ Still, if he ended up with Vinique, he came out ahead. Both avenues would lead to a co-council leadership eventually. Both would ensure his lineage's involvement in matters of the council well into the future.

Ah... Here it is... His fingers came to a stop on *War and Peace*. Grasping it from the shelf by its spine, Kix blew away the dust motes that floated free, highlighted by the spell-powered flames in his hand. After the ensuing coughing fit and a stiff drink to clear his throat, Kix settled in his oversize leather chair with a refill of Jim Beam, his novel, and zero focus.

Papers, books, and miscellaneous items cluttered the space. But he liked it that way. Books he was reading, projects in progress, and papers he'd authored all splayed out in the open, ready for his next steps. He rarely lost anything—it was all here at his fingertips. Tossing the flame into a glass container, Kix refocused, rereading the first page for the third time while waiting on Jack to arrive.

A knock broke the silence. "Come in." Kix stood, meeting Jack's eyes from across the room. "I've been wondering when you'd show. Have a seat."

Jack nodded a hello, his face inscrutable, thoughts locked down tight.

"Drink?" Kix asked. "I remember your poison." He chuckled, reaching for the Jim Beam.

"Sure. I'll not turn that down, so far from Earth."

"Judging from the last time we spoke, I didn't think I'd hear from you anytime soon," Kix began, passing Jack his drink.

Jack didn't meet his eyes as he stared into his glass, swirling its contents, before throwing it back in one gulp.

Kix poured Jack a refill. "I'd hoped you were here to discuss Arista. That you'd reconsidered my offer to be her mate. But now that you're here, and I have somewhat of a reading on you, I think I can rule that out."

Jack's gaze, laced with a cool fury, met his. "Nothing's changed. Arista is off the table. Case closed."

"Perhaps you're here to talk about your son? I heard him again...recently. Maybe we could trade favors."

"Always out for the hustle," Jack huffed, lifting his drink to his lips. "When was this communication? He's indisposed currently."

"Earlier today. He seemed...in a considerable amount of pain." Jack slammed his glass on the table. Raising his brows, Kix poured Jack another.

"Your obsession with my children gets under my skin, but I suspect you already know that."

Kix grinned. "Contrary to your military training, your mannerisms betray you where your offspring are involved."

Jack scrubbed a hand down his face in an apparent effort to rid the emotion evident there. "Down to the reason why I'm here..."

"Please."

"Our paths will continue to cross, it seems. We have unusual traits in common. Our ties to Earth and humanity. You saved my life and, more important, Harry's, while here on Remeon. We each share a commitment to a higher calling—though, from my perspective, yours is somewhat skewed. Still it's there. And last, your involvement with my children, through the council and your status as a warlock. I'd like an opportunity to get to know you better, given all I've just mentioned. If you'd agree, that is."

Kix suppressed a smile. "What did you have in mind? You're welcome to visit me here just about any time you'd like. Peruse through my book collection. We could discuss the affairs of our various worlds. I'm intrigued. What does this look like for you, Jack?"

Jack pursed his lips and shrugged. "My thoughts were along the lines of something more...physical."

"Of course."

"An adventure in the holosuite."

"Interesting proposition. I guess you've spent a considerable amount of time there?"

Jack tilted his head, considering. "The activity has been a good outlet for me. Plus I've been developing training sessions for Stephen, using their programming."

"I see. Well, you have me at a disadvantage here. But I'm up for a challenge. Also I'm interested in the array of talents you'll no doubt put on display."

"If you studied some of the books you have regarding Earth, you'd agree our history is steeped in various forms of physical activities. Like hiking, camping, hunting, fishing, farming, various sporting events, and construction, to name a few."

"Or war. Certainly along those same lines and rich within Earth's history."

"Some might say that. In fact, I've already recreated some past battle scenarios. Combat was surprisingly accurate on every detail. Real to the point of being maddening. My focus has shifted going forward."

"So you want to grow our relationship through our affinity with Earth? Make our Earthly bond stronger?"

"That's the plan, and if you agree, I'd like to bring Stephen along. These types of excursions have been good for him as well."

"Fascinating..."

"Under these controlled circumstances, maybe you could show me what types of plans you have for Simon's training. I've found the environment excellent for exploring different options, weighing the strengths and weaknesses of each."

Kix narrowed his gaze, homing in on Jack. "Like an exhibition of my skills?" Kix eased into Jack's mind, applying a subtle spell, meant to relax his defense against the minor intrusion. No go. The training he'd received at Whisterly's instruction had served him well. Having a daughter for a council chair probably bolstered his skill level along also, not to mention almost dying at Damond's hand during Jack's previous visit to Remeon. The man was cut from tough stuff.

"More like a plan. But call it what you'd like. We can start with one of the other activities I mentioned. Pick one or suggest another. Or we can forget the whole thing." Jack tilted back the remainder of his drink and headed for the bookcase. "I think I'll take you up on the offer of a book though."

"Sure thing, Jack. But hold up." Kix scrambled to his feet.

Jack pulled a book from the shelf. "I think I'll reread *Moby Dick*," Jack announced, arranging his mouth into a smile, before heading to the door with the novel under his arm.

"What about a more realistic experience from Earth? You called me out for claiming a heritage that wasn't really mine. Remember? Let's visit the years of the Depression via holosuite. Part of your life there during that time period. Then we can explore more of my life as a warlock. What do you say?"

Jack lingered by the door. To Kix, Jack's indecision appeared to crease into the deepening lines of his face. "I'll see what I can come up with and get back to you."

"All right. Enjoy the book."

Back inside, Kix clicked on his holographic monitor, zooming in to his view of Earth and its moon, preparing to connect to his family. Having the home planet of his father front and center helped Kix feel a part of a society that he'd never actually visited, as Jack had pointed out not so long ago.

While he couldn't read the man today, more was up with Jack than only a desire to get to know Kix or to build on their common bonds. Kix sensed something much deeper, more ingrained in Jack that was at the center of his odd request. Thus Kix's simple test.

Through the intel Kix had already gained, his tracking of Jack throughout his early years, Kix knew of the struggle and tragedy the years of the Depression held for the man. Was he willing to resurrect those experiences? If so, that would attest to how much Jack wanted what he'd hinted at before—a glimpse of Kix's powers. But why was the real question.

A voice connected and sparked through the speakers. "Yes, I'm here... Go ahead, Kix."

"Good to hear your voice. I'll get straight to the point. I'm about to enter into an agreement which may put your identity at risk. You should act quickly."

～

"YEP. I pretty-near mucked up the whole damn thing. He sensed I was playing him. I felt him pulling away," Jack explained to Whisterly.

"Maybe you could sit down for a minute while we discuss this?"

Jack paused his pacing, shaking his head. "No. You know I work through problems better on my feet, keeps my brain processing."

Whisterly's face softened. "Maybe, but you accept them better sitting down."

"*Humph.*" Jack cocked his head. "When I'm ready to accept, maybe I'll sit."

"What did you learn from the visit?"

"Well, my gut tells me Kix won't give up his contact on Earth, even with Vinique agreeing to mate him. He's a traitor, likely digging himself in deeper and deeper over the years, which is a shame. Back when he intervened to save Harry and me from Damond, Kix still had some integrity left. Now, who knows? But the fact that he went right back at it when he thought you were gone attests to his conniving ways. I don't trust him, which is ironic since, in order to move forward with plan B—erasing his memory and sending him back to Earth—I've got to get him to trust me first. Clearly we're not there yet." Jack's gaze cut to hers. "What is it?"

A hint of a grin tilted her lips. "Nothing really. I just like watching you think."

"*Hmm.*" Jack took a seat next to Whisterly and pressed his lips against hers. "I love doing that whenever I want to."

"Me too. You're sitting, so does that mean you're ready to accept where we are and move on?"

"No. It means I wanted to kiss you." Jack sucked in a breath and let it out slowly, then walked down the floor and back again. "I should do what he asked. That one step will likely move us forward."

"What did he ask of you?"

"When I mentioned the holosuites, he got suspicious. He wants me to take us back to experience the Depression, and when I hesitated, he smelled blood and went in for the kill."

"You could counter with another time period, one that isn't filled with such sorrow for you. No need to drag yourself through that again. You still have nightmares about it. I hear you in your sleep."

"True enough." Jack settled next to Whisterly and laced his fingers with hers. "That was my first thought as well. But maybe a visit down memory lane won't be as bad as I'm anticipating."

"Really, Jack?"

"What if it helps instead? Maybe I could get some closure that I'll never get otherwise. What do you think, baby?"

"I think you need to follow your heart on this one. There are other venues to play in, other places, more experiences than you can imagine."

"I know," Jack said around a grin. "Need I remind you that I've put those holosuites to the test? I've found them to be unparalleled for any type of training I can dream up. As I improve, so do my hypothetical opponents. Except they don't seem hypothetical. I relish immersion in a new experience, then returning to my normal life in seconds. The technology is exquisite."

"But you might feel differently after this trip."

"I might... For better or worse, I'm doing it. Kix will get his inside look into my younger years. And, if I'm lucky, I'll find some peace along the way."

"Jack, you and I know you can't find peace inside a fake reality, only in here," she gestured, her hand on his heart.

"Baby, you've already mended my heart. The peace I'm seeking is more of a reconciliation really, with a past that I wasn't equipped to handle at the time."

"See? And you're sitting—acceptance. What did I tell you?" She beamed.

"I guess we know who wears the pants in this family," Jack said with a teasing grin.

"What does that mean? Sometimes I wear pants."

"It's an expression from Earth, where I hope to be taking you very soon. It means the one who makes the decisions...wears the pants."

"Oh, well, we both do, right?"

"Right. And you are practically perfect, with or *without* pants." Jack pulled Whisterly's legs over his lap. "I'll arrange a time and date for the event in the holosuites with Kix and Stephen and recommend the next venue as well. First part of the plan is in motion."

"I spent some time in the basement earlier, while you were meeting with Kix."

"And? How'd that go? Any change in Simon's condition?"

"No. Still unconscious. Sorry. I know that's not what you wanted to hear."

"The sooner he recovers, the sooner we can get to know our son on our terms."

"Grandmother believes it could be a while yet, months even."

"Months?"

"You were in a coma for months after Damond's attack. Doctors here were convinced you wouldn't recover."

"I wouldn't have without your assistance."

"There was never any question in my mind that I'd try blood magic to heal you. Without you, Jack, my future didn't exist."

"Makes me one lucky bastard," Jack admitted, pulling her closer.

"Those who are telepathic and have magical powers are more sensitive to brain trauma. Simply put, the number of possible issues during recovery are endless, thus the longer time needed to heal from the intrusion."

"Do you think he's aware of his surroundings at all?"

"Based on your experience, I thought not. When I checked on him, I saw no evidence of communication. I attempted telepathic, verbal, and tried to reach him using witchcraft as well. Simon's telepathic pathways weren't responsive."

"Sounds like there's a *but* coming. And you have that cute little line in your forehead that means you've got something important to say."

"Yes, well, Belle came in while Grandmother and I were talking, and she interacted with Simon on a completely different level."

"Meaning?"

"The way she explained it, they communicated with visions."

"I don't follow."

"I didn't either at first. Belle remembered the anxiety Simon experienced during the memory wiping. So, in the hope of easing that feeling, she created a soothing vision and transferred the picture to him through a memory flash. Those are similar to telepathy but in smaller one-time bursts. I would imagine less taxing on brain function."

"Belle never ceases to amaze me. So she flashed him this picture. Then what happened?"

Whisterly's answering grin gave Jack his answer.

"No... How?"

"Yes, somehow he sent one back to her. Belle's picture that she imagined and communicated to Simon was of a stream on her family's farm close to the portal to our world."

"And Simon's?"

"Simon sent Belle a picture of a young boy, from what she understood, his half-brother."

"Incredible. So Mila had a son of her own at some point?"

"I really don't know. Either that or Janus kidnapped another boy and called him theirs also."

"I wonder if this ability of Belle's is a skill we can learn."

"I don't think so," Whisterly continued, shaking her head. "Sounds like what Belle does is an intuitive response to another's injury or need. Like she did when finding her brother among the Night Dwellers and helping you during my reintegration. The way Belle can tap into the essence of another is beyond my magical expertise. Her abilities appear to be a part of her connection to the foundation that drives life fundamentally, especially in the case of the element ground, which provides for renewal through soil and plant life."

"I'm glad she can communicate with him on a meaningful level. I'd like to visit him tomorrow."

"Sure, Jack."

"You know, I've got a little of that mojo that Belle has. The reach of my skill is very specific though."

"It better be." The depths of her gray eyes pinned him in place.

Jack lifted her into a kiss, his mouth bending into a smile. "Let me demonstrate."

∼

STEPHEN KNOCKED SOFTLY, even though the guard's tight nod had granted Stephen access. The man's apparent dislike for humans was only thinly veiled. It was all Stephen could do to not growl back at him. Keeping Arista safe needed to be their top priority, and they'd failed. No... He had.

"Come in."

Arista glanced up as he entered the room, her gaze tracking his progress. Despite his mood, he couldn't help the grin taking over his face. "Hey there." Stephen kissed her softly, lingering, because he could, the influx of emotion from her abduction rushing back to him. All of it had been his fault. "I can't believe you're back at it so soon," he said, leaning back slightly so he could see her face.

"I'm fine. Really," she added, lifting her eyes to his.

He watched an array of emotions play across her features too. "Look. I know you can handle all of this...your ordeal, council leadership, fighting wraiths for God's sake," he scowled, shaking his head. "But you shouldn't have to."

"What do you mean? You were there too. You brought me home."

"Only after putting you at Simon's mercy to start with. And to set the record straight, your father organized the mission to set you free. I just followed his orders."

"I was there, and you guided me out of the cave before it collapsed with us in it." Arista cupped Stephen's cheek. "Without your help, Papa wouldn't have made it to the jeep. The Night Dwellers had caught up to him, and Simon had found his way inside Papa's head. He wouldn't have made it without you, Stephen. Neither would I. Papa needed you for his plan to succeed."

Layers of stress lined her words, but they rang of truth. Arista believed them. But the conversation Jack had with Stephen before the mission pierced him with their cold hard reality. *One hundred percent of the time you need to protect her and love her*. Training with Jack in the holosuites helped. Stephen was stronger, more fit than he'd ever been. Learning from Jack, thrust into the scenarios he'd created, battling foes that Stephen couldn't dredge up himself, well, Stephen was honored to just be a part and soak up all he could, while Jack remained willing to teach him.

And the fortitude he gained... His legs were stronger than ever. Soon he'd be rid of his braces completely; one day in the not-too-distance future, polio would be a horrible distant memory.

Hell, he wasn't a warlock, like Simon; and Stephen didn't have strange powers, like Belle, but he was learning. Day by day, just like Jack had done—well, maybe not *exactly* like he'd done—Stephen could become the man Arista needed eventually.

"Stephen, you're a million miles away. I'm having trouble just keeping up with how fast your thoughts are racing."

He gave an empty chuckle. "You having trouble keeping up with me telepathically? False."

"What is it?"

"Could you spare the rest of the day, love? If only for me? I need to assure myself that you're okay."

"Let's sit for a few minutes. I'll have some food brought in."

Stephen trailed Arista to the couch and took a seat, watching intently as she settled, tucking her legs underneath her and lifting her face to his expectantly. "Food will be here soon. I reached out to the cooking staff."

Stephen grasped her hand and squeezed it tightly. "When we were in the forest, and you were fighting Simon and his minions, all I could think about was getting free of the protection you'd created for me because, in the scheme of things here, I don't matter. You do. And I needed to have another layer between you and Simon, even if that meant me dying. But instead, you sacrificed yourself for me." His eyes searched hers. "I'm not okay with that."

"We love each other, Stephen. When you're in danger, and I can do something about it, I will. It's been schooled into me since I was little, a part of my training to lead the council. On an instinctual level I can't stop it."

"I don't want to be in that position again, but something tells me that won't be the case. So, if there's a next time, I need to be better prepared. I'll never toss spells around, but I sure as hell can do damage in other ways."

Arista tilted her head. "What are you getting at exactly?"

"I hope to keep working with Jack." Stephen ran his thumb over Arista's hand in tiny circles. "But I'd like to train with your forces here at the compound as well. Offer my services, for whatever they're worth."

"Oh!" Arista's eyes rounded. "Are you sure?"

His jaw tightened as he nodded. "I'm a decent shot and getting better. But I need more tactical experience to make up for my lack of magical ability. Around you and your family, that particular skill comes in handy. Trouble has a way of hanging around, it seems."

Arista laughed, tiny lines creasing around her eyes.

"And I'm sorely lacking. Maybe I can make up for the deficiency in other ways, if I give this new task my full attention."

"You're an excellent shot. My father would be dead right now if you weren't. I'm not of the opinion that you need this extra training. So let me be clear. I feel safe and protected around you always. Simon had come for me. We know now what his plans were. If the situation had been reversed, and you could have guaranteed my safety with a few words and a spell. I have no doubt that you would have."

"Damn straight."

"I won't apologize for protecting you. Without you here, I'd be devastated. You see, my actions were purely for selfish reasons."

Stephen pulled Arista onto his lap, his arms circling her waist. "I intend to be a stronger asset going forward. I don't ever want to be a liability where your safety is concerned, love. While we're waiting for the next steps with Simon, I can get started and maybe still have sessions with your dad."

"This plan of yours will delay your trip home."

"My home is where you are. I won't be returning to Earth until we're ready to marry."

Arista did a small leap in his lap, then pressed her lips against his. "I can't wait," she whispered.

He nibbled at her lips while his hands roamed her back, pushing her tighter against him.

"*Ewww.* You all need to stop that," Belle announced.

"Belle." Arista scooted back to her seat on the couch. "Where have you been?"

"Visiting Simon."

Stephen eyed his sister while keeping a tight grip on Arista's arm. "He doesn't deserve you, Belle."

"You sound funny. What's wrong with your voice?"

"Nothing," he said, giving Arista a glance, releasing her for now, his hungry gaze letting her know they were far from done. "How is the disgusting little pervert?" The deep sadness in Belle's eyes made him regret his words, a little.

"I don't really know. He's not conscious. The old witch said he'll be like that for quite some time. For now he's too weak to travel, even by portal."

"Can't say I'm sorry about that, Belle."

Belle plopped down on the couch next to her brother. "Simon hurt you bad when he had you locked up. I know that. I felt it when I helped Vinique find you, so the Day Watchers could rescue you. But I'm still sad because Simon took your peace."

"What do you mean?" Stephen asked, confusion sweeping through his thoughts.

"Simon took something from you. Me and others can help you, but only you can get that peace back, Stephen. You'll know it when you do." Belle curled a warm hand around his free arm. Her touch washed through him, easing the tension that had been building inside.

"Is this what you do for Simon?"

Belle shook her head. "I just let him know he's not alone. Give him a calming vision. He's got no one. Lost to himself, with nothing to anchor him. All I can do is let him know there's life on this side. Simon has to choose it—or not." Belle leaped from the couch, leaving the solemnness behind, giggling as she tucked and rolled with her landing before jumping back up and disappearing into her room.

"Food's on the way," Arista called out after Belle's retreating back. "I'll let you know when it gets here."

"When did she get so smart?"

Arista's face lit with her smile. "I have a feeling you've chosen to overlook it in the past, and it's always been so."

"*Humph.*" Stephen shook his head. *Peace... Safety... Belle's words make sense. How does she see through people like this? Damn, Belle.* An emptiness brewed in his gut. *She's right. I haven't reconciled myself with the torture Simon put me through, much less what he did to Arista. And I don't know that I ever will, not until he's dead. What would it take to get it back... that peace?* Stephen tugged Arista back toward his lap and dropped a kiss to her nose. "I need a bite before we eat," he murmured, nibbling a path along the column of her neck.

# 5

"They'll be here any moment, Stephen," Arista called out from the kitchen, where she and Belle put the finishing touches on a trayful of goodies. "We need to be of one mind."

Belle ran ahead of the treats as she took a flying leap, landing beside Stephen.

"Whoa there. You really need to get outside, Belle. Run around some."

"That'd be fun. Do you want to come too?"

"Is that what you do with all her energy?" Arista asked, reorganizing the cookies and cupcakes on the platter, after giving the arrangement a critical eye.

"At home *this* isn't an issue," he teased, shaking his little sister playfully. "We have chores to do, and by the end of the day, we're all beat. Being on Remeon though requires a different type of stamina."

"We'll go after Mother, Father, and Vinique leave. What do you say, Belle? I need to gather some herbs. You can show me more of how you connect with the spirits of the ground."

"Okay. Sure."

"I forgot the coffee. Stephen, do you mind? It's already in the kitchen. Just bring it in here."

"Sure. Gives me an excuse to get some now." With his own cup full on the tray, Stephen arranged the rest next to the cookies and cupcakes and took a gulp before eyeing Arista again. "Are you sure you're ready to tell your parents...you know... He tossed a glance to his sister.

"You can say it out loud. And, yes, I'm sure. I have been for a very long time. Just been waiting for you to catch up."

A soft tap sounded on the connecting door to their two suites. "I'll let them in," Belle offered, lunging toward the door.

"Come on in. Have a seat." Arista gestured to the couch. "Belle's pouring coffee."

A few minutes later, everyone set with drink and dessert, Vinique took the lead. "If everyone concurs, I'd like to revisit our timeline." Gathering nods all around, she continued. "Grandmother has indicated that Simon will likely be comatose for months, putting our current plans on hold. We could accelerate other portions of our plan or essentially remain in a holding pattern until Simon wakes—or until such time that it's determined that he won't."

Jack took a large bite of cupcake and gave Belle a thumbs-up. "Did you help with this, Belle? It tastes decidedly un-Remeonlike."

"I did. Do you like it?" Belle grinned.

"Absolutely." He reached for another and winked at her, before returning to the conversation. "Personally I think we have plenty to do here that makes this delay fortuitous. Stephen and I will be scheduling time with Kix in the holo-suites, gaining his trust, then moving forward. Depending on the outcome of the first several sessions with him, we'll reassess."

"I agree, Jack," Vinique interjected. "Our agreement with Kix still needs work also. Plus he's holding out hope of a mating with Arista, even though he's been told no by both me and Jack."

"When hell freezes over," Stephen snarled.

"Amen," Jack added.

"Kix knows it's not happening. Since I've offered myself as a substitute, I'd be a little offended if we actually intended to fulfill and fully implement the agreement. But, with the knowledge that we'll derail before we get to that point, I'm good with further talks with him."

"Thanks, Vinique." Arista squeezed Stephen's hand, then held up the coffeepot in question. "Whatever the costs, we'll make sure a mating doesn't go forward between you two. Speaking of mating," Arista refilled cups all around, "we've started some wedding planning."

Jack's fork fell with a loud clatter to his plate, and all eyes shifted from him to Arista, then to Stephen and back again.

"Perfect timing, little one," Whisterly said, filling in the awkward silence. "I can't wait to help you dig into the details. I was going to ask if either Stephen or Belle wanted to visit Earth though. I'm sure their parents are going a little crazy with no news of their children. But starting to plan early...now, is smart."

"Why are you all acting weird?" Belle asked through a mouthful of cookie. "I'm staying. Great-Grandmother Arista says having me around might bring Simon back to himself quicker. That's what you all want, isn't it?"

"It is," Jack confirmed, finding his voice. "When Simon has amply recovered, Whisterly, Simon, and I will travel to Earth. Not sure how long we'll be staying. And Belle? Maybe we'll talk to your parents about you visiting with us for a while, depending on Simon's condition. What would you think about that?"

"Wait a minute... What?" Stephen asked. "It's one thing to have Belle helping Simon in the basement with a coven full of witches at her disposal, if she needs backup against that monster. It's quite another to have her on Earth with him."

"Stephen, don't you think Whisterly and I could properly take care of your sister?" Jack's eyebrows rose to his hairline.

"Well... y-yes..." Stephen stammered. "But you've made it clear your focus is Simon, and I know what he's capable of. I'm not sure being around him 100 percent of the time is best for Belle."

"I assure you, Stephen, we would watch after Belle as if she were our very own daughter." Whisterly squeezed Jack's hand. "We practically feel that way already. Without Belle, it's likely Jack wouldn't have made it through my reintegration. I'll be eternally grateful to her for that."

"Not only that, Mother, but Belle also performed her own elemental magic that day, in order to obtain your true name from Papa," Arista added. "Belle was instrumental throughout the whole process."

"I need to get back to work," Vinique announced. "Sounds like, from what I'm hearing, that everyone will remain on Remeon until we're ready to transport Simon off planet, correct?" The small gathering nodded, except for Stephen and Jack, who remained fixated on each other. "Right. Well, thanks, Arista."

"Sure, Vinique."

"Mother, would you like to join Belle and me for some fresh air?" Arista eyed her father and Stephen, then yanked her head toward the door.

"I'd love to. What do you say, Belle? May I join you two?" Whisterly asked.

"Sure." Belle got to her feet and grabbed one more goody for the trek outside. "No telling how long these two will sit here and stare at each other. Let's go."

Whisterly leaned in to kiss Jack's cheek, along with some

intense words via telepathy, or so it appeared to Arista. She pressed her lips against Stephen's. "We won't be long."

"Take your time, little one," Jack encouraged, standing and straightening to his full height. "We have a few things to discuss here."

Arista's gaze raced from her father to Stephen, her stomach tightening at the thought of leaving the two men she loved most alone right at that moment. A thread of tension rippled between them, taut, the delicate balance precarious but holding.

"We'll be right here, Arista," Jack said, gifting her with a smile. "See you when you get back."

She nodded, then met Stephen's gaze. The passion and love ignited there made her heart stutter.

*I love you, Stephen.*

*Everything is all right, love. I promise.*

Arista ducked inside her parents' chamber, where Whisterly and Belle waited.

"Ready?" her mother asked. After Whisterly's reintegration and subsequent change to her telepathic signature, her mother appeared to everyone else to be Yara, a supposedly newly recovered Remeonite who'd suffered brain trauma. Since the magical reintegration, Whisterly's consciousness had occupied Yara's body. This fact allowed Whisterly and Arista to appear in public as "friends," when in fact they freely nurtured their mother-daughter bond. But right now, sticking close to the compound seemed like a better idea.

Arista tossed another worried glance over her shoulder.

"You've got two men in there who love you fiercely. They'll be okay,"

"I hope you're right, Mother."

"Of course they will," Belle chimed in. "Mr. Jack loves Stephen, just like his own sons. I don't know what all the fuss is about. Am I the only one who has eyes that can see?"

"Thank the gods for Belle," Arista murmured.

"Got anything stronger than coffee in this place? Please tell me you do."

The last thing Stephen wanted was to tell the man no, but he and Arista rarely drank alcohol. "I don't think Arista keeps anything like that around."

"Change of venue then. Follow me."

"Sure."

Stephen followed in the man's wake, like the shadow he truly felt like behind Jack's massive frame. Anytime Stephen was in Jack's presence, the feelings of inadequacy returned. But this wasn't Jack's fault—he'd been understanding, caring even, and the two had bonded somewhat over the similarities they shared with their common ties to Remeon, Whisterly, and Arista.

If Stephen could model his life after someone's, it would be Jack's. Of course Stephen admired his own father, but Jack's journey had turned him into a model of strength and self-assurance, and his authentic nature couldn't be faked. His strength of character and his desire to bend his world toward good were uncanny. Stephen wanted it—all of it. Along with Arista of course.

Jack led Stephen into the quarters he shared with Whisterly. While the set of rooms appeared similar to Arista's at first glance, some differences grabbed Stephen's attention, like the huge holographic monitor he could make out through the open door leading to their bedroom, and the bar, laden with liquor, where Jack stopped to pour two drinks—his obviously a double.

Jack pushed the drink into Stephen's hand, then gestured

toward their seating area. "Look, Stephen. You and I are friends," he began, with a long exhale, "but—"

*But?* Nothing good could be coming after that... "Wait. Let me," Stephen rushed to interject, earning a startled glance from Jack. "Arista is excited. We both are," he added. "We should have waited before announcing beginning our wedding plans. I don't claim to know the proper procedures for planning an interplanetary wedding. Don't even know the first place to begin, except focusing on the one thing I've been meaning to do since bringing Arista back from the Night Dwellers."

Jack took a large swallow of his drink then sucked in a breath, and Stephen held up his hand. "Could I finish first? If I don't now, I'm not sure I'll get this out."

"Sure."

"Two things. First, I've talked with Arista about joining the military forces here on Remeon. I'd like to have training that could mold me into more of strategic fighter, Jack. Like you are. I've got a long way to go, but I'll get there eventually. I can shoot, hunt, and fight better than most, thanks to Pa. And my time on Remeon has helped me learn that I can make it through a life-or-death scenario, although, if it's by skill or dumb luck, I'm not sure which.

"Second, I want to ask you for Arista's hand in marriage." Stephen swallowed his own drink down in two quick gulps, appreciating the burn as it slid down his throat, and the few seconds the liquid courage gave him to pound down his nerves. "I see my future a lot different than I did even a few weeks ago. I want to aid the forces here in any way I can and become a better soldier in the process. With my lack of skill in the magical department, I'll need to depend more on building my tactical skills and firearms training to be the partner Arista needs. More important though, these decisions will keep me here with her while she leads the council. We want to be together now, not in some distant future, when Earth and

Remeon align and everything is perfect. 'Cause that won't ever happen."

Jack's mouth twisted into a grin. "You got that right."

"Then there are my parents. I don't want to hurt them. They don't understand all this. I need to give them a little time to get used to the idea while we and they plan, so that especially my mother will feel a part of everything. And since I don't know the first thing about weddings, that's probably a good thing."

"Can I jump in here, before you lay out your plans for the next thirty years?"

With a quick glance at Jack's easy smile, Stephen released the breath he held. "Sure. Uh... Sorry."

"You seem to have the idea that I'm upset." Jack strode to the bar for a refill, lifting a brow to Stephen in question, then filling only his own, acknowledging the shake of Stephen's head.

Jack continued. "Surprised a little, sure. But, as Whisterly often reminds me, you two are already formally mated, according to Remeon customs. We knew the ceremony on Earth would follow. I'm new at this specific piece of parenting. I want to protect Arista yet give her each new experience at just the right time." Jack laughed. "The reality is Arista and Whisterly have been doing fine at that piece without me. I need it for myself though. So I'll take it where I can.

"I am surprised by your announcement to join the service here. No doubt it helps with you two being together on Remeon. I know little about the strength of the program in the compound though, other than, with Whisterly recently at the helm, I'm sure the people there are some of Remeon's finest. I can vouch for the marines at home, should you choose that route instead. Stephen, you're more qualified than most young men who make this decision on Earth. You already know what it's like to have to fight for your life. You've already killed to save the woman you love. You've participated in undercover missions and come out on the other side successful. You'll succeed in a more formal environment as well, I predict."

Stephen reached for his drink, his throat suddenly dry, unsure which of Jack's points to address first. A coughing fit seized him, and Jack rushed to refill Stephen's glass. Slowly swallowing the amber liquid, a calm filtered through, giving the chaos inside him time to settle under Jack's watchful eye. "I'm fine. Thanks."

"Good." Jack's eyes wrinkled with concern. "Like I've said to you before, this decision to marry or not is Arista's. For what it's worth, I give my blessing. You're smart, tough, and you'd give your life to protect hers, plus you have a good work ethic. And are damn good with a blade... I don't think I could have chosen better for her myself, which I can't."

"Wow... Thanks Jack. Not sure my pa would agree about the work ethic though."

"Sure he would. Especially if he knew all the good you've done here. As I mentioned earlier, I plan to talk with him about Belle." Jack shifted in his seat. "Ah. The tables have turned."

"Protecting my little sister has literally been pounded into me. I'd be stupid not to be concerned with her spending significant time with Simon—who I still want dead, by the way."

Jack's mouth set in a thin line. "I believe, when Simon wakes, if he wakes, he'll be a totally different person."

"I don't care. I'll never trust him, Jack."

Jack met Stephen's gaze. "Understood. But know, if Belle agrees to spend time with us, that I'll protect her as I would my own flesh and blood."

"If she does, I hope that's good enough."

"You've sat at my table. We've traded stories, fought alongside each other, loved women from the same line of witches. I already love you like a son, Stephen, and I trust my daughter's judgment. We're already family in my book."

"What?"

Jack smirked as his eyes danced. "Which part of that didn't you hear?" He got to his feet, Stephen followed suit, and the two fell into a hug.

Stupefied, Stephen straightened his back, so he could stand a little taller, his gaze drifting to Jack's. How would he ever measure up?

"What do you think Arista would say about having the ceremony at my house? Wouldn't that be something?" Jack pulled away with a thud to Stephen's back.

Turning his thoughts back to the grandeur of Jack's home, the entrance, the unique carvings, the raised ceilings and striking wooden beams, windows engineered perfectly to catch just the right amount of light, Stephen responded without thinking, "That'd be beautiful, Jack."

His answering grin left no room for further debate as Jack's chest puffed up while refilling both of their glasses again.

The fuzzy feeling in Stephen's head grew. *Oh boy...* With none of the women involved consulted, it looked like their wedding venue was set.

VINIQUE PUSHED the contract to the side. She'd examined it several times, looking for loopholes, technicalities she could use to get out of mating Kix. Hopefully it wouldn't come down to that. But if it did, everything was spelled out here; she'd be forced into a union with a warlock, who, by the way, also wanted to have a baby with her. This part of the agreement currently prevented finalizing the deal.

In his mind, Kix probably didn't see this pledge as out of line. After all, in the past among their people, arrangements like these had been fostered as a matter of course. Those destined for the council needed to produce an heir to assure the line continued, no matter what. As a sister to Whisterly, this mandate included Vinique.

Whisterly had broken this mold though, giving herself and those who came after her another path to follow. Since curing PR 251, society had been slowly changing as well. Breeding directly, without medical intervention, was now encouraged. But this change in societal norms would take a while to enact in actuality.

A return to sexual intimacy after so many generations of ingraining the opposite approach among their people made for an uphill battle, even though the dispensing of medication to subdue these natural urges was no longer an edict passed down from the council to all Remeonites.

A pivotal point in their history had arrived. Vinique wanted to lead this wave, like her half-sister before her and her niece, however Kix didn't measure up. Arista's personal tactical team had uncovered a recent communication from Kix to Earth, and while Vinique and Arista had gained the warlock's assurances that no more data transmissions would occur while they hammered out a contract, nothing was stopping him from doing just that.

Under Whisterly's guidance the two had maintained a balance of power between witch and warlock. Now, with Whisterly supposedly dead, in Kix's mind the prior agreements were null and void. His thinly veiled grab for power riled Vinique's anger to the core.

With Simon's recovery time frame uncertain, Vinique and Arista had more opportunity to let this play out. Additionally they had more resources: Jack, Belle, and Stephen could also be committed. All had confirmed yesterday that they'd remain on planet, at least until Simon's health allowed for off-world travel. Now this pause in their plans could be put to good use.

"Ma'am, your next appointment."

"Thank you. Come in, Jack. Please sit."

"Hi, Vinique. Whisterly is with Arista. Quite the commotion yesterday with talk of wedding plans on the horizon. And apparently I'm the expert on weddings?" Jack scoffed. "We're not trusting something this important to the likes of me. That's for sure. I'm only aware of the basics...ceremony, party, followed by lots of drinking to accompany the aforementioned activities."

"Sounds like quite the event coming up."

"Well, we'll see," Jack said, the hint of a smile working across his mouth. "Mother and daughter are determined to get started though. As a result, you've got just me for now."

"No problem. Initially what I want to discuss involves mostly you and, to a lesser extent, Stephen."

"Still just me. I'm afraid he overindulged after you all left yesterday." Jack's attempt to suppress a laugh failed.

"Jack, what happened?"

"I'm used to drinking with grown men...who are used to drinking hard liquor, like me. I'm used to Harry, for God's sake."

"Oh no."

"Yep. I led him astray. He's out of it, probably won't feel up to much today. I feel awful about it. Really I do."

"You humans and the things you do to each other... Fine. You can bring him up to speed later."

"Will do."

"I've had my team trace Kix's latest communication with Earth. From what we can tell, no data changed hands. His contact resides in the Washington, DC, area."

"Certainly makes sense politically, if Kix is still dealing. It is possible that his family lives in the area, right?"

"Yes. I believe they do. However, since we discovered Kix's continued duplicity under Arista's leadership, we've been monitoring his communications carefully. We've uncovered two sets of coordinates. One set appears much less often than the other. And that's the contact he reached out to after your latest meeting with him."

Jack steepled his fingers under his chin, lost for the moment in thought. "We need to narrow this down further. I could use my contacts with the Freemasons in the DC area, and we'll have it figured out in no time." A smile inched up Jack's mouth. "Harry can help."

"Please, thank him for me, if he's willing. I'd understand if he'd prefer not to get involved, and in that case, we'll find another resource. I'll transfer the coordinates to you tele- pathically."

Jack leveled his gaze with hers. "Harry will be happy to help, but I'll confirm with him after our meeting."

"Next on my list...are you ready to schedule an experience in the holosuite with Kix and Stephen? Our elongated time frame allows you, him, and Stephen to create a bond over a longer period. As Kix grows to trust you, you'll have more insight into him, his family, and his magical abilities—that's what we need."

"I've scheduled our first holosuite adventure with Kix for the day after tomorrow. Stephen plans to attend as well. Speaking of Stephen, has Arista talked to you of his plan to join with your military?"

"Only briefly. I'm investigating the possibility. This would be quite a milestone if it occurs—if Stephen, a human, joins our armed services."

"Given the fact that Arista is here and that, when her mother and I travel to Earth, Arista will remain on Remeon, I'm all for it. I don't want to see their lives torn apart like ours were."

"I happen to agree with you, Jack. In fact, with Stephen's celebrity status, I don't see him joining as an issue. I think it will be a win-win."

"If my future son-in-law learns to handle his drink, that is." Jack trailed off into a string of laughter. "I'm sorry, Vinique. I just can't believe I derailed him so. I feel responsible," Jack explained, wiping his eyes.

"I don't think I've ever seen you so unrestrained, except for your visit with Whisterly after Arista's birth and your return to Arista most recently. But laughter, Jack, looks good on you."

"Thanks for that. One day at a time Whisterly and I are learning to laugh. For so long we've spent our lives waiting on each other. We've vowed not to do that anymore. No matter what, we'll be together for whatever time we're blessed with. And that means we have so much life to catch up on, so many moments to experience, and I want each and every one with her and Arista. If my daughter chooses Stephen, and it seems she has, that includes him as well."

Vinique studied the expression on Jack's face, his eyes sparkling and full of love for his family. Simon hadn't been mentioned in Jack's litany just now. Was that because Jack had started to let go of his son or perhaps due to the fact that Simon's status was on hold, waiting for what came next, if he even woke up. Or quite possibly Jack's unrestrained joy drilled down to sharing bits and pieces with his whole family, including Simon and whatever future potential their relationship together held. The prospect was more than he'd ever had before. Fatherhood looked good on Jack too.

"What is it, Vinique? Is something wrong? You're staring at me."

"No. Everything's right. I can't help it. I'm so grateful you're here."

Jack stood and opened his arms in time for Vinique to fall into them. "We're going to be okay, Vinique."

Somehow, silly as it was, coming from Jack, she believed his words.

## 6

*a* sharp ache pounded throughout his head, sliding down to his eyes, where it pulsed out a beat, like a drum. Stephen opened his eyes to a blur of pain. An awareness dawned as he rubbed his forehead—a meeting—he had some-where to be. Throwing his legs over the side of his bed, he attempted a stand. Oh no... Pain shot upward, centering on his eyes, each blink of his eyelids feeling like needles had found a new home inside his skull. He slowly lowered himself to the bed again and eased into a horizontal position.

Flashes of telepathic messages popped into his thoughts, most of them from Arista, a few from Jack. He should get up and get moving, but his stomach had other ideas. Why in God's name had he tried to keep up with Jack? To impress his future father-in-law? Fat chance of that, if the number of drinks downed was the measure of his success.

*Arista? I'm here. Just not feeling so great right now is all.*

*I'll be right there.*

*No!* Stephen cringed at the loudness of his own thought banging around in his head. *I mean, no. I'll be fine, love.*

*You don't sound fine. Papa said you weren't awake when he
popped in after the meeting you missed with Vinique.*

*Can you whisper, if there is such a thing in telepathy? Every
word hits inside me like a fist.*

*Sure... Is this better?*

*Much. Thanks.*

*Let me get you something. You don't sound well at all.*

The last thing he wanted was for Arista to see him like this.
He crawled under the sheet and flung it over his head. Under
the thin veil of darkness, he eased out a sigh. Better, just barely.

*I'll get some more sleep. Maybe that will help. I'll let you know
later.*

*All right. But I'll come check on you, if I don't hear from you
tonight.*

*Got it. Thanks.*

Stephen groaned and flipped to his side. The meager
contents of his stomach shifted, and instantly he realized his
mistake. *Ugh...*

The door clicked open.

No... Did she come anyway? "Arista?"

"Uh, no. It's me—Jack. I still have credentials to get in, since
this was my room too."

Pushing the cover down slightly, Stephen cracked open one
eye and closed it back again. "Sorry, Jack. I feel like shit, and I
think I'll feel like shit for a very long time."

Jack's answering chuckle floated through the room, and
even with his eyes closed, Stephen could feel the man's presence close by as he placed something on the nightstand with a
loud clatter. "I'd prefer to feel like shit all alone," Stephen
clarified.

"I feel somewhat responsible for your condition. So, here
are a few things that might help."

An intoxicating aroma, smelling like coffee, pulled Stephen
out from under the sheet.

"As you know, this isn't exactly like our version from home, but it's close enough—and hot and strong to boot. It'll settle that heaviness in your head." Jack passed Stephen the cup filled with the hot drink, watching as he downed three large swallows.

"Thanks, Jack."

"Sure. Now this." Shoving a plate with toast to him with one hand, Jack grabbed Stephen's cup with the other.

"No. I don't think that's a good idea."

"Eat it slowly. You'll need something in your stomach before you take these." Jack pointed to two pills on the plate beside the toast.

Stephen scrunched his nose. "What is that on top?"

"Jelly. Remeon style," Jack added, suppressing a smile.

"Well, it looks gross, and nothing like my ma's jelly."

"I'm sure it's nowhere near as good as hers but eat it anyway." Jack eased back into a nearby chair, adjusted, and raised his eyes to Stephen again.

"You just gonna sit here until I do?"

Jack crossed his arms and blew out a breath. "Yep."

"Great." Stephen reached for the toast. "Here goes." He chewed and swallowed. It tasted odd on his dulled taste buds, but the stuff wasn't horrible, and when the first bite slid down Stephen's throat, his need for a little sustenance became clearer.

Jack's eyebrows lifted. "Well?"

"It's not completely awful."

"All right, good. Chase it with some more coffee, then the meds."

Stephen followed Jack's instructions. "I'm fine. You can go. I'm sure you've got better things to do."

Jack leaned over, his arms balanced on his knees. "I will, when you can get yourself to the shower under your own steam."

Tossing a glance toward the bathroom, Stephen nodded. "I'll go in few minutes."

"No rush." Jack leaned back again, crossing his legs in front of him. "Not that I recommend it, but you'll build up a tolerance over time. *Over time* being the key. I didn't mean to lead you here."

"I'm fine," Stephen countered around another mouthful of food. "Do I remember correctly that you agreed to host our wedding?"

"Yes, I did. Whisterly is thrilled also. Why?"

Stephen refilled his cup as he polished off his first piece of toast. "When my parents hear about this, they're gonna skin me alive, if they can't help with the planning. Not to mention your plan to have Belle stay with you guys."

"It'll be good to meet them. Talk this through."

"If you say so... I'm gonna give this shower thing a try now, so you'll go away."

"Sounds good," Jack said, waiting, making no move for the door.

"Here goes." This time when Stephen left the bed, the excruciating pain in his head had dulled to a manageable throbbing ache.

"You made it."

Stephen paused, tilting his head slightly, not wanting to unsettle the precarious progress he'd made with any quick movement. "Thanks, Jack. I haven't felt that bad since..." His mouth clamped shut, a shiver running down his spine. Silence stretched between them.

"Since you were Simon's prisoner, right?"

Stephen gave a tight nod, still not turning to face Jack.

"I won't let that happen again to any of my family, and that includes you. If it comes down to it, I'll kill him myself first."

Tears pricked Stephen's eyes. Surprised by the unexpected turn in the conversation, and not wanting to fall apart in front of Jack, he trudged on to the bathroom. "Thanks again, Jack, for everything."

"You bet. Glad to see you back on your feet. Keep the coffee going."

"I'll do that." The door slid open and closed again. Stephen leaned against the tile in the bathroom, pushing down on the sudden burst of hurt that had risen so quickly to the surface. He swallowed down the knot of emotion stuck in his throat, shutting his eyes tightly against the memory he'd accidentally willed back to life and into his thoughts.

Taking deeps breaths, he stepped into the shower and let the water wash away his sadness while he reined in his wayward thoughts and gained some semblance of control again.

*Arista?*

*How are you feeling?*

*Better, love. Thanks to your father. Can I see you?*

*Sure. Come on over. I'll fix us—*

*Coffee. Please, just coffee.*

*I'll have it ready.*

*Be there soon.*

He dressed quickly and headed out. Only one thing was stronger than the hate he harbored for Simon, and that was the love he had for Arista. Even if only for a little while, he needed her in his arms.

WHERE THE HELL did that come from? Suddenly Jack's skin felt too tight. Would he really kill his own son? The experience inside the Night Dwellers' cave, where Jack and Simon had engaged in their first physical confrontation, had been surreal. His aim then had been simple—to get Arista *and* Simon out and proceed from there. Hopefully, eventually finding a path toward resolution of their differences. Simon... The man was the antithesis of Jack in all the ways that truly mattered. Evil, controlling, hateful, sadistic, barbaric, authoritarian—the list was endless.

A tiny seed of faith still existed that Simon's defenses would be torn away with the memory wipe—if he ever woke again, that is—and his son would have a fresh start. The knowledge of this bone-chilling certainty steeled his spine. If Whisterly, Arista, Daniel, Stephen, or Belle were to face imminent death at Simon's hand, Jack would stop Simon's wrath by whatever means necessary.

Clarity rang true as it melded within him. Jack hadn't been forced to face this exact scenario in the Night Dwellers' cave. The blow, if it came, would hurt like chopping off his own leg, severing Simon from this life and sending him to the next one, where the supreme being would take care of what Jack could not.

Time would tell.

Jack raised his head to find himself at the basement door. Down below Simon rested, hovering somewhere between life and death, his feet not firmly planted in either realm. Jack unlocked the door and trekked into the inner sanctuary. Simon still lay there, as unmoving as the stone that held him. Jack didn't know what he'd thought might be the case instead.

His son was a warlock after all; maybe he could free himself of the prison where magic held his consciousness captive. Or maybe this was all that would ever be for his son, their relationship forfeited for the good of the remaining family around Jack. Well then, so be it. At the least, wiping Simon's mental slate clean had prevented more deaths at his hand.

Belle popped up from the edge of the wall, her body cloaked in shadows.

"Belle, I didn't see you. You here all alone?"

She giggled. A sweet sound counteracting the darkness of

Jack's thoughts. "Of course not, silly. The coven's here." Her gaze flashed to the ceiling, where the squirming mass shifted in answer.

"Of course." Jack huffed a laugh. "My mistake. You don't have to stay, you know," Jack continued. "Or even visit him."

"I know, Mr. Jack. I stop by every day, but I don't stay long. Each day I sense changes in Simon. If he reaches back toward this life, I want to help him find his way."

"Why would you do that, Belle? Simon has hurt so many people."

A sadness washed over her face while Jack watched her struggle for words. "That's true, but being here with the coven is changing him. For good or bad, I don't know. I see flashes, visions that he shares with me sometimes. In return, I want him to see the light and life surrounding him and all of us. I would do the same for creatures in the forest. Shouldn't I do it for him?"

Jack reached out to Belle and folded her into his arms. "Thank you, Belle, for sharing your light. Your touch might be the only thing keeping Simon from falling into total darkness and chaos."

"No, I don't think so." Shaking her head, Belle withdrew from the embrace. "Even with his memory gone, I feel you and Whisterly there too, inside his head. I don't know if Simon recognizes you're there though."

Belle's smile lit the room. Despite his own confusion, Jack laughed. "I don't understand any of it. But good to know. Now why don't you get out of here for now? Go upstairs where you can get some real sunshine, not only the memory of it in your thoughts."

"Sure, Mr. Jack. See you later."

"Incredible," Jack muttered as Belle ducked out of sight. He heaved an exasperated sigh, her footsteps echoing through the stairwell. How could a young girl affect Jack's view of life in such a profound way?

Perched on a rock, still mired in speculation over his son and Belle's influence, Jack reached for his best friend.

*Harry?*

*Jack... God, I miss you, man.*

*Same, Harry. What's up? You sound worked up.*

*Hell yeah, I am. Some days I feel like it's hard to breathe. This impending fatherhood thing is freaking me out. I could use a talk and some stiff drinks with you right about now.*

*Rain check on the drinks, but I'm always here for you, even while I'm "here."*

*Maggie takes this all in stride, even seems to be getting more confident as our child grows inside her. For me the opposite is true. It's like a miniature time bomb, ticking down until my secret is out. I'll screw up bad. I just know it.*

*You will.*

*Thanks for the vote of confidence, Jack.*

*Just being honest. I'll not sugarcoat it. You'll mess up. Fatherhood is the hardest job there is, and you never have a day off. But you're also gonna be the best dad ever, Harry.*

*How do you know, Jack?*

*Because I know you, what makes you you. And I see how good you are with Daniel. You can't fake that. Relax. The pieces will fall into place as you need them. I'll be there too, however I can, and I can't wait to be an uncle.*

*Means a lot, Jack. Thanks, man.*

*You bet. Now I've got something I need you to do for me.*

*Sure. Anything, you know that.*

*Reach out through the Freemason network. We need to find some contacts in the Washington, DC, area.*

*Really? Why?*

*A scheme that Kix is involved in and evidently has been working for years. I don't know what you've pulled from my thoughts about him lately, but he's a warlock, part human and part Remeon, and trading Remeon space tech secrets with the US. We're trying to shut his ass down.*

*Good God... Your thoughts are a nightmare, Jack. I mean, an army of wraiths... Really? Most days I just jump in and out to make sure you're still alive. I don't make it a habit to stay there.*

*Yeah. I'm with you.*

*Name it. What do you need?*

*I'll give you some coordinates in the DC area, and we need to find out exactly where they lead, as well as businesses and homes within a small perimeter. The local Freemason lodge can handle some of the heavy lifting, thus the need for contacts.*

*Send me what you got, and I'll get to work. It'll give me something else to focus on besides the little human growing inside my wife. I'm totally in awe of her, by the way.*

*You should be. Speaking of little humans. How's Daniel?*

*He's great—a smaller version of you, Jack. I keep wondering how that's possible with him having none of your genes. And he's completely wrapped up in things for the baby. Maybe you should consider another, Jack.*

*Baby? Maybe. Right now I've got my hands full though. Especially with a wedding on the horizon as well.*

*That means you could be Grandpa Jack before too long.*

*Hey, don't rush them.*

*I guess you'd tell me if there was a change in Simon's status. I sense nothing new in your thoughts.*

*No. Not yet.*

*Any way you look at it, Jack, we're two blessed bastards.*

*Yeah. We are. And Harry, don't let Daniel forget me. It would literally kill me if I got home and found him calling you dad.*

Jack heard Harry's hearty laugh through his thoughts. *No chance in hell of that. He talks his mouth off about you every day and carries your picture around with him. You'd think he loves you or something.*

*Thank God, he does. I'll get those exact coordinates for you, Harry. Keep in touch.*

*Jack, you stay safe, brother.*

*You too, Harry. Give my love to your better half.*

*And mine to Whisterly.*

JACK WOKE, dread and longing pooling within him in equal measure. In a short while, he, Kix, and Stephen would enter the holosuite, stepping into 1930, revisiting the devastation of that year. Facing that period in his life was painful enough to experience once. But twice? Being a willing recipient again had him avoiding the day, something Jack never did.

Maneuvering Whisterly on top of him, he resettled her and released a sigh, easing into her thoughts.

*Mmm, Jack what is it? You seem anxious.*

*Yeah.* He stroked her hair and pressed a kiss to her forehead. *A little. This holosuite adventure has me riled up.*

Blinking her eyes, not quite fully awake, Whisterly leaned on one elbow. "Oh, yeah."

"I've come so far from that point in my life. Feels wrong to willingly return."

"Ah, Jack..." She laid her head on his chest. "You're a completely different person now. Those years forged you into the strong loving man you are today."

"Loving you turned me into the man I am today."

"True, but would you have made it this far without Sam to show you how to be that man?"

"No. Most likely not. If he'd not taken me in when he did, I'd probably have turned to a life of crime just to survive."

"Look at you now." Whisterly ran her fingers through his hair.

Jack tracked Whisterly's appreciative gaze down the length

of his body and grinned. "You do know how to grab my attention."

"You're not that starving teenager anymore. You're mine, Jack Livingston. So hurry back from that holosuite. I need you in the here and now."

"Yes, ma'am, Mrs. Livingston." Jack's eyes cut to hers. "I'm counting on you to hold that thought till I return."

She raised a brow and gave him a sleepy smile. "You bet I will."

JACK, Kix, and Stephen had a prearranged time to meet; despite Jack's late start to the day, he arrived first. After spending a good bit of the night weighing which memory to summon for their recreation, Jack was undecided. Lost in thought, and still uneasy with the memories this outing had dredged up, he signed the prerequisite paperwork and jerked his chin to Kix and Stephen as they approached. Sasha, the same attendant who helped Jack on previous occasions, walked Stephen and Kix through the formalities.

Hopefully Stephen's presence would serve the purpose intended, to alleviate the tension between Jack and Kix. Jack had spent some time bringing Stephen up to speed regarding the direction of their plan, since he had missed the meeting with Vinique. They needed Kix to feel at ease, so the next time the three of them gathered here, Kix would share a few spells, show off a little, under the guise of Simon's training, giving away his hand just enough to allow the council to maintain their advantage.

Jack tossed his attention to Kix and Stephen, currently leaving Sasha with smiles on their faces. Kix's resolute gaze met Jack's, the man's thoughts locked down tight. Falling in line with Kix's agenda wasn't Jack's plan; the plan was Kix bending to Jack's. Didn't feel like that though, as he offered his painful past as a sacrifice.

Rubbing his hands together like it was dinnertime and Kix had just sat down to a feast of Jack, drawn and quartered, Kix leaned to the side, attempting to peer around Jack to the suite prepared and waiting for them. "Jack, what's the hold up now? After hearing that lovely lady talk up this tech, I'm ready. I can't believe I haven't tried this yet."

"Hey, just give him a minute, why don't ya?" Stephen cut in.

"Sorry, I don't think you two have met formally."

Stephen shrugged and shook his head. Knowing his part in the plan, he didn't seem to care about the niceties. But they did matter. Building a camaraderie this quickly required commitment to the details and focus.

Jack reminded Stephen of the stakes with a directed thought. Kix had magic on his side. Jack and Stephen had only their will and wit. It needed to be enough. Stephen reached out to Kix, offering his hand. "Nice to meet you, Kix."

"You as well, kid. Your name's been batted around the council for so long I feel like we had to have met already."

"I feel sure I would remember meeting a man such as yourself," Stephen said, still pumping the man's hand.

"All right, now that we all know each other, let's go in." The doors slid open, and the three walked into the room with the now familiar silver metallic background. Still grappling with what came next, Jack's hand hovered over the palm scanner.

A heavy hand landed on Jack's shoulder. "It's okay, Jack."

Jack nodded his agreement, although Kix didn't know what the hell he was talking about. In truth, all *would* work out fine. The only problem... Getting from here to there. "We're going to the coal mine where I used work with Sam, back to his last day."

No matter how many times Jack had replayed this day in his head, he'd always felt like some clue had been missed.

That somehow he could have stopped the horrible tragedy from happening. Would a visual recreation give him more objectivity to see the facts of that day exactly as they had truly been?

"Gods, Jack, just get it over with, man." Kix covered Jack's hand with his and mashed them both onto the scanner. A crackling sounded, and the room buzzed to life.

Jack rounded on Kix, his words spilling out in a hiss. "Do not interfere with my actions. I'll not give another warning."

Stephen sidled up to Kix, leaned in to say a few words that Jack couldn't hear, then stood between Jack and Kix.

*Smart kid.*

"What do you need, Jack?"

"Just a minute and some space." Sucking in a breath, Jack looked on while the vision that had been seared in his brain all those years ago took shape before him. Writhing, twisting, bending, and shaping, the array of muted tones settled into place, the images solidifying as it had been back in 1930.

Suddenly it was like Jack had been thrown back in time, given a precious slice of life to talk to these people, many of whom wouldn't live to see the next sunrise. Of course Jack's actions today wouldn't really impact the past, but could they heal some of the hurt still inside him almost two decades old? Allow some closure? Many here were like a second family. Had given him food, clothing, and friendship. The lump in Jack's throat grew; his shoulders tensed.

"Jack, this is fantastic." Kix sniffed. "But what exactly is that stench in the air?"

"Gases from the mine. It'll get worse as we come closer. Follow me. It's almost time."

They walked along the boardwalk of the tiny town, the businesses bustling with activity, selling produce, advertising their goods. And the diner where he and Sam had frequented —the one where Sam had bought Jack's first meal here, when

Jack had come to town, nothing but skin and bones, determined to support his mother...

But there wasn't time.

Any second now the men would start pouring from the mine. Jack set off at a run, leaving Kix and Stephen to follow, or not. Cresting the hill brought the tree in sight where Jack and Sam ate lunch, where the crew gathered, where Jack and Sam had somehow connected in a real way after his death.

The whistle sounded, freezing Jack in place. His gaze darted to the mine's entry. A man waved, an infectious grin flashing across his face.

Sam...

## 7

*U*ntil Jack had prepared for this visit to the holographic suite, he hadn't considered maintaining this experience, dropping in on his and Sam's life here every now and then. But seeing his mentor before him, Jack struck that thought down quick. Time here was bigger...more sacred than that.

Lunch. Sam would be hungry from the morning's work. Jack shot a glance to their tree. Sure enough, their lunch pail was there and Jack's treasured book, *All Quiet on the Western Front*. That well-thought-out gift from Sam had impacted Jack's views on war, although not in the direction Sam had hoped.

Jack's feet ate up the distance separating him from Sam. A slow smile spread across his lips, amusement flickering in his eyes.

"You finally got your sleepy ass outta bed, I see." Observing Sam through Jack's perspective as an adult caught him off guard. His time-tested instincts earned honestly during the war and trials of hard manual labor kicked in. Men stopped Sam as he walked up the hill, some for a friendly chat, others to discuss the schedule for the day or other mine business. Sam offered a smile, a word, a handshake, or a combination of the three to all but Gene, the supervisor.

Dipping his chin in response to Gene's two-fingered wave, Sam hadn't slowed his pace up the hill to meet Jack.

"I did." Jack laughed. "And you're lucky I managed, or you wouldn't have any lunch, since I brought it."

"You got me there, Start-Up," Sam admitted with a solid thump to Jack's back.

Hearing Sam's nickname for Jack again flooded him with the memories of this time and their original meeting. On that occasion Sam had laughed, reprimanding Jack for "starting up" a conversation about washing Sam's clothes, when he obviously didn't have the resources to do so. Immediately after that, seeing Jack's need, Sam had fed him and taken him in, over time offering the pieces of himself which helped to mold Jack into the man he was today.

Sam eyed Kix and Stephen. Suppressing a grin, Jack couldn't help but notice Sam's immediate acceptance of Stephen and the apparent trepidation with Kix. And it only took a couple seconds. Sam had them sized up before his greeting. "Friends, Jack? Nice to see you getting to know people and not just stuck with your head in that book." His gaze drifted to Jack's copy of his favorite book, then to Kix and Stephen. "Well?"

"Oh. Sorry. Sam, this is Stephen and Kix. They're, uh, new to these parts."

Stephen and Kix shook the hand Sam offered. "You're welcome to join us, if you like. It's not much."

"Oh, you mean, 'cause of the Depression," Kix stated.

"Huh?" Confusion filtered across Sam's face. "There's always someone hungrier than me. Right, Jack? Why, we don't know what these men might have been through. What it took them to get here."

"They already ate, Sam." Jack directed a thought to the two

to make themselves scarce, adding the sternest facade he could muster.

"We'll take a look around and leave you in peace while you eat," Stephen offered.

"Suit yourselves. Only steer clear of the mine, or the guy below with the clipboard might recruit you."

Kix glanced at the soot covering Sam's clothing and face and wiped his hands down the front of his own shirt, like being in Sam's presence had dirtied him in some way.

Jack yanked his head to the side. "Go on."

"Interesting pair you got there," Sam said, watching them go and settling into a spot under their tree while he chugged water.

"Yeah. That's one way to put it." Jack divided out the food and served Sam, Jack's thoughts on the words he wanted to say before setting them free. They chewed in silence until Sam enjoyed every last lick of honey.

"Taking you out tonight, Start-Up. Too much time with books, especially that book, isn't good for you. You need a date."

The look Jack gave Sam told him that he'd be on his own, but Jack remembered this conversation. Sam wouldn't accept a no.

"Hey, Sam, hold up. How about we leave town? Pack up now. I know it sounds crazy. But you've been talking about us hitting the road, going to where the work is. Let's do it!"

Sam paused, his gaze reaching for Jack's. "What's gotten into you? You don't like to go out on the town, much less leave town."

"I'm convinced. Come back with me. Let's pack up and leave."

"Son, I can't leave in the middle of shift. If you're serious, I'll talk to you more about it after I clock out."

"No, now, Sam," Jack contradicted, adding a tone that he

hoped conveyed the desperation he felt, looking back now on this tragic day.

Sam's eyes narrowed, scrutinizing Jack. "Good to know you've been listening." He laid a hand on Jack's cheek and crooked the thumb of his other hand toward the mine's entrance. "This life isn't for you. That's for damn sure. You're going places, son."

"We're going places together. Remember?" Jack corrected.

"You're preaching to the choir." The horn blared, signaling the end of lunch break. "We'll talk later. I'll skip out on the plans I had tonight."

Jack shook his head, gritting his teeth as he spat out his next words. "I'll leave without you. You need to come now."

Sam's eyes widened. "This change of heart...is it because of your new friends? 'Cause the older one is no good. You hear me? Don't listen to or go anywhere with him."

Jack nodded, his eyes filling. No matter what he'd said, Sam would have finished his shift. The little bit of peace that thought brought Jack eased through him. Of course, in hindsight, Jack could conjure something more devious to lure Sam away. But back then, as an almost seventeen-year-old kid, what he'd done just now would have been crossing a hard line.

Sam gave Jack a stone-hard glare. "Promise me. No decisions today. Tomorrow after we talk. Okay?"

"No decisions tonight."

Yanking Jack in tight against him, Sam clapped Jack's back while they lingered in their embrace. "Damn, Start-up. We're really doing it. Soon."

"Soon," Jack murmured.

"See you later."

"Wait."

"What is it? Gene's about to lose his shit."

"Gene can go to hell." Jack caught up to Sam in two lengthy

strides. "I'll take the cage below with you. Check on the guy's supplies."

"Suit yourself." Throwing an arm over Jack's shoulder, the two headed into the mine.

Dread rose in the pit of Jack's stomach, even now as an adult in a recreation of one of the worst days of his life. Clinging to the cool metal of the cage, he closed his eyes, concentrating on Sam's steadying hand on Jack's shoulder as the rickety basket swung side to side, descending into the darkness below. Landing with the finality of the knowledge of the death to come, Jack and Sam plodded through the tunnels, eking out a path to their team working in the alcove ahead.

The light on the hard hat Jack wore illuminated only a few feet ahead before blackness would swallow the pair again. As they routinely did, Jack and Sam worked in tandem, adjusting the rays, pooling the light for spotting any danger ahead. Soon the banter and clatter of the group of men reached them.

Jack and Sam ducked inside the room. "Look who I brought down."

Smiles peeked out from under the soot-covered faces of the men, their eyes glistening, showing the appreciation for the role Jack filled for them. He spotted George, not long for this world now, and reached him in two long strides, thudding him with a hug that brought on a coughing fit. "How ya been, George?"

"Fine, Jack. Better with some water, huh?"

"You bet. I'll load it up and bring it right down." Jack noted the short list, then gave hugs all around. Their confused expressions swung to Sam, who shrugged it off, but, in Sam's mind, he probably chalked up the odd behavior to the impending discussion and the decision to leave this place.

"See ya in a while, Start-Up."

Jack nodded, taking off his hard hat for a hug, mirroring Sam's action. "I'll wait for you by the tree. Don't be late, Sam."

Sam mused Jack's hair, sending dust and debris flying, the toxic stuff quickly finding another surface close by to cling to. "I'll be there. I'm never late. You know that." A cocky self-assured grin rested at the corner of Sam's mouth. "Later, Start-up."

"Later... Under the tree," he added, entering the tunnel, donning his hard hat again for the solitary ride to freedom and life, escaping the tomb below. Swiping at his eyes, Jack stepped into the cage and shuddered.

Kix and Stephen waited for Jack aboveground, engaged in a conversation with Gene. "Let's go," Jack yelled.

Gene's gaze drifted to his paperwork. "Where are you going, son? Get back here. You've got supplies to deliver."

"Go to hell, Gene."

Kix and Stephen fell silently in line as Jack rushed them forward. Anytime now the blast would sound. He cringed. Unable to wait another second, Jack uttered the word to stop it all. "Halt!"

STEPHEN HAD A DAD. A great one. Unless hell froze over, Jack would be his father-in-law. But in addition, after today, Stephen saw Jack as his very own "Sam." Mentoring him in similar ways as Sam had done for Jack. More than anything, but his love for Arista, Stephen wanted to fill that role for someone. What a presence Sam was. Stephen could see the love that Sam had for Jack, even in the little bit of time they shared. Sam's words and actions told the story.

The bay doors to the holosuite opened. Jack kept walking, not a word, not a glance over his shoulder as he beat a path away from the heart-wrenching scene they'd been cast in the middle of. So real, so full of life, Jack drew others toward his spirit—just like Sam must have.

"Seeing Jack like that, knowing he was leaving those men dead in that underground tomb...horrible. Nobody should contemplate living on that planet without magic by their side," Kix scoffed. "How humans ever made it past the Neanderthal stage, I'll never know. Dumb as dirt most of them."

"Looks like you got what you wanted—to see more of the real Jack."

"Yes. I did. Helps to see how his brilliant military mind developed, wouldn't you say?"

"I think, whatever you saw in there today, you already knew about Jack."

"No, not really. Watching life-defining events like that, knowing the transformative power those scenarios can preclude can bind you to a human's soul. As a result, magical powers find new outlets."

Stephen watched while a smile took over Kix's face then spoke his part. "You're up next. Let's see what kind of life-defining moments we experience in your holosuite adventure."

Kix let out a throaty chuckle. "I'm looking forward to it too."

STEPHEN PAUSED at Arista's door, knocked, and nodded to the guard on duty, who waved him on. At least they knew him now. Unless she was in a meeting, he typically got the green light. Since her recent abduction, thank God security had tightened up. Vinique, with counsel from Jack and Whisterly, had made that happen immediately. Even though Arista's attempt for solitary time was more heavily monitored, she'd relented on this point at Stephen's and her parents' urging. Of course with the Night Dwellers currently imploding, since the loss of their leader, from the looks of it, the danger, for now, appeared to be less.

Arista lifted her head from the mound of paperwork littering her desk. "Stephen, you're back."

"Come here." He crossed the floor toward her.

"What is it?" she asked, on her feet and moving on an intercept path. In her rush, Stephen caught her in his arms and pressed their bodies together before covering his mouth with hers in a deep, slow kiss.

"Wow." She gasped, coming up for air. "More of those throughout my day please."

"That can be arranged. Just be careful what you wish for."

Arista wove a path to her couch, towing Stephen behind her. "So, tell me. How did it go?"

He grabbed her hand and brought it to her lips.

Her eyes wrinkled with concern. "Stephen?"

"What Jack went through so early in life...well, I guess he was my age now, when Sam was killed."

"That's about right."

"So awful. Judging from what I witnessed today, it was just luck, or more likely divine intervention, that he wasn't below when the mine blew, and all hell broke loose. If Jack had died, I'd never have known you, Arista."

She lifted his chin with her forefinger. "But Papa didn't die. That's the best part of that horrible story. He's here with me, and I have you too."

"You sure do." Stephen leaned in and tasted her neck, kissed a line up her throat, and nibbled softly on her earlobe.

"I'll be worthless for the rest of the day if you keep that up."

He slid Arista to his lap. "Then my plan is working." Bringing Arista in for a soft, tender kiss, the curve of her lips teased him. "Love, I wanna be more like him, now more than ever."

Arista ran her fingers through his hair. "You're already on your way. I admire you, all you've done, the trials you've been through, coming out stronger on the other side. Think of what you've accomplished already—healing our race from PR 251. The impact you've made on our civilization in the past year is more than some people have during an entire lifetime."

"Thank you for saying so. All my father's words over the years are starting to make some sense." He paused, staring into Arista's eyes as he dragged her palm to his mouth and kissed it. "But what I want to do now has more to do with your father and his influence."

The sparkle swimming in Arista's eyes kept him talking. "I can't go back and be molded by the hardships of the Depression, but I think I've had a few similar experiences on my own. And like we've discussed, joining the military here will help me hone my skills and learn new ones...will make me worthy of you," he said on a whisper.

"You already are."

He shrugged. "I look up to my dad. He's always been a role model for me. But I wanna be like Jack. To learn to be a mentor for others. Maybe what I've been through will be useful."

"Useful? Of course. You've come through illness, capture, imprisonment, stealth missions, training missions. Stephen, you're already there."

"Not yet, love. I've got a long way to go." His smile broadened. "But I think I'm off to a good start. I need to be up to the task 100 percent. Arista?"

"Yes, sweetheart?"

"Your father is my mentor. I realized that today, watching him. Jack's been leading me and helping me since I met him at his house in Utah. And I don't want to let him down."

"My father has let me know how proud he is of you, Stephen. He's excited about our marriage. You've got me, and I can't wait to marry you. We're on our way."

"Feels so good to hear that, coming from your lips. Tell me again."

"I. Can't. Wait. To. Marry. You."

Arista's words rippled through his veins, heating him from the inside out. He leaned into her kiss. A second before he reached her, Arista's breath hitched. "I love that I affect you this way."

"And I love that you don't doubt my feelings for you any longer. Now, *shhh*, and get on with it."

Stephen grinned. "Yes, ma'am, Council Chair."

JACK TOSSED AND TURNED, fighting the revival of old ghosts in his sleep. With each twist and turn, the sheets knotted tighter around him. Jolting upright, his eyes wide, he screamed, "Run!" His breath stuttered, his heart racing. "Damn it!" he muttered, throwing aside the covers.

"Jack?"

"I'm sorry. I should have slept on the couch. I had a feeling this was coming."

"It's okay. Come back to bed."

"I don't think I'll be able to sleep."

Whisterly smiled, canting her head. "Then we'll not sleep together."

Jack chuckled, raising a brow. "That doesn't sound so bad."

She patted the space beside her, and he tunneled back under the covers. "Was it worse than you expected?"

"No. Not really." He settled Whisterly against his chest. "Odd having an audience though."

Whisterly kissed his shoulder. "You don't have to talk about it. Might be easier to sleep if you didn't."

Jack shrugged. "I'm used to it now, I guess. My talks with Sam under our tree keep me attached to the place, so all it takes is a thought or a smell, and I'm right back there. Some of the experience I liked—seeing the old businesses and restaurants we used to frequent as a group—where we had made some happy memories. I'd forgotten that, so reviving the not-so-bad parts was a welcome distraction. But the smell of gas in the air, the coal dust that clings to every person and surface, the icy bone-deep chill that sucks you under as you descend into the mine, those parts will always stick with me. Till the day I die probably."

"You said you were going to try something different yesterday, so that the simulation might not control you."

"Yeah." Jack ran his hand through his hair. "I did. I wanted to see if I could prevent Sam from returning to the mine after we had lunch that godawful afternoon and before everything went to hell."

Whisterly's fingers stilled on his chest.

"I couldn't convince him. I said we'd go explore—travel, like he'd been talking about to me for months. The only catch was that we would leave right then, not after the shift change. I tried after we ate, then again when I went below for supply orders. Maddening that the very thing Sam wanted more than anything—to travel—was not enough to convince him to make it happen. Short of drugging the man and dragging him out of there, he wasn't interesting in leaving voluntarily right then."

Whisterly released a breath, like Jack had just passed a difficult test and come through successful on the other side.

"It does feel good to work out that piece, even though it all comes from the same place—inside my head."

"Are you saying it helped you to go back?"

"In this instance, yes. You see, I've always felt like I should have done more. But looking back, playing all those scenes over and over in my head, the only option was keeping Sam from his shift that day. The realization brings me a little peace." Jack massaged Whisterly's back. "True to himself, Sam returned to finish his work. My guess is, if I couldn't change his mind that day, nobody else could have either, except for maybe one of his buddies in need of him."

"That's progress, Jack."

He nodded and pressed a kiss to her forehead. "Some. His death that follows next never seems to be too far from my thoughts."

Whisterly wrapped her hand around his before continuing. "It sounds like the experience this time was different from your nightmares."

"I think so too. Maybe because of time, distance, or reflection? I'm not really sure."

"What about Kix? Do you think you and Stephen accomplished our goal?"

"I hope so. I'm not up for another go anytime soon. Without a doubt I've given the man more avenues to exploit me within his craft. Kix was enthralled with the whole scene. Stephen kept him engaged in the people and activity around us while I was busy with Sam and the guys. From my read of Kix before we left the holosuite, he wanted to stay longer and experience more of the actual tragedy through my eyes. All about the death and destruction of course."

"You enjoyed seeing the guys from your work team?"

"Yeah, George especially. He was closest to my age, and we were good friends." Jack shrugged. "Bittersweet."

"Can you leave it for a while now? Sleep a bit more before our meeting with Vinique?"

"Go ahead, baby. I'll be right here." As Whisterly snuggled against him, visions of Sam popped into Jack's head. Ones where they'd both been very much alive and engaged in planning their travels beyond the cesspool of the coal mine. The flashes of memory stretched before him. And grinning back at Sam's antics, Jack gave in to sleep, the words in his head falling from his lips before drifting off. "I love you, old man."

∾

LATER THAT MORNING, from across her desk, Vinique faced Arista, Whisterly, and Jack, after delivering the news they'd all been expecting. During Kix's last communication with Earth, he'd sent another data file, but this time the transfer had been intercepted. As far as the team knew, Kix wasn't yet aware they'd switched his file for an innocuous version—one full of general information regarding Earth's solar system, which included none of Remeon's classified data.

"I think we all saw this coming." Vinique unleashed a deep sigh. "I, for one, don't mind admitting I'm extremely happy that I won't need to make good on my promise to mate him."

Arista locked eyes with hers. "I am as well, Vinique. Your willingness to do so goes above and beyond my expectations. But we must act quickly now to finish what we've started. Papa, will you reach out to him and plan another holosuite experience? The day after tomorrow would be perfect."

"Absolutely, little one."

"Meanwhile, Vinique, Mother, and I will plan his unique experience. One that, by all appearances, will seem to be held in a holosuite but in actuality will take place in the basement with the full support of the coven. We won't show our hand until he's expended plenty of energy, casting spells for you and Stephen. So encourage him to keep going, and we'll step in during a pivotal point in one of his incantations, hopefully catching him totally unaware. Questions, anyone?"

A whirl of emotions played inside her head as Vinique listened to Arista's final instructions. Was it relief over her close call with the warlock that washed through Vinique, threading her with an uneasiness she couldn't shake or something more sinister? If Whisterly and Arista felt it as well, then the question had an answer.

*Whisterly... Arista...*

## 8

*A*ll a little on edge, Arista, Vinique, and Whisterly had been sequestered in the basement for most of the afternoon, setting up, verifying, and testing the digital, holographic, and telepathic links needed to recreate Kix's holosuite experience inside the witches' domain, all without actually having a holosuite here. Once Kix initiated the experience in the real holosuite, the three of them could recreate the session via links within the holosuite systems, anchored by telepathic links to Jack, Stephen, and Kix also.

Masterminding this event required the magical talents of the whole coven. Not only would they duplicate the experience and transfer it to the basement but getting Kix here had to integrate within the session itself as well. Vinique would remain above, rendering spells on the fly within the magical bubble she'd created, cloaking the three from any passersby until they were safely hidden below. All of this would need to transpire without alerting Kix to the deception. If all went as expected, the coven's space would act as an extension of the holosuite, adapting to the actual scene ongoing inside the simulation.

"This is quite a feat that we've undertaken, Arista."

"I would agree. Fortunately Great-Grandmother and the coven have our backs."

"We do," the old witch cackled with a natural wickedness embedded in her tone. "We're all set here. I have to say, it will be a pleasure to send this man to the humans to deal with for good."

Above, the mural twisted and slithered as the coven members communicated, eager to begin, their robes swaying free of their bindings and their voices carrying, mingling with their sisters in excitement.

Arista released a breath, nodding to Vinique to take her place upstairs, then turned to Whisterly. "Ready, Mother?"

"You bet I am, and since we'll be concealed from his view, all of us will have a front-row seat to the spells he conjures, learning his unique style of magic as we go." She angled her head, listening. "Jack is close, little one," Whisterly warned.

Arista beckoned to the waiting coven. Floating down to join them, the witches took their places, hoods draped over their heads, whispering to one another as they gathered. Expectation hung heavy in the air while they lingered, waiting, the anticipation ramping up with each moment that passed.

"We're on." All eyes homed in on the ancient witch, whose grin spread from ear to ear. "Watch and listen. Now...silence," she finished on a slow hiss.

Panic seeped into Arista's thoughts. "Belle, I've forgotten Belle. Her human connection is an accessory we can utilize."

"Easy, dear. I brought her with me. She's been visiting with Simon, hidden from view, in preparation for today's activities."

"Thank the gods, Mother. I want to exploit every advantage we have." Arista scanned the perimeter, spotting Belle among the congregation of witches, the wise child taking in her surroundings with a watchful eye.

"Center yourself, little one. All is well." Grabbing her mother's hand brought instant relief as her calming presence permeated Arista, flooding her being. Tension slid from her shoulders, just as the door leading to the basement burst open.

"Thank you, Mother."

Were they ready for any contingency? Had they anticipated Kix's responses? Would he learn of their deception too late to interfere with their plan? All those questions needed an answer in the affirmative to guarantee success. And their magic needed to be spot-on. No room for error today.

Voices carried through the confines of the basement while the small group traversed the steps, and then the cobblestones, all built into the elaborate specifications of the holosuite. A whoosh of air accompanied Jack, Stephen, and Kix as they entered, and the congregation watched the action unfolding through the thin mist-like veil that separated them.

One aspect of the holosuite had not been replicated: the integrated safety features. In order to allow the casting of spells, and for those spells to work as intended, protection from real harm couldn't be upheld here. In fact, they were counting on Kix's vulnerability, when, at the last moment, he understood whom and what he faced.

Jack and Stephen appeared to be enthralled with the warlock's spells as Kix conjured them one after the other.

Through the thread of the group's telepathic connection weaving among the coven, they quietly went to work. Taking turns, the witches rotated, counteracting Kix's spells and balancing his energy with their own, effectively neutralizing his power. Inside the simulation, the incantations still achieved the warlock's desired results. Here, the coven worked through his battery of magic, ensuring a counterspell existed to overpower each of his spells.

Hours of learning passed before Kix showed signs of weariness, and Jack and Stephen had almost run out questions it seemed, judging from their longer stints of silence.

"Well, Jack, do you feel like you're more in tune with me

now? You and Stephen know more about me than almost anyone here in the compound, with the exception of the council and my own family."

"The session has been enlightening for sure. Not that I understand it all of course, but I feel a certain kinship between what I've witnessed today and the enchantments I've seen from Arista and Whisterly."

"Kinship, yes. But we warlocks have our own brand of magic, unique and set apart from witches. Where we are alike is the source of our magic, knowledge passed down through the families and entrusted to the new generations as time passes. We only have to connect with our power, learn to harness it, then direct it for the greatest impact. After what you've seen today, I hope you'll agree that I'm qualified to help your son in ways that no one else here can."

"You've given me a lot to think about, that's for sure."

"Jack? Do you hear that?"

"Hear what? My ears are still ringing from that last explosion you created."

"No... This is different."

"Hey, I wouldn't mind seeing that last thing again," Stephen interjected.

*Nice try, Stephen. Ready yourself. He's breaking through*, Arista warned.

"Jack, where is your son? He was captured, but surely he's too big of a threat for the general infirmary. And I don't recall hearing from the council. Of course we haven't had a formal meeting since Simon's imprisonment."

*Simon... Kix can feel his presence, Miss Whisterly. I can sense the flashes of thought through my connection with Simon*, Belle communicated.

"His accommodations are classified. I'm sure you understand why."

Kix let out a sinister chuckle. "Normally, yes. But I'm a

council member. His whereabouts should be at my fingertips. Even now as I browse through prisoner records, in-patients under doctors' care, and residents of the compound, I've got nothing."

"Security has tightened since Arista's abduction and rightly so. I suggest you take it up with them."

Kix's eyes narrowed, and he edged to the boundaries of the magical oasis. "He's close. So close, I can feel his energy radiating, pulsing in his need to reach me." Awareness dawned on Kix's face. He sauntered toward Jack. "What are you not telling me, Jack?"

"I don't need to tell you anything," Jack growled out, meeting the surprise in his opponent's eyes.

*Belle, can you occupy Simon's thoughts with those visions you've been talking to us about? Anything. Just keep them coming. We don't want Simon—unconsciously or consciously—lending strength to Kix while we go head-to-head with him.*

*I sure can, Arista.*

*Good girl. Do it! Time to act.*

The shroud of mist dissipated. Kix's mouth fell open.

A booming voice split the silence.

"Warlock! You've been judged, and your sentence determined," the hag bellowed. Her hand cut the air, and Kix stumbled, his hands and feet instantly bound tight, where he leaned now against the rocky wall.

Kix surveyed the room, blinking, his eyes adjusting to the dim light. "Jack? Did you hijack my simulation? What's with all this?" he asked through a nervous chuckle.

"No." Jack blew out a breath. "This you brought on yourself."

"Stephen, you too?" Arista stepped front and center,

followed by Vinique. Farther back, Jack stood with Yara? His new mate?

"Of course. I'm with him," Stephen said with a jerk of his head toward Jack.

"Arista, now that you've lured me here..." Kix let his gaze wander the perimeter of the space. This time observing, lingering... "To your coven. What now?"

"Warlock. Was I not clear enough? You've continued to defy the council, despite repeated warnings. You sent another transmission of data to Earth, which was intercepted and nullified. This time we'll wipe your memory, then send you to spend the rest of your days there."

Kix yanked at his bonds, mouthing a spell.

"You'll find your powers don't work here in our coven. Only within the space of our own creation, wrapped inside the holosuite technology were your spells permitted. Here, we won't tolerate them."

"No, no, NO! We have a contract. I'm to mate with Vinique. Vinique..." Kix pleaded, giving her his full attention, "you have more integrity than this. I know you do. Honor what we set out to do."

"You have the gall to speak of integrity? You, who have continued to defy your council chair? Not only have you betrayed the oath you took as a council member, you've let down your own people."

"You can't do this. My future *is* council leadership," he murmured, his voice spilling out in a slow, sinister sneer.

"Your future no longer involves Remeon."

*No. Not after all my work. Not with all that is yet to come...* "Somebody...anybody... Listen to reason. The council needs me." Kix dragged his attention to the woman Yara, who spoke in soft tones to Jack. "Jack, why is Yara here?"

Yara lifted her head, leveling Kix with an icy gaze. "You never learn, Kix."

Closing his eyes, Kix thrust the full weight of his powers inside Yara's head, pushing against her boundaries, searching for a crack in the armor of her defenses in order to eke past. "Don't mess with me, Kix. You'll find I'm more disagreeable than Arista and willing to end you in the here and now, instead of waiting for your new home to take care of it for me."

A remnant of the witch he'd known hovered in his realm of consciousness. "Gods... Whisterly? It can't be..." The coven had talents deeper, darker, and more secretive than even he knew. *Well done, Whisterly. Well done.*

Arista stepped in between the two of them. "Kix, you'll have your memory wiped today, and our spacecraft will take you to Earth, leave you with enough food and supplies to last you one week, as well as a temporary structure. From there you're on your own to make your way. In the past, you've proven yourself to be extremely resourceful."

"Arista, no. Wait. Let me make it up to you. You won't regret it. I'll serve you here, in your own coven. Just put me to work."

"Silence! It's already begun." The witches surrounded Kix, their robes rustling in the tightening circle. One member lifted one of Kix's hands, baring it for the knife that sliced a path down his palm. Arista paused, allowing the coven the few minutes necessary for collecting his blood and mixing the concoction necessary for the spell.

Another coven member ambled forward, presenting the chalice to Arista while she bowed low. Arista set to work upon the tome's page presented to her, staining it crimson. Then raising her arms high, she whispered the words which would allow Kix's memories to fall away.

A shiver scuttled down his spine, spells that could end this madness racing through his head. Although over time he'd regain his memory, Kix would be on Earth, with no way to return to the world where he'd spent his lifetime. He'd need to forge a new path now. Pick himself up and begin again. Hells, they couldn't do this to him!

"Arista!" he screamed. "I beg—" Kix fell forward, writhing and squirming under the magical power binding him. Visions paraded inside his head, then cascaded away as he lifted his chin, basking in the stray thoughts of old, before they slid away from him. One by one, he shook the memories loose, mumbling, spouting off spell after spell, attempting to thwart Arista's incantation in progress. But Vinique and Whisterly, along with the coven, were fighting against him too. He sensed their collective power, counteracting his spells, he surmised, just in case the magic he conjured proved productive in this controlled environment.

Grasping, flailing, he reached for the last pieces of himself. But only nothingness remained.

The coven swayed, chanting their assent as their incantations merged with Arista's, the old witch the driving force at their core, conjuring, spinning spell after spell through the magical space.

Kix leaned his head against the wall, babbling nonsense, his face bereft of emotion. Inside, his mind was a pristine page. Held in the coven's tome under lock and key and bound up tight were the memories spanning the man's lifetime, tucked away until such time as his consciousness healed from this intrusion, and they returned to him in a painfully slow march. That or powerful magic could force them back, at risk of death to Kix. Either way, by then, Kix would be only a distant recollection of himself to the people of Remeon, instead making his way on Earth. His human heritage would need to guide him now.

Arista checked his pulse, scrutinized his eyes. "He never lost consciousness. His powers are formidable. Fortunately we have the strength to overcome his kind. Lay him down there," she directed the coven. "Give him food and water. In a day, he should be able to travel."

"I'll arrange for the transport," Vinique said.

"Great-Grandmother," Arista began, "I felt startling differences in the way Kix handled this process versus Simon, yet our work was virtually the same in both instances."

"True, dear, but Simon had only just begun his walk as a warlock—a complete novice to the arts. Kix, on the other hand, is fully trained in his craft and a significant power to be reckoned with. Even residing on Earth, I'm confident he'll find some way to reach us, once his memories have fully returned."

"We'll need to determine a way to monitor him."

"A prudent move, Arista. And after today, one step closer to our goal. Good work, all of you," the old witch exclaimed. "We've neutralized a threat for the time being."

STEPHEN UNBUTTONED the first two buttons of his shirt and sighed a heavy breath. Exhausted from the last twenty-four hours on duty and spending last night in the barracks, he couldn't wait to see Arista. Over the last seven months, life on Remeon had eased into somewhat of a routine, if there could be such a thing here at the compound.

Stephen felt more comfortable in his decision now, with some experience under his belt, his military training ongoing. As a result of his initial training and testing, he'd been assigned to the Intelligence branch of service.

Arista had been relieved at this, glad that he wouldn't be first in harm's way in the event of an attack. Stephen understood that, if such an event occurred, he could very well be pulled into a first wave of response to any act of war perpetrated against the compound. But, for now, he enjoyed this niche, reveling in the troves of data stores he'd been reading, the tech he'd been learning, and the tools of investigation he'd been privy too.

And thankfully Jack still worked with Stephen in the holo-suites, typically once a week. No longer scared of these sessions, Stephen was eager for them instead, soaking up all Jack could offer, notably in the forms of technique and strategy. Because, good God...Jack was a master.

In so many ways life had moved on. Kix had been banned to Earth only days after the confrontation in the basement and dropped off by a starship, back in service after a brief respite due to tight resources, before the cure had freed those constraints once again. So far, so good... Couldn't believe that would be the last heard from the warlock though.

Days slipped by, and though Stephen remained busy, thoughts of home, his real home, were never too far away. Guilt racked him. If only he could reach out telepathically to his parents, let them know he and Belle were all right. After so many months they would be torn up with despair, with the tortured emptiness of not knowing.

Initially Arista, Whisterly, Jack, Belle, and Stephen had planned a trip to Earth. After all, that had been part of the arrangement, before they'd known that Simon would be out of it for so long. Arista, Whisterly, and Jack would have the chance to meet Ma and Pa, and Stephen and Arista's wedding planning could begin anew.

At the same time, Simon would travel to Earth, then begin the rehabilitation that Jack had such faith in—something Stephen didn't share. With no idea when the evildoer would finally grace them with his presence, the group committed to set a date to move forward. Life couldn't be put on hold forever for his future brother-in-law.

Jesus... The words disgusted him.

This morning brought new revelations on that front, however. Waking in a cold sweat, gasping for breath and clawing at his head, Stephen had no doubt that Simon was coming out of his coma. He'd not spoken to Stephen though. Were his memories truly gone? Or maybe the ass-wipe was just continuing where he'd left off.

Either way this turn of events meant the trip to Earth was back on track, sooner rather than later. But did Arista know of this latest development? Or was Stephen the only one privy due to his and Simon's...connection. He would know soon enough. His visit to Arista this morning was a surprise, hopefully anyway.

Stephen gave a nod to the guards congregated by Arista's door. With an audible *whoosh* it slid open.

"Whatever it is will need to wait. I'm covered up in weeks of work and—" Arista lifted her head. "Stephen!"

"Surprise, love," he announced with a smile, sweeping her up in his arms as she met him halfway across the floor.

"You feel so good," she whispered. "Two days away is a long time."

"I was sure I'd mucked up my surprise. Your telepathy skills are eons ahead of mine. I figured you'd know anything I tried to hide from you instantaneously."

"Not this time. I had no idea. You're improving."

"Where's my sister?" Stephen tossed his gaze around the room. "I want to kiss you properly."

"In the basement, with the coven."

"Of course she is."

"Focus," Arista instructed, using a finger to drag Stephen's attention back to her.

"You don't have to tell me twice." He pressed his mouth against hers, caressing her lips slowly before deepening the kiss. Arista let out a tiny gasp. "Ah...did you miss me? I don't mind telling you that feels good."

"You know I did. Come have a seat." Arista led him by the hand to the couch. "We have things to discuss."

"All right, after another one of those first." Stephen buried a hand her hair, steadying Arista as he leaned in for another kiss. "*Mmm.*" He grinned against her mouth. "Two days without you is entirely too long."

"No argument here."

A familiar pull throbbed inside his head, and he sat up, disgust twisting his lips.

"What is it? Me?"

"God no, love." He leaned his forearms on his knees and sucked in a breath. "I figured you'd already know. Simon appears to be coming out of his coma. I can feel him reaching inside my thoughts, but it's different this time."

"How?"

"Almost like he's testing our connection somehow. Before his, uh, procedure, he'd yank on the link between us, and then there would be instant pain, followed by an inability to breathe, before he'd hold me immobile, prepared to do his bidding."

Arista squeezed his hand.

"I'm waiting, expecting him to do all those things I mentioned, but so far he's just hanging out in my head. Strange, right?"

"Yes, but assuming the memory wipe worked, he won't remember all that he's done. The connection he forged with you is hardwired, it sounds like, sorry to say. So his brain is reconnecting to familiar pathways but not in an intention to cause you pain. Does that make sense?"

"No. Not with him. I guess I'll see what happens. The good news from all this is we can go to Earth, have you meet my parents, get the wedding planning underway, and Simon off Remeon for a while, though I'm still concerned about the possibility of Belle being around him constantly."

"Have faith in my parents. They'll keep her safe."

"I'm trying, love. Really I am. She's my sister. It's ingrained, and I love her. I'd rather focus on us, if I can, and preparing for our wedding, getting us where we need to be so we can marry."

"I want that too, sweetheart."

Stephen took her hands in his. "Then let's get going. With your parents or not, let's travel to Earth and set our wedding date. Then come back here, where our life is now, and work on us. I don't want to wait for you and me to be *us* any longer."

"Yes. Yes, to all of it." Arista circled her arms around Stephen's waist and leaned her head on his shoulder. Tilting her chin up, he brushed his lips against hers, his fingers sliding from her waist, inching higher.

Arista let out a soft moan.

"I want you—"

"Stephen?" came a soft voice.

"Belle." After going back for one more quick taste of Arista's lips, Stephen straightened. "What is it?"

"Gross."

"What do you want, Belle?"

"Miss Whisterly wanted to speak to you and Arista. We talked downstairs among the coven. I'm going back down now."

Arista raised her brows. "Good. It's a sign. Let's put some action behind our words."

His smile lingered in the corners of his mouth as he bit back a groan. "So many ways I'm interpreting that right now. I'm all in, love."

histerly entered her sanctuary, lost in thought. What they'd been waiting on for seven months had finally come to pass. Simon was awake. Anxious and jittery to a degree she rarely experienced, she reached for his thoughts. Simon's eyes held dark pools full of questions, but no ill will or animosity on his part that she could detect. A breath left her as she stood here, stunned. She'd prepared herself for this not to work. Did the three of them really have a fresh, albeit temporary, new start?

"I'm your mother," she began tentatively, awkwardly placing a hand on his shoulder. "If it feels strange to call me that, you may call me Whisterly. You'll be fine. I'm sure it's odd, not remembering much for the time being. But try to rest, and know your feelings are normal. Your father and I will help to fill in the blanks. How are you feeling?"

"Confused...frustrated. Nobody's telling me what's going on, or why I can't remember anything."

"Try to be patient. I'm guessing most of what you'll want to know will come from us, your father and me." Navigating Simon's empty stare, Whisterly shifted before continuing. "This is Belle." Whisterly reached out her hand and pulled Belle in to face Simon. "She'll stay for a bit while the coven monitors your progress. Assuming all is well, we'll take a trip in two days' time. How's that sound?"

Whisterly looked on while an array of emotions warred for control of Simon's face. Surprise, excitement, wonder, even a touch of fear, all registered in Whisterly's thoughts from her brief read of him. All very normal emotions to experience given Simon's condition.

His gaze snapped from Belle back to Whisterly, as if evaluating. "Fine, I guess." Simon turned his attention toward Belle. "You've been here, in my head, keeping me grounded with visions that eased my pain. I'm not sure why you'd do that. I sense we aren't related. But I thank you."

Belle nodded. "True. We're not, but I understood I could help. The unrest in your mind called me."

He chuckled. "Well, I appreciate you stepping up and into the clutter in there. I'm sure no doctor could have done the same."

Whisterly's heart beat a little faster. Gods, that was pure Jack. His facial expressions. His laughter. She'd get used to this, right? "I'll be back soon, Simon. Belle will be here a while longer, and the coven is evaluating your fitness for travel, so we'll talk again when they've finished that process."

"Good to know, Whisterly." With a cant of his head he added, "Please tell me I'm here among the coven because I possess powers as well."

"What do you think?"

"My insides...the surge of energy and commotion I feel there, plus my communication with Belle, tells me that I do. But I want to hear it from you."

Whisterly nodded her agreement. "That's the truth. Part of why we're here is to help you manage your powers."

"Excellent. Thank you for your part in my recovery."

"You're welcome, Simon. Belle, you'll need to leave in a little while. Understood? The coven needs some one-on-one time with Simon, and you have some things to tend to in order to prepare for our trip as well."

"Sure, Miss Whisterly."

Acknowledging the coven members at work as she passed, Whisterly initiated her communication. *Grandmother, the procedure appears to have worked. I sense no ill will or animosity. The question is, how long will these effects last?*

*Indeed. We'd love to know. But we don't. Make the most of the time you have, and watch for signs, little things, that Simon might hide as his memories return. If you're attentive, you'll recognize bits and pieces trickling through his thoughts before everything comes rushing back. And, in the interim, he'll regain access to the grimoire and the coven. He'll need it for his study.*

*Understood. And thank you, Grandmother.*

*Get to know your son, child.*

Whisterly hurried through the hall to her chambers, her only concern now— Jack and what this would mean to him. "Jack," she called out, walking into their bedroom.

"Here."

Her gaze searched his in the space between them, and suddenly she let the floodgates loose. The voice of reason all these months, Whisterly hadn't wanted to get Jack's hopes up too high, armed with the real knowledge that their son could die or, worst case, not wake from the coma at all. A smile spread her lips. "He's awake, talking and asking questions. I don't sense the malevolence from before. He seems...normal, open to what's ahead, and...thankful. Jack," she said, hesitating, "Simon was thankful."

"*Shhh.*" Jack crossed the space to Whisterly and kissed her quiet. They eased side to side, lingering in their embrace. "This feels good. I sense now that you wanted this outcome as much as I did."

She nodded against his chest. "I didn't fully realize it until I saw him. My son, for once, not spewing words of hatred. I don't think I allowed myself to hope. I wanted this for you."

"But now you can see you needed it too."

"Gods, yes, Jack. Maybe even more than you did. Watching him talk, move... You're there inside Simon's words, his actions. I want him to be whole again too, Jack, and ours."

"One step at a time, baby." His thumb caressed her cheek, before kissing her again. "Let's pack. I'm taking you home with me. Next stop—Earth!" Jack spun Whisterly around the room to the sound of her laughter, and he joined in, holding her tight, until he collapsed on the bed with her in tow. "Sorry I got a little—"

A tear trailed down her cheek, then another. "I'm sorry, Jack," she said through a weak smile. "My emotions are all over the place. I can't wait to experience Earth with you. I've wanted this since the first time you were here, but I never let myself truly believe that it would happen. And ever since I realized we had a son, I couldn't wait for you two to be together, so we could have a chance as a family. Honestly, with the passing of these last seven months, I didn't believe it'd work."

Her watery gaze met his.

"I know, baby. I had hope enough for both of us." Whisterly gripped Jack's wrists, where his hands rested at her neck as Jack leaned in, pressing a kiss to her forehead. "Let's get you packed," he whispered against her cheek. "And keep in mind that we'll buy you some clothes on Earth as well. All right?"

"Got it. Shopping for clothes in your hometown? Wow..."

"Now let's talk logistics for a few minutes, huh? You, me, Arista, Stephen, Belle, and Simon will all travel to Earth via portal. But you and I are going first, with two days lead time."

Whisterly raised her brows, reading his thoughts, watching fire igniting in his eyes.

"That's right, Mrs. Livingston. Two whole days in my house,

just you and me. I've got so much to show you. You've no idea my plans for us, before chaos descends, and we visit Stephen and Belle's home, later bringing Simon and Daniel home too. So"—he shrugged—"some details to work out."

"I can't wait, Mr. Livingston."

"Glad to hear it," he admitted, snaking an arm around her to keep her close. "Now here are my thoughts on our travel..."

❧

*HARRY, tomorrow's the day, man. Just Whisterly and me at first, followed by Arista, Stephen, and Belle a few days later, then Simon, once we've determined where Belle will stay.*

*That's great, Jack! But why won't Belle be with her parents at her home?*

*Long story. Bottom line—we need her with us for a while.*

*I sense your inner turmoil, but also I can tell the emotion comes from a good place.*

*A very good place. Oh, and as much as I want to see Daniel, our reunion needs to wait until Whisterly and I return from Stephen's house. My return followed by another abrupt departure wouldn't be good for Daniel.*

*Agreed. I'm not even telling him yet, despite the fact that I feel like a little kid at Christmas myself. I can't wait to see you.*

*I second that. Until tomorrow then.*

*I'll be there at the portal on my end.*

❧

"WELL, baby, I think we've got the logistics of who's going where and when all tied down now, so what do you say? You ready to do this?"

"You know I am, Jack." She turned to Arista, Stephen, and Belle. "Two days and we'll see you at home."

"I can't believe we'll be visiting Stephen's parents in just a few days," Arista said, excitement threading through her voice.

Stephen gave her hand a squeeze. "God, I hope that goes well..."

Jack's answering grimace gave away his thoughts on the visit. "Harry's sending a telegram to them. So at least they'll know we're coming, but I imagine there will be a significant amount of explaining to do on my part."

"Yeah," Stephen agreed, the grim set to his mouth matching Jack's.

"I don't blame them. I'd be pissed also. No doubt they've been going through their own private hell not hearing from you guys," Whisterly added.

"You ready?" Vinique interjected. "I'm gonna initiate the portal. Harry's already on the other side."

Whisterly leaned into Arista's hug, then Stephen's and Belle's next, and finally turned toward Vinique. "Thank the gods for you, my sister. I'm as ready as I'll ever be."

"Do you have your universal translator?"

Whisterly tugged on one of the three chains around her neck. "Yes, right here with my key and Sam's dog tags."

"And we have extra translators. Just in case," Jack added.

"Hopefully I'll pick up the language pretty quickly."

"I have no doubt, brilliant witch wife of mine."

"Here we go." With the flick of Vinique's wrist, the wind shifted, picking up speed, and soon the trees bent under the sway of her power, sending leaves and stray branches spiraling into the air with their giddy dance. The portal tunneled a path through the waterfall, instantly spanning the distance between their two worlds.

"Damn, this never gets old," Jack said, a grin lifting his lips. "Ready, baby?"

"This is my first time," she blurted out, eyeing the rush of water with a relative calm through its center.

"I know." Jack looked at her expectantly. "Which means... we run!" Grabbing Whisterly's hand and their one large bag, the pair took off to the sound of Whisterly's laughter.

"JACK, THAT WAS AMAZING," Whisterly spouted, catching her breath.

"I know, right?"

"I can't even put the experience into words. Took my breath away."

"And, just like that, you're here on my world. Incredible, isn't it?" Spreading his arms wide, Jack beckoned Whisterly to him. "Welcome to Earth, baby." He kissed her softly. "There's more where that came from."

"I better never run out," she whispered in his ear.

"Bring your pretty bride with you," Harry called out, "and get the hell over here, Jack. I've got someone I want you both to meet."

"Harry! Man, I've missed you." Jack closed the distance between them, tugging Whisterly along behind him. "No way... Congratulations. You have a..." Jack's gaze met Harry's.

"We have a son."

Jack pulled Harry's forehead to his, joining their consciousnesses. "May I?" he asked, leaning back, his voice gravelly.

Harry placed the squirming mass in Jack's arms. "Jack, meet Harrison Jack."

Jack blinked, trying to stave off the tears brimming his eyes. "God...he's beautiful, Harry. I've forgotten how small babies are. It's been a long time."

Whisterly poked her head around Jack's arm and pulled down the blanket for a better view. "Harry, how sweet, a little Harry Jr. You must be so proud."

He nodded. "We are. Welcome." Harry folded Whisterly

into his arms. "It seems like forever since I've seen you. You look different, but I recognize you in here." He pointed to his forehead. "You're nothing short of a miracle, passing from death to life, from what I hear."

"Thanks to this man here, yes."

"Your love story is one for the ages."

"The two people in this world I can't live without"—Jack lost his battle as a stray tear slid down his cheek—"together on Earth." Jack kissed Harrison's forehead and settled him back in Harry's arms. "My Harry's a dad." A slow grin eased over Jack's face. "We need to have one hell of a party."

Harry slapped Jack on the back. "We'd love that. How about we wait until you all get back from visiting the Stewarts. Then we'll all gather at our place. Daniel will be ecstatic to see you."

"I can't wait. I've missed him so much."

"Yeah, like we discussed, I'm not telling the little monkey until a day before you'll see each other. He'll be climbing the walls otherwise."

Jack laughed.

"You think I'm kidding?"

"No, man. I know you're not. That's probably best."

"Well, shall we head to your place, Jack? Or somewhere else you'd like to go first?"

"I need to buy some groceries, but I can go back out and get a few things later."

Harry opened the car door for Whisterly and handed over Harrison. "Would you mind? You can slide him in the contraption over there or hold him. Your choice."

"I've got him, Harry."

"Oh, Jack, hope you don't mind. I gave Maggie the key to your place. She bought some groceries, so you wouldn't have to go out right away, plus she brought over dinner. We wanted tonight to be special for you two. After all, there's only one first night on Earth."

"Do I mind? Hell no. Thanks, Harry."

"We did it purely for selfish reasons." Harry laughed, and Jack could hear the smile in his voice. "Stick around. Your home is here, you guys."

Harry droned on for Whisterly's benefit about all the "sights" they were passing, the two engaging animatedly with an occasional gurgle interjected from Harrison.

It was surreal for the moment, for Jack or someone he loved not to be one step away from death.

"Earth to Jack," Harry announced. "Come in, Jack."

"Sorry."

"In a couple days we need to touch base on that task you gave me—with the Freemasons."

"Sure, Harry. I'm interested to hear what you've found out. Kix is here now and has gone through a memory wipe. Before he was banished from Remeon, he was fitted with an implantable device, so we could track him. Hopefully that will help the council keep tabs on him."

"Understood."

The car made the turn onto Jack's driveway. Rocks spit from underneath the tires as he stretched his neck for his first glimpse of home. "God, I've missed this place."

Harry threw the car into Park. "Can I help you guys in?"

"Nah. I've got it." Jack leaned into Harry's hug. "I already love baby Harry to pieces," Jack whispered. "Go take care of my nephew. Get the little guy home. And thanks for everything."

"You bet. The key's under the welcome mat."

Jack and Whisterly waved to Harry from the porch. "You know what this means, Mrs. Livingston?" Whisterly raised a brow. "We're all alone. For the first time. Ever. No Remeonites to barge in on us. No council business. No security guards. Just us."

"What should we do?"

"What a loaded question." Jack gave her a teasing grin,

turned the key, and pushed the door open. "First this." As he lifted Whisterly into his arms, she let out a small gasp. "Perfect." He stepped over the threshold, then lowered his lips to hers, tasting, caressing.

"*Mmm*. Jack, what is that lovely aroma?"

"That would be my favorite meal, courtesy of Maggie. Fried chicken and mashed potatoes—with dessert and homemade bread, I'd wager."

"Gods, it smells divine. You've got her wrapped around your little finger."

"Maggie is a sweetheart, the sister I never had, like Vinique. But food is pretty low on my priority list right now." He squeezed her tight. "Can you wait a bit?"

"Sure. This place...wow..."

"*Shhh...* Later," he murmured, kissing the words from her lips.

"Jack, show me your room. Take me to bed."

He headed for the stairs. "Always reading my mind... I love you."

WHISTERLY'S HAND slid lazily down Jack's chest. He moved in for a kiss. "I'm being a horrible host. How about that dinner now?"

"No complaints here."

He unleashed a lopsided grin. "Happy to hear that, baby. But I can't have you collapsing from hunger." Jack swung his legs over the side of the bed and pulled on pants. "I'll go warm up our dinner. You can wait here, if you'd like. It's up to you."

"No way. I'm coming too." She eyed the pool of clothes on the floor. "Can I borrow a shirt? I don't wanna put all that on again."

"Sure. Grab anything in the closet that suits your fancy or in the drawers over there."

"I'll be down in a few minutes."

"Take your time. Doesn't that sound good?" He flashed another smile, then bounded down the stairs.

Whisterly sifted through the options in Jack's closet, evaluating, touching the fabrics, sniffing each one as she tried them on. Finally settling on a flannel button-down, that somehow still smelled faintly of Jack, she tunneled her arms inside and buttoned up his shirt that hit her just above the knee.

Her gaze drifted around the room. Every item had a spot. The only things out of place were their clothes, in their haste recently discarded on the floor. Jack had so many personas... her husband and lover, a soldier, a father, a son, the facade he wore on Remeon, and here, who he was on Earth. Still so much to discover about the man, she realized, as she studied the pictures on the wall, vivid in action, representing people she didn't know—except the ones featuring Harry's smiling face.

Whisterly picked up one of the smaller photos from the bedside table. A little boy grinned back at her. Dark curly hair adorned his head, and the unconstrained laughter on his face was contagious. She couldn't help but return the smile. The boy held open a leather glove, and his other hand spread out to his side, poised for something, anticipating... Daniel—had to be. Adorable.

A fireplace stood ready to chase away the cold, and a leather chair with a blanket and two books on top made it look as if its owner had just stepped away for a moment from their reading. The walls, painted gray, fit with the overall masculine tone of the room. Comfortable, not pretentious, so very Jack.

A clatter downstairs reminded her that her husband was busy fixing food, so she padded down the hallway and took the stairs in search of him. Following the sounds of activity amid the scrumptious aromas of food cooking, she found Jack and poked her head into his homey kitchen.

"There you are. Thought you must have gone to back to sleep."

"No... Jack, I'll need a lifetime to get to know your house."

"What do you mean by that?" he asked, pulling items from the oven.

"I'll find my way around—it's not that. The pictures, books, newspaper articles, other important items gathered here because they mean something significant to you."

"*Hmm.*" Jack cocked his head. "I haven't thought about it exactly that way, but I guess that's true."

"A far cry from the atmosphere of our chambers on Remeon. Your home is rich...full of a life all its own from your time here."

"I like that idea." Jack gave her a pensive smile and served their plates. "How about we eat in the den? I started a fire, already took the wine in there, hoping you'd say yes."

"Of course... What is it? You're staring."

"Oh. Well, you give that old shirt new life, is all. Can't help the staring part—get used to it."

They settled by the fire on blankets and pillows that Jack had pulled from the chairs, then took their time eating the home-cooked meal Maggie had prepared. When they'd finished, Whisterly gathered the plates and put them on a chest within arm's reach. "I hope you don't expect me to cook like that. I wouldn't know how to begin. Maybe with the help of a little magic..."

"No, don't worry. We'll map this out as we go. I'm used to fixing meals for Daniel and me. It's no big deal."

"It is to me. I want to learn."

A smile brightened his face. "We can make that happen."

Whisterly sipped her wine, scanning the clippings and pictures in the room.

"What are you thinking about, baby?"

"The way you're wrapped inside each and every room of your house."

"Our house." He kissed her cheek. "As we built it, I imagined you here with me—the day when we'd make it ours." He chuckled. "I can die a happy man now."

Whisterly swatted him with a pillow. "Don't say such things!"

Jack scooted her to his lap. "I was kidding. I want you to be comfortable here. And I'd like for you to make this house your home as well. That's important to me. So think about what that looks like for you."

"Okay." She let the smile beginning inside her burst free. "I'd really like that."

Jack tugged Whisterly with him as he straightened. Can I show you something else tonight? Is that all right?"

"Sure, lead the way." Jack picked up the plates with one hand and led her behind him with the other, dropping their dishes in the sink on the way through the kitchen. At the stairs leading to the basement, he paused, appearing to struggle with the words he wanted to say.

"I, uh..." Whisterly squeezed his hand tighter. "Wanted to build a space just for you in here. At the time, the work was therapeutic. You see, I was convinced you'd be here with me someday. If I'd known then how long it would take for you and me to be here, together, I'm not sure I'd have completed it."

"Whatever it is, I'm glad you did, thinking of me."

"Well, I didn't finish it yet. The final touches need your expertise, and wiring isn't complete down there, so we have no electricity beyond the stairs, but I've got candles and matches in a basket down there."

"I can't wait. Let's take a look."

"You want to do the honors?" Jack flicked on the light switch at the top of the stairs, then gestured downward.

"Sure." Whisterly took the lead, and when she hit the cobblestones after stepping from the stairs, she knew what Jack had done. "Illumine," she murmured. A ball of light sprung from her hand. Twisting the flames with her fingers, she tamed the blaze into a small glowing mass.

"Straight ahead, baby."

Rocks framed a doorway tall enough to clear her full height. Glancing back at Jack, she smiled.

He shrugged, his eyes dancing in the low light. "I figured, why should you have to stoop?"

"Jack..." she began, spinning in a full circle, once she reached the center of the room. "It's incredible." The walls were rock, the floor covered in dirt. Bookcases lined one wall, and as she turned toward the exit again, an image of a pentagram hung over the door opening. Off to one side, Jack had set up a bed, piled high with blankets. Where she stood in the middle of the room, a slab of rock jutted out, and on its flat surface laid multiple containers of varying shapes and sizes.

"For your concoctions," he added, pointing to the far corner where a desk and chair appeared, ready for her to set to work. Jack strolled toward her, carrying two lit candles that he placed on the slab, his gaze drifting upward.

"No..." Whisterly spread her arms wide, flames bursting from her fingertips to highlight the ceiling. Witches in various stages of activity, draped in cloaks, some with hooded coverings, some displaying a shadowy face, some with skin hanging from their hollowed cheeks, others in the midst of casting a spell, adorned the space. "How?"

"I had it commissioned. Took well over a year... The artist thought I was off my rocker, but who the hell cares." Whisterly reached for Jack. He gathered her in his arms. "Still needs your touch. As I said, it's not quite finished."

"Thank you, sweetheart." She turned her attention to the

bed, raising a brow. "Should I sleep down here while I'm working?"

"I'd rather that and have you warm with blankets than shivering because you've fallen asleep on the floor. To be clear, I want you in my bed every night. The option down here is just in case. Past experience tells me how involved you can be in your work."

"Or for when you come down here to visit me maybe?"

"There's a thought. I like it."

"Jack, I'm speechless..." His eyes, gone soft, melted her.

"Then I've done my job well. Welcome home, baby," he murmured, lifting her into a kiss.

JACK PRESSED his lips to the back of Whisterly's neck and crawled out of bed. It was early and his wife's warmth enticing, but he couldn't miss his first sunrise back at home. Drawing the shade back just enough to let in the muted tones of purple and red, he watched, mesmerized as the kaleidoscope shifted, coming alive, chasing the darkness with tiny bursts of yellow. A warm arm tightened around his waist. He turned and kissed Whisterly's temple, covering her hand with his.

"I almost missed my first sunrise on Earth."

"I wanted to let you sleep." He sighed, lifting his gaze again to the array of colors deepening in the sky. "Damn, this never ceases to amaze me."

"It's breathtaking, Jack."

"You can see the same view from the kitchen. Most mornings I'm downstairs already with my coffee, and I take it all in from down there."

"Then what? What's next in Jack Livingston's typical day?"

Jack pulled Whisterly into the window seat and wrapped his arms around her. "Well, before your, uh, transformation, I'd talk to you for a little while, drink more coffee, read for a bit, then wake up Daniel."

Whisterly backed into the crook of his neck. "Sounds positively terrestrial."

Jack's mouth quirked up. "How would you know?"

"All my research on your planet of course, and a special someone gave me a book once, all about Earth."

"And now you get to experience everything firsthand."

"I can't wait. But why would you ever want to leave this place?"

"You know why... To reconnect with Arista. To see Simon. To be nearer to you." Whisper soft, Jack's fingers glided down Whisterly's arm, raising tiny bumps along her skin. She snuggled closer. "We have one more day before our privacy ends and others descend into our little world."

"That's okay—there's room."

"How about that coffee?"

"Yes, and I want to hear all about your plans for me today. In a little while..." She eased her thoughts into his.

*Mmm. Perfect... I like the way you think, baby.*

Thirty minutes later, the two sat down at the cheery kitchen table with hot mugs of coffee. "Smells divine, and you're right. This coffee tastes different from the Remeonite variety. I'm not an experienced coffee drinker, but your version is definitely my pick."

"I'm glad you approve." Jack swallowed a large gulp. "First up today—shopping for you—a few items so you'll blend in a little better. Not that I mind, I just want you to be comfortable. Plus we need to buy train tickets for the lot of us to visit Stephen and Belle's home. I promised Arista she could have a quick tour through the house before we go, so we need to plan to fit that in tomorrow. Listen... We may get a few questions from neighbors...others in town. I've given our situation some thought." Grabbing Whisterly's hand, he hesitated, not sure how to put what he wanted to say into words.

"Besides Harry and Maggie, people around here don't know about you. Hiding such a big part of myself—you to be exact—has become second nature. Since I've been away for a while, coming back with a wife won't seem odd to people...maybe... I'm not sure." His brows knitted. "But I want everyone to know we married. I hope you're not disappointed."

"No. Of course not. I'd shout it from your rooftop if I could, Jack. I'll follow your lead with this Earthly custom."

"All right. We're all set. We'll finish your tour around the place, then on into town. But first, Daniel's favorite, hopefully yours too—pancakes."

"I'm intrigued. I could get used to this..."

"That's the idea."

## 10

*T*he bumpy *clickity clack* of the train lulled Arista into an easy stillness. This adventure of hers didn't seem possible, but here she was on Earth, with her parents and Stephen accompanying her to meet her future mother- and father-in-law. Being the head of the council on Remeon was easy compared to waiting for this encounter.

She fidgeted nervously with the universal translator hanging around her neck, twisting it back and forth as she thought of all the ways this visit could go horribly wrong.

Stephen—Thomas as he was known here on Earth— assured her repeatedly that his parents would welcome her, but anxiety plagued her just the same. The Stewarts should have received Harry's telegram by now, so thank the gods, they'd had *some* warning. Call it instinct, witchcraft, or telepathy, but she expected trouble.

"You're not on Remeon. Quit worrying," Thomas had said, encouraging her. But his thoughts told a different story. And the deep lines across his forehead, along with the ridged set of his mouth when he thought she wasn't watching, confirmed her fears. He was worried too.

After answering some initial questions of hers, he'd fallen asleep, and at least for now, the tension in his face had relaxed. Belle sat across from them, gleeful, her legs suspended from her seat, kicking back forth in the air, oblivious to the irritation of the travelers who attempted to pass by her in the aisle. Papa and Mother sat behind Arista, completely lost in each other. Finally together, happy. But how long would that last with Simon on the way in only a few days' time? Would he destroy their newfound joy once and for all?

Papa seemed blind when it came to Arista's twin brother. With faith to spare, he continuously spoke of the miracles that could occur if Simon were only given a fair shake in life. Papa's wisdom when it came to people and what made them tick was beyond Arista's vocabulary in both languages, English and Remeon.

Time and time again he stood up for others, and he'd fight for his beliefs as he'd done throughout his lifetime, most recently for her own freedom. Arista wouldn't contradict him. Instead she'd bleed her brother dry with a special spell she'd conjure just for him, if the situation warranted, if Simon hurt her father in any way.

A cold indifference threaded through her as she shivered. If she focused too long on Simon, this often happened. Her mother's voice filtered through Arista's thoughts.

*Relax. Breathe in through your nose, out through your mouth.*

*I know. I'm trying...*

*Try harder, little one. Let it go.*

Her mother was well aware that destructive thoughts could be a terrible thing if they got free... Something easily accomplished by a witch. Leaning back against the seat, her eyes closed, Arista imagined herself back in Papa's house. She'd had only a quick glimpse. Oh...she'd wanted more time there...in the huge great room, a roaring fire casting its warmth on her back, and magnificent wooden beams appearing to hover from the ceiling above, all welcoming her inside. The house Papa had built was unique, a far cry from the stark facilities of the compound, with their hard uncompromising lines. In Papa's home she could feel the love infused in every inch of its creation. A perfect place for Thomas and her to marry. Thomas... How about they just skip to the wedding part.

*That's better. Keep it up.*

Arista focused on the list developing in her head. So much needed to be accomplished in the few days she and Thomas had here before their all-too-soon return to Remeon. Yet another thing on the long tally of items Thomas's parents would find disturbing—for the foreseeable future, Arista and Thomas would make their life in the Remeon compound—her managing the council, Thomas training with the military.

Along with those fun pieces of news for his parents, Thomas wanted her to go dress shopping, with Mother and Mrs. Stewart, of course, and dive into wedding planning. And just what did that mean exactly? As if Arista had any clue. Her chest tightened. A quick visit to another planet and back again. So why did she feel the life draining from her, breath by breath?

"Come with me to the dining car for a drink, little one."

"Mother..."

"Let's go. Belle, would you mind keeping Jack company for me for a little while?"

Belle flashed a smile, instantly lighting up her face. "Sure, Miss Whisterly."

Jack patted the seat next to him as Belle scooted in. "How about a card game?"

"Okay. But look out 'cause Thomas says I'm pretty good."

Jack pulled out cards he had stowed in his pocket. "Show me what you got," he said, laughing as he shuffled the deck.

Arista led the way to the dining car, amid the hustle and

bustle of the humans' activity. Could she ever fit in among all of them?

*No, Arista. Don't even try. Be yourself with those you meet on Earth. The ones who matter will fall in love with you, like we are.*

THE GROUP TOOK a cab to Thomas's house but not before hitting up some sightseeing spots in his quaint hometown of Lexington, VA. Seeing the town through the eyes of a visitor cast a different light on the people, Thomas's old stomping grounds, and institutions like VMI, the Virginia Military Institute, and nearby William and Mary University in Williamsburg, Virginia.

While Thomas spouted off what little he knew of the colleges, he quickly found that Jack had more knowledge, especially regarding VMI. *Of course he does.* Thomas chuckled as Jack told funny antidotes of some of his war buddies who'd graduated from the college. And why the hell hadn't Thomas known that Jack and Harry had graduated from Texas A&M?

Surely Jack had evidence of that fact on the wall in his den in Provo. Admittedly, that day hadn't had enough hours to fit in all the words the two of them had needed to say to each other. They had spent most of that afternoon speaking about topics that most people didn't discuss. Awful things the two of them had in common—their torturous experiences on Remeon and of course, Arista, the light in both of their lives.

Although Thomas had suffered some of the most horrific injuries, mentally and physically on Remeon, he'd always be grateful that his abduction had led him to Arista, then to Jack.

The car lurched as a long stretch of road poured out in front of them, and the driver threw the car into fourth gear. Thomas rolled down the window and let the fresh air rush in. Scents and sounds of home that he'd never thought he'd miss suddenly pulsed inside him, like lifeblood. The smell of the fields at harvest. The sun's warmth on his skin. Fresh hay laid out in the animals' stalls. The familiar aromas billowing from Ma's kitchen, morning, noon, and night. Even Pa's prayers echoed through Thomas's thoughts, reminding him that a higher power watched over all of them.

The foundation for life that he'd learned here was sound, with a mixture of hard work, respect, and a healthy dose of faith in the unseen—be that the assurance of crops making it to harvest, or God, who his pa, and Thomas as well, believed guided us all. And Thomas hadn't fully understood that fact until now, after being away for a time and returning. He missed the farm and its annual renewal of life that still pumped in his blood.

The driver downshifted, the rev of the engine as they slowed and the fields sprawling out ahead telling Thomas they were close. The urge to throw open the door and run through those fields he knew like the back of his hand almost overtook his will to stay put.

Later. So much more...later.

The barn came into view, and Thomas leaned over to Arista, whispering, "Remember your first motorcycle ride?" Arista's lips lifted. "I'm taking you on the real thing before we leave."

Curling her fingers around his hand, she bounced in her seat. "I can't wait."

Not knowing the reception they'd receive, Thomas had made Jack aware of accommodations in town, as a backup plan. Plenty of room for them all at the house though. With Mary gone, Jack and Whisterly could take her room. Arista could share with Belle or take his bed. Thomas could sleep on the couch... or not... What, was he out of his mind? Arista did it to him...

She gifted him with a shy smile. She'd read him just then.

Kissing her temple, Thomas grinned. His thoughts were

never far from every inch of her, especially with her nestled so close.

The car puttered and jerked to a stop. Jack unfolded his long limbs from the car, stretched, then leaned back in to pay the cab driver. Thomas helped Arista from the back seat and waited while Belle crawled from her spot in the middle. Whisterly stood by Jack, when Thomas straightened, just in time for Shep to come running.

Their dog had never been so happy, yipping and licking at Thomas's feet before darting to Belle and starting his little tirade all over again. Jack headed to the porch with Whisterly and Arista following, Belle and Thomas still tangled up with Shep and his welcome home dance.

Something wasn't right though.

With Shep making such a racket, Pa knew they were here. Where was he? And Ma? She was usually first to greet visitors. Maybe Thomas and Belle didn't rank as visitors, but Jack, Whisterly, and Arista sure as hell did. The telegram that his parents received yesterday told them everything; Thomas knew, since Jack had recounted every word.

Jack tugged on the screen door to reach the front door to knock.

"Hey, hold up just a sec," Thomas called out, amid the barking and giggling in the yard.

The door swung open in a sudden jolt, Pa's frame standing tall, blocking the entrance. What the...

"You must be Jack... The one responsible for my kids' disappearance."

From behind, Thomas observed while Jack's stature changed instantly from relaxed to a defensive posture, and he took a half step back, throwing one arm to the side to keep Whisterly from going any farther. Never had Thomas seen his father like this. In all his buying-and-selling dealings in town, and the disagreements that would invariable pop up, Pa had always been calm, businesslike, respectful. Thomas set off at a run, his legs eating up the distance between himself and Jack.

But Pa must have planned this, and catching everyone else off guard, his punch connected with Jack's jaw before anyone else could react.

Inside, Thomas heard Ma scream, and Pa shook his head, then turned to the scene on the porch. Out of breath, Thomas inserted himself between his pa and Jack. "What's gotten into you, Pa? You just hammered into a decorated marine. What's wrong with you? He could literally take you out."

"I'm fine, Thomas." Jack wiped blood from his split lip and straightened. "I'd probably have done the same, had the tables been turned." Thomas looked on as Jack sized up his pa. "And I'm not sure I could take him. It's all right."

"The hell it is, Jack. Pa?"

Belle took a running leap into Pa's arms. "We're okay, Pa. Mr. Jack and Miss Whisterly, they've kept us safe, and Thomas too, a course, just like you told him too." Pa lifted Belle up and crushed her to his chest, swaying as a silent sob racked his body.

*Well, once again, thank God for Belle.* Just what Pa needed. Thomas grimaced, still in disbelief.

Ma squeezed Pa's shoulder, kissed Belle's cheek, then opened her arms to Thomas. "Welcome home, son."

Thomas let his ma wrap her arms around him. Stiff against her at first, he gave in and buried his face in her hair.

"You've been well and truly missed. Your pa's been beside himself with worry, me too, with no way to reach you both."

Taking a step back as Pa released Belle, Thomas's eyes locked with his father's. "Jack, Whisterly, and Arista are my family as well, Pa. If you can't accept that, then I'll leave right now. Arista and I will marry soon, and we'd prefer your blessing, but I don't need it."

Thomas cleared his throat and closed the remaining

distance to his father. "Because of your guidance and that man's over there—who you just decked for no reason—I'm standing on my own finally, with a direction in my life. I won't let you or anyone else take it from me."

Thomas paused, proud that his voice didn't sound shaky, because he sure was. The silence that stretched on could have been minutes or hours for all he knew. But he wasn't budging, even though his mother's shoulders shook with silent tears.

Pa took Ma into his arms, kissed her softly, and whispered something Thomas couldn't hear. Pa cupped Ma's cheek before turning and approaching Thomas. "Son, you're right. I've behaved abominably. We've missed you both terribly. The first four or five months weren't so bad. But then, I don't know"—he shook his head—"it was like something snapped inside."

Thomas narrowed his eyes, considering his pa's words. Was he really talking to him, man to man? His pa seemed...raw... honest, and real.

"All I can do is ask your forgiveness. Maybe one day, when you have children, you'll understand." Pa extended his hand toward Thomas and stepped closer. He would only need to close the gap. Belle nudged his butt from behind. He swatted at her and missed when she scooted out of reach.

"Forgiven, Pa," Thomas muttered, letting Pa's strong arm yank him into a hug.

"I'm proud of you son." Pa walked to Jack, eyeing the ground, before meeting Jack's steady gaze. "I'm sorry, Jack. I, uh...have no excuse, other than I've been outta my mind over these two here."

Jack offered his hand. "I understand. More than you know."

"Thank you for your service." Pa grabbed Jack's palm, pumping up and down, then turned his attention to Whisterly.

"This is Whisterly, my wife."

"Ma'am? Were you the one Belle mentioned was...dead?"

"That's me." She smiled as Pa shook her hand slowly, unease flitting over his features. "And my daughter, Arista."

"Mr. Stewart," Arista acknowledged, dipping her chin.

"Please, call me James." Pa gestured toward the door. "I'd like to start over if I could. I've messed up pretty good here," Pa said, scratching his chin. "But my wife can soothe just about anybody and any situation with her cooking. Come on inside. Make yourselves at home."

Ma led the way, hesitating for a moment before taking Thomas to one side. "Thomas, what do aliens eat? What if they don't like what I've fixed?" she asked, her voice laced with an undertone of panic that he'd never heard before.

Thomas stared at his ma, trying to gauge if she was kidding or making fun of Arista and her family—two things his mother typically would never do, but after what just happened with Pa, Thomas wouldn't be surprised by anything with these two today. "Ma," Thomas began, a smile growing on his face, "they eat what we eat. Just not nearly as well, since they've never had your cooking. I promise they'll love it."

"Thank the Lord," she whispered under her breath, scurrying through the door ahead of Thomas.

*Not a bad idea. Should have started with that maybe.* Thomas bowed his head and offered a silent prayer for this visit that had only just begun, fight and all. A delicious aroma exhaled from the open door, drawing Thomas in; wrapped in its power, he closed his eyes and drifted into the kitchen.

"WELL, WHAT DID YOU THINK?" Thomas asked, pushing the barn doors closed on the 1942 Harley that he'd missed every bit as much as Ma's cooking.

Arista slid her hand in his. "Experiencing that ride in my

head, like I did the first time, was amazing. But this? It's hard to describe."

"Try," Thomas said, leaning down to press his lips against hers.

"*Mmm*. Okay, well, at first, I was a little scared. Everything whizzed by so fast. I shut my eyes."

He grinned. "I could tell by the way you were holding on to me so tight, and I loved it."

"*Hmm*. Then I decided to take a peek, and the feel of the rush of wind on my face, with you next to me, nothing has matched it, except—" Thomas raised a brow, waiting. "When we first kissed."

"You passed. Best answer ever, love. Nothing like the surge of adrenaline I get when I ride." The porch light beamed out a path as the two climbed the steps leading to the house. "I wonder how it's going in there?"

"Dinner went well, and I don't hear any yelling—that's a good thing."

Thomas hummed his agreement. "We'll see. Dinner had the advantage of Ma's cooking."

"Yeah, I could tell Papa loved it."

"Him and me both. Many family arguments have been wrestled and put to bed over that table with Ma's food as arbitrator." Thomas held open the door as Arista walked in. Was that laughter coming from inside? He poked his head inside the family room. Ah, whiskey, the other universal arbitrator.

"Son, Jack here has been telling me about the people on Remeon—how long they'd been sick." Rubbing the scruff on his face, Pa scrutinized his son. Thomas stood at a standstill, not sure where this conversation was headed. At the very least he could dart back outside with Arista. "You and your sister have made a difference in the history of another planet. Because of you, another society was healed?"

"Well," Thomas cleared his throat, "me and others, like Jack."

"No, I was just a prelude. You got it done, Thomas," Jack explained, downing the remainder of his drink. "And as sure as I'm sitting here, I owe my life to Belle. That's an incredible little lady you've got there."

Pa's eyes misted, and he nodded, like he'd known what Jack had said was true. "She's special—no doubt about it. Elizabeth and I will talk it over. If Belle can help your son, like she helped your wife, we don't want to stand in the way. As long as she'll be safe, and we'll hear from her while she's away."

"James, I've come to think of your children as family. Hell, we'll *be* family soon, right?" Jack reminded James, with a jerk of his chin.

"That's true. But it's not the same."

"Agreed. Arista, Simon, Daniel, and Whisterly are my life. I give you my word I will watch over Belle as one of my own."

"You're a hard man to say no to, Jack. So I won't just yet. I'm going to turn in. Anything I can get you all?" Pa asked as he got to his feet, filled his glass, then aimed the bottle toward Jack in silent question.

"Don't mind if I do. And thanks for your hospitality."

"Don't mention it. Son, Belle's waiting up for Arista, but your sister is probably asleep by now. Could you show Arista upstairs?"

Thomas rocked his head.

"Good. Night all." With a jerk of his chin, Pa headed to his room.

Jack unfolded himself from the couch and reached for Arista, kissed her forehead. "I'm on the way to bed too. Going pretty well, don't you think so, Thomas?"

"Uh...what just happened here?"

$\sim$

"I LIKE THEM, ELIZABETH," James began, shedding his clothes. "But believing our Belle saved Jack or that either of them could have anything to do with bringing someone back to life?" A shudder ripped through his body. "I don't really want to think about that too hard."

Elizabeth reached out to her husband; he climbed in bed to join her.

"Our two youngest children have officially surpassed me. I have no idea what to do with either one of them."

"The same things you've been doing for years now— guiding them, teaching them the ways of the world, but mostly loving them. Trust in that, like you always have."

James kissed the top of her head. "We can do that."

"James?"

"*Hmm*?"

"You and I need to tell Belle. Tomorrow. The next day she'll be gone most likely, assuming we agree to Jack's plan. She needs to know."

"I wanted to wait until she was a little older," James said through a grimace. "Maybe then I'll have the right words."

"You'll have them when the time comes, tomorrow, next month, or next year."

"I pray you're right. Today was almost shot to hell, thanks to me."

"I love you just the way you are, James Stewart." Elizabeth sighed, nestled against her husband's chest. "I'd like to learn more about those universal translators that Whisterly and Arista wore. Wouldn't you?"

"Nope. You can ask them while you're shopping tomorrow —one big alien family, God help us all."

Elizabeth laughed. "You always tell me what the Lord brings us to, He will bring us through."

"I do, don't I?"

∼

"THERE YOU ARE, Jack. I was about to come looking for you. Everything all right?"

Jack shrugged and slumped into a wingback chair, setting his drink on the side table in their bedroom. "Took some whiskey, but better than when we first got here." His gaze met Whisterly's as Jack's hand skimmed his jaw.

"Think about what they must have been going through for all that time."

"I know. That's the only reason I didn't obliterate the man. For a second, laid out on the porch, it reminded me of Damond. Me, on the ground, defenseless."

"It took a much stronger will to not fight back today."

"Once I put myself in his place, I knew I couldn't hit back. It got me thinking though. I should have been in communication with Thomas's parents through Harry before now. With everything going on, it didn't come to me to do it." Whisterly quieted. "Hmm. See? You think so too."

"Maybe," she agreed, with a slight back and forth motion of her head. "But neither of us is perfect. It's over and everyone's fine. For the moment."

"Right. And who the hell knows what could happen in that next moment. In any case, the whiskey helped." Jack raised his glass and emptied his drink again. "Plus I genuinely like the man."

"I'm headed to sleep. I've got no idea what I'm in for tomorrow while dress shopping. How about you go in my place?"

"Elizabeth is a dear, baby. You'll be fine."

"Come to bed, Jack. If you fall asleep in the chair, I'll never get you over here."

A wicked smile crossed his lips. "You don't have to tell me twice."

AFTER THE EVENTS of the day, the exhilarating motorcycle ride, plus the excitement of being on Earth, Arista lay wide awake, listening to Belle's soft snoring. Too many jumbled thoughts filled her mind. Magic was nothing compared to...wedding dress shopping. What did that even mean?

*Give it a rest, little one. An adventure we'll go on together tomorrow. Go to sleep.*

*Working on it. Good night, Mother.*

A growl left her throat. *Ugh. No use.* Throwing aside the covers, Arista glanced over her shoulder, murmured a quick spell, then traipsed from the room.

"Thomas, are you still awake?" A light tapping noise echoed down the hallway. "Gods, I'm going to wake up everyone."

"Yeah, come on in."

Even through the darkness she could see him perfectly. Dappled moonlight shone past the open curtains, bleeding through the darkness, providing a trail of light inside the room.

Thomas sat up in bed. "Are you okay?" Through the dim light, concern wrinkled his forehead.

Arista flung herself on top of the bed on the back of a long exhale. "Sure. I just can't sleep. Do you mind talking to me a little while?"

"You're worried about something. I can tell."

"Yeah. Earth is stressful."

Thomas chuckled under his breath. "Earth's got nothing on Remeon, love." He reached for her hand. "Both of my parents adore you. Given my dad's ruckus, I know things were kinda rough at first, but we'll be okay, one way or another."

"What you did, standing up to your father like that, took courage. I'm proud of you."

"He was outta line. But looking back on it now, I get more of where he was coming from, protecting Belle and me, because"

—Thomas's gaze slid to hers—"even though you didn't need it from me today, all I could think about was your protection. Nothing else mattered." Feet hitting the ground, Thomas yanked his shirt off the chair.

"What are you doing?"

"Putting on a shirt."

"I can see you perfectly by your moon's light. Don't put your shirt on."

"Arista, did you come in here to torture me? Come here."

Sparkling light lifted skyward as Arista flung her arms wide and joined him. "It's done," she admitted. "I've hidden us. All anyone will see here, should they come in, is an image of you in the bed."

Thomas arranged his mouth into a smile. "What about Belle? She wakes up all the time. Sometimes she comes in here and sleeps at the bottom of my bed."

Arista fought a smirk working her lips. "I may have cast a little spell on your sister too."

"My God, Arista." Thomas pulled her close, then turning her around, pinned her against the wall. "My boyhood dreams of having a, um...young lady in my room, don't do you one bit of justice."

"Want to tell me about it?" Thomas swallowed hard, and where her hands lay on his chest, she felt the rhythmic rise and fall, the steady pounding making her fingers tingle.

"No. I was so immature. You'll be my wife. I don't want to do anything that might mess that up. Plus you've got me at a disadvantage," he said, his gaze spanning his bare chest down to his shorts. "What do you want, love? Spell it out 'cause I'm not thinking too clearly, thanks to you."

"You talk a lot." Arista grabbed the delicate strings of her nightgown tied at her throat and yanked them loose. The slinky material fell past her shoulders. Cupping her cheek, Thomas lowered his mouth to hers, barely brushing her lips, then he dipped in again for more, deepening the kiss, when she let out a soft moan.

A shudder rippled through his body.

Underneath her fingers Arista could feel his control slipping.

"God help the last shreds of my sanity, but you need to keep this on," he whispered gruffly in her ear, rubbing the flimsy material between his fingers, settling the gown over her shoulders again.

"But—"

"*Shh.* I'm hanging on by a thread here." Thomas swept his fingers along her spine, pressing their bodies together. He groaned. "Lay with me for a while, love."

~

THE FIRST GLOW of morning light bathed Thomas's bed, chasing the chill in the room. Arista startled awake. "Gods… Thomas?" A smile lifted his lips in sleep. Leaning into his warm body, she pressed a kiss to his mouth.

"*Mmm.* Arista," he mumbled. His eyes snapped opened. "Arista!"

"Yeah. We fell asleep."

Thomas glanced at her, then back to himself. They'd been talking. He'd pulled a blanket over them. Now…this. "Okay. Let's get you back to your room. Too early yet for Ma to be fixing breakfast. But not too early for *little bit*—she's an early riser."

"I'm aware. At home she crawls in my bed all the time in the middle of the night."

"Hopefully that incantation you used on her is still good. Come on."

"Thomas, I can't wait for more between us." Her gaze drifted to the floor.

He lifted her chin with his forefinger and stared into her eyes. "Me either, love. Our time is almost here."

The door let out a giant squeak in the silence of the quiet sleeping household.

"*Shh. Go.*"

Arista slipped from the room into the hallway, took a step, paused, mumbled a few words under her breath as Whisterly opened her bedroom door. Hidden from view now, Arista didn't stop, but she felt her mother's presence just the same.

Breathing a sigh of relief when Arista got to her own room and a still-sleeping Belle, Arista thanked the gods and crawled in beside her. With last night's memory of Thomas's body snug against hers, she drifted back into a restless sleep.

 

## 11

*E*lizabeth would mark today in the win category, so far anyway. Just thinking about the conversation they needed to have with Belle tonight made Elizabeth feel ill. Not because of herself but how Belle might perceive the information. Telling her now was the right course of action; Elizabeth could feel it in her bones.

Before Belle headed out across the country again, Elizabeth and her husband needed to share the secret they'd hidden from Belle since her birth. At the outset, the two of them didn't discuss the topic with her. She was too young...never the right time...just one more year, they had reasoned. Then they would sit her down. Then the information would somehow make sense to their precious Belle.

Despite the looming talk, Elizabeth couldn't fight the smile crossing her face. Today's shopping spree had been fun—unexpectedly so. Strange happenings aside with the two women, Whisterly and Arista were a joy to have around. The delight in Arista's eyes when she'd settled on a dress had moved Elizabeth to tears.

The genuine emotion and love Whisterly and Arista had for

each other were contagious. Thomas would be part of that. Well, watching them interact together, clearly he already was. Going forward, Arista's every happiness would be his and vice versa. The two of them had found something truly unique in each other.

Elizabeth was sold on Whisterly, Arista, and Jack—and, by extension, Simon. James didn't know that—yet.

Jack, Thomas, and James had gone on their own outings today. First, a visit out along the property lines, with stops at the garden and to check in on the livestock, then into town for dinner supplies and more whiskey.

James and Jack had put away some liquor yesterday, but anything that paved the way a little down this bumpy road was well worth the price. Bring on the whiskey and, surprisingly, some honest conversations about life and family. The two men had more similarities than differences, and both of them put their families first in their lives.

Whisterly, Jack, Thomas, and Arista had an engaging game of cards going on in the den—full of laughter and bets set on the side. Dinner simmered on the stove. Belle knocked softly on her parents' bedroom door, just off the kitchen on the first floor, interrupting Elizabeth's thoughts and dragging James from his pile of work at the desk.

Their eyes met; her husband's jaw tightened while a muscle pulsed at his temple. He reached for Elizabeth, pulled her to him, then nestled her between his legs. "Come in, Belle."

Belle opened the door just enough for her head to dart inside. James's face softened, a smile crinkling his eyes. "Come sit on the bed, little bit."

"Okay, sure, Pa." Belle lifted herself up and over atop the bed and, after a hearty bounce, stilled herself there, except for one foot, which swayed back and forth as she waited.

Elizabeth and James shared a glance. At that moment when he reached for her hand, she wished they could read each other's minds, like Belle and Thomas, so James could feel her support through his own thoughts.

James began. "Belle, would you like to visit with the Livingstons for a while and help where you can with their son, Simon? After speaking with Jack, your mother and I are about to make our decision. Wouldn't you rather stay here, after so much time away?"

Belle cocked her head, considering. "I have missed the farm and especially the forest and all our animals. But," she said, with an upward glance, "Mr. Jack has a forest around his house too. That makes me really happy," she exclaimed, punctuating her sentence with a smile.

"And? You didn't answer my question, Belle."

"Oh, I want to go, Pa. I already know I can help Simon. On Remeon, I helped get rid of some of his pain. He said so, when he woke up from his coma."

"Maybe we should charge for her services, huh?" James murmured under his breath to Elizabeth. Battling a smile, she nudged him to continue. "Belle, we'll give it a couple weeks and see how things go with Simon...with you there helping. A few weeks, then we'll see about longer."

A smile warmed Belle's eyes as she lunged off the bed. "Really, Pa?"

"Only if you promise to write and call," Elizabeth added. "Do you understand?"

"Sure, Ma. Pa, was that it?"

"No. Sit back down for a minute," he instructed, his tone turning more serious.

"All right... What is it? You seem sad and hurt all at once." In the midst of the short silence, Belle reached for James's hand, and he covered hers with his own. "You're sad, Pa. Why? Because of me? I'll be all right, and I'll do what you've asked. You don't have to worry."

"We believe you, Belle. There's something else. Something that might be hard for you to hear, but that we need to say."

"Okay." Belle inched onto the bed again.

"Belle, you're our daughter. You always will be. But"—he paused—"you weren't born to us."

"Huh?"

"Your mother and I are not your actual birth parents. You have another mother. We adopted you when you were a tiny baby, just born."

Belle looked from her pa to her ma.

More than anything Elizabeth wanted her daughter to say something, to scream or cry. Anything. They waited, giving her time to process her father's words.

Tears filled her eyes when Belle spoke. "You mean, I'm not yours? You're not mine? Why?"

Elizabeth joined Belle on the bed, draping an arm around her shoulders, pulling her close. "You'll always be our Belle. And we are yours. Forever. I promise. The only difference is, I didn't give birth to you."

Belle's chin wobbled as she listened. "Thomas and Mary— are they really yours?"

"I gave birth to them, Belle, and they're ours, just like you are."

"They don't know about me?"

"No, dear. We went to the hospital to have a baby, and that baby...died. That same night, another mother, with no family, died while having her baby. We believed that was a sign from God. So we adopted you. And, as they worked through the details, we agreed to be your foster family while the papers were filed. Eventually everything worked out, and the adoption was finalized."

"That's so sad, Ma."

Elizabeth nodded, amazed at the sensitivity of their

youngest child. "In some ways, but it also brought us all together."

"Remember how I told you I'd always protect you?" James asked, joining them on the bed. Belle bobbed her head. "I meant that, for always. Belle, in all the ways that matter, you're ours."

"I guess this explains why I'm different. Why I can do strange things sometimes."

"Maybe, sweetheart. But your wonderful talents aren't strange. They're a gift from God to help others. Do you understand?"

Belle sniffled. "I think so. I'm sorry, Ma and Pa."

"For what, sweetheart?"

"That your baby died. You must have been really sad."

Elizabeth swayed as she spoke, her words almost a whisper. "Yes, but I was the very first one you healed with your special gifts, Belle—just by you being you."

"Really?"

"Really. Both of us," James added, his voice gravelly.

Wrapping her arms around her mother's neck, Belle breathed, "I love you, Ma." Then she glanced at her father. "Pa." With a loud stomp she jumped from the bed, out the door, and trudged up the stairs.

Elizabeth reached for James, exhaling a long sigh. "That went way better than I expected."

James nodded his agreement. "That's our Belle. Always one step ahead of us. Let's close this circle and talk with Thomas and Mary also. We don't have to keep this secret any longer."

The relief from years of worry regarding Belle's parentage washed over Elizabeth, leaving her like a cleansing spring rain. "Yes James."

∼

JACK SCOOTED BACK from the breakfast table. "Thank you. I can't tell you how long it's been since I've had food this good." He huffed a laugh. "I hope you were taking notes, baby, 'cause I can't cook like this. To be fair, my mother taught me. I can cook. Doesn't come out tasting like this though."

"Elizabeth shared her biscuit recipe with me. We'll see how that goes."

"It's a start anyway."

"You're welcome, Jack," Elizabeth said. "Maybe I could bake for the wedding?"

"Oh, no, ma'am. We'll have that catered. Our turn to have you both as our guests."

"So exciting," Elizabeth beamed, glancing toward Arista and Thomas. "The big day will be here before we know it. More coffee, Jack?"

"No, thanks. We need to catch our train, after seeing these two to the portal."

James cleared his throat. "I'll drive you all, Jack, and I'd like to accompany you to the portal as well."

"No need. We can manage with a cab."

"No, I insist," James said, the set of his jaw leaving no doubt that the issue had been decided.

"Thank you, James. We accept." Whisterly turned her attention to Arista. "I hate to see you go, but I know you must."

Thomas kissed the back of Arista's hand. "*We* must..."

Belle cleared the plates, then dashed to her father, squeezing him by the waist. "I love you, Pa. See you soon." James bent to her level and cradled her to his chest. "Be good, little bit, and be safe."

"Of course, Pa."

He chuckled and ruffled her hair. "I'll help you load up, Jack."

Privy to the loving exchange, Whisterly understood the heartache of watching a child leave. James would miss Belle every bit as much as she and Jack would miss Arista. Through the facade of the elder Stewarts' smiles, the deep lines cutting across their foreheads told a different story. Worry and sadness warred for control of their faces, like a never-ending battle.

James and Elizabeth had confided in Whisterly and Jack, sharing the difficult conversation they'd had with their youngest daughter, making the two of them promise to get in touch if they believed Belle needed her parents, if only to talk for a few minutes on the phone.

That one conversation went a long way toward explaining Belle's extraordinary abilities. One of the child's parents had not been fully human. Whisterly was almost certain. Little by little she could help Belle develop as well, concentrating on her strengths while also exploring the child's untapped potential. Grandmother was right. Belle's exceptional talents needed much more study.

Belle led the small group to the portal. Arista hung back so Thomas could have a few minutes with his parents.

"Son..."

"Pa..."

"Wait. Let me finish," he continued, his hand cutting through the air. "We want you to know we're proud of you and your commitment to join the military service there on Remeon. From what Jack's told me, you've been holding back. Said that you'd saved his life on multiple occasions. Is that true?"

Thomas averted his eyes and kicked at the dirt. "Yeah, I guess it is."

"Be safe, son. I'm happy you're living your dream."

Thomas appeared to struggle for words, then met his father's watery gaze. "You taught me that, Pa, years ago with the very first seeds we planted together. To have a plan. To work hard for it. I'm finally getting there."

A satisfied smile stretched his lips. "Yes, you are, son." The two collided into a hug. "Watch your back, son, and take care of that pretty young lady."

"I will, Pa."

The wind shifted, bending tree branches to its will and sending leaves swirling in a spiral, as a vortex formed over the water ahead. "It's time! Hurry, Thomas," Belle yelled.

"Leave it to my sister. She loves this part."

Shep barked and clamped his teeth on Belle's clothes, pulling her backward. "Okay, boy. Just Thomas and Arista this time. I hear ya."

After another exchange of hugs, Thomas and Arista stood before Jack and Whisterly. Whisterly closed the distance to her daughter. "You'll be back here before you know it. Take care, little one."

"You too. Both of you."

Jack leaned in, kissing Arista's forehead. "Now go on before the portal collapses. I miss you already."

"Bye, Papa."

"Jack." Thomas grabbed Jack's hand for a quick shake, dipped his chin in acknowledgment, then raced ahead, hand in hand with Arista.

James stood still, staring at the spot where the portal had initiated then vanished, with stray tree limbs and leaves littering the ground, attesting to their rough treatment in the relative calm now. "Unbelievable, right, boy? You know what I'm talking about." Shep barked his agreement and padded toward James.

Elizabeth strode toward him with a confident gait. "Our son's getting married, James..."

He squeezed her close. "Yes, he is, sweetheart." James turned toward Whisterly and Jack. "Ready to head out the old-fashioned way?"

"You bet," Jack answered.

"Let's get you two, I mean three, to the train station."

Whisterly and Elizabeth chatted the whole way to the station. Who knew weddings could generate constant conversation? While they talked, Whisterly sensed Jack sinking into his own thoughts. This trip had been an intense whirlwind of activity, with the promise of more to come.

As they stood by the car, Jack extended his arm, and the two men shook hands. "Thank you for your hospitality, James, Elizabeth. Looking forward to seeing you again."

"Likewise." James and Jack shared a glance. "Take care of my little girl."

"You can count on it."

～

"WELL, that was emotional and brutal in ways I'd never dreamed possible."

A lopsided grin took Jack's mouth, amusement on his lips as he assisted Whisterly on board the train, then Belle. "You ain't seen nothing yet. Just wait until you have the full-blown Earthly wedding experience. You can't use ours to gauge what's in store for us in December—a Christmas wedding."

"Jack, our wedding was perfection."

"Agreed, baby. But in my mind, nothing could have gone wrong that night, once you said yes." Jack sought out the porter, tipping him in advance to make sure Arista's wedding gown would be properly stowed for their travel. "Okay, what seat will it be, little bit? With Whisterly or me?" Jack growled, wrenching his mouth to one side in his best imitation of a monster.

"You're so funny, Mr. Jack."

"Funny? Huh... Works with Daniel."

"Then he's a scaredy-cat." Squirming around Jack, Belle climbed into the empty seat next to Whisterly.

Daniel... Jack had tried to keep his fears at bay during the long months away from his son. What if he didn't remember him? Worse...what if Daniel wanted to stay with Harry, Maggie, and their new baby? Jack let that last question marinate in his thoughts for a few minutes, weighing the probability. On several occasions Harry had stated Daniel could live with them...if he wanted. Jack's chest tightened.

*Jack, relax, man. Daniel is bouncing off the walls, chomping at the bit. I couldn't keep him, even if I wanted too.*

*Harry...*

*Sleep, Jack. You sound exhausted. I'm the one with an infant. This trip has been...interesting.*

*Rest. We'll be here.*

*Thank God for you, Harry.*

*Yeah, yeah. See you soon, Jack.*

THE DAY so far a continuous blur of packing and instructions, Simon awaited the next step in the journey as he trailed Vinique along the banks of a river he didn't remember, like everything else. Certainly he'd recall regal trees such as these, whose branches draped over the water with a relaxed dominion while gnarled roots clung tight to the rocky shore, preventing its sudden demise from one moment to the next. Simon gazed, taking in the view. Breathtaking didn't quite do the site justice.

"Where to from here? Throw me in the river and be done with it?"

"At least for now, no. Your visit to Earth to meet up with Jack and Whisterly requires this special form of travel."

"I see. Interesting what I still recall, even though I'm experiencing memory loss." Simon didn't miss the flash of panic skirting her face. *Hmm.* "For instance, I can't remember experiences, events, people, beyond those I've just met recently. Yet history and certain facts seem to have stuck with me, for the most part."

Vinique nodded her agreement. "Sounds about right. Here's where you'll pass through the portal. Jack and Whisterly are already on the other side, waiting for you. If you don't have any questions, I'll get you on your way."

"You don't like me much do you, Vinique?"

"I'm trying to keep my feelings neutral where you're concerned."

"How's that working for you?"

Vinique broke her concentration needed to initiate the portal to answer. "Somewhat limited success, if you must know. You've hurt those I love."

Simon tilted his head, considering. "Seems as if this fiasco is a performance for judging later."

"No, Simon, it's a gift. Accept it. Learn from those two people waiting for you on Earth. Lucky for you, they've never given up on you."

"And you have?" Simon asked, with a twitch of his mouth.

"Let's get started." Through a sudden shift in the air, the trees surrounding them shivered and shook in an oddly misplaced dance. At the heart of the disturbance a whirlwind spun. Surrounding that, a vortex opened, growing larger by the second.

"I'm going in there?"

"Yes. Now. Hurry before it collapses."

"Thank you, Vinique." A single bag in hand, his gaze never left the unruly water as he put one foot in front of the other, heading for the disturbance.

⁓

JACK POUNDED BACK AND FORTH, pacing, wondering what the hell was taking so long. *Vinique, everything okay over there?*

*Absolutely. For better or worse, here he comes.*

*Thanks, Vinique. We owe you a debt of gratitude.*

*Just remember. Underneath this whitewash, he's still the same. You've just got a temporary reprieve. No matter where you take him or how you dress him up, he's still Simon, a ruthless sadistic killer.*

*Understood. Still gotta try, Vinique.*

*I know. It's who you are. Watch your back. And never forget what Simon's capable of.*

The portal whooshed open, and in the sudden burst of light, Jack watched his son emerge. Simon's brows knit in confusion; he tossed a look over his shoulder, then righted himself, before continuing on, until he was toe to toe with Jack.

"Simon, welcome to Earth." Jack shook his son's hand, the motion awkward and slow as Simon focused his gaze elsewhere.

"*Hmm.* I expected something grander, I guess, after seeing Belle's images."

"Give it more than three seconds before rendering a decision, huh?" Jack said.

"It's all new to me as well, Simon," Whisterly added. "Humans are fascinating."

"Whisterly. We meet again."

Jack continued. "My friend Harry has planned a party to celebrate our return, your arrival, and we'll be picking up our other son, Daniel, who's been staying with Harry, while I was away on Remeon."

"You have another son?" Simon asked, the obvious question left unspoken, hanging between them.

"Daniel is our adopted son but no less our son."

"Where's Belle?"

"Here I am. I've been exploring."

The lines of tension on Simon's face relaxed as Jack watched his son's reaction to Belle unfold.

"What did you think of the portal? Pretty neat, huh?"

Simon shrugged, visibly biting back a laugh. "Yeah, I kinda liked it."

Jack and Whisterly exchanged a glance. "Ready, you two?" Jack held the car door open, and they crawled inside, settling in the back seat.

*Look out. On our way, Harry.*

*You damn sure better hurry. Daniel has been counting down the hours and now minutes. The kid's like a time bomb.*

*Apologies in advance for whatever mischief comes your way tonight.*

*We can handle it. And I've got whiskey for the duration.*

*Good news right there, man.*

Right on cue, when Jack pulled up and stepped from the car, the front door burst open, exhaling Daniel, who took a flying leap toward Jack.

Stunned into action, Jack plucked Daniel from midair, the force sending them both tumbling to the gravel-covered driveway, flipping in circles from the momentum, until finally rolling to a stop. "Hello to you too, buddy." Jack pushed to his elbow, meeting the intensity of Daniel's gaze. "God, I missed you, son. You okay? I mean, besides the fact that you've given up baseball to become an offensive tackle."

"Huh?" Daniel's forehead scrunched, his expression turning stormy. Jack wrapped him in a hug. "Don't leave for so long again, Papa. Do you promise?"

Jack held Daniel, silent tears trickling down the boy's cheeks. A shuddering sigh shook his chest. "I'm sorry. I'll only be away if I have to. I can promise you that much."

Daniel nodded slowly. Grabbing a handful of Daniel's shirt, Jack wiped his son's cheeks. "Now look. You got both of us all wet."

Daniel let loose a giggle. "Hey, I really did."

"I've got two words to make this all better." Jack's attention flashed toward the doorway, where Harry stood. "Food. Now."

Daniel's eyes, focused on Jack, went wide. With a sudden twist, he faced Harry. "Really?"

"Yep. Really. Go wash up, Daniel."

"You got it."

"His mood's improved, thanks to you, Harry."

"Looks like he got you good."

Jack sighed. "Damn near tore me up, and I'm not talking physically."

"Get off your ass, come on in, and I'll get us that drink." Harry slapped Jack on the back. "I sure as hell hope you're staying put for a while."

"That's the plan. Oh, I need to introduce Daniel to Whisterly and Simon, and you and Maggie to Simon..."

Harry pinned Jack with his gaze. "We've gotten some of the initial awkward introductions over with. The rest we'll handle with food. Oh, and Jack, Simon is the spittin' image of you. I'm gonna need to be careful 'cause my instinct is to trust him."

"Yeah. You should, Harry. Months ago I almost killed him myself."

"Damn, Jack. You've gone through hell."

"But I've got Whisterly, Arista, Daniel, and you, so I'll face whatever's coming. But I'd really like that drink you keep promising me first."

A grin took over Harry's face. "I did, didn't I?"

# 12

---

The disarray of the unruly group of humans made Simon uneasy. They were loud and, from the little interaction he'd had with them so far, rarely serious. Pondering the gathering further, he looked on while Maggie and Harry piled the table with plates of food. A hand landed on his shoulder, interrupting him from his study in human dynamics.

"Simon?"

"Jack."

"Simon, this is Daniel, also my son. I've taken the liberty to tell Daniel you've come from out of the country and that we've been apart since your birth."

Simon nodded, evaluating the smaller human. He would have guessed the boy and Jack weren't genetically related even if Jack hadn't told him outright. Strange. Why would he call him his son? Daniel stuck out his arm, and the two shook hands.

"We're already alike." Daniel grinned.

"No. I'm sure you've got that wrong."

"I don't remember much about the father I had before Papa. But Papa reminds me of him all the time through stories."

"Is that so?" Simon felt himself drawn to the young boy, suddenly so serious and direct.

"Yeah. Maybe Jack has some stories for you too."

Simon lifted his head to find Jack's steely-eyed gaze homed in on his. "I don't think so. I outgrew fairy tales long ago."

"Papa says you're never too old to lose yourself in a story. Right?" Daniel glanced to Jack for affirmation.

"That's true, son."

"I guess we'll be spending some time together. I look forward to it, Daniel."

"Why don't you go find a seat for dinner, Daniel?" Jack squatted and whispered, "I think Maggie saved you a spot next to her and baby Harry. See?"

"Yeah." He took a step and swiveled back to Jack. "Come on, Papa," he demanded, his voice filling with all the feigned authority he could muster, his unsteady gaze swinging back and forth, clearly uncertain of Jack's compliance.

"I'll be right there." Jack tried unsuccessfully to stifle a laugh as Daniel took off.

"You haven't told your son about Remeon?" Simon questioned, losing the battle to keep the accusatory tone from his voice.

"Yes. In bite-sized chunks he can understand. No, to all the details, although I'll get to it all over time. I'd appreciate you letting me give him specifics as I see fit."

"Works for me." Simon shrugged. "Especially since all the particulars escape me at the moment."

"Damn. I forgot to introduce Daniel to Whisterly. Excuse me."

*This should be good.* Hovering close by the table, Simon evaluated the seating options while keeping an ear out for Jack. Tugging Daniel to his feet appeared to take some doing, but Jack succeeded.

"What, Papa?"

"Real quick, before we eat, I wanted you to meet Whisterly."

Bending down to Daniel's level, Whisterly offered her hand. "Hello, Daniel. Nice to meet you."

"You too." Daniel replied, his eyes silently pleading to be turned loose to eat.

"Whisterly is my wife, Daniel. She lives with us now."

Daniel cocked his head. "Whisterly..." He rolled out the name, practicing the syllables on his tongue. "I've heard you talk to her before. When you don't think I'm around."

"*Hmm.* You probably have." Jack rubbed the scruff on his face and appeared lost in thought. "You see, I've missed her so much over the years that I talk to her in my thoughts all the time."

Daniel met his father's gaze while Simon focused on Whisterly's reaction. Was his father always this brutally honest? The intensity of emotion between his parents hit Simon out of nowhere, and he drew in a breath, trying to steady his step. Something snapped together deep inside him. What the hells was that?

"Simon?" Belle repeated.

"What?" he asked, yanking his attention from Whisterly and Jack.

"I said, are you okay?"

"Sure, Belle."

"Come on. Sit beside me. Nobody gets to eat till we're all sitting down, and Mr. Harry says grace."

"So many rules." Simon rolled his eyes, gaining back his composure from whatever the hells that pain was. "Why can't we just eat?"

"Really?"

The conversation settled—all eyes on Harry for the prayer.

"I think I prefer to eat in solitude." Faces around the table turned, their eyes shifting to Simon in a room gone utterly quiet.

"Sometimes I feel the same way, Simon, especially after having this little guy over here." Harry made weird faces at their kid, blubbering nonsense in Maggie's lap. "We're a lot to handle at times. But also good company." Harry winked at Daniel. "Daniel, would you like to give thanks?"

"Sure, Uncle Harry." Squeezing his eyes shut, Daniel bowed his head.

Like everyone else, Simon followed suit, the action feeling foreign and wrong.

"Dear God. Thank you for this food that we can finally eat. Thank you for new friends and family. And mostly thank you for bringing Papa back." His voice lowered. "Please make him stay. Amen," Daniel said, finishing the last word stronger.

"Amen," they repeated.

"Can we eat now, Uncle Harry?"

"By all means." Harry grinned. "What are you waiting for, Daniel?"

~

"Harry."

"Yeah, Jack?"

"How about a refill? Need to talk to you in private for a few minutes, before we head out."

"Sure." Harry eyed Jack's empty glass. "Bring me one of those and grab your own, then come on into my office." He waved Jack through. Harry grabbed his bottle of Jack Daniel's and poured fresh drinks for the two of them.

"Thanks for tonight, Harry. Nobody's killed anyone with a wayward spell yet. I'd call that a win. Now for the real test— alone, together under one roof."

"Simon seems...subdued."

Jack studied the amber liquid. "He does. One of the many

effects of the memory wipe. Our real work with him starts tomorrow. Filling those memories back up."

"I'm sensing that's not why you wanted to speak to me though."

"Right. It's not. What do you hear from the Freemasons you contacted?"

"Ah. Well, I have had some communication back." Rummaging through paperwork in a drawer, Harry paused, reading. "Here are my notes. You were right. A man matching Kix's description has been located near those coordinates by our Freemason contact in the area. Seems he's taken up residence there."

"Figured as much. Anything else?"

"Yeah. These." Harry handed Jack a stack of photos.

"Who are the people with him?"

"Not congressmen or senators, but close. People well connected on Capitol Hill."

Jack leaned back in the chair and crossed his leg over one knee. "How does a man with no memory manage that?"

"I don't know, Jack. The man already had roots within the Freemason network. You mentioned his father was a member. And, since you said he was a warlock, possibly that has something to do with it also."

"Maybe... Or he's had help from said warlocks. Recovered now perhaps? And, if the data has found a home, could be they're running with it."

"I'm expecting more intel any time now."

"Thanks, Harry. I'll communicate this information to the council. We should assume Kix has regained his memory going forward."

～

JACK DIDN'T TRY to fill the silence during the drive home. Daniel and Belle dozed while Simon stared stoically into the darkened night sky. Daniel needed to be brought fully up to speed about Remeon, Whisterly, and himself before someone else beat Jack to it. He'd already laid the framework for more substantial conversations to occur.

If Belle could handle all this, Daniel could as well. Right? Jack debated with himself back and forth, considering the impact of this discussion too late, with everything else he'd been dealing with. The two kids were close in age, but Belle seemed older, mature in ways that Daniel—and Jack—couldn't comprehend yet...probably because she wasn't fully human.

Whisterly reached for Jack's hand. *Tomorrow.*

He gave her hand a squeeze. *Tomorrow, baby. We're as ready as we'll ever be.*

SIMON BLINKED, a path of sunlight streaming through the curtains, hitting him just right with its sliver of warmth. Still groggy, he scooted to sit up and let his gaze travel the room. A vision of another space flashed in his mind for an instant, then was gone again. From Remeon most likely, he reasoned. A chill coursed over him as his gaze swept through the tidy harsh lines, eloquently furnished and outfitted for any need. Here... This place—he searched for words, exhaling a breath— brought comfort. He padded about the room, sat in a chair, poked around in the closet, delved into a chest of drawers, examined the pictures, and stared out a window, taking in the serenity of just *being*. Instinctively he realized nothing comparable to this right here had ever been his.

Noise and laughter from downstairs drew him, made him want to take part where happiness sparked such a response. Instead he took his time, dressing slowly, spending more time watching at the window and perusing a shelfful of books he couldn't read.

"Simon," someone called. *Daniel.* He raced down the hall, sounding as if he might plow through the door but stopping just short in rapid steps. "Come eat. Papa says we can't start without you, and Belle and I are starving."

Simon chuckled as he finished dressing. "Be right there."

"Hurry." Then the running repeated in the opposite direction.

Aromas drifting toward him led Simon to the source—the kitchen. Whisterly and Jack leaned against the stove and each other, drinking from large mugs. The two of them looked so happy it was jarring. Daniel and Belle fidgeted at the table, their frowns lifting when Simon walked in.

"Finally," Daniel announced. "Now, Papa?"

"Sure. Dig in, tiger."

"Simon. How'd you sleep?" Whisterly pulled herself from Jack's side.

"Why?"

"Oh, just wondering if you were comfortable in the new surroundings."

"Is this a test?"

"What?" Jack's brow knit in confusion.

"A test—whether I meet your requirements to stay."

"Of course not." Jack thumped him on the back. "You don't have to meet any requirements to stay here. Whisterly only wanted to be sure you were all right with your room and bed."

"I see." If the contentment surging in his chest was any measure, the answer would be yes. For right now it might be best not to share that information though. Otherwise, someone might yank Simon far away from here and the oddly pleasing sensation settling within his soul.

"Ready for some pancakes?"

Daniel leaned in, laughing. "She burned the first batch. You can still smell it."

"True, young man," Whisterly agreed. "You're used to your father's expert pancake-flipping skills. I'm new at this. The second set was better."

"Yes, ma'am." Daniel raised his plate. "More?"

"Coming right up. Simon, here ya go."

"Try 'em with syrup," Belle chimed in, smothering the stack with a gooey dark mixture.

Silence descended with all eyes riveted to Simon as he brought the first drippy bite to his mouth. What if he hated it? "*Mmm.*" A warm, fluffy sweet goodness sparked inside his mouth. "Really good." Cutting into a second bite, his lips eased up. "These right here are worth the trip to Ear—I mean, uh, here, entirely on their own."

"There you go, Jack. Proof I'm improving."

"I had no doubt. Plate the next one for me, baby, and I'll give it my personal taste test."

"Yours and mine, coming right up."

Jack and Whisterly joined the others at the table. "Papa, I'm done. May I be excused?" Daniel asked.

"Sure. Rinse your plate and Belle's, while you're at it." Daniel's chair screeched on the floor. "Why don't you take Belle outside and show her around?"

"Okay, Papa."

"These are quite good Whisterly." Simon swallowed another bite, watching Daniel and Belle sprint out the door. "Thank you."

"You're welcome."

"Nothing I'm aware of on Remeon quite matches this breakfast treat. Well, not that I...remember anyway."

Whisterly eyed Simon over the rim of her cup. "Simon, your father and I would like to get started tomorrow with discussing your heritage and some basic lessons in magic."

"All right."

"You've already been immersed, so even if you can't remember that experience or recall individual spells, all the information you need is at your disposal. Here." Whisterly pointed to her head.

"I would concur. Something's up there, trying to break free. Not sure if or how I should make that happen."

"I'm not a warlock, but I can help with the basics. We'll see where that takes us. How's that sound?"

Shuffling to the coffeepot, Simon caught a glimpse of the kids at play. "Such freedom here." He lifted the pot in silent question. When they nodded, Simon refilled Jack's and Whisterly's cups, then his own. "Is it like this everywhere on Earth?"

"Yes. For the most part. Kids should be allowed to be kids. Don't you agree?" Jack asked.

"In theory, yes. But what if even the children have to fight for survival?"

"You don't have to do that here."

"But I sense that I have in the past."

"Look, Simon. We don't know exactly how this process will work, how soon memories will resurface, how you'll feel about us once you have both the old set of memories and the new, whether you'll want to wield magic any longer once you learn of its practical, yet safe usage for you and others around you."

"Sounds complicated."

"Highly likely." Jack rose, gulping coffee as he eyed Daniel and Belle through the window. "I'd like to share some knowledge of my work with you also—construction. I've built a small business since returning from the war. Doing quite well too." Lines furrowed in Jack's forehead.

Simon could almost hear the gears turning, bursting with the need to have Simon participate in what Jack knew.

"I need to expand though. Hoped to have Harry on board

by now. With the new baby, he's waffling on me. I think I'll get him to agree eventually."

"Without magic? Without the help of telepathy for communication? You build things?"

"Exactly. Like this house for instance."

Simon took in the details all around him with a new appreciation, nodding. "Sure. No harm in listening."

"I was hoping for a little more enthusiasm. But I guess you don't know enough to have an opinion yet. I'll fix that."

Simon shrugged, raising his cup. "I love this."

"It's the caffeine. I have three or four cups a day. Sometimes more. I'm headed outside to play catch with Daniel. Care to join us?"

"I guess. Uh...what should I call you both?"

"Whatever feels right for you."

"I'll take care of the dishes," Whisterly announced. "Jack, you two go ahead."

He disappeared, returning with two gloves and a ball. One of the gloves came hurtling through the air. "Catch."

Simon plucked it from the air. "Is this all there is to it?"

"Watch and learn. You're about to get bested by a nine-year-old."

SIMON LOOKED on as Jack and Daniel engaged in a pointless exercise of throwing a small ball back and forth. Belle's giggles increased in conjunction with their throwing speed, the ball smacking with a loud *thwack* proportionate to the pair's efforts. Lowering himself to a seat in the grass next to Belle, Simon gave her elbow a shove. "Do you understand the point of this?"

With one glance, Belle's face conveyed a joy Simon didn't comprehend. They were, after all, just throwing a ball in the air.

"Fun." The smile deepened on Belle's face. "To have a good time, silly."

"*Hmm.*" Simon tore a blade of grass and munched on it, threw it on the ground and grabbed another. "How did you learn to do what you do, communicate using pictures, visions through your mind?"

"I'm not sure. It happens when I'm trying to help someone."

Simon turned to face Belle. "It's an extraordinary gift, and you're not even a witch."

"True. I'm not sure what I am. Some on Remeon believe me to be part Fae."

"I was thinking the same. Healing is in your nature, but you accomplish it in a most unusual manner."

Belle cocked her head. "I guess so, but it's different for everyone, since they all have different needs."

"I see... So you communicated those visions that I needed because that was the only way to send me help at the time?"

"Right."

"And you've had no training?"

"Only with the little people in the forest and later with the witches on Remeon."

"I'm pretty sure, without your help, I'd still be in the basement on Remeon in a coma. You reached out to me when it seemed very few cared."

Belle lowered her head. "Just because you've done some bad things doesn't mean you deserve to die. There's always hope." Belle flashed her teeth with her broad grin. "Best thing—it's free. You just need to grab it."

"You two ready to give it go?"

Simon jerked his gaze to Jack's. "Sure. Why not?"

Jack pulled Simon to the side while Daniel gave Belle instructions. "Take it easy on her," Jack muttered to Simon. "I don't know if she's ever thrown a baseball."

"Neither have I. But I'm betting Belle will be just fine."

Daniel demonstrated for Belle in the distance, his motions exaggerated. Watching with a laser-like intensity, Simon memorized the movements, going through the few steps in his head.

"Come on, Belle. Right here." Simon threw his fist into his glove, demonstrating, just like he'd seen Jack do it. Arcing powerfully through the air, the ball hit Simon's glove in the center, delivering a sting to his hand.

"You've done this before, Belle." Jack clapped for her from the sideline.

"Yeah. Thomas thinks he's Jackie Robinson. We play all the time."

Simon tossed the ball back, falling short by several yards.

"You got more than that, Simon," she yelled.

Simon shook his head, concentrating on Belle's open glove a few seconds, before focusing, then letting go.

Lunging for the ball, Belle snatched it from the air. "That's it."

Why did it make Simon so happy that he'd succeeded at this silly human game? Belle's laughter was contagious. Maybe that was it. Pretty soon Simon was missing more often than catching the ball.

"All right. My turn," Jack announced. Belle gave up her glove. "Good job, Belle." Jack nudged her toward the sideline by Daniel. "Thomas has done a good job with you."

"Look out, Simon," Daniel taunted. "Papa's got that look."

"Ready?"

"Show me what you got, Jack."

Daniel whooped and Belle clapped as Jack wound up and loosed the ball.

∼

"The end." Closing the third book of the night, Jack added, "That's all for now."

Daniel squirmed by his side. "I had fun today. Lemme stay up longer."

"So you like having more people around, more than just us?"

Daniel met Jack's gaze, gauging the seriousness of his words, Jack was certain. "Sometimes, Papa."

Jack ruffled his hair. "I get it, son. More people can spread more happiness. Sometimes."

"What do you mean, Papa?"

"I don't need more than a few people in my life—you, Whisterly, Uncle Harry. But Simon is my son also and Arista my daughter. Having them around won't mean I love you any less. Understand?"

Daniel's forehead furrowed.

Jack smiled as his son lost himself, mulling over Jack's last words. If he could read his son, those thoughts would be flashing by a mile a minute.

"I think I do. I'll bet they don't want you to be away from them either, just like me." Daniel wormed his arms around Jack's waist.

Kissing Daniel's forehead, Jack continued. "Soon you'll meet Arista. And one day in the future I'd like to take you to visit where Simon and Arista live, where I met Whisterly. But, if I do that, you'll have to promise to keep it between just us, our family. Like the bedtime stories I've told you before."

"Sure, Papa. About the faraway place you've visited?"

"That's right."

"You haven't added to the story in a long time, Papa."

"I know." Jack inhaled a deep breath. "For a while it was too painful. But I'm ready again now. We'll start tomorrow. I'll continue to tell you about where Whisterly, Arista, and Simon are from."

"Wow... Okay. The place where magic is real?"

"Yes, it is, son. I promise."

"Neat. Tell me more about Arista."

"Okay. For a few minutes longer. Let's see... She's beautiful, like her mother. Smart like you—"

"And I bet she sees inside people, like you do." Daniel yawned.

"What do you mean?"

"You know about people, Papa. It's what you do best. I think Arista is just like that."

"Aren't you the wise one?" Jack tickled Daniel's stomach. "I think you're right." Straightening, Jack stretched. "Don't let all that smartness go to your head."

"I won't, Papa," Daniel mumbled, sleep already taking him under. "They're not stories...real..."

Jack kissed his son's head, drawing in his scent. This kid had Jack's heart wrapped up tight. One day, God willing, all three would be here under his roof—Arista, Simon, and Daniel. That would be a very good day.

"Night, son," Jack whispered, then he clicked the door shut.

"What a serious face. Your thoughts are all over the place."

"That's about right, baby. Is Belle settled?"

"She read me a book. Talked about Thomas for a while, but her thoughts are calm, peaceful."

Jack met Whisterly on their bed, pulled her close, and kissed her softly.

"*Mmm.* That was nice." Her fingers brushed hair from his face. "What is it, Jack?"

"I've decided to talk to Daniel more directly about Remeon, you, Arista, and Simon. Before now, we've discussed some of my experiences but disguised behind a story format. Seemed an easier way to share bits and pieces with him of what I was going through. Now I want him to hear the truth—even visit one day. Well, what do you think?"

"I'd love to help you, if you'd let me. You'll tell him about magic and telepathy also?"

"Yes. And after he visits, he could learn telepathy as well. I miss that with him, after experiencing it with Arista and Simon." As his words sunk in, Jack watched for Whisterly's reaction, wanting to see the expression on her face before reading her.

"This step could help Daniel and I bond. Jack, I'm all for it."

Relief worked its way through the tension in Jack's shoulders. "Thank God. Starting to bring him into our world feels right...now."

"It does."

Jack's throat tightened. "I still worry sometimes that we won't be in sync, even more so where Daniel is concerned. After Simon..."

"*Shh.* I know Jack. It'll be easier though. We don't have to think everything through on two separate worlds anymore. Where you go, I go."

Jack's gaze drifted to hers. "Where you are, I'll be also. Always."

# 13

$S$leep wouldn't come. Simon leaned against the window, peering into the darkness outside, comfortable in its shroud-like covering, clinging to him like a second skin. Humans were funny, in an odd sort of way. Their silly games, running around, chasing balls... Why? The images he'd captured in his head of the day just past flashed before him now. Laughter, fun, joy—all foreign to him. And something else... Belonging, acceptance. He'd felt those things, yet he had no right.

Questions riddled him.

The odd feeling blooming in his chest grew, due to no action of his own. Probably what was keeping him awake right now. Pacing back and forth, he let the day's activities roll through his head; they'd been busy at nothing really. Maybe that was the point? Whisterly's delight while making pancakes, Jack instructing Daniel, Belle as she'd pummeled Simon with that damn ball, and her giggles when she'd bested him.

A half smile tilted his lips. Belle was different. Maybe because she wasn't fully human. Maybe because she'd helped him on Remeon, despite how messed up his past had evidently been.

He needed answers.

Throwing on a shirt and pants, he left his room for more space to roam. Accustomed to the darkness, he made his way down the stairs, his fingers gliding over the wooden banister, reminding him of the fact that his father had made this house... with tools, wood, time, and his own bare hands.

Even Simon understood wood, hammer, and nails didn't make it what it was now though. Filling it with those he loved made it a home.

Moonlight spilled through a window in the front door, bathing him in its nocturnal light. Lingering for a moment, conscious of the power at work humming through his blood and needing a connection, he sought a bond. He closed his eyes, hunting the source.

A ripple pierced his blackness, a tug of something familiar waiting for him...

Like a bolt of lightning, sudden recognition led the way. Through the hall, into the kitchen to a door tucked out of the way, he paused, his hand hovering over the doorknob. Unease coursed through him because he needed what was behind the door, in that it had seized him first. So his next steps were clear. Twisting the knob, he followed the steps to another doorway, then ducked inside.

"Illumine," he murmured, the word coming from nowhere, tumbling from his mouth to light the dark musty room. Tracing a slow circle in place, the tightness in his throat lessened, taking in the intricacies of the space, his in a way, but not, he instinctively reasoned. Dirt covered the floor, and rock lined the walls. Shelving along the walls held books that screamed for his attention, but the rock slab in the center drew him from somewhere deeper, more primal.

A rhythm sprung to life, unbidden, pounding in his head as

his eyes drifted shut, and chanting, a multitude of voices strong, filled his thoughts. He clung to the solid rock at his fingertips, needing its strength. Bit by bit he pulled the force to him, shoring up his fortitude. This ancient call erupting from within him, centuries old... Simon had experienced it before. Powerless to deny what he inherently knew to be his, he moved back and forth, letting it wash over him instead.

"Simon."

*Whisterly.* Snapping his eyes open, he stood transfixed, trapped in her gaze. Words jumbled in his brain, fighting to get out in the right order. To explain why he was here. "I...I'm sorry. I just...felt like I needed to be here." Silence stretched between them, and as the minutes passed, he felt each one slip slowly by.

Simon's body jolted forward when her thoughts brushed his. So many others had linked with him, wanting something from him, and he recognized them as that realization hit. The tendril of thought reaching for him again had been a part of him once, then had broken of no accord of its own. He sighed, Whisterly's touch like the covering to a festering wound, the fragile pieces finally weaving tentatively together.

Stumbling backward, he rubbed at his forehead, confusion clouding the reality standing before him. *Whisterly?*

"You belong here, Simon, just like me. You recognized the call. You do fit here." Whisterly closed the distance between them. "I'm glad you found your own way."

Simon exhaled a long breath, letting go of the dread that had twisted his stomach upon his mother's arrival. "You are? Why?"

"The pull you experienced means your powers are intact and are reminding you that your sorcery yearns for oneness with you."

"Well, I can go now, if you want to be alone. I get it."

A smile spread over her face. "Simon, I'm here because I

sensed your presence. Tomorrow I'd planned to bring you here anyway. To introduce you to the magical sanctuary that Jack built."

"Oh. Good. So I can stay a while?"

"Yes. Do you feel any discomfort being here? Any traces of memory returning?"

"A ceremony of some sort." Simon refocused inward, seeking the connection again. "But it's gone now. No pain," he assured her, shaking his head. "Just a feeling that there's so much more, and I'm only scratching the surface."

"Then we'll have no trouble getting started."

"Wait. You said Jack built this this?" Gazing again at the totality of the space, his jaw dropped. "Imagine all the work, all the time."

A faraway look transported Whisterly away for a few seconds, and the peace in its wake let Simon know whatever it was held a deep meaning for her. "Jack said it was therapeutic at a time when he was missing me, you, and Arista."

Simon cocked his head. *Could Jack really have missed me?* "I'm not sure I'll know what to do when you begin lessons."

"I have a high degree of confidence you will."

"How long do you think it took Jack to build this?"

"Years, off and on."

"I can't even imagine how it would feel to be a part of something like this. To make it come alive. How did he do it?"

"From his memory of my sanctuary on Remeon, that's what got him started. His love for us kept him going. But he didn't make it come alive. He couldn't create that feeling you and I have inside."

"How did it happen then?"

"We did that, Simon. You and me."

SIMON TRUDGED up the basement stairs, pain nagging him from the inside out. It was better to have than not, acknowledging the part of him that made him feel most alive. It also hurt like the hells had opened wide after a grueling session with his mother. The pounding in his head didn't seem to dissipate after that first night of recognition. Instead, the ache just ramped up or scaled down, depending on the level of activity for the day. But having an outlet for the magic that lived and grew in his soul gave him a peace he didn't know how to name.

What had he done with this force before? Before the witches had erased his memories? When he'd confronted Whisterly with this question today, she'd said they'd discuss it over time, almost like he was some kind of fragile instrument that she might strain and break with use. Her answering tone had been light and quick, her face hastily devoid of emotion. All of which meant not good things.

With all the power at her disposal, she couldn't mask her face fast enough. As she peeled back his layers, exposing him bit by bit, he'd have to wait and let her feed the information to him in the morsels she deemed him able to handle.

Telepathy hadn't worked on Whisterly's steel trap of a mind, neither had the threads of magic that he'd tried to slip by her—no such thing. Plain as day now why he heard his father occasionally call her the master.

Frustration got the better of Simon, coming out in a groan.

Belle skipped through the kitchen, turning toward the noise. "Simon? What's wrong?"

"Nothing, Belle. Go on."

"Why don't you come with me?"

Simon shook his head. "I don't think so. Got things to do."

"Like what?" She smirked. "Sulking in your room? Come on." Grabbing Simon by the hand, she dragged him out the door, where Daniel waited perched on a step, eyeing them both expectantly.

*Great...* "Where are you going?" Simon asked.

"Into the forest. Daniel knows the way."

*A tromp through the forest with two kids...* "Tempting, but I think I'll pass." Simon pivoted to head back inside.

"No, you can't," Daniel pleaded. "Belle promised to find the little people."

"No promises, Daniel. They'll only show if they want to and only if you don't scare them."

Simon paused, his interest piqued. This ability Belle had intrigued him. It wouldn't hurt to find out more. "All right. Let's get going then." Simon caught up to them, just as a small animal lunged for Belle. "Look out, Belle."

Snapping her attention to the perceived threat, her body relaxed. "Only a cat. Take it easy, Simon."

Daniel jumped up and shrieked like a girl. "Shadow!" Daniel scratched the scruff at the animal's neck as the cat leaned into his touch, emitting a soft rumbling sound; then it traced a path around Belle's legs, before puddling at her feet. "She likes you," Daniel exclaimed, a grin growing on his face.

"She belongs to you guys?" Belle asked.

"Not really." Daniel shrugged. "I don't think she belongs anywhere. When she comes around, Papa feeds her, but I haven't seen her since we've been back. I thought she'd left for good. Probably thought we'd abandoned her. Poor kitty." Scuttling inside, Daniel returned in no time with a saucer of milk.

"Are you still coming, Daniel?" Belle asked through squinting eyes, turned toward the sun. "In a few hours, it'll be dark out, and I wanna be back before then."

"Yeah. Sure. Shadow will be fine, right, Simon?"

Simon rolled his eyes. "You bet, squirt."

The trio tromped through the undergrowth, heading toward an area dense with tall pine trees. "You guys aren't quiet at all," Simon called from the rear, cutting at a stray tree branch with his hand. "Are we about done?"

Belle shushed him. "They know we're here." When they came upon a fallen tree log, she dropped onto it. *"Shh,"* she repeated.

"She means you," Daniel mumbled to Simon.

After another eye roll, Simon complied, stilling, except for the in and out of their breathing, which he could easily hear from all three of them in the silence.

Dark clumps of dirt squished through Belle's clenched fists, and even though Simon couldn't make out the words, her lips moved ever-so-slightly. A soft breeze meandered between the trees, its whisper changing, adjusting as it roamed between the three of them.

Daniel jerked, sucking in a sudden breath.

Simon's hand landed solidly on Daniel's shoulder, letting him know in no uncertain terms not to move. Then, like he'd done many times before, Simon eased his way into Belle's thoughts.

The excitement in her smile worked its way through the nooks and crannies of Simon's mind, before he heard her voice communicating in a language Simon guessed wasn't programmed into the universal translator. The syllables sounded like an ancient verse or song.

Letting his eyelids fall, Simon felt the foreign communication flow through him. The tiny beings were...happy, elated to be in communion with Belle. Simon dug in a little further, wanting to get at the essence of one of the tiny creatures, to know its thoughts and desires. Because if he knew that he could...

Sinking deeper into her thoughts and the creatures, Simon sensed light, joy, and something else... Peace? Whatever it was, he needed more. Craved the high that being right here held for him. Pressing on, he slammed into a barrier. *No, Simon. No more. The little people bring healing through their calmness and harmony. But you can only have what they give freely, so all may share.*

Belle whispered something again and threw her arms up high, painting the air with pinpoints of sparkling light. She chased the small throng, and powerless under their enchanting spell, Simon followed, with Daniel in the rear. Pulsing higher and higher, their brilliance eventually faded from view in the darkening sky.

Whooshing out a breath, Simon shook his head to clear it, wondering if he'd been under a spell, whisked away by those tiny things somehow.

Daniel's laughter echoed through Simon's ears. "Wow, Belle. That was neat. I can't wait to tell Papa. When can we do it again?"

"Not sure, Daniel. For now, we need to head back," Belle insisted.

How long had they been out here? At the time it had felt like minutes, strolling among the tiny souls. In reality, closer to two hours had passed, judging from the sky.

Daniel took point, weaving a path among the trees, finding his way easily, where Simon would have struggled to find the house again without the aid of magic.

"Well, what did you think?" Belle asked Simon through a smile as they approached the house.

"Your 'little people' healed something inside me I didn't know was broken," Simon murmured, more to himself than Belle. "That was incredible."

A contented smile rested on Belle's lips. *This is only the first step, Simon.*

"You channel that energy somehow?"

"Yeah." Belle bobbed her head. "Everyone needs something different. That's where I come in."

~

JACK DOWNED another mouthful of whiskey, enjoying the burn as it slid down his throat. The fire crackled in the fireplace, hissing and sputtering as the tongues of flame reached higher, chasing the chill from the room. He glanced up from his book, *Dark Carnival*, concentrating instead on the conversation he'd had with Daniel before he'd gone to sleep.

Determined to bring Daniel up to speed slowly regarding Remeon, telepathy, and magic, their storytime had become somewhat abstract, as he'd guided Daniel into a fuller under-standing of the stories Jack had told his son over the years. Oddly enough, these were more fact than fantasy, as bit by bit, he'd indoctrinated Daniel to Remeon under the guise of make believe.

"So, you're saying magic is real, not just a part of a fairy tale?"

"Well, the energy is real, but only some people can access it and give it life."

"You can't, and I can't." Daniel paused, eyes round, waiting for affirmation.

"That's right."

"But Whisterly, Arista, and Simon can."

"You got it."

"Doesn't seem fair, Papa. I'd like to learn too."

"Arista and Simon inherited the ability from Whisterly, just like you gained certain traits from your parents. For example, you're good at sports. Better than Simon, I'd wager, and you can roll your tongue. I can't because I don't have that ability."

"Yeah, but magic is *way* better."

"Eh, sometimes." As Jack had kissed his son good night, he had displayed his tongue-rolling skill again. "Show off."

Jack settled in the den, his thoughts turned toward the next day. Telepathy would be much harder to explain. Tomorrow night they'd begin to tackle that one. A creak sounded, followed by footsteps. "Are you done, baby? Come join me by the fire."

A hearty chuckle followed. "Sorry, not who you were expecting..."

"Simon. Sorry, Whisterly was to join me after her conversation with Vinique."

"Headed to the kitchen for a snack. I'll leave you to your, uh, reading."

"How about a nightcap instead?" Jack raised his glass.

"Okay, sure, I guess."

Jack filled a glass at the bar. "Jack Daniel's will be all right, I trust? I've a fully stocked bar with alternatives. You're welcome to take a look."

Simon shrugged. "Whatever you're having is fine with me. I don't think I drink much, on Remeon, I mean."

Jack cocked his head and handed Simon the whiskey. "Probably wise. Alcohol is strong in the compound. I assume it would be the same where you were."

A smile spread across Simon's face.

"Good, isn't it?"

"Yes." Simon lowered himself to the couch, the two sitting in silence, watching the fire pop and hiss as it danced. "I can see why this is one of your favorite rooms in the house." Simon's gaze swept the space, then settled on Jack. "It's comfortable, has a lived-in feel, but is richly furnished."

"You have a fine eye for detail. Everything here I expressly chose, and honestly, expense wasn't so much a factor as comfort and the feel of the room. This place is more *me* than any other spot in my home."

*It shows. Well done.*

An authentic compliment from his son—something Jack never expected to hear. Telepathy didn't lie. Jack had felt the honesty in Simon's words, just like he'd experienced Simon's hatred via this same mode of communication on Remeon. Progress?

Simon scanned the pictures and articles that covered the walls. "Looks like you've had a long, distinguished military career."

"You could say that, although *distinguished* is a matter of perception. Some wins. Some losses. Through it all, I remember most the people who didn't come back. No one really wins at war."

"Now that we're connected telepathically, I can sense, even though I can't remember on my own, that you and I have fought on opposite sides."

"That's true." Taking another swallow of his drink, letting his thoughts drift back, Jack continued. "I hope, given time, when your memory returns, you'll see that battle in a different light."

"*Hmm*. After visiting the forest with Belle today, many outcomes are possible that I didn't even know existed."

"She's one extraordinary young lady, Simon."

"One I don't fully understand, even with the help of magic."

"Me either. I've been the recipient of her healing talents as well."

Simon turned up his glass, emptying the remainder. "I guess I'll leave you in peace now to get back to your book. Thanks for the drink."

"Simon"—Jack cleared his throat—"what would you say to a card game? Harry and I get together every now and then, and we're meeting day after tomorrow at a tavern in town for a couple beers and a game or two of twenty-one. You're welcome to come along."

"Me? I don't even know how to play. Plus I don't want to interfere."

"Easy enough to learn, if you're interested."

"Okay... I guess. Why not? I'll give it a go."

"Let's get us another round, and we'll move to the kitchen. The cards are in there."

Seated at the kitchen table, Simon opposite Jack, he shuffled the cards. "Remember when we play, you, Harry, and I use telepathy—be careful not to give away your hand."

Simon battled a grin.

"Haven't even started yet. What's so funny?"

"You and Harry might have to be careful, but you don't need to tell me that. Shielding my thoughts for a game of chance, or anything else for that matter, comes naturally. As a human, I get that it'd be more difficult for you."

"Oh...this will be fun." Eyeing his son across the table, Jack shuffled the deck, the cards sliding back neatly together in well-formed stack. "We'll play a couple rounds for practice, then place some bets." Jack leveled Simon with his gaze. "Try and keep up."

## 14

*T*he tavern he and Jack often visited loomed ahead. Harry picked up the pace, wanting to get there ahead of Jack and Simon to order a round of beers for them and have a shot and a beer himself. Something besides his son's screaming all night had him on edge, and he was pretty sure it was Simon.

Jack was vulnerable where his son was concerned. Lost in hope for what might be and an endless stream of what ifs. That was a big *if*, knowing all that the kid had done. Fact: Simon was a coldhearted killer, whose memories would come flooding back soon enough. This playing nice in the interim was creepy as hell. Why other people didn't see it that way, well, Harry didn't know. Desperation maybe?

But for the sake of his friend and brother, Harry would do absolutely anything, including laying down his own life. Like always, Harry would have Jack's back, especially when he wasn't thinking clearly where Simon was concerned. The shit would hit the fan, and when it did, Harry would be there to slog through the crap with Jack. Harry needed his friend to come out whole on the other side of whatever this was with Simon. Whatever it took.

Halfway through his beer the pair showed, right on time of course. Harry smiled, not because he was happy to see them necessarily, but that the world's clocks could be set based on Jack's punctuality. The man was never late. If he wasn't on time, past experience had proven great concern was warranted. Only twice in Harry's life had he known Jack to be late. The first, he'd been deathly ill with a case of the measles; the second, fighting for his life on Guadalcanal.

Lifting his chin, he acknowledged Jack and Simon as they made their way toward Harry and Jack's regular table. "Good to see you, Harry." Jack slammed his hand against Harry's. "Looks like you've gotten a head start."

"Well, yeah. Soothes what ails me." *And gives me some liquid courage when it seems I'm already failing at this father thing,* he added telepathically.

*No chance of that, Harry.* "Thanks for ordering the first round." Jack and Simon dropped into chairs. With a quirk of his lip, Jack produced a deck of cards. "Shuffle them up, Harry." Jack took a gulp of beer, followed by another, then wiped his mouth with the back of his hand.

"We gonna make this interesting, or are we playing just for fun?" Harry dealt the cards.

"Sure. We'll add bets after a couple rounds. Simon only learned two days ago."

Harry raised his eyebrows. "Whatever you say, Jack."

"Hit me." Jack peeled the card back, then tapped his cards, instantly rewarded with a second one, even though Harry's focus was elsewhere.

"Simon?"

"Huh?"

Harry and Jack followed Simon's gaze to the bar, where three young ladies were having drinks. One had her eye on

Simon. "Why don't I go order us another round?" Simon polished off his drink and stood without waiting for a response. "Three beers, right?" he asked, pausing for confirmation.

"You got it. Add it to my tab, and uh, come back with the drinks," Harry added with a gesture toward the girls gathered at the bar.

"Right, uh, be back in a few." Simon glanced absentmindedly at his cards, then back to the bar.

"We'll deal you in next hand. Go. Return with the drinks." Jack's mouth lifted in a half smile.

"You're not a little worried about that, Jack?" Harry jerked his head to the scene unfolding at the bar, Simon's attentions consumed by one of the young women.

"Not yet. A guy interested in a girl? Simon's lost his memories. He's not dead."

Two of the women resettled with their drinks at a table while Simon and the one girl remaining eased onto stools. "Maybe I should go rescue our drinks and nonchalantly check out this situation. What do you say, Jack?" Harry asked, in full-on protection mode now.

"If anyone's gonna check this situation the hell out, it'll be me. Just hold up a second."

The door opened, and two young men sauntered in, looking to be about eighteen or nineteen. Their faces went taut when they saw Simon with the girl. And with a sudden purpose in their stride, they beat a path to him.

"What about now, Jack?" Harry and Jack straightened, in sync without words or telepathy. Harry homed in on Simon's face. His eyes gleamed with a chilling cunning. Piercing and strong. Not particularly reminiscent of Jack. Instead, it reflected what still shone behind Whisterly's eyes just before...magic.

Busy talking to the girl, but obviously aware of the two headed for him, Simon appeared to be playing a part, and Harry watched Jack's son work. "Jack, that kid of yours... He's got the same tell you have right before you throw a punch. Wait for it... It's like reliving our first fight a lifetime ago in that old diner."

"It wasn't like that," Jack growled. "And it won't be a punch either, not in the typical sense anyway."

"Agreed." Harry and Jack headed for the bar.

Both young men crossed the floor toward Simon, his head bent in a heated conversation with the young lady, when the newcomers yanked the girl from the stool and steered her to join her friends.

"Fellas, how about I buy you two a beer? You can join our friendly card game, over there." Jack jerked his chin toward their table. "What do you say?"

"I don't think so. Got a little matter to clear up here first," the larger of the two answered. "This kid had a hand on my girl's thigh. He'll need to answer to me for it." The man raised a fist, aimed for Simon's jaw.

Jack gave a slight nod.

Harry flew into action, grabbing the second man, interrupting his lunge forward, occupying him instead with a one-two punch. Jack temporarily subdued the first, easily blocking the punch intended for Simon, then delivering one of his own straight to the man's gut, leaving him doubled over and heaving for a breath.

An eerie tinkling sound descended on the place, grabbing Jack's attention.

"What the hell?" Harry muttered, pausing in the middle of throwing a jab. His eyes widened, witnessing the wall of glasses behind the bar burst in a sudden cacophony, rattling and shattering into small shards, flying like tiny missiles throughout the space. Harry hazarded a glimpse at Simon.

Eyes clamped shut, Simon moved his lips at a furious pace as miniature pieces of glass embedded into the bodies of the two dazed young men.

The owner came flying over the bar, bat in hand, confusion marring his face. Winston was an old friend of theirs. The only trouble they'd brought to the tavern over the years coming from some rowdy gatherings with servicemen, sometimes celebrating along with a little too much drink. Typically these days it was just Jack and Harry, throwing a few back with a friendly game of cards, always welcoming the occasional outsider or two in their midst.

Now Winston stood warily beside Jack, ready to swing in defense of his longtime friend and his place.

"Enough!" Jack screamed, inserting himself in between Simon and the man still recovering from Jack's blow. Neither Jack, Harry, Simon, the owner, or the girls—who now crouched under a table—had been hit with the flying shards.

But the two men, covered with pockmarks, blood flowing from tiny wounds caused by the broken glass, gazed at Simon, eyes round in stunned horror.

"Jack, I've got this." Harry whisked to Jack's side. "I'll be sure the girls get home, then come back here to help clean up, as well as, uh, settling up with Winston. Get Simon out of here."

Jack nodded, squeezing Harry's shoulder. "Winston, meet my son, Simon," Jack offered, twisting Simon around to face the owner, bat still in hand.

"Your son?"

"That's right. He'll be back to work off the cost of the damage he caused today. Give it some thought. Maybe you've got some roof repairs that need fixing, or maybe the outside could use a new coat of paint? Personally I think you should have him clean your bathrooms too, top to bottom. I'll see to it that any task you request receives his undivided attention."

"*Hmm.*" Winston glanced at Simon, then Jack. "Yeah, I see the resemblance now. Okay, Jack," Winston said with a sigh, "if you say it, I'll take you at your word."

Harry slapped Jack on the back and leaned into his ear.

"Magic aside, Jack, we've done a hell of a lot worse than this and with no girl on the line. Keep that in mind."

"I know, man. I know..." Jack's brows creased with his frown. "But so has he."

Harry tracked Jack's and Simon's exit through a path cleared in the glass, presumably by the men who'd escalated the fight. Harry exhaled a deep breath, and crunching over the scattered bits of broken glass, he picked his way to the girls, still hunched under the table. "Come on out." Harry extended an arm, helping them to a stand. "You three okay?" They silently bobbed their heads. "All right, my name's Harry. Let's get you home."

KIX LEANED back in his chair, closing his eyes against the pain still rallying in his head from the recent tracker removal. The warlocks who'd found him said he'd been lucky. But that didn't make a lick of sense. How did being torn from your life and your home world—left on Earth to die—add up to luck? He rubbed his forehead, unable to keep a moan from escaping. The site where he'd been sliced open hurt like hell. Going forward at least, he hoped to not be announcing his every move as it happened.

Bits and pieces of memory were returning, more and more each day. Disjointed thoughts floated around in his mind, comingling into a jumbled mess, none of them quite fitting together. Confusion still clung to him like a dense fog. How he'd gotten here, how long he'd been here, and who took the thing from his head were the questions utmost in his thoughts when he had a lucid moment.

Only one thing was clear. Magic and the paramount place it had in his life. The stirrings of that force trickled through him, sparking recognition, and he hoped healing along the way. The supernatural power pulsed through his veins, certainly what was responsible for keeping him alive from one moment to the next.

Thinking back, what he did remember since his arrival clicked easily in place; after all, his mind was a clean slate. Apparently he'd wandered for several days. So the warlocks who'd sensed his presence and had found him had estimated, based on his level of dehydration and hunger. Immediately identified as one of their own via his telepathic signature, they'd taken him in and cared for him while he slept for two full days. When he woke, they'd told him his name, and Kix had gone back to sleep, hopeful for more information when he came to again.

The next time, another two days had passed. Three from the group had stepped forward, identifying themselves as his family—one witch and two warlocks—his brother, his brother's wife and son. Could it be true? After being relegated to Earth, others like him had searched him out? But his elation was short-lived.

Their healer had discovered a tracking mechanism fused inside Kix through magic. Undoubtedly this procedure occurred on Remeon, the planet of his birth, his relatives had told him. And even though its removal carried grave risks, no other alternative existed other than getting the contraption out of him.

The device, enchanted with spells to inhibit the return of his memories, also made magical study difficult, more complex, with this extra layer of bewitchment confounding his tasks. Turns out the chances of Kix surviving the removal of this tracker were close to 40 percent. He'd beaten the odds, yet again. Fate seemed to smile on him as the days passed, each one giving him more of a sense of comfort in his own skin.

The door to his bedroom squeaked open. "Brother, are you awake?"

"Painfully so. I find myself wishing for the nothingness of before, just to make it go away."

"Your body is fighting back. Rebuilding itself. A good sign."

"So you've said, Eliphas. In a few days' time maybe I'll see it in the same light." Kix pushed himself up to sit. "Have you come up with anything to take my mind off this searing pain?"

"Quite possibly. But I can return later." Flashing a tooth-bearing grin, he wheeled around to leave.

"Don't you dare. Get back here."

Lines cut through Eliphas's forehead. "The universal translator we found in your pocket is an amazing piece of technology. Soon we'll uncover even more about planet Remeon and your parents who blessed us with their knowledge. "Here, I wanted to return it to you."

"All right. If that was your idea of news to rid me of pain, you've underestimated my torment."

"Nah. That wasn't it. Best part of this—we stumbled upon it."

"Eliphas, if I had the strength, I'd knock that smile right off your face. Hells, get on with it."

"Sorry, brother. Upon coming to us with the prospect of certain death to where you are now, arguing, fighting to get stronger, well, it's changed our coven. So here it is... We've isolated a trace of magic from another warlock distinctly different from any of the others we've previously identified in the US."

"And? You said earlier that warlocks could be found throughout the nation."

"I did. But we know of their existence. The signature trail this form of magic leaves is unique, and it closely aligns with yours."

"I can't think straight. Gods, spell it out for me. My brain feels like mush."

"You and this warlock are both from Remeon, brother."

"*Hmm*... Can you track him? Find him?"

"No. Not based on only today's activity. But the man's a warlock. We'll be ready next time it happens. And as long as the magic isn't performed underground, we'll have a decent chance of determining a general location."

"Sounds somewhat iffy, but a good bit of news for this pain-infested day. Now I'll try to pull from memories I don't have to recall the man. What a vicious cycle."

"If you don't recall this about our magic, let me remind you. The more you relax, the easier it'll flow."

"Uh-huh. I'll work on that too, with the hole I've had ripped in my head."

"We're on the precipice of busting this wide open. When we do, you'll be further along in your healing and your memory recovery. We'll get answers. Next we'll get revenge."

When sleep finally came, it brought only a short fitful escape from the pain. Dreams haunted Kix. Words scrambled in his head. Memories unwound in short clips, dissipating again without any focus or retention, only scattered scraps of garbage.

A faint smile curled his lips. Then the name tumbled from his mouth.

*Jack...*

JACK SAT up straight in bed, pulled from a deep sleep. A shiver shot up his spine. *Kix...* He buried his face in his hands.

"Jack?" Whisterly's hand landed on his back. "What is it?"

"Nothing, baby. Go back to sleep."

"Jack... I sense him too. It can only mean one thing. Kix is regaining his memories."

"Great..." Jack swung his legs over the side of the bed. "Just great."

Whisterly scooted in beside him, her hand curled around his bicep. "I meant to tell you tonight, after I spoke with Vinique, but I must have fallen asleep before I could."

"You knew?"

"Just tonight. You've been so busy with Simon."

"Yeah." Jack ran a hand through his hair.

"We're both awake now..." Whisterly joined him. "Let me tell you what she had to say."

"Okay. Shoot."

"For a while we could track him. He'd been in the DC area, since we dropped him off, where we already knew his family lived. Sometime during the past few days the tracker inside his head was disabled. He must have had help. That's no easy feat."

"So you're saying magical help."

"Most likely. He's probably severely incapacitated about now. Even with the aid of witchcraft, death is a likely outcome when attempting a removal of these devices."

"I guess we won't know, will we? Until we do. Since we can't track him."

"Well, Simon might assist—" In the half light, Jack pinned her with a glare. "Hear me out. Simon's come so far already. Control with so much power at your fingertips is...difficult. Granted, I know nothing about raising boys, but I assume this specific element must be worse with boys. I missed the immersion of both of my children, but I remember from my own experience that the resources which are yours to command are overwhelming. And despite what you think, from what I heard of the confrontation in the tavern, Simon didn't do so badly."

Jack shook his head. "We don't know what he was about to unleash on them, after shattering all the glasses."

"Shattering the glass came from holding himself back, Jack. He was attempting control so hard that the energy came free another way. You've experienced me at my magical worst, when I attacked you. If you hadn't been there..."

His facial features contorted at the memory of Whisterly's possession by a corpse. The event had been a test of her witchcraft, but they both could have died that day. Jack drew Whisterly into a hug. "Okay, baby. I get what you're trying to say."

"You were there for him, like you were for me. He's learning by doing, with boundaries in the basement and in real-life situations, he's holding himself at bay. Progress. Anyway, back to what I was saying. We can use Simon's status as a warlock to gain a sense of where Kix is."

"We knew we'd face this, one way or another, from Kix when he regained his memories and from Simon as well. I just didn't expect it so soon."

Whisterly nodded. "Kix has had help with that too, accelerating the process of regaining his memories—a very dangerous course of action."

"Speaking of help, I need to talk with Harry again. Our contact within the Freemason network has received information confirming off-world communication to an individual associated with an organization known as NACA—the National Advisory Committee for Aeronautics—quite possibly the benefactor of Kix's data streams over the years."

"Sounds like Harry's getting close."

"Yes. The depth of Kix's deception will soon be fully known. But ultimately we'll have to face his wrath, like a never-ending story. You, Simon, Belle, all in danger from what's to come."

Whisterly took Jack's head between her hands, locking her gaze with his. "We'll be ready. Simon's power is strong. Belle's an incredible help, soothing both of us after a hard day of lessons. When it comes, we'll face it, as we always do."

Jack leaned his forehead against hers and pressed a soft kiss to her lips. "Did Vinique have any good news? If so, let's hear it."

"Yes, as a matter of fact. Arista and Thomas are doing well. Fully consumed with wedding planning and using Vinique as a sounding board. Me too of course. It's different for Vinique, being there in person, and she's enjoying that role, since she can't be here on Earth for the ceremony."

"I'd love to have her here too."

"You know Vinique. She thrives on chaos. She's right where she wants to be."

"On that topic, would you like to meet with the caterers I have in mind for the wedding?"

"Yes, Jack. In fact, I insist you turn that responsibility over to me."

"Happy to," he said with a small smirk. "Also I've been giving some thought to our wedding gift for Thomas and Arista. What do you think about paying for an overnight stay in town after the wedding and then a weeklong getaway for them?"

"Sounds wonderful. Something we never had."

"Right." The muscles in Jack's jaw tightened. "After we get those two settled, and Simon's outcome is...clearer, we're next. I plan to whisk us off somewhere far, far away, but still on Earth, I might add."

"I can't wait. I'll hold you to it. Jack?"

"Yeah?"

"Don't worry. Arista and Thomas are good together and deeply in love. They'll find their way."

"I know. No one measures up for her in my eyes. But Thomas is a good man, and I've grown to love him as a son. We're fortunate in that regard."

"I agree. Sounds like a *but* is coming though."

Jack's lips curved up. "But...time moves so quickly with children as a yardstick, and I've missed out on Arista's entire childhood. Makes it difficult to cram everything into this small window of time I've given myself."

"We'll do the best we can for them. Then move back and let

them take the reins. You'll need to work on how to hand them over."

"Yes, oh, wise one..." Jack's mouth twitched in amusement. "I haven't figured that part out yet."

"How about you give it a rest for now, and go back to sleep with me for a while."

"Deal. I'll give it a rest." He tunneled them both under the covers and wrapped his arms around his wife. "But sleep can wait."

$\mathcal{L}$ ife, oddly enough, settled into a rhythm. Simon spent his days, for the most part, either at the tavern in town, helping Winston to fix up the place, or in Jack's construction office, always with time set aside for magical study in the basement. Sometimes with, sometimes without Whisterly. Today, however, their small overnight house guest had garnered everyone's attention, even Simon's, though he'd never admit it out loud to anyone.

Whisterly paced the kitchen with Harrison on one shoulder, screaming his lungs out. "He's not hungry. He's not wet, just woke up from a nap. What's wrong? I used to be good at this," she said with a faint chuckle.

"It's what babies do. They're here to make your life hell."

Three pairs of eyes turned to him.

"Thanks for the bit of wisdom, Simon. Maybe you can take a spin with him around the house? See if he calms down." Jack encouraged, his mouth settling into a smile.

"I'll pass. I only came in here for the coffee."

"You're doing it wrong, Miss Whisterly. Let me try," Daniel

pleaded. "I help Aunt Maggie *all* the time. Baby Harry knows me."

"All right. Have a seat, and I'll hand him over."

Daniel's forehead wrinkled in concentration as Whisterly lowered Harry into Daniel's arms. Swaying the baby in his gentle grip, Daniel added a subtle bouncing motion while he moved back and forth.

After one more cry of protest, Harry quieted and snuggled deeper into Daniel's chest.

"See?" Daniel's grin spanned ear to ear. "He loves me."

"I have no doubt. You're great with him, Daniel." Whisterly filled her coffee cup and let out a long sigh, Jack close on her heels.

"You do know he can feel your tension," Jack added, glancing at Whisterly. "You were up all night with the little lad while he pitched one fit after another."

"He has a stronger set of lungs than Arista, I do believe. I can see why our Harry's done for." Jack grunted a laugh, squeezing Whisterly's shoulders. "To say nothing of Maggie."

Simon silently took in the tender scene, intuitively understanding, deep in his gut, that he'd never been the center of anyone's world—not like this. He found himself absentmindedly mirroring Daniel's movement as if Simon could offer some small comfort to the child. Horrified by his actions, Simon stilled his motion and drank down a swallow of coffee, tearing his gaze from his adopted brother and the baby, now making tiny smacking noises, lost to sleep.

"It's okay, you know," Jack spoke softly in Simon's ear. "It's okay to want to hold them when they sleep...when they're peaceful." Simon shook his head but didn't answer yes or no. Jack took the sleeping bundle from a triumphant Daniel and lay him into Simon's arms. Transfixed, Simon stared when the baby nuzzled closer as if seeking a heartbeat before settling again. His little chest rose and fell in a steady rhythm while a deeper sleep took him under.

A gentle rapping sounded on the door. "That would be Harry. I'll get it." Jack left the kitchen. Simon thought about handing the baby off but reconsidered with the unusual warmth blooming in his chest.

"Wow. Which one of you hit my kid over the head with a bat?"

Daniel giggled, raising his hand. "It was me. I got him to sleep."

"Well, pack a bag. You're coming with me for the night."

"Really, Uncle Harry?"

"As long as your dad agrees."

"Can I, Papa?"

"Jack, I almost feel human again. You know what I mean? Thanks for keeping him last night."

"Sure thing, Harry. How's Maggie?"

"Out like a light. Going on twelve hours now."

"Sure. Go pack a bag, son." Daniel's steps echoed down the hallway, ending as his door slammed shut. Jack cocked his head. "You sure you want another kid for the night?"

"God, yes, Jack. Daniel is a natural with the baby." Harry turned his attention to Simon, the man's movements tentative —or apprehensive. Simon wasn't sure which as Harry reached for his son. Simon released the sleeping bundle. "Thanks." A smile formed on Harry's lips that had nothing at all to do with Simon. "You all seem to have the touch here."

"Uh, seriously," Simon insisted, "the kid was screaming his lungs out ten minutes before you got here."

"Sounds like my son, that's for sure."

Simon nodded, barely listening as Harry and Jack droned on, the conversation taking on different twists and turns the longer they stood here. Careful not to attract any undue attention, Simon emptied his cup in one final swallow and slipped outside.

A welcome chill washed over him after being inside, closed in with so much...togetherness. He took in a breath and shook off the feelings before they could run too deep—the fragile sleeping baby, the easy happy banter, the warm cozy kitchen— all of it too much.

A noise like a small motor sounded; at the same moment Simon felt movement between his feet. Shadow traipsed in and out, taking her time, puttering her contentment. Off to one side lay an empty, abandoned little bowl. *Belle.*

Jack's office—that's where she was. Simon pushed through the door to Jack's construction office, Shadow close on his heels. Curled on a bed, lost in the pages of book, Belle lifted her head and gifted Simon, or more likely the cat, a smile. Shadow leaped up to Belle's lap, circled twice, then plopped down onto the book's pages. To Simon the office had an air of familiarity about it now.

He and Jack had already spent many hours poring over plans for Jack's next projects, in addition to those he hadn't quite finished yet. And despite initially fighting Jack's offer to give him a glimpse into the business, Simon found he couldn't get enough of it now.

Accomplishing something so significant with one's own hands, without the use of magic, felt meaningful, powerful on a whole other level. Jack had laughed at that, telling Simon it was good to hear the human side of him talking. Pondering Jack's words again, Simon wondered if his human DNA drove his desire to create something new, molding it from nothing, with only materials, a set of tools, and a plan. His energy needed a place to land, so with a few hours yet until a lesson with Whis- terly, Simon dropped into Jack's desk chair. "Mind if I hang out here for a while?"

"A course not." Before returning to her reading, Belle lit

several candles, brightening up the room and chasing away the dreariness outside.

Bending over Jack's desk, Simon dug in where he'd left off. Shadow took turns, first burrowing into Belle's lap, then prowling at Simon's feet, but later when the commotion started, she couldn't be found.

~

WITH ONE LAST wave to Harry, Daniel, and Harrison, Whisterly breathed a sigh of relief. "Remember what I said about wanting another baby?"

Jack gave her a crooked smile. "Yeah."

"Well, I'm officially not sure I could handle it. Arista's baby-hood was a long time ago. I was so much younger."

"And dealing with a PR 251 diagnosis of your own, plus the betrayal of your council members, you'd be fine... We'd be fine. In fact, it's an option I'm quite looking forward to." Jack swept Whisterly off her feet and pressed a kiss to her mouth.

"Hold that thought. I need more coffee. Now." His answering chuckle made her heart feel light, happy, despite her lack of sleep. Groaning into her cup of aromatic liquid energy, she closed her eyes, inhaling its dark goodness. Jack's gaze was all over her; she felt his focus trickle over her body, even with her own eyes shut tight. Inside, he was laughing at her. The sensation threaded through her. "Jack Livingston, quit that this instant."

"I can't help it. Who knew drinking coffee could be such a sensual experience? The anticipation... I love it."

"Well, it's your fault I'm hooked on the stuff to start with."

"Baby, hurry up and finish, or I'll not be responsible for my actions."

Slowly she opened her eyes, lowered her cup, and raised her nose to the air. "Jack..."

He leaned toward her, pressed deeper into her thoughts. *God, what is it?*

*Fire.*

They threw back their chairs and raced outside. Grayish smoke billowed from under the door of Jack's construction office. "Simon... Belle... Are they in there?"

Whisterly nodded. "Wait, Jack. There's nothing you can do. Let me..."

"The hell there isn't." He raced forward.

On the opposite side of the small building, glass shattered. When Jack reached the pair, Simon had Belle clutched tightly to him as they rolled on the ground, extinguishing the fire still burning their clothes and singeing their flesh. Jack pulled a limp Belle free. "You all right, Simon?" Jack yelled while shaking Belle and checking her for injuries, over the din of more breaking glass.

Simon nodded solemnly through a soot-smeared face, then pressed a book into Jack's hands. "Here. It's all I could grab. I was reading about your plans..." He coughed, shaking his head. "I turned, and everything was on fire... I tried to put it out, but it got too hot, too fast."

Jack muttered a curse. "Come on, Belle! Wake up!"

*Simon.*

Lifting his head amid the smoke clouding his vision and searing his throat, Simon straightened to answer Whisterly's summons. Behind him, Belle coughed and sputtered, managing only one word. "Shadow?"

Tongues of fire streaked through the broken glass, and as a blast sounded, a section of the ceiling caved in. Jack crouched over Belle, protecting her while flaming bits of wood and shards of glass rained down on them from the darkened sky. "Everything's gonna be okay, Belle," he shouted through the confusion.

Whisterly searched Simon's face and connected their consciousnesses. *Feel it, Simon? Let go. Pull it to you.*

The wind picked up, leaves and tree branches relenting under its steady sway.

Whisterly murmured a spell, clenched her fists to the sky; tiny water droplets plopped to the ground. First only a few, then they multiplied.

Following suit, Simon tilted his face upward, joining in the enchantment, commanding the rain to him. Steady drops fell, until water slid from them in sheets of pounding pellets. As they gazed past the charred remnants of wood, glass, and furniture, relief flooded Whisterly with the onslaught of water. A hiss sounded in the rain's aftermath, mingling with the rising mist, imitating the trill of insects as it permeated the air.

Jack carried Belle inside, then returned for Whisterly, Simon, and the book. "It's out," Jack mumbled, covering their shivering, rain-soaked bodies with blankets. "Rest you two. You've done all you can."

Black smoke still drifted to the heavens in dark plumes through the leftover glow of smoldering embers. Jagged pieces of wood littered the ground from the unnatural deluge, tossed from their original location, revealing a gaping hole in Jack's office. Whisterly scanned the ruins, partially burned books, a desk cleaved in half, sections of mattress, the headpost from the bed. The remains of the structure sagged, half of one wall sighing in the back-and-forth whisper of the wind.

Jack followed the two inside, guiding them through the back door. On the table a drenched and tattered book lay. Simon stumbled, caught himself on a kitchen chair, then dropped to it. He peeled back the cover. Inside, though the edges were frayed and the paper somewhat damp, the page was mostly intact. Thumbing through the rest, Simon's lips edged up.

*Good work, Simon. You got Belle out and saved Jack's plans.*

Simon dipped his chin, his face a black sooty mess. *Thank you...Mother.*

Whisterly's breath caught, her gaze on her son as he scaled the stairs, heading to his room, shedding wet, smoky layers of clothing as he trudged along.

"Baby?" Jack's eyes wrinkled in concern. "Are you okay?"

"I'm fine. We all are. Let me get Belle into a warm bath."

"Then you next."

"Then *us* next," she corrected.

"Us..." Jack trailed his thumb across Whisterly's cheek. "Simon saved years' worth of my work. My designs and plans are all in that one book. Harry still has everything regarding our in-progress jobs at his house, since he's been completing the follow-up. That," he said, gesturing outside, "I can fix. But the heart and soul of my business is right here in my plans and drawings."

"He did good, Jack."

"He did good, baby."

"But you're wrong about one thing—the heart and soul of your business are here." She drew Jack into a hug.

Belle padded into the kitchen. "Did you find Shadow, Mr. Jack?"

Jack and Whisterly shared a glance. "Not yet, sweetheart. But cats are quick. I'm sure she got away. Probably just hiding away somewhere. She'll come back when she's hungry."

"But what if she's hurt? She didn't mean to start the fire. And Simon yelled at her when she knocked over the candles." Belle gasped for breath, her eyes glistening. "I'm sorry. I never should have lit them." Two giant tears slid down her cheeks.

Whisterly took Belle's hand and guided her up the stairs, cradling her body against her own. "It's nobody's fault, Belle honey. Time for a warm bath. Doesn't that sound good?"

Belle jogged her head. The two disappeared with only the squeak and squish of wet shoes in their wake.

Jack headed to the back door, eyed the wreckage of his office. So much time he spent there, working, planning a future. His gaze settled on the book, soot blackening the table around it. And it's all right here... Thanks to Simon.

TRACES OF POWER still thrummed through his veins, like a live thing seeking more. How to get rid of it, Simon wasn't sure exactly. He wrestled out of his wet clothes and tugged on dry pants and a shirt. Darkness enveloped him, matching his mood and the smoldering disaster still belching smoke outside his window. He'd done the best he could, so why did a vague uneasiness still nag at him? Like something undone, simmering inside him, the same as the wreckage in the yard.

He traced back his actions. Was there something he could have done to prevent this mess? To stop that stupid cat? And why the hells did it matter to him so much? *Belle... Belle? Are you there?*

*Here, Simon.*

*Good. Just wanted...*

*Yes. I'm fine. Tired...*

*All right.*

*Simon...thank you.*

*You're...welcome.*

*Will you help me find Shadow tomorrow?*

*That damn cat...*

*Promise me you will.*

*We'll see, Belle.*

Even in his mind the words felt awkward. Forced. He scrunched his face, pushing back at the tide of thoughts rushing toward him. *No. Not here.* Downstairs, Whisterly had charmed the space. No one could get in besides Whisterly, Jack, or Simon. Plus, any creature not human or Remeonite would be safely contained. Simon headed down the stairs in the now eerily quiet house, not stopping until he reached the basement. Here, if needed, he could let some of the demons loose, where they could scatter among their kind.

He breathed a sigh of relief, dropped to the bed, and let the memory take him under. A crash clamored through his head. Jerking his eyes open, his surroundings appeared to him through the eyes of a child. The basement with its spells, books, witches, herbs, and solid walls drifted into the background. In its place, a shadowy chamber loomed, sparsely outfitted with a bed, dresser, desk, and chair. A man yelled, his voice interspersed with intermittent muffled cries.

Simon sat upright intuitively understanding this was only one in a long line of similar memories. The woman's voice rose again, in time with another sound of items smashing to the ground. Fear gave way to anger, making him move. Simon loosened his grip on the damp bedsheet between his fingers and slid to the floor. Maybe he could help. He crept to his door, opened it a crack, admitting a sliver of light inside. A fresh bout of fear returned, perking his senses, and when a door opened, then slammed closed again, Simon peeked outside to investigate.

A woman pressed her way inside, backing Simon against a wall. The yelling outside quieted as she leaned against the door; shivering, panting for air. She crumpled to the floor. Cloaked in the relative safety of the corner, Simon gathered his courage and crawled to the woman.

"Simon!" She flung her arms out wide. Terror made his limbs shake, but he settled on the woman's lap while she rocked them back and forth.

"Everything will be okay," she whispered over and over, swaying with her words. "He won't get to you. I won't let him."

A metallic odor filled the space. With Simon's eyes adjusted to the limited light, he took a closer look, running his hands up the woman's neck, then along her face. "You're bleeding." He gasped. "I can get help." Simon struggled in her tight grip.

"No, Simon. You'll be okay. I'll see to it." Tears slid down her cheeks as she straightened and locked the door.

"But what about you?" Simon held her watery gaze, the weight of her hurt pounding inside his heart with every beat.

"Everything will be okay," she repeated, scooping him up, depositing him under his covers gone cold. A groan tightened her lips as she adjusted next to Simon on top of the bedcover, nestling him as close as she could.

"I'm not a baby anymore. Your thoughts tell me we're not okay. He's a monster." Mustering his courage, Simon jumped from the bed, making a beeline for the door.

"Simon! Don't make me run after you." Her voice came out in a desperate cry, stilling him in place.

Stifling his own tears, he rushed back to her and threw his arms around her neck. "I'll stay. We'll—" The door burst open to a fresh round of screaming. Cowering, Simon covered his ears, squeezing himself against the wall.

"Don't you dare!"

Simon's eyes widened more with each successive stomp of the boots that approached.

*Simon.*

A voice cut through the old memory processing through his thoughts. He blinked, focused.

Whisterly stared back at him. Worry creased her eyes, and even though the ash and soot had been washed away, the smell still lingered from earlier, along with the burns that littered her skin in red splotches. "We heard you call out."

Simon tossed a glance to the door, where Jack hovered.

"I can go," Jack offered.

Scrubbing his hand down his face, Simon shrugged. "I don't care if you stay. I had a memory come back. At least I think it was."

"Yes. I read your thoughts."

"I don't know her name though."

Whisterly stepped closer to her son. "Would you like to?"

"Yes."

"Her name was Mila. She used to work for me. She was... instrumental in stealing you from us after your birth. But I do believe she loved you very much."

"Gods..."

"She was in over her head from the beginning," Jack added.

"I can sense the tension and apprehension rolling off both of you."

"Well, it's earlier than we anticipated for you to start regaining your memories."

"Just one memory, Mother. I can handle it. You're actually worried about me?"

A hint of a smile raised Jack's lips. "She is."

"And you?"

Jack rubbed his chin. "Yeah, me too."

"I'm fine." Simon turned his attention to Whisterly. "Down here, I don't feel as crazy, when a memory hits me like that." He shook his head. "Not sure that even makes sense."

"Makes perfect sense to me," Whisterly said. "Some believe past scars to be hideous. I disagree. The one you just relived will help you. Otherwise, hidden inside, never confronted, they are often worse, much more easily ignored as they fester and grow. Use them to make you stronger. Each one is a badge of courage—a sign you went through a struggle and came back on the other side, changed somehow."

"Take these memories as they come, Simon. We'll be here, if you need us. I'll head back up and leave you two to it."

"Uh, hold up, Jack. That man. The one who beat Mila and raised me, I guess. I don't want to think of him as my father."

Jack paused, eyes narrowed, waiting.

"I still remember next to nothing about my life before

waking up with the coven, but...uh..." Simon cleared his throat and started again. "I need an anchor... Something I can hold on to, no matter what. Maybe that could be you two? Since I was born to you before Daniel was yours, could I...? Hells... Nevermind—"

Jack's shocked expression made Whisterly's heart skip a beat. "I'd like that Simon," his gravelly voice bit out.

"You read my thoughts."

"Still feels like I imagined it."

"No, *Papa,* you didn't."

## 16

*B*elle?
        *There was a fire in Mr. Jack's office. I'm okay. We all are.*

Stephen shivered, sensing the fear behind his sister's words. *What happened?*

*It's all Shadow's fault.*

Stephen pushed back from the table and the dinner he and Arista had just prepared.

*Who the hell is Shadow, Belle?*

*Mr. Jack's cat—she started it. Poor thing ran away, I think.*

*Are you burned? Injured in any way?*

*A few burns and cuts, that's all.*

*Cuts? How bad?*

*Not too bad. Hurts though. Simon grabbed me and crashed us both through the window 'cause the door was blocked by flames.*

*Good God, Belle...* His skin crawled, his lip rising in a snarl. *Simon rescued you?*

*Stop yelling at me. I can feel you screaming. You're not helping me.*

*I'm sorry, Belle. I should be there. I'm usually the one who helps you with anything.*

*I'm fine. I promise. So is Simon. I'm just not sure about Shadow.*

*Cats are damn good at taking care of themselves. She'll find her way back to Jack.*

*I gotta go now. I'm taking a bath. Then Miss Whisterly said I should call Ma and Pa.*

*That's a good idea. Would you like for me to come see you?*

*Nah. I'll see you soon for the wedding.*

*True. But I could visit you before. Just say the word.*

*Don't worry.*

*I'll try. But you know, Belle, I love you.*

*I know you do. Love you too.*

HEAVING A SIGH, Stephen plopped on the couch.

Arista dropped next to him. "What happened?"

"There was a fire in Jack's construction office." Stephen held up his arms, then slapped them to his side. "Everybody's okay. Apparently Simon saved the day. Just not the cat."

"Glad Belle's all right. Go see her, if you want to. You could get leave to go for a day, maybe two."

"No. She doesn't want me to. I could tell." His sigh ended in a growl. "I've been replaced—by Simon."

"Don't be silly."

"I feel decidedly unnecessary. Pa had to beat responsibility into me for my little sister, and now Simon takes over?"

"Would you rather he jump from the burning building and leave your sister inside?"

"Of course not. Still don't trust him." Stephen narrowed his eyes at her. "You've got a point though, I guess."

"We've got to try and keep an open mind. I'm having difficulty with that also. I hope Simon can change, but we'll need to wait and see. I'm glad he was there for Belle."

"Yeah, me too," he groaned. "It's just...Simon is so despicable, and that's the nicest thing I have to say about him." Arista silenced him with a soft kiss. She knew just how to bring him out of his dark thoughts.

"So can we finish eating, since everyone's okay?" She squeezed Stephen's hand, and he could feel her mindset shift. "We need to get our final decisions to my mother tomorrow on our menu choices for our wedding dinner. I need your input tonight. The date, location, my dress, food almost all done. Invitations in the works—thanks to your mother and big sister."

"A Christmas wedding... I'm like a little kid during the holidays. Showing you the sights will make that time of year even more fun."

"I absolutely cannot wait."

"Yeah, patience isn't one of my virtues, but you already know that about me. Do you know how much I'm looking forward to making you mine, permanently?"

Arista raised a brow. "I have an idea, yes."

Stephen slid Arista onto his lap. "I want to show you more of Earth. Travel for a bit after we've tied the knot. We haven't talked much about a honeymoon. It's hard for you to commit to time away from all this, all your responsibilities here. I get that. But I need for you to experience my world, the way I do. Does that make sense?"

Arista cupped his cheek. "After all my people have put you through—"

"Mostly the Night Dwellers..."

"The Day Watchers grabbed you first in holographic form, remember? Anyway, you've committed to a life here with me, training with our military... I want to make those same types of commitments to you too. After all, our children will be half human."

A slow grin inched up Stephen's cheek. "A baby Arista someday in the future sounds perfect—"

"Or a baby Stephen..."

"More witches and warlocks...just what we need. Let's make some more decisions tonight, love. Our trip...West Coast, California, or East Coast, New York?"

"Okay. After dinner. Two more decisions to be finalized. Deal?"

"Agreed."

Stephen raised Arista to her feet, pressed a kiss to her forehead. "Maybe the reintegration of the factions will be finalized before we return to Remeon, but I doubt it. Still so much left to do. So much death and trauma. God, they've been through hell. The conditions that Simon and his minions forced the Night Dwellers into, all while Simon saw to his own personal needs above everyone else's, makes me crazy. He should be put to death for his war crimes, but wait, no... He's living in the same house as my sister."

"Belle's all right, and she's prepared more than most to fend for herself. Not that she should have to. You'll need to trust this one to my parents."

"I'm trying."

"Focus, Stephen. Dinner. Decisions. And what comes afterward."

His eyes met hers. "I could be convinced to skip to the after-dinner part of the evening."

"No, you gave me your word."

"Did I though?" Wrapping her into his arms, he whispered, "It's all about determining priorities. And of course, efficiency in carrying out duties." He smirked. "I'm excellent at both."

"But dinner." Arista shot a glance toward their cold food on the table.

"Doesn't even register on my radar. *Shh*, love. Come here. I want you to do something with me."

Laughter danced in her eyes.

"Well, of course *that,* but I'm talking about this." Stephen held her in a tight embrace, his left hand grasping her right, his other hand against her lower back, keeping their bodies close. "Go with me to the holosuites. I've been practicing dancing for the wedding. Will you join me?"

"This is nice." Melting into his arms, she followed Stephen's gentle back-and-forth sway. Next he twirled her in a circle, then yanked her close again, stealing her breath while he kissed her neck. "Yes. I'll go." She pressed her lips to his. "Definitely. You've convinced me."

SIMON GLANCED at the sun through narrowed eyes, gauging the time. A crisp wind blew, scattering the shriveled fallen leaves in its wake and drying the sweat from Simon's body. His shirt he'd worn this morning lay crumpled in the grass, where he'd dropped it hours ago just so he could catch these cool breezes as they drifted by. The weather was mild for mid-November, so Papa said. Doubtful there would be many more days like this one before colder weather returned and stayed.

Work proceeded per plan to have the new construction office, which would do double duty for overnight guests, finished at least one week before the wedding, scheduled for December 11th. The household was totally consumed with planning, especially Belle. Preparing to see her brother, Arista, and her parents threw her into a whole other level of excitement.

Simon preferred to focus on this more solitary role. He'd found over the past weeks that working with a hammer, nails, and a ruler, with Papa's design as his guide, centered him, when almost nothing else in his life held the same power.

His studies in the craft and slowly returning bits of memory kept his days and nights right at the edge of chaos. Peace was elusive, except for here. Nodding, satisfied with his work, he descended the ladder for a drink. Jack's office was shaping up nicely. In fact, with another two weeks or so, the exterior would be complete. Shadow purred at his feet, keeping him company, since Belle wasn't close by.

When Shadow had returned several weeks after the fire, Belle and Daniel arranged a welcome home party for the creature and had insisted on Simon's participation. He'd grumbled at that, but truthfully he would do anything for Belle. On days when everything seemed too much, she could bring rest and calm to his soul with a thought or a touch. Her power and her connection with the forces inside the earth went beyond his understanding. Simon was just a welcome recipient.

After the fire's devastation, Harry had arranged what he called "a good old-fashioned barn raising."

Translation? A hell of a lot of neighbors and friends came together and raised the walls and roof on the new office in under two days. For Simon, the adventure was a trial by fire, immersing him in the tools of the trade. The camaraderie with Harry and Papa and others present that day made Simon feel not so stupid when he'd asked construction-related questions, and the activity lit a spark within him that hadn't been squelched since. The whirlwind weekend had strengthened his basic knowledge, giving him a solid base to expand upon.

The weekend had other pluses as well. Harry had eased up on Simon since then. Going back to his first day here seemed as if Harry had been waiting for Simon to screw up. And he did.

Lots.

But not purposefully to hurt his parents.

Simon had other bright spots in his life. Ones he wanted to explore further. Since the brawl at the tavern, he'd seen Rachael—Rae—from time to time, making that mess of a day worth so much more than the hell he'd caused. At least she'd kicked that asshole out of her life, leaving the field wide open for Simon. They had a good time together, but he had no plans currently to clue her in on Remeon.

Leaning against a log, he sucked down water, then lay his head back, basking in the sun's rays made cool with the wind chasing a path through the day's heat. Shadow jumped to his lap and spread out. At the moment he didn't even care. Right now it felt good just to be.

"Wow. Nice view." Rae let out a loud whistle, startling the cat from her perch.

"Rae? Wasn't expecting to see you today."

Her bottom lip stuck out in a cute little pout. "Didn't think I needed an appointment."

Simon crossed the few feet between them and pulled her into a hug. "Of course not." The warm press of her arms against his skin and her lips on his neck made him forget what he wanted to say next.

"I made sure you were alone first."

"You're the one who wanted to keep this quiet, not me."

"And I still do."

Not able to wait another second, Simon kissed her, hovering a beat in the air between them before taking her lips. "*Mmm.*" He smiled against her mouth. "It's a nice surprise. But I do have work I need to finish."

"So I see."

"Want to keep me company for a while?"

"No, really, I can't stay." She pulled away, taking a slow step backward, her fingers lingering on his chest.

Simon grinned, letting loose a low chuckle and starting his climb up the ladder again. "Tease."

"Someone asked about you at the tavern. That's the real the reason why I stopped by."

"Me? That's strange." Simon paused, his back against the ladder for support.

"I thought so too. The man described Jack to a T, you somewhat less so. Anyway, Jack's so well known around here, the man would have found his way eventually. This way I could give you a heads-up and find out a little for you."

"Maybe it's Jack he wants to see after all."

"No, he was specific. *Jack's son, Simon.*"

"*Hmm.*"

"Said he was an old friend of your father's, so I assumed from the marines, but he didn't seem like the military type, you know? And he knew literally nothing about the war."

Simon listened, a smile pasted on his face, the oddities that Rae pointed out making him more and more uncomfortable as she continued to speak. The details about his father's early life, the fact that Simon had a twin, the man's strange speech, the unusual apparatus around his neck.

"Like yours," she'd commented.

*He's from Remeon.* "Thanks for letting me know, Rae."

"For sure, Simon." Her gaze roamed his chest again, and Simon couldn't resist jumping to the ground and taking another kiss to tide him over.

"Later." She winked, walking backward. With a final wave and a smile, she was gone.

The afternoon wore on, Rae's words foremost on Simon's mind. The man had said he'd stop by today. Maybe it was all a ruse, but why? Simon didn't have much in common with his father, other than Remeon, his mother, and Arista. And, well... telepathy. A thread of unease wound through his thoughts, raising more questions, making him wonder if somehow he'd put everyone in jeopardy yet again.

Some days he wished for more of the mundane existence the humans around him enjoyed, walking around day to day in blissful ignorance. Then remembering his father and mother, and what little he knew of their lives, their struggles, how could he be less? More waited for him. He could practically taste it.

The sun hung low on the horizon, casting some of his work-space in shadows. Pride surged in his chest, taking in all he'd accomplished. Despite the disruptions, Papa would be pleased at his progress. Simon stowed the ladder and the other supplies, but as he turned toward the house, a man watched him in the distance from the property's edge.

"Who are you?" Simon shouted. "Can I help you with something?"

"Simon? We've a few things to discuss. I've been searching for you for weeks now."

"Do I know you?"

"In a sense. Yes. Could you spare a few minutes?"

"For what?"

"The truth you deserve."

With an eerily familiar cut of the man's hand, a spark electrified the air.

KIX CROSSED THE PROPERTY, coming to a stop a few feet from Simon.

"I sense your thoughts...the essence of magic flowing from you," Simon spoke up. "You're like me, from Remeon."

"More like you than you realize just yet."

"What's your name?"

"Think of me as a friend from home, one who has your best interests at heart."

"A friend? You're blocking your thoughts and hiding behind magic. Coward seems more fitting. How about I go with that?"

"Call me Seer."

"We're done here." Simon strode purposefully toward the house.

Kix followed, thinking of options as he walked. Hells... This wasn't going as planned. He'd only recently gotten back his own memories, "helped" along in the process by other warlocks. All he'd lost at the hands of Arista, Jack, Stephen, and Vinique suddenly abundantly clear... A potential mate. Protection for his family. Position as council chair.

Gone.

Since coming to Earth, pain had been his constant companion, stalking him like a ruthless predator. First, the removal of the tracking device had nearly killed him. Second, the spells which brought back his memories over the course of weeks instead of months, when they would naturally return for most warlocks, left him with a searing throbbing ache in his head.

The enchantment the coven had used would hold permanently with most species. Humans, for example, were the easiest to control. For witches and warlocks, these types of spells progressed at a different pace. Fully up to speed with his restored memories, Kix lived in pursuit of one goal—revenge. And a singular focus for his wrath.

Simon.

Jack and his family would experience the same. This little reunion was about to have an unwelcome guest.

What else was left for him now? Whatever the coven had done to his head, or maybe the damage that had come afterward, left Kix unable to communicate with Remeon telepathically. His magic, thankfully, remained intact, strong as ever. "Simon. Wait. I can help you."

"I don't need your help."

"I'm betting you do. You reached out to me once. But you don't remember, do you? Because your memories were stolen, right?"

Simon slowly twisted around to face Kix. Anger augmented the strong lines of Simon's face, his muscles pulsing along his jawline.

*Gods...if I didn't know better, I'd swear this was Jack in front of me on his first visit to Remeon.*

"Good. Let's use that anger."

"Leave," Simon gritted out through clenched teeth.

"I'm a warlock, better equipped to help you than anyone else on Earth, or Remeon for that matter. What's more, I know what you're going through. The disorientation. The betrayal. The hatred. I've been there and can help you come out on the other side, whole again."

Simon wavered, his forehead creased, silently considering his options Kix wagered.

When their eyes met, Kix knew he'd hit a nerve, even with Simon blocking his thoughts.

"How?"

"Now you're talking. Let's start with a show of what I can do for you—the return of a memory. A more recent recollection will hurt somewhat less. Sound good?" Simon gave a curt nod. "When we're through, if you don't want my help, I'll leave."

"Get on with it."

Kix waved him forward, inwardly smiling in victory. Part of the beauty built into his plan was the full access to Simon's thoughts. All of his blocking mechanisms had to be down for the magic to work. Of course Kix could break them down. But less pain for Simon meant a higher likelihood of more memory retrievals in the future.

Kix sucked in a steadying breath because what he was about to do would hurt him almost as much as Simon. Reveling in the aftermath would be sweet, worth it, and only the first step in the journey of what was to come.

"Okay. The process will go easier for you if you willingly let me into your thoughts." With hands on either side of Simon's head, Kix eased through. "That's it." The delicate procedure wove through Kix's own thoughts. He could easily kill Simon at this point, but that would be too easy and relatively painless for all involved. Kix had much bigger plans.

Murmuring the spell his family of warlocks had perfected

on him, a sigh eased past his throat. *Right there...* Behind his closed eyes, Kix witnessed tiny sprinkles of light popping up within the maze of Simon's cerebral cortex. With a tendril of his magic, Kix reached for the closest one and gently set it free.

With any luck the released memory would relate to Simon's latest reflections regarding the invasion of the Night Dwellers. As a council member, Kix had been privy to the attacks. At the time, Vinique had made the council aware of Jack's rogue attempt to save his daughter. If luck was with Kix, this memory would show Jack in a not-so-pleasing light with his son. "Done. What do you see, Simon?"

Simon stumbled backward, like he'd been physically assaulted.

Kix helped Simon to sit and watched the memory play across his face. After what seemed like minutes, he exhaled a breath, shaking, wiping sweat from his forehead.

"Well?"

Simon blinked his eyes open. "I want to see more."

"All right. In time. This wasn't easy on either of us. Ready to learn more about your craft as well?" Here it was, the tipping point. Had Kix sold himself well enough? Had the memory held the shock value he'd hoped?

"If I can have more of this, I'll consider what else you have to say."

Kix inched into Simon's thoughts again, disguising his path. He shook his head, incredulous. A rare treat, indeed. Jack, his son, and wife. Ah, Whisterly... Always a force to be reckoned with, and he would. "I'll be back in a day or two. Rest up, Simon. You'll need it for what's to come."

## 17

The perky gurgling of the coffeepot intruded on the silence, the only happy sound of the morning as the men of the household gathered around the breakfast table. Simon glared at his father over the rim of his cup as he downed another swallow. Papa filled his cup, a thermos, and turned off the stove, before sitting down to finish the remainder of his eggs and sausage.

"Papa, I wanna go... *Puleess!*" Daniel whined.

"You can take my place, squirt," Simon answered, head bowed, not meeting his brother's pleading gaze.

"Next time, Daniel. We talked about this. Why don't you go on back to bed for a bit?"

"*Ugh,*" he groaned, slamming his head dramatically on the table.

"You ready, Simon?"

"Uh, sure, I guess." Simon turned up his cup, draining it, wishing he could crash in his bed again. He glanced at the still-dark sky and sighed. It was too damn early, and the memory from yesterday had kept him wide awake all night while he'd tossed and turned, examining it and the strange man who'd visited.

Papa swatted Daniel on his backside. "Hey, next time. Take care of Whisterly and Belle while we're out, okay?"

"Okay." The two clasped hands and fell into a hug. "See you later." Daniel disappeared, dragging his feet down the hall in a slow meander toward his room.

"Well, all right," Papa said with a chuckle and shake of his head. "Grab your sack and let's go."

The chill of early morning wrapped around them, shotguns perched on their shoulders, their breath coming out in small puffs of steam, a flashlight illuminating their path as they walked.

"Just so you know, I'm not all that interested in hunting."

"Is that so? I couldn't tell from your attitude this morning."

Simon increased the distance between them.

"What's on your mind, Simon?"

"Nothing."

"How's Rachel?"

Simon turned to face Jack. "What?"

"Simple question. You're seeing her—right? I used to be young and in love."

"Stop."

"Still am."

Simon rolled his eyes. "Well, I'm not. We're just having a good time."

"Don't disrespect her, Simon."

"Leave it alone."

"Say it. Whatever it is. Something is on your mind."

Simon squared off with Jack. "Maybe if you hit me, you'd get your point across better. Not much different from the treatment I received at the hands of Janus over the years from the way I see it." Simon dropped his sack and leaned the shotgun against a tree.

"What are you talking about?"

Simon crouched low as Jack perched his gun alongside Simon's. Simon jerked back, the newest memory of Jack's blows echoing other beatings in his head from his adopted father. Simon circled, his breath heaving out in gasps, noisy in the relative serenity of the woods. He faked with his left and swung hard at Jack with his right. Jack blocked the hit and tackled Simon. Crashing to them both to the ground, Jack lifted to his forearms and hovered over Simon's face.

"Just like in my memory. This is exactly what you did. Go ahead. I know what comes next."

Jack blinked. "Do you? Do you also know what came before? Did you see the whole memory?"

"I'm...not sure. Just saw you giving me hell and then me unconscious."

"Sit up, Simon." Jack dropped beside him. "When you came to in the basement of the compound, we didn't hide the fact that you'd had issues that needed addressing. Didn't really want to tell you this, here, now. But here's one of the more recent ones—you, uh, kidnapped your sister. You wanted to have the sole heir to the council chair. I had no other choice that day. You left me none. Later we heard directly from your own mouth how you had plans to use her eggs and your...input to create a baby in the lab."

Simon's face scrunched. "What?" Shaking his head, Simon's next word left him in a hiss. "No..."

"Your telepathy skills are excellent. Read my thoughts. I've experienced your probing firsthand. You can sense if I'm being truthful or not."

"Gods..." Simon ran a hand through his hair, got to his feet, soft wisps of black smoke curling up from his clenched fists. "Why do you care what happens to me?"

"You're mine. My flesh and blood. I'll always care. No matter what."

Snatching his sack and shotgun, Simon stalked off, heading deeper into the woods.

"Wait. Hold up."

"Leave me alone."

Jack waved him back. "Hand me the shotgun. Anything you come upon out here you can handle with the knife there in your boot or a spell. Just keep your wits about you."

Simon paused, giving Jack a chance to catch up, then turned on him, averted his eyes, and shoved the shotgun in his hand. The first rays of sunlight peeked out from along the horizon, interrupting the darkness, etching out a path of light between them. Simon lifted his chin tentatively and held his father's steady gaze. But where he'd expected to see horror or anger instead lay sorrow, his father's eyes brimming with concern. Stomping away again, Simon held on to Jack's last words as they rang out clear and strong.

"I'll be waiting for you, son."

WATCHING his son trudge through the woods, an electric blue aura surrounding him, made Jack wonder if he was doing the right thing, leaving Simon, giving him space at this moment. After all, Simon had the power within him to wreak havoc like this town had never known. But Simon was an adult and had been handling Night Dweller matters for some time now, even if his methods had been sinister, to put it mildly.

Over the course of years, Simon's techniques of persuasion, bending others to his will, had been his calling card. He didn't just wake up evil one morning; he'd been molded, pushed, conditioned by Janus to follow in his sadistic ways. If there could be any hope of change, Simon needed to see his deeds from another perspective, beginning now. And later? As more memories returned, he'd need to reconcile them in order to move forward.

His chest aching from a sadness he couldn't define, Jack turned from his son's course and made the short trek home in the growing light.

He ducked into the quiet house, stowed the guns, started a fresh pot of coffee for Whisterly, then headed to his bar. Despite his mood, a grim smile took his face. Not the first time, by a long shot, that he'd gone for a shot or two this early in the morning.

After starting a fire to chase the chill from the room, Jack poured a whiskey and grabbed his journal from the cabinet, then settled in his chair to get his thoughts out on paper before they tangled further in his mind. Some days he wished for it among his most private thoughts—the mundane. A life without constant struggle and pain. Then, as he always did, he let it go, since his battles had led him back to Whisterly.

The flames sputtered and hissed, fingers of fire licking away the cool air. Whisterly joined him. Wrapped in a blanket with a cup of hot coffee in hand, she kissed him, before settling into the chair nearest to Jack, watching the fire in silence as they waited. The minutes ticked by, and their telepathic conversation flowed back and forth while he silently debated. Had he made the right choice for Simon this morning, giving him space to deal with a memory foreign to him? Hurtful to him?

Whisterly left to supervise breakfast for Daniel and Belle, and when the children were off to individual activities of reading, which Whisterly insisted they do every morning, his wife joined him again.

"He's barred me from his thoughts," Jack began, "which I expected, but it's been two and a half hours. I can't sit here any longer. I'll go look for him."

"Wait, Jack. I can sense trace bits of magic. He's not far."

"Thank God," Jack whispered as he poured another shot of whiskey and sat down again.

The back door opened and shut. Boots, first one then the other, thudded to the ground, followed by the sound of a sack, slapping the floor.

The pair's steady gazes pinned each other in the stillness.

"I don't want to be that person from my memories," Simon announced without preamble, his eyes a deep abyss of anger and sadness all at once. "I, uh, am though and don't know how to stop it. He's me."

"That's true, but you have options now. Choices and the will power to change."

"I don't know if I can. Only one memory hit me yesterday. Look what happened."

Jack rose to his feet, meeting his son head-on; he rested his hand on Simon's shoulder. "I, for one, am glad the memory impacted you this way. Made you think."

Whisterly joined them. "Remember on days when old memories hit, and the hurt meshes with your soul that they don't have to define you going forward. The love that brought you into this world is stronger than the power those memories have over you."

Jack gathered Simon into a rough hug, his son's focus on the flickering blaze. "I'm here. Your mother's here. Together, the three of us, we're a force to be reckoned with. It won't be easy, but we'll keep the demons at bay."

"Yeah?" Simon pulled back and studied his father's face. "I'll hold you to that."

～

THE SEER'S latest visit churned in Simon's mind, making focus on work difficult. The man's motives were clear—binding Simon to him through magic. Yet they were already affiliated through their common bond as warlocks. His mother's teachings warned of this powerful magic. How all-consuming it would eventually become, until Simon would be completely under the Seer's control. His to command. Simon shuddered as a fleeting image grabbed him, then, just as suddenly, let go again a few seconds later.

A young woman on her knees before him, crying, her clothing torn, Simon's hand easing down the slope of her neck, exerting just enough pressure at her throat to keep her stationary. Simon's intentions had penetrated her thoughts, bending her to his will. Gods... *This is who I am? Or was?* Did the distinction even make a difference? The fog in his mind cleared, but the effects from the vision still clutched him tight.

Heart racing, gasping, he considered the impact of the Seer's words. Simon belonged with his kind to reach his full potential. Made sense. The steps he already took with the man had moved him closer, but to be a full-fledged warlock would require living, training among his own kind. Dread curdled in his stomach.

In the not-too-distant future, a choice lingered. Yanking on a tendril of magic, Simon pulled his thoughts back in line. The exercises his mother had him practice daily worked, most of the time. He eased a shaky breath in and out and lowered to the newly built steps leading to the construction office. Soon he'd talk to his parents about the Seer, but for now, the visits stayed locked out of his thoughts, concealed by Simon's barriers.

"Simon?"

Lifting his chin, Simon brought Belle's worried gaze into focus. "Belle, I forgot you were down there."

"Me and Shadow are hurt."

He grunted a laugh. "Shadow doesn't care about anyone but Shadow."

"You've hurt her feelings. Look." Shadow darted up the steps, then stalked Simon from behind.

"Somehow I don't think so."

"How's it going upstairs?"

His father's plans for a new office had gotten hijacked as construction had progressed. Now Papa's office would reside on the second floor. The plans were modified to accommodate his mother's vision of a full guest suite below, complete with its own bathroom, putting the time line for completion by the wedding in jeopardy. The planned structure of the room remained basically the same, just moved one floor higher. To his credit, Simon had suggested a few changes—which his father had incorporated—that made the square footage work harder toward a more efficient use of the new space.

In his head, Simon saw the room as it had been, prefire, then now, everything reconfigured to where it fit, with space for future expansion of the business built in. Simon recalled a recent conversation with his father. *Opportunity exists here for you. You've an innate talent for construction and architecture. I've sensed it, seen it in your work. My guess is you do too.*

The truth made Simon feel bare...exposed...so he'd acknowledged that fact only with a silent dip of his chin, when words and even telepathy had failed him. He wanted to be a part of something like this, tangible and real, so much so that it made him ache inside.

Simon turned, glimpsing the progress from his vantage point, where his gaze could span the entire upstairs. "It's going good," he answered Belle. "If the plumbers hold up their end, we should finish with a week to spare before the wedding."

"Looks much better than it did. Don't you think?"

"Not sure Papa would agree, with the space doing double duty, but I like the organization upstairs, and the guest bedroom is shaping up nicely too. You've put a lot into it. Well done, Belle."

Belle beamed back at him, the effect of Simon's words evident. Then, like a sudden change in the wind, she cocked her head and stared, her eyes piercing and fierce. "Something's changing inside you, Simon. I can feel it. Tell me you can too."

"Yes, I can." He raised a brow. "Maybe you should stay outta my head, Belle. I'm not even sure how much control I have from one moment to the next. Inside, my thoughts, my memories, all feel so...fluid. Like I can't quite hang on to anything."

Belle's brows furrowed, her lips turning down into a frown. "Stop treating me like a little kid."

"You *are* a kid, Belle."

"Come with me, but be quiet, Simon. Listen for their call."

Treks through the forest with Belle had led Simon right to the edge of his sanity, wondering sometimes if their excursions did, indeed, happen. Today would be more of the same, Simon expected. Her abilities were impressive and difficult to define. Whisterly thought so as well, and the time she and Belle spent together in the basement one on one, Simon wasn't privy to. But he was sure of one thing: Belle's abilities were growing.

Belle's control over one's psyche defied magical explanation, since she wasn't a witch, but her powers seemed equivalent. Her connection to the earth and its life-giving essence meant no boundaries for her.

Simon obeyed and followed her to the woods. "Belle, I've never heard them. Only through you have I experienced their power."

"You will today," she whispered. "Eyes closed."

Belle led him deeper into the forest and spoke in soft tones, as if in conversation or maybe a calling forth; Simon couldn't tell. A rich earthy scent filled his nose, followed by the fresh smell of newly fallen rain, and as he relented control to Belle, they tromped deeper into the woods. The wind on his face, the brush of leaves against his cheeks, the flicker of branches as they passed all filled him, until the sensations surrounding him were his singular focus.

A tiny voice emerged, then another, and he heard them all

as they merged into thousands...maybe more... They called to him. Eyes wide open now, his jaw dropped, and the little people descended, touching Simon with their lifeblood, joining with his. They spoke to him, not with words, but through their energy-giving power. The forest breathed a collective sigh with the beings' presence, their movement like a heartbeat, strong, steady, alive...

Belle twirled, laughing in the small clearing, where they communed with the beings. A soft yellow glow emanated from Belle—her aura, Simon surmised. As it shimmered in her wake, the Fae-like creatures appeared to bask in its warmth. Surrounding him as well was Simon's own deep blue aura, the little people jubilant in the power-giving light. Later, when Simon blinked, minutes or hours could have passed by, both of them now perched on a log.

"What was that, Belle?"

"An invitation into their world."

SIMON PACED in the darkness of his room, still too keyed up from the events of the day to sleep. This evening, after he and Daniel had finished the dishes, Belle had gifted Simon with new images—ones separate and apart from his returning memories. Inundated with spells, caught between flashbacks and incorporating the new, experiencing consciousness with the little people on a different plane, well, being overwhelmed would be an understatement.

Soon he'd collide in a crossroads. *When* would only be a guess. But with the intensity inside his head ramping up with each passing day, he found himself wishing that the memories would hit him in a final gigantic wave. At least at that point the influx would be over, instead of the constant inundation happening over and over again.

Climbing in bed, with the moon beaming a path into his room, Simon willed sleep to come. He expected, or was it dreaded, a visit from the Seer tomorrow—another grueling lesson, most likely. What if Simon decided against living with his kind, instead choosing to return to Remeon or a life on Earth, anonymous among the humans? Worse things, much worse, could befall him than putting down roots here with someone like Rae, for example. If she'd have him. Maybe he could clear outta here for a few hours. *Mmm... Rae...*

A knock sounded on his door. "Yeah?"

"Can I come in?" Daniel asked.

"Sure. I guess."

"Wow...it's dark in here."

"Well, it's nighttime. Besides, the moon gives off enough glow to find your way around. What do you want, Daniel?"

"Papa's in the middle of something. He said maybe you could tell me a story about Remeon tonight."

"About Remeon..."

"Yeah. Someday I'm gonna visit. Papa said so."

"Uh-huh... Where did he leave off?"

Daniel's voice lowered to just above a whisper. "A really cool part when all the people split up. Papa and Uncle Harry were there. Whisterly too."

"The thing is, I wasn't born then, so not sure I can help with that."

"But you know about it, Simon. Papa said you were taken to the Night Dwellers. Taken from Papa and Whisterly."

"You know I still don't remember everything, Daniel. Might be best to wait on Papa."

Daniel squirmed onto Simon's bed, arranged himself along the bottom, and turned his face toward his brother, Daniel's eyes full of anticipation.

Simon really didn't remember anything he'd been told about the turbulent time that had defined the Day Watchers

and Night Dwellers. Those particular memories were fragments, incomplete. "Your father was there. He'd be the better
one to tell this part."

Daniel crossed his arms, held up his chin defiantly. "I'm not
leaving until you tell me what you *do* remember."

"*Ugh*," Simon groaned, throwing his head back onto the
pillow. "You win. But just a quick story, then back to your own
room."

Daniel's eager expression tugged at Simon's heart. Through
the moonlight, bright on Daniel's smiling face, Simon felt the
little guy's hope—what would soon turn to disappointment.
The pieces Simon could remember weren't a happy bedtime
story. The kid deserved better. For Simon, it fit though.

"Well, like I said, I still don't remember much. Mostly places
and feelings... Here goes... The nights were strange, not like
here on Earth, when people sleep with the moon's rise. On
Remeon, we have two moons, so the nights are well lit, and the
Night Dwellers did most of their work during this time. As soon
as I was able, my adoptive mother took me out foraging, gathering food and other items that we needed. I do remember
looking forward to the time with her, one on one. Even though
I don't recall the details, spending time away from all the others
made me feel...special."

"Sure. I know what you mean. Like when Papa and I play
catch."

Simon nodded. "In a way, I guess. But when you play catch,
that's fun, recreation. Our nightly gathering was more of a job.
Everyone helped, unless they were sick. Because so many were
ill, all were necessary in the effort, even kids. We had quotas to
meet when we went out at night."

"What's that mean?"

"*Um*...objectives or numbers."

"Like when Papa tells me to read ten pages?"

"Are you punished if you don't finish?"

"Of course not, silly."

"Then, no, not the same."

Daniel's eyes widened.

"Again I don't remember specifics. But, when I got out of the cave at night, I was focused more on exploring, especially if I was alone, without someone to help me concentrate on the task at hand."

"Where was your mother?"

As Simon spoke, more details filtered in, rising from the clutter of his thoughts. "Some nights she was needed among the Night Dwellers. Most of the time I didn't mind being alone, from what I recall. The freedom to roam, to get away from all the people, the sick ones especially, well, I couldn't wait. Returning without meeting expectations was another matter though. My adoptive parents were sick eventually, like a good majority of the Night Dwellers."

"That's sad."

"Yeah. The more the number of the sick increased, the more that meant those of us who were well had to do."

"But you were only a kid."

Simon scoffed. "That didn't matter. I was hungry. Always hungry—"

"Papa says growing boys can eat a horse."

"When I didn't meet my quota, I had to miss a meal, sometimes two, since I wasn't working hard enough and since I was letting down those who couldn't fend for themselves. I had sticks under my mattress I kept to gnaw on when it got really bad. At least it was something..."

Daniel sniffled, interrupting Simon. "That's just awful. I'm hungry sometimes, and I eat all the time."

"I hear ya, little brother. At least talking about this helps me pull more from that time so long ago."

Tears rolled down Daniel's cheeks.

"Aw... Now don't do that. You said you wanted a story. This is all I got. It is what it is."

"I know I did. But you called me *brother*. I've always wanted a brother." Daniel crawled on his hands and knees along the bed, until he sat beside Simon.

"Now what are you doing?"

"I'm sorry, Simon."

"Don't be. I'm fine. It happened a long time ago."

"Can I stay here a little while longer?"

Simon looked into Daniel's tear-streaked face, a silent plea hanging on his lips. "Yeah, sure, I guess so."

Daniel scrunched in closer to Simon, curling up against his chest, then Daniel shuddered out a shaky breath. "Simon?" he whispered.

"Yeah?"

"I like that we can eat all we want to here...and...I like having a big brother."

Simon sighed and rested his head against the bedpost as Daniel's breathing settled into an even rhythm.

## 18

S imon fought sleep, letting the night swallow the feelings rising within him from the story Daniel's request provoked. A spark of memory flashed. A brother—he'd had one among the Night Dwellers, Simon was almost certain. As fragments of their time together formed in his head, Simon's eyelids drooped shut.

Darkness surrounded him, a deepening abyss sucking him in. Where was he? This wasn't right. Where was the Night Dwellers' cave? All the people? His brother?

*Simon?*

Goose bumps rose on his skin. He jerked his head toward the familiar voice. Only her and him suspended in an inky black void.

*I remember you.*

*As well you should.* She cackled. *I'm your great-grandmother.*

*We've spoken before.*

*We have, Simon. I'm returning this memory to you. Because you can't afford for it to come to you last—or not at all. As the foundation for all others, this one binds you to your family, solidifies your place in the realm of sorcery.*

The vision before him cleared, the blackness fading to a dull gray. A cool dampness gripped him as the memory invaded. The multiple times he'd been here, in this place, the basement in the compound, rang with a new clarity.

*You abandoned me.*

*No, I kicked you out. There's a difference. You were a danger to the coven.*

*And now?*

*Now you're facing a true enemy. One who can end you for good.*

*What can I do?*

*Remember...*

The room before him shifted, shimmering with an eerie glow as the hooded figures descended and planted themselves in a circle around him. A murkiness formed, then slowly cleared. A much younger version of his parents stood facing the old witch as she prepared for what appeared to be a blood magic sacrifice.

He strained to see more, but the veil returned, eclipsing the area in shade and gloom.

With a mumbled word from the hag, an apparition formed —his mother giving birth, Mila close by. The details came rushing back... His mother alone and vulnerable, her baby taken. His father's gentle care of Arista. Simon's life would have been significantly altered if he hadn't been used as a pawn.

The circle enclosing him swayed, and urged on by their chants, the coven moved, dancing about him while new visions raced through his head. The images of Simon, in captured moments of his life, paraded by. But even as he tried, he couldn't catch any of them. Finally Simon's body jolted to stop. Once again he experienced the onslaught of information, viewed his pointless attempts to battle what came natural to him.

*You were meant for this journey before you were born. Bound to the tome by blood magic and, at the appropriate time, called to the book to immerse and become one. You must remember all this to stand against the foe, whose magic chips away at you now.*

Simon gasped, his thoughts peppered with the warning inherent in his great-grandmother's words. *I remember. Something brought me here. Joined me with the book.*

*Yes. But temporarily you've been restricted. Your actions will determine your passage forward.*

*Why are you helping me now?*

*We could be stronger, together, fighting against the same adversary.*

*How will I recognize it?*

*Your soul is already battling it, Simon.*

*Will I remember this—what you've shown me?*

*The memories I've restored...your binding with the tome before you were born, your birth, and immersion...yes. The rest is uncertain, except for the will to fight. I've awakened that within you also. You'll feel it and hopefully aim the urge in the right direction. But in the end, the choice is yours. You are a warlock, Simon. Use Whisterly's teachings. Become the seer you were meant to be.*

A smile inched up his face. *From what I do recall, Great-Grandmother, fighting is an instinct I already possess in abundance.*

*We'll see, when the time comes.*

*Why can't you restore all my memories now?*

*They were wiped away for good reason, so you could have the opportunity that a fresh perspective might offer. Gaining them back too quickly could cause great harm. Time to experience small fragments of what was lost to you as a child will provide ammunition for the uncertain future you face.*

The chanting that had quieted surged again. The tide turned as Simon soared higher with the beings. A stray glimpse revealed their hollowed faces, their deep-set eyes, the thin layers of skin covering protruding bones—his people. *His people...* Simon reached a boundary where the witches couldn't pass. Higher and higher he floated, the rich, throaty cackle of his great-grandmother echoing in his head.

*Simon... Remember...*

"My people," he murmured. "My people..."

A small form rustled beside him. Startled, Simon sat up. *Daniel...* Fighting the smile lifting his lips, Simon shook his head. Somehow, his "little brother" had scooted over just now and fully occupied two-thirds of his bed. In his sleep, Daniel murmured something unintelligible and snuggled closer into the little bit of space Simon occupied on the bed. "Uh-huh... Shouldn't really call you *little*, when you've taken over the whole bed. Papa shouldn't call you 'little guy' anymore either, squirt."

Simon stretched and shuffled out of bed, reaching back to cover up Daniel, who'd settled into a soft snoring rhythm again. Simon's thoughts, not cleared from the dull haze he couldn't quite shake, still caught the muffled voices just the same. Pulling the door open, he hesitated at the entryway, listening. Uncle Harry was here. *What time is it anyway?* Simon lifted his chin to the clock. *Eight thirty...* He never slept that late. Simon tossed a glance to Daniel. *It's all his fault.*

The aroma of freshly brewed coffee drifted up the stairs. Thank the gods for his mother or father, whichever one made the addictive concoction. After tugging on pants and throwing on a shirt, Simon slipped down the stairs. Halfway down, Harry's voice rose, and his father's to meet it. Must be in the den.

Simon slowed, catching snippets of the conversation. As badly as he needed coffee, the tone of the two men interested Simon more at the moment. He stilled, dropping to sit on the stairs and tuned in, easing gently into Harry's thoughts.

～

"WHAT'S THE LATEST INTEL, HARRY?"

"Well, Jack, our old 'friend' has had quite a run of bad luck, so it seems."

"Can't say I feel too sorry for the guy."

"He came close to death, our source tells us."

"Death? They last reported Kix had been recovering from his memory wipe."

"Indeed." Harry smirked, flailing the letter in his hand. "Much has transpired since then."

"Well, all right. Let's hear it."

"Don't you ever feel any remorse over all this?"

"Huh? How do you mean?"

"The man saved us from certain death. Damond almost snuffed us out during that doomed trip to the shooting range on Remeon. We were so stupid."

"Speak for yourself, Harry. The reality was the council still needed us. At that point they were far from done with the needles... the invasive tests... Kix was protecting his own future —no more."

Harry shrugged. "Maybe. But he kept us alive, and that's what we needed right then. Almost makes me feel conflicted. If I'd never gotten home, I'd never have met Maggie. Had a son—"

"Okay. Reel it back in, Harry. I get what you're saying. But the man had no real feeling for us. The overriding concern was always what we could do for them. When they were done with the medical procedures, they'd have gotten rid of us. If it weren't for Whisterly intervening when she did, I'd have been just another dead Earthling, sacrificed along the way toward a cure."

"Call it whatever you want. The man's intervention allowed us to live another day. I'm grateful, now, here, on the other side of it."

"I'm grateful too—just not to him. Back to the letter, Harry...

You left me on the brink of death."

"Yeah. Kix's family helped him ditch or disable the tracking device that Vinique had put in. A doctor treated him for serious injury over a period of weeks."

Jack shook his head. "Too bad. Confirms what we knew from Vinique already. I had hopes that whatever procedure occurred, magical or otherwise, had finally ended him."

"There's more. Kix reached out to additional contacts among the Freemasons, suggesting that portions of his memory may have returned."

"Maybe his family connected them."

"I thought the same at first. But then Kix had conversations, about you and your whereabouts. Easy enough to determine in this day and age. However, this alone lets us know, at the very least, that some pieces of his memory are intact, proving what we already believed to be true."

"His warlock family could have some counterspell against the memory loss."

"Who knows? Lastly he's on the move. Hopped on a train over two weeks ago, heading initially to the Chicago area."

"So he's already here most likely."

"That's my thought too."

"Time for a more detailed discussion about Kix with Simon. Maybe it should come from Whisterly though."

*I guess it's no coincidence that your son is currently pushing into my thoughts. He probably thinks I'm an easier target, what with you being married to the former head of the council and all.*

*Did he make it through?*

*Hell no. Not beyond the barriers I've had set up. But I'm guessing he hasn't given it his full magical efforts yet.*

*He's heard us, Harry—*

"Papa, Harry..."

Both of their heads turned to the intrusion.

"Morning, son."

"That's my cue," Harry said. "I'm leaving the letter with you, Jack. Put it away."

"Don't go on my account, Uncle Harry."

"I'm not. Had my coffee, a little verbal sparring with your father, and now I have a full list of to-dos waiting for me at home. Jack, Simon." With a final nod, Harry headed out the front door.

"Have a seat. I'd like to discuss something with you."

Simon plopped into a chair. "Okay."

"I'm guessing you heard part of the discussion we were having, and it's fine. I'm glad you did."

"No, not really. I heard you talking on the way to the kitchen."

Jack's mouth quirked. "*Hmm.* So you didn't try to read Harry's thoughts just now before coming into the room?"

"Yeah, I did. Only up to the point where he'd closed himself off though."

"No need for any of that. Come in and ask directly."

"I believe that's what I'm doing right now."

"Okay. Fair enough." Jack joined Simon, lowering into a seat next to him. "A new threat is here, one I'd hoped would be neutralized, but it's not. The man's from Remeon, a warlock, and was ousted from the council for crimes against your planet, then sent here, where he has family he hasn't known until most recently, from what we can confirm."

"So, an outcast warlock, like me."

Jack scrutinized Simon, studying his body language, careful not to attempt telepathy. Men told their thoughts in a multitude of ways. If one was attentive, words weren't always necessary. In face-to-face discussions, this method rarely failed Jack. "An outcast and a warlock, like you? I disagree." Simon crossed a leg over one knee but kept quiet. Waiting. "Kix had an upbringing of privilege, yet he chose a life of deception, exposing his people for personal gain."

"I had more than most, and deception is the least of my offenses from what I've gathered."

"Can't really compare the two of you, when you were stolen at birth from us. I don't want to rehash this part with you, Simon, but you need to know the man is a danger to you. He wants to hit your mother and me where it hurts us most—through you."

Simon narrowed his gaze. "I see. I'll be looking out for him."

"His powers are significant."

"So are mine, especially with my mother's additional teachings. And maybe I could learn from this man, take what I can, even with his evil disposition. If you have hope for me, why not him?"

*Hmm. Sounded like the old Simon talking.* "I'd advise against it. He wants us dead, Simon."

"I won't let that happen."

"I won't either. You'll let me know if he gets in touch, telepathically or otherwise?"

Simon's quick scowl twisted into a smile. "I will. I'm starving. How about I attempt to make us some eggs?"

"Sure. I'll take a front-row seat to that." Jack's gaze cut to Simon's, reading the unspoken language buried there. Jack had little doubt—in fact, he'd bet his own life that his son was hiding information specifically related to Kix.

"All done here, Winston. I'm headed home for now."

"Home?" Winston asked. "Taking that pretty little thing with you?"

Simon followed the owner's gaze. Rae was early. A smile graced Simon's lips as their gazes locked, and her answering grin took his mind far from work. "That's up to her, but I sure hope so."

"You know, Simon. I could use another pair of hands around here. You've stayed even past the point where your debt was paid, and I appreciate that. What would you say to a longer-term arrangement—a job?"

Simon walked to the maintenance closet and put away his broom, searching for the right words. The man had been kind in the handling of matters related to Simon's fight in the tavern. Winston could have had Simon arrested. "Thanks for the offer. I'll be pretty busy for a while, helping with arrangements for my sister's wedding. After that, my father has given me some construction jobs to tend to. But if you need something, I'll be around. Just let me know."

"Ah... That's right. Isn't the wedding about two weeks away now?"

"A little less. I guess Christmas closing in has made the time even more stressful, but I wouldn't know really."

"Really? Why's that?"

"Well, I've never celebrated the holiday before this year."

"You don't say..." Winston shook his head and whooshed out a breath. "Hard to believe, you being Jack's son and all."

Simon shrugged and turned to leave. "Yeah. I get a lot of that."

"Wait just a minute."

Winston met Simon at the door. "Here," he said, shoving a wad of cash in Simon's hands.

"You don't owe me anything, Wilson. If anything, I'm indebted to you. I've learned a lot. Plus I had the chance to make things right between us."

"Keep it. Hiring help to do the jobs you've completed would have cost me much more. I want you to have it."

Simon dipped his chin. "Thank you."

"Go on. Use it to buy her a nice Christmas present."

Simon gripped Winston's palm, shook firmly, and chuckled. "I guess I should. See you soon."

*Damn. Who can tell me about this Christmas thing and not laugh in my face? Daniel...* "Rae, you're early," Simon scolded, pushing through the door. The mischievous glint in her eye sent his heart racing. He grabbed her hand, and at the first intersection, tugged her down the alley. Crushing his mouth against hers, their bodies met brick.

"Simon," she whispered, coming up for air. "I can't stay."

"I wanted to take you on a real date today."

"I know. Me too." She drew him to her again, tasting his lips, her fingers digging into his back, sending chills up his spine, until Simon groaned and pulled away.

"This was a bad idea." His mouth lingered on her neck.

"I disagree. The time I have with you, however long, is nothing short of...magical."

*What if*s churned in his head. He ached to have more with her. The half-truths he had shared with Rae felt more like lies now. But letting her in completely would probably send her running. Besides, he still had so many questions that needed answers about his own life. Keeping her at a safe distance made more sense. Didn't it? Was he crazy to want a life with her with so much undecided? Giving these thoughts time in his head sent a streak of fear shuddering through him. "Will you walk with me?"

"Sure. For a while. Is everything okay?"

"*Mmm*," he hummed his agreement. "Come on." More physical space between them allowed the blood to start pumping to his brain again. "We're having a small party next week, mostly family, but I'd like you to come, if you can. A tree-trimming party. I, uh..."

"I'd love too. Sounds like fun, if you're sure your family is all right with me being there."

"I'm not all right with you *not* being there."

"Oh, I guess it's settled then." Rae bowed her head, hiding her face.

"No. Don't do that," Simon said, lifting her chin with his forefinger. "I like you. A lot. We've had fun. We can keep it that way, if that's what you want. But I'd like more with you. More time... As well as more of this..." He brushed his lips with hers. "I just needed you to know where I stand."

"Simon," she murmured with a gentle squeeze of her hand, "I want the same thing."

"You do?"

"Yeah. It's hard to admit I have feelings for you because of that jerk I'd been seeing before. It scares me I didn't see it coming. So I pretend. It's safer that way."

"Back up to that part again about you having feelings for me. Tell me more about that."

"You knew that already," she scolded softly, her voice gone quiet.

"I'd hoped. And I always want you to feel safe around me."

"I do, Simon."

"Good. Here's where we part for now." Simon lifted her into a kiss. "See you soon."

On an information hunt, Simon picked up his pace. When he got home, he headed for Daniel's room. "Hey, squirt."

"Hey." Daniel's forehead folded in confusion as he closed his book. "What are you doing here? You never come to my room."

"Never?" Simon thought back. Might be true... "So..." He shrugged. "I'm starting today I guess."

"You want something."

Some days it seemed as if the young human in front of him could already read minds. If his father had his way, Daniel would soon enough. "True."

"I knew it! That means you need to give me something in return."

"What did you have in mind?"

"Depends on what you want."

"Okay. Here goes. I want to understand Christmas, quick."

Daniel smirked. "Oh. That's easy, but it will still cost you. I want another story about Remeon, sometime this week."

Hells. The kid had him. Simon was desperate, and he didn't have much time to get it all figured out. "You drive a hard bargain for a child. Deal. But only if you start explaining now, and provided you answer all my questions, from now up until Christmas."

"Sure. Ask away."

Simon pulled a chair next to Daniel's bed and dropped down. "The first question I have is why does a fat man deliver presents to everyone and put them under a tree?"

"That's an easy one. It's tradition. The gifts stand for so much more though."

Simon listened, silenced, in awe of Daniel's knowledge. But maybe Simon needed another source. Because all this couldn't be true...

## 19

*H*er chores finished, Belle dashed out of the newly completed construction office. She wasn't hiding exactly. With the upcoming frenzy of the wedding, along with food preparation and plans for company, even she could feel the tension pumping through the air. Her parents would be here of course; she missed them something awful, especially at night when all was quiet.

At that time, when the house was settled and all the animals bedded down for the night, her ma would read to her. Other times they might only talk in the stillness of the day just past. Even though Belle could read on her own, the special time was hers alone with Ma—time Belle sorely missed now.

Miss Whisterly, Mr. Jack, and Daniel were nice, but they weren't Ma, Pa, or Thomas. Belle was needed here though, and the odd connection she felt with Simon became harder to deny the longer she remained. Simon's evil past complicated everything, but since his memories had been cut away, what was left made him vulnerable, lost, and hurt as he tried to connect the pieces left over. His emotions washed over her more than anyone else knew, Simon included. But that was because she could help.

Air burst from her lungs as she ran for the tree line. No one chased her; the exertion felt good. Besides, Simon was close, and she hadn't seen him since this morning at breakfast. Her heart felt light, knowing she'd see her brother and parents soon. Most guests would arrive next week and stay close by in town, but Thomas and Arista would come through the portal tomorrow, just in time for the cutting of the tree. A smile slipped over her face as her cheeks rose. *Christmas!*

Broken bits of conversation drifted in and out as she trampled through the underbrush. Straining to hear, Belle softened her steps, and as she did, two distinct voices became clear—one unfamiliar, the other Simon's. Intuitively she disguised her telepathic signature, a little trick Arista had taught her. Even though Belle wasn't a witch, Arista had delighted in guiding her through this task.

Witchcraft wasn't necessary, only excellence in telepathy and discipline. Arista had bragged that Belle possessed both in abundance. And, to Arista's credit, she'd been right; the skill had come in quite handy. Belle's smile broadened; the stranger and Simon wouldn't sense her coming.

From her position crouched next to a tree, Belle could make out Simon, feeding wood to a fire while the man opposite Simon spat out instructions in quick succession. Belle's breath caught as Simon's deep blue aura glowed, burning a shimmering perimeter around him. She crept closer, the wind whistling through her clothes, but bringing her nearer to warmth and more mumbled conversation as well.

A cruel sneer, aimed at Simon, twisted the other man's lips. Simon, lost in the enchantment of his spell didn't appear to take notice. "Power isn't yours unless you use it. Practice it. Let it consume you. Otherwise what good is it?" Simon slumped to the ground, the man groaning his disappointment. "Several more memories gained, at least there's that."

"Yeah," Simon scowled, a frown creasing his brow as he eased his body against the closest tree, hissing in pain.

"We'll need to try this again soon. Prepare better next time. You're a warlock. Act like it."

The stranger disappeared in a bustle of swift movement and flowing fabric. Simon shuddered, his gaze trained on the space for what seemed like minutes, before he called out, "You can come out now, Belle."

"Simon!" Belle whisper-screamed. "You knew I was here?"

"Yes, and you shouldn't be."

"I didn't follow you, Simon. Just happened to see you, so I disguised—"

"That doesn't stop me from sensing you, Belle. Telepathy is kinda my thing. Mother says it's one of my greatest gifts. You can't beat me at it, and you can't hide from me." He grimaced, sucking in a deep breath.

Belle scurried to Simon's side. "Who is he? He's not a nice man. You don't need to be a witch or warlock to see that."

"He's a seer, a warlock. Someone who can teach me my craft, and he's helping me recover my memories faster."

She had seen the hatred in the seer's eyes. Felt its intensity. Couldn't Simon? "Whisterly's helped you with that, right?"

"Sure," he shrugged, "but not fast enough."

Angry blisters puckered the skin on Simon's hand, his lips drawn back in obvious agony. "I can help with the hurt. Try and sit still." Belle hummed as she worked, connecting with the earth's healing essence, coating her hands in moist rich soil interspersed with tiny pieces of decaying leaves and moss. "Here we go. This might hurt a little before it gets better." Belle surrounded Simon's hands in hers, applying gentle pressure to transfer the mixture to his tender skin. "Can't you see what he's doing to you?" she chided. Holding their hands in place with the cool salve, Belle dragged her gaze to his.

"Honestly I'm not sure if it's bad or not. Maybe I'm just not strong enough, like he says."

Belle shook her head. "How's the pain?"

A hint of a grin fell to his lips. "Better. I guess you're stuck here now. That's what you get for sneaking around in the forest."

"I wasn't sneaking. You know I come here every day I can." She slowly withdrew her hands, bits of dirt falling between them. "Move your fingers. See how it feels."

Gingerly at first, Simon squeezed his hands together, forming a fist. "Amazing. Good as new."

Sighing her relief, Belle joined Simon against the tree. "You should tell Jack and Whisterly about the seer. You know that, right?"

"I will. Once I've gained what I can from him. I promise."

"What if that time never comes? I'm worried about you, Simon."

"You see me, Belle Stewart, the real me, like no one else ever has, and I'm grateful, but deep down in my gut, I know I need to do this and that I'll be stronger on the other side because of it."

Belle listened, biting back the words on the tip of her tongue as the gloaming stole the sun's rays from the forest. She inched nearer to the fire. "I'm here, and whether I'm right next to you or on another planet, I always will be. Remember that, okay?"

Simon jogged his head, then paused. "They're here, aren't they, Belle?"

She nodded. "You can feel it too?"

*Shh. Yes. Let them come.*

Closing her eyes, Belle sensed the first twinkle of their light, then let their ancient lifeblood flow through her.

SIMON DROPPED INTO THE BOOTH, waiting for Rae to join him. Business was buzzing, the lunchtime rush in full swing at the Covered Platter. His father and Harry swore by the burgers at this place, so when Simon needed to get outta the house, plus he wanted to see his girl...hells, why not?

His girl? Was Rae that? He'd not seen her since they'd both agreed to be a couple. But did they really agree to that? Thinking back on their conversation, Simon wasn't sure— about any of it. Except for the feelings that rose from somewhere deep inside him whenever they were together. Navigating this...whatever it was, put him in unfamiliar territory, especially among humans. Lost in his thoughts, Simon raised his head to the noise as the bell danced a hello to the incoming customer.

*Rae...* Her lips lifted in an easy smile when she saw him, and Simon rose in an awkward half stance midbooth. "Hey, you," Simon murmured, leaning across the table to meet her in a kiss that Simon had been anticipating for two days. "I missed you."

The words slipped from his mouth before he could stop them. They were true, but he shouldn't say everything on his mind, like all the other humans, because he wasn't...that. Simon cleared his throat and sat back down.

"I love it here. Food's great. Your company is even better." Rae reached out a hand, covering Simon's.

"Yeah?" Her smile told Simon all he needed to know. No words or telepathy needed. "Order for me, will you? Whatever you want, then times two for me. I promised Daniel I'd bring back any leftovers."

"Sure. I can do that. Don't even need a menu, except to choose the flavor of pie for dessert."

A heavyset woman, her forehead dotted with sweat from working the lunch crowd, hovered at the end of their booth, filling glasses with water and lifting a pot of coffee in question. Simon nodded, turning his cup right-side up while Rae shook her head. "Ready to order, or should I come back in a few?" she asked, her eyes drifting to the chairs filling around the couple.

Her name tag read Marie. Simon imagined that the name fit the woman. She'd be efficient, a good cook most likely, but not a pushover to work in a place busy as this. Simon allowed himself an inward smile. In some ways he was improving assessing his human counterparts, even without using his telepathic abilities.

"No, we're ready. Give us three of your lunch specials. Two for him," Rae whispered and pointed, plenty loud for Simon to hear. "And pie, which would you recommend?" Rae asked, eyes lowered, perusing the menu.

"Apple," Marie offered without hesitation. "Made it myself this morning."

"Excellent. We'll have three pieces. Go ahead and wrap the third to go, please."

"You've got it. Your food will be up in a jiffy."

"So, today's the big day. Right?"

*The wedding couple arrives.* Simon met her gaze, gulping a swallow of his favorite Earth beverage. "Yeah. Glad to be anywhere but home right now."

"Bad, huh?"

"Awful. The wedding is four days away. You can't walk down the hall in the house right now without getting assigned another job. So I work to stay outta sight. That's my plan for the duration."

"But it's your sister. You're not close?"

Memories of Arista were still a jumbled mess in his head, but a few pieces had fallen into place, and they hadn't jived with the typical brother-sister bond. In fact, quite the opposite. Clearly Papa didn't want to discuss it further, until Simon's memories of his sister fully returned, because his father avoided speaking of Simon and Arista in any light whatsoever. So it must be pretty bad, and what he already knew from the discussion of his recovered memory with Papa was awful enough.

When Simon had woken among the coven on Remeon, one of the initial emotions he could feel was Stephen's hatred. Well, Thomas's, as he's known here. And clearly it had to do with Arista. Dread worked its way up Simon's spine as he gave his concerns renewed life on the subject again. Even though he'd begun to unearth some of the reasons behind why he was the person he became on Remeon, it didn't make the disappointment in himself any less. "We, uh, grew up apart. So we don't really know each other. We're strangers, more or less."

"Oh, that's tough."

"Yeah. Uh, thanks for agreeing to come tomorrow, for the tree-trimming party. A friendly face helps with all that's going on."

"At least it's Christmastime. Everyone loves Christmas." Rae's eyes twinkled, filling with some emotion Simon couldn't identify. "What's wrong?"

"Well, I've never...celebrated Christmas before."

"Oh. Okay." She swallowed hard, sipped her water, then slowly put the drink down again. Turning the glass between her fingers, she watched the condensation make tiny puddles on the table. Minutes passed in silence.

Simon didn't know what to say, so he kept quiet.

"Here we go, folks." Marie slid the plates on the table, Simon's piled twice as high with burgers and fries. Marie glanced at Simon, then Rae. "Sorry, did I interrupt a seance?" she joked. "You two all right?"

Rae offered the woman a smile, a genuine dazzling all-Rae smile, to her credit. "Looks wonderful. Thank you."

"Sure." Marie's gaze still bounced back and forth between the two of them, like she wasn't sure if she should stay to ensure the issue didn't concern the food. "I'll be back to check on you in a little while." Met with more dead air, Marie encouraged them. "Go on now. Eat up."

Sinking her teeth into her burger, Rae gave the woman a thumbs-up, sending Marie on her way finally. Rae chewed her bite fifteen times. Simon counted, waiting, watching her throat work as she swallowed. "I'm honored to spend your first Christmas with you, Simon. This time of year is magical. You should spend it with those you love."

"What?"

A grin inched up her face as Simon's gaze collided with hers. "You heard me."

"No, I'm not sure I did. My imagination's playing cruel tricks on me."

"Here it is again. Listen up 'cause I'm only saying this once." She leaned in closer. "I'm falling in love with you, Simon. Christmas and love—they go hand in hand. I can't wait to spend the holidays and the wedding with you."

Simon's mouth hung open while Rae giggled. "Your food's getting cold," she announced through bouts of laughter. "You might want to start eating it."

Simon's gaze spanned the diner, double-checking, in fact, that they were still here in the restaurant and her words weren't a trick of magic or telepathy gone haywire in his head. A tornado of emotions churned through him as he reached across the table and pulled Rae toward him. He didn't care that the restaurant had gone quiet when his lips crashed with hers. Rae smiled against his mouth and took a breath. "I'd like a second helping of that please."

"Plenty more where that came from. And I love it when you ask so...nicely." Simon grinned, kissing her again, muttering a curse due to the table between them.

Unaware of the audience they'd attracted, catcalls and clapping eventually separated the pair.

"Sorry to disturb your lunch, folks."

Marie refilled Simon's coffee, a smile stretching her mouth. "Now that's what I call a kiss. Dessert on the house for you two."

His hunger the overriding need now, Simon ate a huge bite. "Gods, this is amazing." A few minutes later Simon had moved on to the second burger.

"Don't forget to save some for Daniel."

"*Mmm.*" He moaned, pushing aside the plate. "The rest is his. Moving on to the pie."

"Well, what did you think?" Rae quirked up an eyebrow, surveying their plates, empty, except for sprinkled bits of pie crust.

"We'll be back. Soon. Best place I've eaten on Earth, by far."

"Wait. What?" Rae cocked her head. "On Earth?"

The bell jingled again, this time exhaling lunch patrons and admitting one all too familiar face. "Rae, isn't that your ex?"

Drawing in a breath, she swiveled, then gasped.

Simon watched her mouth move, easily making out the cuss word by reading her lips. Funny, all he wanted to do was kiss the obscenity from her mouth, regardless of the man stalking toward them.

"Simon, he hates you. We've already paid the check. Let's just go. Hurry."

"I'm not running from him, Rae. What's his name again?"

"Jesus, Simon... Mike, his name's Mike. Please, can we go now?"

"Save the begging for later, huh? I promise you I want to hear it again, but not when you're scared." Simon met her eyes and winked, considering his options... Lunch crowd almost gone. But just the thought of Rae getting hurt further ignited the growing fire within him. This confrontation needed to resolve quickly, or he might easily end up killing the man.

Simon shook his head, silently scolding himself. Hadn't he

learned anything? Paying off another bill for wrecking the place wouldn't do either. And there was Marie to consider. Her day was about to go downhill—fast.

Fleeting thoughts of Papa flashed in his head. *Okay, we'll try your way first. Then it's all me.*

*Simon, is everything all right?* His father's voice sparked to life in his head.

*We're about to find out.*

*Simon...*

Simon stood, offering his hand as Mike approached the table, his lip lifting in a snarl.

THE DINERS CLEARED a path for the man on an intercept course with Simon. A determined set to his jaw, Mike plowed through the restaurant, oblivious to anything or anyone in his way. "Mike, isn't it?" Simon asked, confident the man had no interest in talking.

He flung away Simon's hand, stealing a glimpse of Rae in the process. "Come on, Rachel. You don't belong here with him."

Plastering herself deeper into the booth, Rae lifted her chin toward the door. "Go on back to the rock you climbed out from. Not interested."

Ignoring Rae, Mike didn't miss a beat. "What are doing with my girl...again?"

Rae and Simon shared a glance. "I don't believe she's your girl, but what's more important—*she* doesn't. Turn around and get outta here, and let these nice people eat their lunch in peace." Simon waited, hope lingering in the quiet, hanging over the room.

People hovered between bites, eager for what would come next. Hells, Simon didn't want this extra attention. But it was a little too late for that now with all eyes in the restaurant flickering between Simon and Mike.

"We're through, Mike," Rae said, her voice breaking the stillness. "I told you that."

"Nah." Mike shook his head. "We'll never be through. Guys like this one here, they don't understand and need a personal lesson," he spat out, his tone dripping with icy disgust. "I'll be the one to teach him."

Simon caught Rae's shudder in his peripheral vision and steeled his stance.

"Where's your daddy and his trusty sidekick? Don't see them lurking around this time."

"I don't know. It's not my job to watch them. Last chance. Why don't you reconsider before you ruin everyone's day here?"

A cocky grin slid along Mike's face. "You seem to be under the misconception that I'm afraid of you. Jack and Harry were doing you a favor before, at the tavern."

"Is that right... How so?"

"Protecting you, by keeping me away."

"You see, I remember that day differently. Jack and Harry were trying to protect you—from me."

The man's laugh, hearty and deep, barreled up from his chest. Eyes watering, he fought to maintain control. No matter. Mike would see soon enough. Unfortunately, all of the patrons would see some of what would befall the human creature as well.

Concentrating on the spell he needed, Simon pulled the fingers of his right hand into a tight fist and squeezed. Within thirty seconds, Mike's smile turned to concern, and when panic sparked in the man's eyes, Simon still held his clenched fingers together. As he watched Mike turn varying shades of red, then purple, the man fought for the air Simon withheld.

To the crowd, Mike's actions seemed odd. Probably like he

was having a fit of some kind because Simon didn't actually touch the man. At about the two-minute mark, Mike collapsed, clawing at his throat and smacking a chair on the way down. Simon really didn't want Mike dead, just incapacitated and frightened enough to leave Rae alone, so Simon relaxed his fist, allowing the flow of air again in Mike's chest.

He sucked in a shaky breath, followed by another.

*A damn useful spell.* "Hmm. Must have been something he ate. Ready to go, Rae?" Simon tossed a glance toward the booth, where she still sat, speechless.

Bending over where Mike lay, Simon placed his hand on the man's shoulder, appearing to offer comfort. "If you want to use that body of yours to monotonously inhale and exhale, that's up to you," Simon rasped. "But if you bother Rae again, I'll find a more creative use for your organic matter, like garden mulch. Understand? Just nod. I know your lack of oxygen is compromising your brain function as we speak."

Silently Mike flopped his head in an up and down motion.

"Good. Glad we've cleared that up." Simon stood and turned to the booth. "Rae?"

A tiny gasp left her lips. Clearly petrified, her eyes round, she seemed unable to move. Mumbled voices filled the room.

"Rae"—he took her hand—"it's okay, honey. Let's go."

At his words she snapped out of her trancelike state and scooted from the booth, her gaze fixed on Mike, struggling for breath.

Thank gods the term of endearment worked. Simon had witnessed its use in action several times with his father and Harry. Without exception his mother and Maggie had complied with the situation at hand. His word choice did something else unexpected though—drew him closer to Rae.

Simon's heart hammered as he closed the distance to the door, Rae in tow. Marie stood by the exit, holding the door open for them. Digging into his pocket, Simon pulled out some additional cash and pushed it into the waitress's hands. "Sorry for the commotion. Loved your pie. Best I've ever had."

She nodded, shoving the leftover food into Simon's hands. "Come back anytime. Not sure how you managed that, but the man had it coming. Take care."

"Let's walk." Simon trudged along the boardwalk, Rae barely able to keep up. This pent-up energy inside... Simon wasn't sure how to get rid of it, so he increased his speed.

"Wait. Simon. I can't keep up with you."

"Sorry." He slowed and they inched along now at a painfully lethargic pace.

"What happened in there, Simon? Do you know what affected Mike like that?"

Simon's mind bolted. He couldn't tell her everything. Not now. Not like this. She'd run, and he'd never see her again. Now more than ever, Simon couldn't bear that. "It's hard to explain. And I'm pretty sure you won't want to know, once you do."

"You're scaring me. Don't get me wrong. I'm grateful to have Mike away from me." Rae yanked Simon closer. "Simon... Simon!"

He wrapped her in his arms and kissed her quiet. "I would have done just about anything to get you outta there and away from that idiot human."

Rae ran her fingers through his hair as Simon's thumb slid down her cheek. "Why did you just call him *human* like that— like you're not?"

"Rae...I am...different. Can we just leave it at that for now?"

"You had Mike under your control somehow in the diner, didn't you?"

Simon rocked his head and sighed. "Yeah."

"*Ooookay*...okay...okay..."

Rae paced nervously, mumbling to herself until Simon pulled her to him again, nestling her against his chest. "*Shh.*" He pressed his lips against her forehead while they swayed.

Simon wasn't sure how long they stayed like that, until the tension in her shoulders and back gave in to his touch, however long that was. "That's better. See?"

"Simon..."

"Rae, in time I'll tell you everything. Just let me do it at my own pace. All right?"

She nodded her head against his. "Don't disappear on me, Simon."

"I won't, honey." *That time it just slid out. Felt right.*

"This is nice. But you've got family at home, waiting to see you."

"No," he chuckled. "No one arriving today wants to see me, but I am expected back home. I do need to head that way." He lifted her chin until their eyes met. "I'm not leaving until I'm sure you've calmed down though. I'm still me, Rae."

"I'm fine. I don't usually need a knight in shining armor. Today I did. Thank you."

"You're welcome," he whispered, brushing his lips with hers once more. "See you tomorrow?"

"You will. We're gonna decorate the most perfect tree. I can feel it."

After Rae disappeared inside her house, Simon headed for home. *Yeah... I'm feeling something different than that.*

The laughter reached him first, way before the house came into view. By the time he arrived, the late-afternoon sun had faded, giving the December chill a head start on the night to come. A bonfire burned, its tongues of fire reaching out to swallow the remains of the day. From Simon's viewpoint he could take it all in. Around the pyre they gathered. Thomas and Belle grinning ear to ear on one side, Arista gazing into Thomas's eyes from the other; Daniel, snug against Papa, and Mother who leaned into him, probably whispering something in his ear, causing Papa's silly smirk.

Simon's face flushed from the intimate scene, where he had

no place. His presence would cause tension, and the sounds of laughter would die on their lips. Circling around the back of the house, Simon slid inside the rear door and dropped the leftovers and pie in the refrigerator for Daniel as promised. The fresh aromas of soap and balsam filled the air.

He fought against the urge to go farther into the house, to linger among the now familiar rooms that brought him comfort and an alien sense of belonging. Instead, he turned back toward the door and stepped outside, ignoring the want in the pit of his stomach, drawing him toward family and the ordinary everyday moments he craved.

*Illumine.* The light spun in brilliant cords as Simon twisted the blaze into a tight burning mass, shining a path among the trees ahead.

*Simon, come join us.*

*Maybe later, Papa. I need time.*

*You've been away all afternoon.*

*I have.*

*Drinks then in the den. Don't be long.*

## 20

*J*ack couldn't deny that the next week would bring highs and lows like he hadn't experienced since his own unorthodox wedding. No less wed though. If he had it to do over again, he wouldn't change a thing. He had his perfect match beside him and his children gathered close. One lessoned he'd learned—none of it would last. The happiness in his heart at this moment was fleeting, but the joy his soul experienced would echo in this time spent forever.

"Simon's here somewhere," Whisterly whispered in his ear.

"Yeah, he'll be along later." Jack shrugged. "He needs to find his own way through this. We can't do it for him."

"I just hope we all live through this wedding. Quite the event you've decided to take on here, Jack."

"My family's happiness is important to me."

Daniel wiggled free, ran around the fire, and plowed into Thomas. He absorbed the impact of sprawling arms and legs, moved Arista aside, then tackled Daniel to the ground where Thomas pinned him, only able to lift his head now.

"Jack, maybe you should help?"

He huffed a laugh. "Na, baby. Daniel got himself into it. He'll be fine."

"It's nice to have Arista here and for her to finally meet Daniel."

Jack nodded. "I can't tell you the number of times I've wondered how our lives would have been different had Arista, Simon, and Daniel all been raised here."

"I had a council to run, a society to heal. You were busy fighting a war and later with a business. We could only hazard a guess. Time and fate play cruel tricks on all of us. Granted those years were...torture. Now on this side of the divide, I'd rather live it the way it's been dealt. We've loved, learned, grown, experienced happiness like most never will, here or on Remeon. Our lives are exactly how they were meant to be. And it's only the beginning."

"You're pretty smart for a witch, you know that?"

"I do." Whisterly squeezed Jack around his waist and leaned her chin on his shoulder. "Want me to cast a spell so our night will seem longer?"

Jack's eyes widened, and he turned abruptly toward her. "No, promise me you won't. Let it be as is. No spells affecting our time together."

"Okay Jack, as you wish."

Daniel had wriggled his way free from Thomas, or more likely, Thomas let him loose, and currently, Daniel held Arista's attention. Even from here Jack could hear his son trying to impress her with his knowledge of Remeon. Thomas maneuvered toward Jack. "That's a fine young man you have there. His head is already full of all things Remeon."

"As my son, that knowledge will be part of his heritage. I'll see that he's well versed in it. Someday soon I want him to visit, and he'll need to be prepared."

Thomas rubbed his chin. "I thought you wanted to keep Daniel out of the politics of the planet?"

"I do, while he's young. But he'll be growing in knowledge in the meantime to participate on both worlds, Earth and Remeon. Thanks to people, like you, Thomas, that's possible."

He barked a laugh. "Thanks to you is more like it, Jack—and Harry of course. Will he be joining us tonight?"

"No, he wanted us to have today for just us." Jack's eyebrows rose. "Wise on his part. Would you agree?"

"Sure. He's hoping to escape the fireworks. I get it. I don't blame him. Personally I'd like to get the initial meeting with Simon out of the way. Until I do and get a feel for where we stand, I'm not leaving Arista alone. Where is he?"

"He'll be along."

Belle raced by, out of breath from playing tag with Daniel. "Simon's on the way back to the house. He told me so."

"Would you like to join me for a drink inside, Thomas? Nothing like some liquid fortitude to steel the night. What do you say?"

"Sure." Thomas waved Arista over. "How about a drink, love?"

"Sounds good."

Jack snaked one arm around Arista and the other around Thomas and led them toward the house. "What about Daniel and Belle?" Thomas asked with a backward glance.

"Let them run off some more energy. We'll call them for dinner."

"By the way, Jack, if we ever settle here on Earth, I'd love to have your help with plans for a house." Thomas paused, his gaze roaming the entryway before sweeping to the wooden beams high above. "Your workmanship is incredible."

"You've got a deal, Thomas. I've been working with some of my clients since we've returned. Not digging in too deep though, since I don't know how long we're here for just yet."

"I see. I'd hoped you'd both be back on Remeon soon."

"I think we'll be interplanetary travelers from here on out. What'll you have, Thomas?"

"Whiskey."

"Me too, Papa."

"Coming right up. Thomas, if or when you settle here on Earth, maybe you'd like to consider throwing in with Harry and me. For now Harry's carrying the burden, so we're keeping our client list manageable. Something to think about though. For the future. Even with Simon's help, if he stays here, we'll need more manpower."

"Simon?"

Jack gave a curt nod. "Yes. Simon. He's got a knack for carpentry. Pretty much completed the work on my new office after the framing was done. I'll be taking him into business with me."

"That will count me out, Jack."

Jack swirled the amber liquid in his glass, then swallowed the contents, poured another. "Your decision, son."

The back door slammed shut, sending Shadow scurrying through the house. "Look who I found," Belle called out.

Simon stood at the entry to the den, poised as if deciding whether to enter. Whisterly's light touch from behind eased her son into the room.

"I can leave," Simon offered, arcing his thumb back the way he'd come.

"No. Come sit by me," Daniel begged.

"And *meeee*," Belle added.

"So much for you two kids running off more energy. What would you like, son?"

"Whatever you're having, but make it a double."

"Sounds like a good idea." Jack gave a humorless chuckle.

Simon plopped onto the couch and was immediately surrounded by Belle and Daniel. And as Thomas glared,

Shadow leaped onto Simon's lap and settled, purring contentedly.

"Hell, even the damn cat..."

"Relax," murmured Arista.

"I'm trying. It's not working."

"Dinner in five," Whisterly called from the kitchen. "Refill, Thomas?"

"Yeah. And, on this one point, I agree with Simon. Make mine a double too."

*Whisterly, baby, we've got a night ahead of us...*

WHISTERLY ROSE to clear the dishes.

"Daniel, hop up and give her a hand, son."

"Sure, Papa. That means I get to taste-test dessert."

Jack stood, set to give chase, before Daniel grabbed a few empty plates, yelped, and ran from the dining room to the kitchen. "The kid's all about sweets."

"Not just him. Let me give you a hand in there, Mother. Just hope I can still fit in my wedding dress in a few days."

Thomas's gaze followed Arista until she disappeared into the kitchen, then darted back to focus on Simon again. Belle kicked Thomas under the table. "You're being rude, Thomas. Give him a chance."

"You don't know what you're talking about," Thomas countered on a long exhale.

"You're wrong, Thomas. I know him better than you now. He's changed."

Thomas's mouth set in a thin line. "Or you just think he has. He's got you all fooled. The sadistic bast—"

"Thomas, pie?" Arista asked, shoving the plate in front of him.

"Yes. Thanks, love."

"Try to relax. I'd like to enjoy my time here with Mother and Papa." Arista's tone softened. "I can take care of myself. Remember? Plus, with you, Papa, and Mother here, Simon couldn't hurt me or you, for that matter. Thomas... Please?"

He shook his head, pulling his gaze from Simon. "I'll try. My brain is in overdrive, in protection mode with you and Belle so close to that monster."

"I understand. But we're fine. You know I'm not a fan of my brother either, but I sense that he's changed, just like Belle says."

Thomas kissed the back of Arista's hand as she sat down, then shoveled a bite of pie in his mouth. "This is excellent, Whisterly, second place to my mom's, of course."

"I'll take that as a compliment." Whisterly slid into her seat at the table. "After all, it's only the third pie I've ever made. How many has Elizabeth made?"

"Oh, wow... I don't know. Do women keep track of that sort of thing?"

"This one does," Jack chimed in, doling out another round of whiskey for everyone.

*Good plan, sweetheart. We'll pour them all in a bed here in a little while. Sooner rather than later, okay? We need to talk.*

Jack cocked his head in silent acquiescence.

"When will Rae be over tomorrow?" Whisterly asked.

The vacant look in Simon's eyes retreated. "Not sure exactly. Sometime after breakfast. She's so excited to be involved with Christmas decorations and holiday planning."

"But you're not," Thomas mumbled.

"Actually I am." Simon lifted his chin, meeting Thomas's gaze.

"*Hmm. Who is she?*"

"Simon's *girlfriend*." Belle grinned. "She's pretty."

"Well, that's a mistake..."

"You think you get to decide that, Thomas?" Shadow scurried from Simon's lap when he stopped scratching her ear. "She's one of the few people who gets me, despite my messed-up head. Your sister is another. Rae and Belle have helped keep me sane. Well, them and working with my hands."

Thomas's gaze snagged from Simon to Belle, a look of betrayal written on his face.

"Thomas, what's wrong?" Daniel piped up.

"Nothing." Thomas shoved his chair back and threw back the remainder of his drink, Arista following suit. "Thank you, Whisterly, Jack. At least I'm pleasingly sloshed."

"You bet," Jack said. "Belle, can you show your brother to my office?"

Thomas's eyebrows rose in silent question.

"Best accommodations around. Newly finished. Complete with a bathroom suite." Jack beamed at Simon, whose mouth inched up at the indirect compliment.

"Come on, sweetheart." Arista guided Thomas, falling into step behind Belle. "Let's go."

Belle's voice lingered as they tromped through the kitchen. "Your room is *beeautifulllll*, Arista. Just wait till you see it! Mr. Jack's been working on it for years. Miss Whisterly told me so."

*Meet me upstairs, baby, after I get everyone settled in their separate corners for the night.*

Thirty minutes later Jack strolled into his bedroom.

"Well," Whisterly asked, "do you think they will make it through the night and wake up in one piece?"

Jack grunted a laugh. "I used to wonder the same thing each time I got a new batch of recruits to train. Yes, I do, as long as those of you with magical tendencies keep your spell-making to a minimum for the night."

"Watch out, a well-timed spell could be our saving grace."

"Good point, baby." Jack's arms threaded around Whisterly's waist, his forehead wrinkling with a frown. "What's got you so upset you'll only settle for a verbal private conversation?"

"Come sit down." Whisterly tugged him toward their seating area, her mouth bending to match Jack's. "Tonight, while Belle was so focused on Simon, I read her thoughts. Before you say it, I know, I shouldn't have, but her concern for our son was so overwhelming I had to seek the source."

"Go on."

"Kix is here. Been here for a while, from what I could pull from the conversation Simon had with her."

"God, already? Could you tell if Simon knew who Kix was?"

"Around Simon, Kix calls himself *the Seer*. It's likely he's forcing back memories and accelerating a training plan according to his own personal agenda."

"Or vendetta. We almost killed the man."

"I've let domesticity cloud my judgment while that warlock got his claws into our son. We'll have eyes on him soon. In the meantime, I'll spend some time with Simon tomorrow, after you all bring the tree back. Find out more from him."

Jack took her hands. "We won't quit fighting for him. Ever. The transformation Simon's experiencing is nothing short of miraculous. We can't let Kix snatch it away. Anything else from Belle?"

"Only that Simon believes he's learning from the man what he can before cluing us in."

"When you're young, you think you can take on anything and win. I know I did."

Whisterly cupped his cheek. "You did, Jack. You won."

"By the grace of God, I got you back. He'll see us through this too."

"I'll be raising the power of our coven in Simon's defense. Your God's welcome to join in."

"I think you've got that backward, baby. But throw it on the fire, and we'll use it."

∽

ARISTA'S EYES BLINKED OPEN. *Three days. Only three days until our wedding.* Dappled rays of light peaked through the curtains, bathing her in warmth from the December morning sun. She turned over, letting her body sink into the mattress as she squeezed her pillow. Beds like this didn't exist on Remeon. The four-poster mahogany bed, handmade by Papa, made her feel...regal.

Wrapped in the comfort of this room—from the silky sheets to the blankets that had held her snug during the night—she felt Papa's love. Her father had fought for words when he brought her upstairs last night. For him, working on her room over the years had been cathartic, a way to aid his healing—his only hope that she would one day visit and sleep here.

Stretching, she pondered the items Papa had chosen for placement in here. The wooden floorboards chilled her feet as she meandered around, soaking up the rich textures and coordinating fabrics throughout. Complementing the bed, in the same style, the dresser matched perfectly, topped with an ornate mirror, and on the dresser's surface lay the book that Arista had given her father—the one with Remeon's detailed history, alluding to their family's magical lineage. A bookcase lined one wall, and as she'd perused the selections on witchcraft, she wondered at her father's ability to locate books such as these on Earth. Surely they'd be difficult to come by.

A painting of Remeon's two moons hung over her bed, stunning in the way the light captured the moons' rise. Her gaze swept to the next piece of art, a pentagram, which adorned the space over the door, so that the room was steeped in the craft and covered in protection. Her father had told her that last night too.

A recent picture of her mother and father decorated the dresser. Their happy faces turned toward each other, Papa mentioned this was taken the day after he'd brought Whisterly home. A tear slid down Arista's cheek as she recalled him telling her last night, his voice thick with emotion while he'd held her tight. Her parents had been through a long rough journey to have a life together, one filled with disease, heartache, separation, and death. And the chaos wasn't through with them yet. But somehow they'd endured.

Every element of her bedroom had been painstakingly put together. Glancing around the space, she could feel her father's love woven within each minute detail.

"The process gave me a way to keep you close when you were far, far away. Honestly I think it was as much for me as you," Papa had told her, before kissing her on the forehead and leaving. "Welcome home, little one. Know that you'll always have a place here."

Arista padded to her sitting area and dropped into the mauve wingback chair. Her father mentioned he'd waited on this item the longest of all the pieces to complete her room. But he'd insisted on the color, since it reminded him of her gentle heart, yet fierce spirit. She glided her hand along the unique fabric and pulled the blanket draped on the back of the chair across her lap, settling in to lose herself in one of the magical books her father had chosen.

A smile edged up the corners of her lips, just before a knock sounded. *Thomas...* "Come in."

Thomas poked his head in. "Look what I've got."

"Coffee?" she asked, sniffing the air. "Bring it on over, if you dare. I feel positively decadent, not yet dressed for the day."

A grin crossed his mouth. "Move over a bit, and we can be decadent together. I missed you last night. You seemed so far away."

Wrapped in her blanket, Arista stood as Thomas sat down and rearranged her on his lap. "*Mmm.* I love it. Tastes different though."

"I added a little cream for the perfect balance, in my opinion. What do you think?"

"I agree. Soon you'll be moved into my suite in the compound, and we'll always wake up together." She smiled, leaning in for a kiss.

Thomas cupped her cheek as their lips met. "I can't wait," he murmured.

"You seem to be in a better mood this morning."

"Not really. My thoughts regarding your brother haven't changed. We'll endure the next few days, so we can come out married on the other side. I can do that, love, with my eyes on the prize."

"Tell me about papa's office."

"You really should see for yourself this morning. I'll admit Jack and Simon have done good work. It's two stories, where it used to be one—the bottom level devoted to a wonderfully comfy guest suite." Thomas's gaze skimmed Arista's room. "I don't know that it's as lavish as all this, but I don't think I've ever slept in a more comfortable bed."

"Isn't my room just perfect?"

Thomas covered her mouth with his. "*Mmm*."

"What was that for?"

"I needed a taste of your happiness to save for later...during my trek through the woods for a Christmas tree. With Simon."

"Ah, yes."

"It's beautiful. Jack has obviously spent a long time making it perfect for you."

"I love it." Arista's breath caught, her eyes filling with tears.

"None of that, love." Thomas stood, taking her with him. "Get dressed, meet me downstairs for breakfast, before I'm sent out with all the men in your family to kill a defenseless tree."

"Okay, I'll be right there."

Thomas kissed the length of her neck and unbuttoned the top three buttons of her nightgown. "See? I've got you started..."

"You sure have. Now out, before I beg you to stay."

"Arista..." he growled out.

"Go."

Fifteen minutes later Arista plodded down the steps, following the cheerful sounds of laughter and family, together with the aroma of a feast she couldn't name.

"There you are," Papa called from the stove, a kitchen towel thrown over his shoulder, his focus on the source of the delightful smells driving her forward. "Hungry?"

"Famished."

"Good. Pull up a seat. Pancakes and sausage coming right up."

"He makes the best pancakes," Daniel sputtered around a mouthful of food.

"I'll bet he does." Arista refilled her coffee cup.

"Arista... I saved you a spot. Come sit by me. *Puleess...*" Daniel drawled.

"Sure, be right there, Daniel." After kissing her father's cheek and accepting a plate piled high with pancakes and sausage, Arista squeezed between Daniel and Belle. Eating beside the wiggly two offered its own challenges, but as she savored each bite, something else strange grabbed Arista's attention. Her twin's nervous anticipation pulsed through her veins, like it was her own.

*You've opened your thoughts to me, Simon.*

*Yes. I have. I can't remember all that's happened between us in the past, but the situation can change going forward. Rae doesn't know about us. Be nice please. She's important to me.*

Arista scrunched her forehead, confused, until Simon left the table, ahead of a knock on the door.

*Rae, her name's Rae, and she can't wait to meet all of you.*

Silence engulfed the room, so the woman's awed whispers drifted into the kitchen before she did. "Rae, you remember my parents, Jack and Whisterly."

"Of course. Thanks for letting me crash your family gathering."

"Nonsense. Lovely to have you," Whisterly flashed Rae a quick smile. "I'll accept any and all offers of help with decorating for Christmas and the wedding."

"Great, Christmas is my favorite holiday."

Jack passed Rae a plate of food. "For all the men in the room, here's your ten-minute warning."

"Rae, across the table is my sister, Arista, her betrothed, Thomas, and the two wiggly ones are Daniel and Belle."

"So nice to meet you all. I feel like I know you already from the tidbits Simon has shared with me."

"Ladies, I'll see you upon our return, and to the rest of my crew," Jack winked, "don't keep me waiting."

*She's charming, Simon. Don't worry. Looks like she can hold her own.*

*You've no idea.*

Simon brushed Rae's mouth with a quick kiss. "Be back soon."

Rae beamed a smile. "They're lovely, just like you said."

Thomas swallowed the last of his coffee as he and Arista shared a glance.

## 21

"*W*ish me luck." Thomas pressed a kiss to Arista's mouth. "Truly I'd rather stay here with you in front of the warm fire than go off tromping through the woods in the cold. Plus it looks like snow, which makes the whole outing all that much worse."

"Get yourself in the spirit of Christmas, for me, Mother, and Father. Look at Daniel. He's so excited to be one of the guys."

The boy could hardly be still. Daniel was practically dancing by the front door. Excited was an understatement.

"All right, almost wife and mate of my soul, you've shamed me into compliance. I should be a better conduit of the Christmas spirit. Your enjoyment of the season and all the magical moments mean everything to me." A flash of a smile came and went. "Christmas magical moments, I'm talking about here, just to clarify. Your personal magical moments have the highest priority in my life, but I expect a front-row seat to those—always, not just at Christmas."

"And you have it." Her laugh squeezed Thomas's heart. "Now go, or you'll get left."

"Again that's an outcome I could get behind."

"Go... Expect to be dazzled by the Christmas decorations on display when you return."

"I expect to have you all to myself when I return, if only for a short time. Promise me."

"Done. Now go. They've officially left without you."

One more too-quick kiss later, Thomas found himself in the chill of late morning, wrapping his scarf around his neck and mouth, tucking the remainder inside his coat, already cinched tight. He sniffed the air as lazy snowflakes drifted their way to the hard ground. More was coming; he could feel it in his bones. Hopefully their little posse would beat the storm home.

Thomas adjusted the sack on his back, grateful for the warm coffee that Whisterly had stored inside, among a few other supplies. Ahead, Jack carried a light lunch of sandwiches for them and, of course, the ax to chop down the tree.

Trudging along, Thomas made no attempt to hurry or to catch up with Jack and his sons. He was stuck with them for at least a couple hours. From here, they looked picture-perfect. From here, nobody could guess the secrets they kept hidden between them. Moving pictures came alive behind his eyes. The cold, the hunger, the isolation, the control, and the mind games that had delighted Simon as he'd dug deeper and deeper into Thomas's head. He gritted his teeth, reliving the horrid pain, a growl rumbling up from his throat, when someone grabbed his arm.

"Thomas? You okay?" Daniel's forehead scrunched.

Thomas blinked and wiped the snowflakes from his eyes. "Yeah, sure. Why?"

Daniel continued to shake Thomas, apparently unconvinced. "You stopped. Papa wanted me to check on you. Make sure your leg was all right."

"I'm fine." Daniel hung back, matching his pace to Thomas's. "You can go on back up with them," Thomas encouraged with a jerk of his head.

"No, I'll stay." Daniel glanced longingly ahead, his face the picture of gloom. "I'm good with bringing up the rear."

Braces weren't the reason Thomas didn't want to follow so closely. The last time Thomas had worn them had been months ago. His legs were stronger than ever before. Just in case though, the metal reminders of his illness took up space in his travel bag, on the off chance he'd need them. And wouldn't that just beat all... Braces on his wedding day.

Nothing would keep him from marrying Arista, including the weakness that had become so much a part of his life since his polio diagnosis. That chronic weakness less now, his training on Remeon and the passage of time had both been effective at increasing his strength.

Thomas pulled the coffee from his bag, drank deeply, and offered Daniel a drink. He wrinkled his nose. "Go on, have a swallow. It'll warm you up." Daniel took a tentative sip. "*Ugh*," he gagged. "Tastes like dirt."

Slapping him on the back, Thomas continued, "You'll think back on today and remember this was the day you started to love it."

"Look." Daniel pointed. "I see it." Shielding his eyes from the nonexistent sun, Daniel beamed. "The perfect tree."

Squinting, Thomas followed Daniel's gaze. "Looks like it could be. Maybe you've found *the one*."

"Papa, wait. There it is." Daniel rushed ahead, then stopped and turned, as if remembering he'd been told to stick with Thomas.

"I'm right behind you."

After they'd all given approval, Jack began the process of chopping down the tree, offering Daniel some guided swings before passing the ax to Simon. He swung hard once, twice, and a third time, an audible *crack* echoing through the woods as the tree fell onto the light layer of snow with a *whoosh*.

"But what about Thomas?" Daniel asked. "He didn't have a turn."

"I'm good. Now can we eat and head back?"

Simon scoffed. "Thomas is too busy steering clear from me to be bothered with cutting down our tree."

"You made quick work of it, son. I'm sure Thomas doesn't mind missing a swing or two of the ax. No doubt he's done this task many years in a row."

Thomas leveled Simon with a glare. "Don't mind in the least."

Jack cleared the nearby undergrowth from a circular area and stacked wood while Daniel gathered more and fed those to Jack. With a murmured word from Simon, a flame sparked to life between his fingers, and seconds later the fire sputtered and crackled between them. Surrounded in warmth, they munched on their sandwiches and drank coffee.

The fire jerked with the blowing wind, stretching, arcing, bending, as if seeking more fuel to add to its hungry blaze. Thomas stomped a spot clean with his boot, digging farther till he hit the mud beneath the surface. The insanity of this gathering struck him. Lifting his chin, he bore his gaze into Simon's.

Spinning thoughts turned loose in Thomas's head, his anger rising, mingling with the raging emotions, all seeking freedom, bottled for too long. *Thomas...* The word came out as a streaming hiss, a memory of when his actions were not his own as a gleeful Simon imposed his will on Thomas instead by invoking his true name.

Rising to his feet, Thomas watched his own motions like a bystander. Straightening to stand, Jack and Simon stepped back from the fire. Daniel wormed a path between them. "What's going on? Papa?"

"Get back, son." Jack pushed Daniel behind him. Simon nodded, and Jack jerked his chin, in some silent acknowledgment of their communication.

"Here's one of your memories back for you. I relive it frequently," Thomas bit out. "Now you can again too." Thomas let his thoughts flow to Simon, advancing on him at the same time, cornering him against a tree.

Simon shook his head, shoving Thomas to the ground and tossing a wary glance to Jack.

"For Arista, 'cause she comes first," Thomas muttered, scrambling to his feet. His initial punch landed squarely on Simon's jaw, the force sending his head backward into the tree with a loud cracking sound. Simon answered with a fist to Thomas's chin, the impact lifting him high, then splaying him out flat on his back.

In the corner of Thomas's mind, voices stirred, Daniel's... and Arista's. *Arista?* Simon crouched, waiting, as Thomas got his feet under him again and rammed into Simon in a bent-over dash, both of them slipping, unable to gain traction in the new fallen snow.

Arista. Terron, Thomas's friend from the Night Dwellers. All the women Simon had undoubtedly tortured on Remeon. And Thomas himself... Somehow representing them felt right as he hammered Simon in back-to-back blows, the revenge freeing for the mere seconds it lasted.

Pleading sounds broke through his manic fog, but they'd not come from the man bearing the brunt of Thomas's fists.

Locked in a choke hold, Simon thrashed and rolled to a stop. Thomas released him, then straddled Simon.

Breathing hard, Simon relented, relaxing underneath Thomas's grip. *No...* Thomas fired off an uppercut, followed by a hook and cross. Still nothing. "Fight! Do it!"

Through the blood trickling down his face and pouring from his split lip, Simon groaned, "No."

Boots came into view, Jack's boots. Following the path upward, Thomas met Jack's hardened gaze. "Enough, son."

Daniel threw himself between Thomas and Simon, sobs racking his body. "Get off him, Thomas. Now," he yelled.

The presence of full awareness stunned him as Thomas stumbled off Simon. "Jack, I...I don't know what happened." Thomas absentmindedly swiped at his own bloody lip. "It hit me from nowhere. I was back on Remeon, cowering before him except, this time I got free. I was free..."

Jack nodded. "I understand, unfortunately all too well. Let it go now, if you can. If you can't, the pain will eat at your insides until you have nothing left."

Thomas mouthed the words that wouldn't come, then turned his gaze to Simon's haunted eyes, where a quiet horror rested on his face. Sinking into the path of Simon's thoughts, witnessing Thomas's own experiences through Simon's eyes shook Thomas yet again, the combination sending a shudder through him, all of it too much to bear with the experiences coursing through him.

Jack pulled Daniel to his chest, murmuring soft words of assurance while the boy cried. Thomas reached down, offering his hand to Simon, not knowing if he wanted Simon to accept it or not. Thomas paused, searching for words. "I need to be done with this. This hatred between us... I can't let it into my life with Arista. It ends now."

Simon nodded.

"I don't want to cause you the same pain you inflicted on me. I did, but I don't anymore. I know now that I couldn't stay true to me if I did."

Simon clasped Thomas's hand. "You didn't. Nowhere close." Scooping up handfuls of snow, Simon grimaced as he scrubbed his face clean.

Thomas followed suit.

Jack's lips thinned to a straight line, looking from Simon to Thomas. "So, can I trust you two to behave now? Or should I put the tree between you?"

"You need to punish them. Both of them," Daniel insisted, his body still heaving from his cries. "That was awful."

"You have a point there, son. What should it be?"

"Same as you give me when I fight."

Jack's eyebrows climbed up his forehead. "A day full of labor... *Hmm.* That can be arranged."

"And make 'em do it together."

Thomas's eyes narrowed. "You fight a lot, do you, Daniel?"

"Not anymore." The boy's eyes glistened before he turned, fisted the tree trunk as best he could and began dragging it in small steps through the snow. "I learned my lesson. Why haven't you? You're older than I am."

Jack canted his head, his gaze speaking for him. With Daniel leading the way, Simon and Thomas on either side of the freshly cut tree, supporting its weight, and Jack guarding their six, the bruised and bloodied crew headed home.

*Love, we're on the way back.*

*Are you all right? Are both of you all right?*

*Can't speak for Simon, but I'm better than I've been for a very long time.*

WHISTERLY AND JACK had been expecting the confrontation at some point, but her breath caught at the intensity of emotion hitting her as it flowed through her from Simon. Better now than during the wedding, she and Jack had reasoned, hoping the timing would align either before or after the main event. Arista locked eyes with her mother, stunned to stillness in the midst of unwrapping an ornament while Rae bounced and sang to an unfamiliar Christmas tune on the record player, blissfully unaware of what was happening in the woods.

Their morning had been productive. Greenery adorned the entrance. Bouquets of pine, magnolia, and eucalyptus, trimmed in holly, welcomed potential visitors, the trail of scent beck-oning them deeper into the den, where tables would replace furniture for the reception after the exchange of vows. The grand entryway with its high beamed ceiling would be where the ceremony took place. Poinsettias, in a combination of white and red, expected to arrive the morning of the wedding, would line the perimeter of the entryway, with final touches of greenery to be added throughout the house the morning of as well.

But the tree, in addition to formal decorations, needed to be finished today. Tomorrow would mark the arrival of many guests, including Thomas's parents, and that meant more entertaining. Jack was a master at these sorts of things.

During her limited time on Earth, Whisterly had marveled at the way he engaged with humans and how they were effort-lessly drawn to him. Whisterly loved Jack, of course, so he had her, but everyone she'd encountered who knew Jack was pulled into the charisma that she'd claimed as hers alone. The command he held over humans wasn't magical but enchanted just the same.

They'd need that and more to pull off the wedding Jack had been planning for decades for his daughter. Hopefully it would live up to her husband's expectations. In his mind, the extrava-gance helped to make up for lost time—all the years away from Remeon and Arista. Why couldn't he see that the genuineness of his love had more than filled the void of his physical pres-ence over the years?

The booming baritone of Jack's voice, mixed with the higher tone of Daniel's, cut into her thoughts. *They're home.* The song rang out clearer as they approached—"O Come All Ye Faithful," one of Jack's favorites. No wonder Daniel knew all the words. Arista had prepared hot chocolate and more coffee, when she'd heard from Thomas they were returning with the tree.

Rae descended from the ladder, where she'd been hanging greens and arranging candles. "Let me give you a hand in the kitchen, Arista."

"Sure. We deserve a break. What will it be? Coffee or hot chocolate?"

"Hot chocolate for me. Thanks."

"Okay. I'm fixing Daniel and Simon a cup also. My guess is Thomas and Papa will want coffee."

"Don't forget me!" Belle yelled, running down the hallway. "I want hot chocolate too."

"How's it going back there?"

Belle had been tasked with bringing Christmas cheer into the bedrooms with strategically placed ornaments and candles. "Almost done. Just need to go outside for Mr. Jack's office."

A blast of wind swept through the kitchen as the back door opened, admitting snow and freezing rain, along with Jack and the boys. Stomping their feet and shedding their outer layers, the small group groaned, making their way into the kitchen, one by one. "Remember what I said," Jack warned, before Daniel popped his head into the kitchen.

"Smells so good in here." Daniel rubbed his hands together, blowing on them for additional warmth.

"Come on in here, by the fire. Rae has drinks set up for everyone."

Whisterly hugged and kissed Jack and Thomas; then she lingered, examining Simon's injuries, before pulling him into a tight embrace.

Belle looked out the window at the tree in the snow. "Good job you guys." Then, letting her gaze rest over the whole group, she rolled her eyes. "Why can't you all behave?"

"You know what? I asked them the very same thing, little bit," Jack added.

Rae glanced up after getting Daniel settled while the entourage entered. Her mouth fell open, her eyes shifting from

Thomas to Simon, trying to put the missing pieces together. "Oh my... What happened?"

Simon took the lead, accepting the forgotten cup of hot chocolate from her hands. "Looks worse than it is. I promise."

Her eyes filled, her fingers sliding gently over the lacerations and bruises coloring his face. "Why?"

Kissing her palm, Simon met her gaze. "It's okay. We're okay... Let it go for now."

Her gaze scanned the room, everyone hesitating in the pause, waiting for Rae to absorb the events that had transpired, those that everyone else had foreknowledge of. Rae gasped and sank into a chair, nodding her agreement.

Filtering in behind Simon, Thomas, Arista, Whisterly, Belle, and Jack each took seats near the fire, solemn, while sounds of Christmas music filled the emptiness.

Jack drank down his coffee and headed for the bar. "Anyone else?"

Thomas answered with a nod and handed over his cup.

"Thomas and Simon didn't plan to fight this morning, but some things can't be healed with words, Rae." Jack passed Thomas his drink and settled in his seat again. "Fighting is a poor answer as well in this case, but I'd wager it did bring a bit of clarity. Simon? Thomas?"

Both gave a silent jog of their heads.

"Can't guarantee it's over. Not by a long shot," Thomas added.

"Maybe not"—Jack sipped his drink—"but, at least now, some healing, a long time coming, can begin, son."

"What's their punishment, Papa? Tell them." Daniel shook his head, a well-placed look of disgust beyond his years plastered on his face. "You're gonna let them off, aren't you?"

"Daniel"—Jack laughed—"when have you known me *not* to follow through with what I've said?"

"I don't think ever."

"Well, I'm not starting now. Finish your drinks, you two. Then bring in the tree, set it up, and alone the both of you will decorate it this year. Daniel will give you direction, if you need it. Have it finished before dinner. Any questions?"

Daniel snickered. "So I'm in charge?"

"I think that about covers it. Yes."

"Wow." Daniel's grin grew. "You all need to get in trouble more often. Can I have more hot chocolate, Miss Whisterly?"

"You bet."

Thomas waved Simon out the door. "Let's get this moving. I don't plan on spending all afternoon tied up with you."

"Same."

With a squeeze of Rae's hand, Simon tromped back into the kitchen.

Dazed, Rae watched the chaos unfold further. "I really don't understand..."

"Jack?" The front door slammed shut.

"Harry?"

"We couldn't wait any longer to see Arista. She was smaller than Harrison here when I saw her last." Harry burst into the den, baby Harry and Maggie in tow. "Oh, good, we haven't missed the tree trimming."

"No, you're right on time. Come on in. I'll reintroduce you."

"Maggie, how about some coffee?" Whisterly asked.

"Sounds lovely. Could I give you a hand with the decorating?"

"Oh! I'd be forever grateful, Maggie. My focus has been a bit off-center this morning."

Maggie's face softened into a smile. "That's what I hear. You don't think our timing was purely coincidental, do you?"

⁓

Simon glared across the tree limbs to Thomas's half, fully decorated and illuminated, then Simon scanned his own in comparison. They'd agreed to split the decorations and stick to their own individual sides of the tree, in a divide, conquer, and not interact strategy for their task completion. Rae joined Belle, the pair of them staring at the uniquely decorated tree.

"It almost looks like two different trees, depending on which side you're looking at," Belle exclaimed.

Rae tilted her head side to side, evaluating. "Pretty, but, yeah, I agree."

Jack sauntered by, passing through from the kitchen. "Gentlemen."

Simon and Thomas joined Jack on either side of him, quiet while he scrutinized the tree.

"I think you've missed the point of the exercise."

"You gave no additional instructions. Just to decorate. We've done that," Thomas explained, with a side glance to Simon.

"Belle, Rae, would you mind lending a hand? Talk them through some changes? They need a vision—a *unified* one." Jack's smile seemed to warm the space between them as he stepped back and looked on for a few more seconds, before being drawn back to Arista's meet-and-greet currently underway in the kitchen.

"What's wrong with you, Thomas? You've done this so many times."

"Yeah, well, never with him, Belle."

"Look, guys," Rae began, "this isn't so hard to fix. The way you've taken the decorations out of the box, they were all segregated, and that's how you hung them on the tree. Mix them up a little. Go on. Thomas, take some from this side and intersperse them over there. Simon, you do the same. Wait, back up. You need to fix the lights first. Be sure to circle the *whole* tree this time, not one half or the other. And for goodness sake," she heaved an exasperated breath, "put decorations down this path here in the center. It looks so isolated, very un-Christmacy."

Thomas slapped his arms to his side. "Looks like we're starting over."

"Great idea, Thomas," Belle added.

An hour later, the four-person team looked on, evaluating the redecorated tree. "Well?" Thomas asked, his eyebrows raised. "What do you think?"

"I like it." Simon nodded.

"You don't get to decide," Thomas shot back, irritation creeping into his voice.

"No decision. Just an opinion. You all know I'm no Christmas expert."

"Much, much better," Rae agreed. "We'll let Belle make the final call, before Jack takes a second look."

"I love it, with one small exception."

Thomas groaned. "What is it?"

"You forgot the most important part." Belle's eyes sparkled, her gaze centering on the very tiptop of the tree. "The star..."

"Oh, right."

"Here it is." Simon pulled out the ornament, climbed the step stool, and attached the star. "Now?" Simon asked, his gaze returning to Belle.

"Perfect. Everyone will love it."

"Not that I haven't thoroughly enjoyed your company, Thomas," Simon said dryly, "but while we're waiting on Jack's final verdict, Rae, there's something I'd like to show you."

"Oh. Sure. Where?"

"Come on. Follow me." Murmuring a spell as they walked through the kitchen, Simon cloaked them from sight. Whisterly's gaze, however, met with Simon's, following the pair before they turned the corner to descend the basement stairs.

"To the basement? Why? Do we need more decorations?"

"No. I wanted to show you this." Simon stood in front of the door, indecision suddenly sweeping through him.

"What's wrong? Open it."

"Well, what's behind that door is big, and it's something my mother and I share. So it's a risk for her too."

"Oh. Sounds like you're afraid I'll expose you or your mother. Is that right?"

"You might want to once you see. Yeah."

"Or you could be confident of your trust in me."

With one hand he palmed the back of his neck then eyed her warily. "A hard concept for me, I'll admit."

"If you're not sure, let's go on back upstairs."

"No, Rae, I want to let you in, so you'll start to know the real me. Well, what little I know myself."

Rae took Simon's hand. "Okay. Ready when you are."

The door creaked out a welcome, swinging wide open at Simon's nudge. "*Igni*," Simon muttered. Fire sparked to life in his hand, and as he tamed the burst of flame, Rae jolted backward, her mouth moving with no words coming out. Dumping the shimmering mass into a glass container, Simon led them to the center of the room. "I know. It's a lot to take in."

Rae nodded mutely, spinning in place for a better view. "So... You perform magic?"

"That's right."

"Your mother too?"

"Yes. And Arista as well."

"Sure. I guess that makes sense... She's your sister. Wait, no, none of this makes any kind of sense."

"There's more."

"More beyond your magical ability?"

Simon squeezed her hand. "Yeah. Rae, I'm not from here."

"You told me that. Said that you were from far away."

Simon focused on the shadows dancing across the walls. "Really, really far away. Another planet."

Rae stumbled backward. But Simon's hands steadied her, keeping her upright. She shook her head, one hand lifting to her mouth in awe. "That day we met, in the tavern, when all the glasses broke... That was your doing then...right?"

"Right. I was angry at how your creep of a boyfriend was treating you. Whisterly is helping me learn better control."

"And the other day in the diner..."

"Yep. That was me too." Simon dragged in a deep breath. "I'm all kinds of messed up. Forgotten some things. Other memories are slowly coming back. Today Thomas reminded me of how horrible I've been in the past. Rae, I'm not a nice person."

"You are from what I've seen. So I'll make up my own mind. But, Simon?" Rae's voice lowered to barely above a whisper. "Are you controlling my feelings for you—hexed me somehow? Is that why I can't stand it when you're gone?"

A grin inched up Simon's face. "No. But I love hearing you say that. I feel the same way, Rae. You're becoming a part of me, in here." Simon thumped his chest, punctuating his words. "And that's not something I know how to conjure."

Rae stepped into the space between his legs, where he sat on a large slab of rock in the center of the basement. "Tell me more."

"You tell me something first... Are you scared of me because of all this—because of what I am?"

"I am."

The hope in Simon's heart dimmed; he hung his head.

"But not because of all this." Rae's gaze darted around the room, lighting for a few seconds here and there, before moving on and finally resting again on Simon. "I'm afraid because of how you make me feel, way before I saw any of this."

"Oh, thank the gods, Rae." Simon rubbed at the tightness in his chest.

"Gods?"

"*Shh.*"

"No. You have to explain all this." Rae's hand cut the air.

"I will in time. First, give me your word you'll keep our secret."

"Sure, you've got it. Is there a secret handshake or what? Please don't tell me you're gonna cast a spell on me."

Simon shook his head and pulled her closer. "Just this." Straightening to his full height, Simon cupped her face, kissing her softly, letting her set the pace, before he deepened the kiss. "*Mmm.*" Simon pulled back. "That told me all I needed to know."

"Did it?" Rae tilted her head.

Simon couldn't stop the grin playing at the corners of his mouth. "It did."

"'Cause I have so many more questions."

Simon patted the rock next to them. "Sit and fire away."

Thomas peered out the window. Light snow had been falling for almost two days, lending the countryside and homes in the area a cozy Christmasy quality. The ride to the train station had been mostly quiet. He preferred it that way, under the circumstances. But before they added his parents to the mix, Thomas had to know, as much as he feared the answer.

Alongside the turmoil going on inside him, he literally felt sick. The next few days would be some of the most important of his life, and besides his parents, and Arista of course, Jack was the next most influential person in Thomas's world. After yesterday, it was possible he'd wrecked the relationship between them that Thomas valued so highly.

They'd been through life and death together. Jack remained his mentor. More than anything Thomas wanted to change the world with the quiet strength that Jack so easily wielded. Thomas watched and learned from the man constantly, but that wasn't enough. Thomas needed Jack's love and respect also, since he'd be marrying his daughter. Had he ruined everything for the few minutes of physical release he'd unleashed on

Simon? He prayed not. But God help him, it had felt good in the moment. "Jack?"

"*Hmm?*"

Thomas glanced outside again, gathering strength and steeling himself, willing an inner peace and calmness inside him that he didn't possess. "How's Simon?"

"Fine, as far as I know. I didn't speak with him before we left."

*Great. Just great...* "Jack, read my thoughts. Will you? I don't know how to say what I need to. Besides that, I feel like I've broken something between us, and I don't know how to fix it."

Jack nodded. "I've been where you are. Except, as you know, Whisterly and I killed Damond, the council member who almost killed us both. I'll admit this scenario is more complicated with the intricacies of the relationships involved." He shook his head and grimaced. "Being so close to your captor, in these unique circumstances, must be a living hell for you, Thomas. I feel horrible putting you through that."

"Yes. That. Exactly." Thomas released a long sigh.

"I'd want to kill Simon if I were you too. Hell, some days, knowing all he's done, I admit I feel that way to a certain degree. But it's also my job to protect him, and long ago I flat-out failed at that, Thomas. I need to do what I can now to fix it. You've had loving parents all your life. Simon hasn't."

"I don't know what to say, Jack, except I haven't been seeing the situation from your eyes."

Jack laid a hand on Thomas's shoulder and squeezed. "I wouldn't expect for you to, son. Honestly I understand where your head's at more than my own some days."

The tension released in Thomas's shoulders, and the unease in the pit of his stomach lightened a bit. "Thank God," he whispered. "I wouldn't change what I've done, but I'd forever regret it if I'd lost you in the process."

Jack threw the gearshift into Park. "Not gonna happen.

You're family, Thomas. I love you, like Arista, Simon, and Daniel. Understand?"

"No... Not really." Thomas added with a shake of his head. "But I'm grateful. I love you too, Jack. You're like a giant to me."

Jack let out a hearty laugh and wrapped Thomas in a hug. "Far from it. I appreciate the sentiment though. Now let's go give your parents a proper welcome. Huh?"

Thomas said a silent prayer as he slid from the car. *Thank God for you, Jack.*

WHISTERLY REFILLED HER CUP, then Simon's, before sitting down to her own breakfast of bacon and eggs. First up, early this morning, had been Jack and Thomas. After they left for the train station, Arista, Daniel, and Belle ate a hurried breakfast before they'd dragged Arista out to play in the snow. She'd groaned under her breath but had given in.

Whisterly didn't need telepathy to interpret the dark circles under her daughter's eyes. With yesterday's upheaval between Simon and Thomas, Arista and Thomas had struggled through a predictably long evening filled with discussion, lasting into the early morning—just like Whisterly and Jack had experienced.

The confrontation between Thomas and Simon wasn't unexpected. But the work in repairing relationships due to the emotions dredged up was far worse than any physical scars. Simon narrowed his eyes, searching Whisterly's face from across the table. "What is it, Mother? Go on. I feel you ready to pounce. Let's get it over with."

"Good instincts." Whisterly inhaled a calming breath. "To be clear and fair to Belle, she didn't have any idea what hit her when I read her thoughts. And I wasn't intending to invade her privacy. Belle's discomfort drew me to her. Such an unusual emotion for her. I wanted to help."

Simon nodded, the clues easily adding up in his head. "I've been found out."

"We promised each other honesty."

"Technically speaking, I wasn't being dishonest. Well, maybe a little during my conversation with Papa." He leaned back in his chair, silently contemplating. "Threats are everywhere. My plan was to assess his knowledge, then come to you both, when I had something to share."

"And?"

"And I'm not quite done yet."

"Fill me in with what you do know."

"He calls himself the Seer, and he's a warlock, as you're aware, giving him a unique perspective on me. So far his methods have proven more successful than yours in bringing back my memories."

Whisterly trapped Simon in her gaze. "This is tricky business to trust to a warlock you don't know. Are the memories true or could the man be planting partial truths in your head? How would you know the difference?"

"Well, we share a bond—information—back and forth. I see his thoughts. He sees mine."

"This man is extremely skilled. He allows you to see what he wants you to see, Simon, just like you've done with others of lesser skill than yourself."

"Possibly true, I guess. But I have increased the speed of my learning."

"Yes, but at what cost?"

Simon spread out his arms, emphatically punctuating the action with his fists. "Look at me. I'm fine."

"Quicker in this case isn't better. An overload of your synaptic patterns could happen quickly and without warning."

"I can't remain in this sinkhole filled with half-truths and limited knowledge. I want more. He offered me a way, and I took it."

"Sounds like the old Simon."

"Maybe all this was for nothing. Maybe I'm destined to be exactly who the seer tells me I am," Simon answered simply.

Whisterly leaned in closer. "You are destined to be who *you* want to be, Simon. Not who your adoptive mother and father pushed you to become through what amounts to abuse and slavery."

"Once I unlock all the doors, the possibilities are endless. Don't you see, Mother?"

Whisterly grabbed Simon's hands and trenched a path deep into his thoughts. Hope, love, desire, shame, remorse... All lived inside him and warred for dominance on Simon's face. "You agreed to trust your father and me. To give us this time. Do you still trust us, or have we lost that to the seer too?" Whisterly held her breath, waiting.

Nowhere within him did she sense the hatred so deeply embedded when Simon had been first captured and brought to the compound. Maybe all of them *had* made an impact... She, Jack, Daniel, Belle, and Rae, who loved him for who he was, not for what they could get from him. Rae's feelings were so transparent. All of them could see what she felt.

"It's because of your love and Rae's, because of your help and Belle's, that I've managed to put myself back together at all."

"Then we can still fix this. I need to hear the spells you've been practicing, word for word. We need to get to the root of their meaning quickly. Grandmother, along with the coven, will lend additional aid. We'll be prepared when he appears next time. When is he expected?"

"I never know. He shows up without warning."

"Promise me—a blood oath this time, Simon. Do not engage the seer without me."

Simon yanked the knife from the sheath at his waist, cut his own palm, Whisterly following suit. Shuddering as they clasped blood-streaked hands together, the magic charged between them. "I promise, Mother. I want to build a better life, for Rae. It's becoming clear that there's no place for her in who I used to be."

Whisterly pressed her forehead to Simon's. "Together."

JAMES LET his mind wander as the countryside whizzed by from his vantage point in the back seat. He reached for Elizabeth's hand, and she squeezed back reassuringly. For the life of him, he didn't understand how two of his children had gotten so wrapped up in Jack and his family, and James had heard all the explanations from his children. What they'd gotten into seemed far from the settled farm life that had served him and his ancestors well for many decades.

Intellectually Thomas and Belle surpassed James now, communicating in ways he'd never dreamed possible. The two of them had seen things, experienced things they'd never dreamed possible, all due to a strange planet that people on Earth had never heard of.

Every step of the way, James and Elizabeth had expanded their beliefs to incorporate the truths that their own children had proven. How had the two of them been chosen as guardians for their gifted offspring, or was it cursed? Honestly he wasn't sure.

The trials of Thomas's polio diagnosis and the months mired in the haze of doctors and hospitals that came afterward... Watching their two youngest children being sucked into a world full of danger, witchcraft, and telepathy... Had they failed as parents completely, or were they uniquely suited to mold their offspring for these...adventures? James couldn't help but chuckle at the Creator's sense of humor. Thankfully only God knew these answers, especially on those days when it seemed as if their two youngest children were lost to him forever.

Some bright spots existed. He and Elizabeth had tried to focus on them in their uncertainty. As husband and wife, their relationship had not only endured but strengthened throughout their children's trials.

Coming out on the other side, their family unit had been more open than James could have believed. Too open maybe? A son and daughter who participated in saving another race... James shuddered as he warmed with pride at the same time. How could he not allow them to fulfill their chosen destinies? He couldn't rule over them, just guide them along the way. And so he and Elizabeth had acquiesced.

Watching the events unfold had been truly magical, as all had aligned exactly as Thomas and Belle had foretold.

James stood in awe of his son, who lived his dream on his own terms with the discipline and love that James had fought to instill, just as he'd always hoped. And Belle, who defined her own path, each day gaining new knowledge which James and Elizabeth couldn't even begin to understand but only stand by, while Belle grew into her potential.

Since finally unveiling the news to Belle of her adoption, they'd only spoken to her a few times over the phone. As if the child had already known, Belle adjusted to the news, taking it in stride, seemingly the information confirming what she'd known all along—she was special, and her parents didn't know how to name, or identify the source of, the unusual talents their daughter possessed.

Maybe society on Earth wasn't ready for his children. Maybe the lessons on Remeon had been the teacher that James and Elizabeth never could have been. Had they made the best decisions for their children, for their future? God, he prayed so.

Elizabeth nodded her head against his, like she'd heard the silent argument in his thoughts, and then kissed his cheek.

Mere coincidence that they were in tune to each other as never before? James didn't believe in coincidence. He kissed her back and then gave his full attention to Jack as they drove closer to his home.

"Thomas here thinks the snow will continue throughout tomorrow. What do think, James?"

James had barely given a thought to the weather as the snow steadily came down, shrouding the landscape in an additional layer of white. Frankly his mind was fully consumed, and the conditions outside didn't make the cut. He rolled down the window, intuitively sniffing the air and lifting his gaze to the cloud cover. "I agree with Thomas. We'll have snow to accent the wedding activities, rain if it warms up."

"So be it," Jack grumbled. "I'd hoped all this would blow over in time for the wedding. "Lots of friends and family traveling for their big day."

"Rain, snow, or sunshine, I can hardly wait for tomorrow," Elizabeth chimed in. "Oh, and, Belle, I've missed her so. She'll be there to greet us, won't she?"

Thomas and Jack exchanged a glance, or more likely a telepathic conversation. Jack nodded. "Sure she will be. But she and Daniel were out playing in the snow this morning and had dragged Arista out with them. They might be quite a sight by now."

"I just wish Mary could be here too."

"How's she feeling Ma?"

"Better, dear. But with her cough lingering still, we all thought it best she stay home and recuperate. She sends her love, heartbroken as she is not to be here."

"We'll find a way to visit with her soon. Nobody knows better than me how awful it is to be sick during family gatherings."

Jack turned down a one-lane road, the pristine white back-drop perfect against the gathering of tall pine trees as they opened to reveal the expanse of Jack's property and his custom-built two-story home. "Jack," Elizabeth gasped, "what a beautiful house. Thomas mentioned you were in construction, but I had no idea."

"Thank you. I continue to customize it as our needs change, but we love it, and thankfully so, my business has expanded beyond my solo capabilities. Harry's deciding if he wants to be a full partner. Simon I hope will join me, and I've asked Thomas as well, although he turned me down."

All eyes flitted to Thomas. "Yes, well, my life will be on Remeon, for the most part, with Arista, as Jack is well aware. I've also formalized my commitment with their military forces for the next five years." With a nod to Jack, he added, "I was grateful to be asked. Someday, with Jack's help, I plan to build my own cabin for Arista and me to settle in while we're on Earth, for whatever length of time that may be."

Jack mussed Thomas's hair. "And you'll have whatever training I can give at that point, assuming I'm still able." Laughing off the conversation, Jack and Thomas got out of the car.

James had studied them while they had danced around the topic though, and it was readily apparent, to this Earthling anyway, that more was being communicated silently between the two of them.

James and Elizabeth climbed from the back seat and reached for their luggage.

"We've got this." Thomas waved his parents toward the house and Belle, who'd run to greet them in snow boots but no coat. Thomas grinned. "She can't wait to see you guys."

But James's gaze lingered on his son. In the stark light of day, the cuts and bruises that littered Thomas's face were glaring and freshly gained. From James's perspective in the back seat, it hadn't been as obvious.

Thomas furrowed his brows under the scrutiny. "What's wrong, Pa?"

"Shouldn't I be asking you that? What happened to your face, son?" Recognition dawned as James and Thomas followed Elizabeth toward the house. "It's just us. Jack won't hear."

"I don't care if he hears, Pa. But can we have this conversation later? Everything is fine." A smile played at his mouth. "Besides, you should see the other guy."

James slung an arm around his son's shoulder. "Sure, it can wait. But I'll ask you again—later." James turned forward just in time to catch Belle as she launched into his arms, a tangle of sloppy boots, wet arms, and legs that latched on tight. "I missed you, Pa," she whispered.

"Missed you too, pumpkin." James fought to keep his tone even. "Shep doesn't know what to do with himself with you two gone. He mopes a good part of the day, unless he's following me around during chores or in the garden."

"Poor thing. I miss him too." Belle slid down and grabbed James by the hand. "Hurry, Pa." Belle kicked up snow and mud, splaying muck while dragging James as he balanced a suitcase in one hand and her in the other.

Thomas kept out of striking zone several paces behind the pair.

Stomping mud and snow off his boots, James crossed the threshold and put his travel bag down, amazed at the simple magnificence of the room he'd entered. Glass accented the log construction, drawing light into the circular entryway which seemed to stretch beyond, spilling paths of brilliance that spun in all directions, leading to various parts of the house. "Why, Jack, I'm fascinated. I can't wait see more."

"You like this area?"

"Sure do. I bet the sun hits just right in here. What a showcase."

"Glad you approve. This is where the actual ceremony will take place tomorrow."

Poinsettias lined the shelves above, sprinkled with holly, magnolia, and eucalyptus; the same pattern repeated below at ground level, except with candles interspersed at regular intervals.

"It will be stunning. Thanks for all your hard work, Jack, preparing for the big day," James said, his gaze still spanning the beam structure above.

"This house was a joy to build, knowing one day I'd bring my family home here."

"From what I've seen, it shows. Your workmanship is top-notch."

"Thank you, James. Whisterly and I are honored to have you here."

"Pa," Daniel yelled, ahead of his arrival. "When are we eating?" His boots, wet with mud and snow, squeaked, smearing a path to a stop. "Oh, hello."

"This is my son Daniel, and Simon is just over there by the banister."

James canted his head. "Nice to meet you both. Thanks for sharing your home with us."

"You look like Thomas," Daniel spouted out, staring intently at James.

"With good reason." James laughed.

"Welcome." Whisterly took Elizabeth's hand, ushering her in. "Thomas will show you to your room. It's just been redone. Hope you'll like it."

Thomas elbowed Daniel. "I'm bunking with you for the night, squirt. Sorry, but that's the way it's got to be."

"Go get cleaned up, Belle and Daniel. Dinner won't be long.

We're eating early today. And, Daniel, get those wet boots off and into the mudroom," Whisterly chided.

"James, join me in a drink? Warm you right up, guaranteed."

"Don't mind if I do."

Simon tilted his head as they passed, lifting his gaze directly to meet James eye to eye. "Mr. Stewart."

Cuts and bruises along Simon's face and arms looked fresh but on their way toward healing. *Saw that one coming. Way to go, son.*

"Join us if you'd like, Thomas and Simon. Harry and Maggie should be here anytime now."

## 23

S imon had grabbed a tumbler of whiskey, participated in Papa's toast to their guests, and at the first opportunity, ducked out of the gathering. "C'mere, Daniel."

Daniel heaved a sigh. "Nah... What'da you want, Simon? It's time to eat, and I'm hungry."

Simon dragged Daniel down the hallway and into his room. "You said you'd answer questions, if I had some."

"Questions 'bout what? Stop messing around. Whisterly's gonna get mad at us."

"About Christmas," Simon answered, lowering his voice.

"Jeez. I thought we'd finished with this."

"As you're well aware, I'm working on gifts, and that's key, right? But—"

"You're making this way too hard, Simon. It's really, really simple."

"I just want to be sure I understand."

"Gifts are because of—the main thing. That's what Papa says anyway. Because of how it makes you feel when you understand what's in the middle of it all." Daniel's grin took over his face. "I LOVE getting gifts."

"The main thing?" Panic sparked in Simon's gut. *Shit.* "Don't think you said anything about this before."

"Sure I did. You musta not been listening." Daniel leaned in and loud-whispered in Simon's ear.

"*Hmm.*"

"Okay, now can we go eat?"

Simon opened the bedroom door. "Scoot, squirt."

"Good job. We're late." Daniel led the way to the sounds of laughter and conversation and slid into his chair without a word.

"Glad you could join us." Whisterly arched her eyebrows in question.

"Daniel never misses a meal," Papa piped up. "If he ever did, I'd think him deathly ill or dead. I was about to send out a search party."

"It was his fault." Daniel hooked his thumb to Simon and all eyes followed.

"Relax. We're all here. That's what matters." Papa bowed his head, everyone else following suit, except for Rae who glanced at Simon wide-eyed with an I-can't-believe-you-left me-alone-with-this-crowd look.

Simon gave her hand a squeeze and whispered, "After the prayer, eat up. I have a plan."

Simon plastered a smile on his face, struggling to remain on the fringe of the conversation as the pleasantries droned on. He teetered the fine line of staying just involved enough to know when to smile or laugh when appropriate but not to get pulled in so deep as to actually have to speak. James and Elizabeth went on more about the house, then raved over Arista's dress. Simon dug into his roasted duck, savoring each bite, chewing slowly to make it last longer, and to give his mouth something to do besides talk.

"What do you think of my new office/ bedroom suite?" Jack asked James. "We rebuilt it from the ground up."

"Oh? That's impressive. You and Harry?" James asked, looking at the two men.

"No... I helped with the framing, like many of Jack's neighbors did after the fire," Harry answered, patting baby Harry, who dozed on his chest. "Jack and Simon did most of the work though. Simon's got a knack for building and woodworking. Takes after his dad."

Simon froze, his mouth and cheeks full of green beans and mashed potatoes while all waited for him to acknowledge Harry's praise. The thick vegetable mixture coated Simon's throat as he gulped water in an attempt to swallow it down faster, his efforts ending in horrified gasps when Simon spewed the mess out of his mouth and across the table, hitting James square in the chest. Simon stifled his cough, trying to keep the remainder down, Rae banging him hard on the back.

Papa threw back his chair. Mother stood with a spell primed on her lips. "I'm fine," Simon gritted out. "Sorry. Uh, sorry, Mr. Stewart."

Everyone froze, hanging on between the seconds of silence that followed, waiting for James's response. "Believe me. Three kids... A farm... Need I say more? I've been covered in much, much worse. No harm done."

*Simon?* Belle began, drawing him into silent conversation.

*I'm okay, Belle.*

*Promise?*

*Promise. I'm gonna get outta here for a while though. Cover for me?*

*Sure. I'll try.*

Mother returned to the table, armed with wet towels, and Harry went around to each guest, decanter in hand, and kept the alcohol refills flowing. As everyone raised their glasses to a toast led by Harry, Simon tugged on Rae's arm, and they disappeared into the kitchen. "Grab your coat and come on." He poured coffee into a thermos, yanked a blanket from the mudroom, and pushed Rae through the back door.

"Wait, Simon. Were you playing around in there?"

"No, Rae. I almost choked, maybe because I wanted outta there so badly."

"Your family isn't so awful."

"Yeah. They have their moments. Enough about them for now, huh? It's all a bit much. How about a few minutes under the stars—just us?"

"Okay. I'm game." Rae tucked her jacket tighter around her neck. "Snow's still coming down. Pretty, but it's starting to pile up. With the sun down now, it'll get cold fast."

"Illumine." Fire licked Simon's fingers and danced erratically with the night breeze.

"Never a dull moment with you, Simon."

A smirk worked his mouth. "I'm just getting started." At the tree line Simon built up his fire. Adding brush and fallen wood, he coaxed the damp pile to burn with a spell. Wrapping the blanket around Rae's shoulders, he guided her to sit between his legs as he leaned against a log. "Ah," Simon sucked in a deep breath. "Feels so good out here. Doesn't it? Have a drink?"

Rae took a generous swallow of coffee, handed it back. "So peaceful and warm, thanks to you."

"I do have an ulterior motive, besides snuggling with you under the moonlight, away from the wedding revelers."

"No... Do tell."

Amusement lifted his lips. "You're gonna be sorry that you made fun of me." Simon stalled, his first surprise materializing as he spoke.

"Look at those stars there. They look different... Simon! Oh, my God... They're moving toward us...getting closer."

Rae's heart galloped underneath Simon's arms crossed over her chest. Closer now, Simon heard their soft whispers through the sway of the wind. "Relax, honey. The little people are welcoming us to their forest."

"The...little people?"

"Or people of the ground...the earth. Close your eyes for a minute. Feel their presence. When you're ready, open them again. You'll see each sparkle of light is a tiny being."

Rae shivered but did as Simon said, seconds later opening her eyes to the twinkling of light showering around her. "Fascinating... I'm mesmerized."

"Good." Simon kissed her cheek and ran his hands up and down her arms until her trembling stopped. "Remember when we talked about Christmas?"

"Yeah, sure. You said this season would be your first time celebrating. Now I understand why."

"Right. Well, Daniel's been teaching me about the holiday, and it's finally all coming together." Simon paused, drinking in her growing smile. "Papa, Mother, Daniel, and Belle, they all want to make me better. I want that for me too and for you, for us, and what we could become together."

"I like the you right here, right now, the way you are," Rae whispered, her eyes meeting his with a halo of brilliance surrounding her.

"I have a long way to go still, and I'm not sure I want to return to Remeon. What I am sure of is making a life with you, once I'm on the other side of this and whole again." Simon adjusted them both, so he could see her face without straining. "From what I could pick up and have heard in discussions with family, especially Daniel, Christmas is a good time for renewal."

Rae tried to blink away tears, but a steady stream fell down her cheeks anyway.

"Don't cry. Maybe I could give you your Christmas gift early? To mark the official beginning of us?" Simon wiped her tears with his thumb. "What do you say?"

"Yes, of course. I love surprises!"

Simon shoved his hand in his pocket and pulled out a wooden box. "Here we go. Open it."

Rae ran her fingers along the etched top of the wooden box. "You carved this?" Simon dipped his chin. "Beautiful."

"Don't think I did them justice," he said, tossing a glance to the sky.

Her shaking fingers lifted the lid on a small emerald ring. "How could you manage this?"

"Working at the tavern and for Papa, saving every penny," Simon explained, a smile tugging his lips. "Do you like it?"

"It's perfect."

Simon took her hands in his. "For the promise of my love, now and in the future, will you wear it?"

Throwing her arms around Simon's neck, she whispered, "Yes."

He slid the ring on her finger. "I'll always be here with you, even if physically I'm not. That's my Christmas promise to you."

"Simon...*shh*. Just kiss me."

His grin grew as she tackled him, and they twisted on the ground, blanketing themselves in fresh snow. "You've got me, honey." Simon marveled, coming up for air from their kiss. Maybe he understood this Christmas thing better than he thought. Daniel had made it crystal clear. *It's all about love, Simon. Once you get that, everything else falls into place.*

What a smart kid...

～

THIS WAS IT. Today was the day Arista would finally become Mrs. Stewart. She dressed slowly, taking her time with the silky garments, evaluating, nodding her approval with each additional layer as she progressed.

The Earth tradition of taking the man's last name still irritated her, but in the end, she'd agreed to abide by the custom while here on Earth, for Thomas. On Remeon, nothing would change. As council chair, her given name assigned at birth would remain. For so many reasons this marriage marked a milestone—becoming one with an Earthling just one of them.

With this wedding, a lifetime of interplanetary travel between Remeon and Earth would commence for the two of them. Family held an important place in their lives, and if Papa and Whisterly choose to make a life on Earth, then Arista would carve out time to visit them and Thomas's family as well.

After a chilly start at their very first meeting, most notably the fight between Papa and James, things had calmed considerably. Their genuine love for their children showed in the unique individuals they had become.

Arista sensed her mother's presence before she arrived at her door, and she couldn't help but compare the vastly different wedding ceremonies. Both surrounded in love, her parents had to wed covertly while the public celebration today was almost overwhelming. What mattered was the love she and Thomas had for each other. Hopefully it was enough to span a lifetime. Enduring a separation similar to her parents'... Well, Arista wasn't sure she possessed that much strength of spirit.

When Arista had initiated the Remeon mating ceremony without Thomas's knowledge, she'd been desperate not to follow in her mother's footsteps but had also known then her life wouldn't be complete without Thomas in it. And thankfully, due to their mating, she'd never be forced to have children as her mother was. That decision could be made when they were both ready.

This past year had been a whirlwind, a mixture of happy and sad. After today, Thomas promised to whisk her away to multiple destinations, scheduled to return in time for Christmas here at her parents' house.

Her heart thumped loudly in her chest. Thoughts of tonight

with Thomas, their trip, their future...so close she could practically taste it. A light knock sounded on the door. "Come in, Mother."

Arista heard her mother's audible gasp when she entered the room. "Sweetheart, you're breathtaking."

"Thanks, but you've seen the dress, Mother."

Whisterly closed the distance between them and stood behind her daughter, together gazing into a full-length mirror. "Yes, but you look different today. Positively glowing."

Arista tilted her head to the side, perusing her form in the mirror. The A-line, V-neck style dress did hug her figure perfectly. Thankfully, additional alterations weren't necessary after the first one. The satin dress—with its ornate beading along the arms, bodice, and the train—accentuated the gown with a sense of timeless elegance. After all the pictures she'd flipped through when shopping, this type of gown had been her number one choice. The small posse with her had agreed —the style suited her completely.

"Come. Sit, little one. I've brought you some wine for a private mother-daughter toast."

"Sounds wonderful."

"To the bride and groom...a long and happy life together."

Arista took a tiny sip. "Tastes wonderful too."

"I just saw Thomas downstairs, and I must say I've never seen him looking more handsome and self-assured."

"I can't wait to see him."

"And despite the snow still piling up, guests have arrived with almost zero no-shows. We have a full house. It's almost time. I wanted to ask if you had any questions. What I mean is, if you'd had a traditional mating on Remeon, your mating night would have been a celebration for a successful pairing and all that those ties could ultimately bring you as the reigning council chair. Here, on Earth, it's much different. You and Thomas will find your way because you love each other and treat each other with respect, but your journey will be unique. Let me know if I can help anytime. There aren't many who have navigated this same path, from Remeon to Earth and back again. So if you have any concerns about—"

"Mother, I know you saw me leaving Thomas's room at his family's farm the morning before we left to return to Remeon, but we didn't—"

"You don't need to tell me this, Arista."

Arista took a large swallow of wine. "As a matter of fact, we've spent many nights together and have never engaged in the human style of coupling. Not that we weren't tempted, for me especially. After coming off my cocktail of meds at home, I practically didn't know myself any longer, but Thomas wanted us to wait until after the wedding. And finally we're here."

Whisterly squeezed her daughter's free hand. "You'll find your way together. You have a healthy helping of all the ingredients you'll need. Take your time with the wine. The guests are lining the entryway as we speak, but they're also enjoying their own prewedding cocktails. Here. I wanted to give you this, for later."

"A letter?"

"I know, little one." Whisterly rolled her eyes. "You've got a whole boxful still to read from me, but this one's different."

"I still plan to work my way through those. Your words over the years, when it was just us, without Papa...I want to take them in slowly."

Whisterly folded Arista into a hug. "There's no rush. Take your time, sweetheart. This particular letter is about love and marriage. I wrote it over the years, adding bits and pieces as I watched you grow. Started it right after you were born on Remeon and finished last night. Not that I'm an expert by any means, but on this special day, I...we...wanted you to have our words of love."

Arista gave her mother a glassy-eyed smile. "Papa?"

"Yes, he added a few lines of his own and signed it as well."

"I definitely can't handle this now. I'll put it in my bag and read it during our trip."

"Great idea. Ready?"

Arista blew out a breath and dabbed at her eyes, then tucked away the letter. "Almost."

Fifteen minutes later, hiking her dress up around her knees, Arista slid into her boots and out into the twilight of the snowy evening, carrying her shoes. Mother offered a steadying hand, while they walked from the back door around to the front. "Your father's waiting for you by the entrance."

Arista felt like a baton being passed as she went from her mother's hand to her father's, with a kiss on the cheek from Mother. Papa kissed Whisterly before she slid inside, his gaze still lingering on where she'd been after she'd disappeared from their sight.

"Your mother made me the happiest man across the galaxies when she married me. I wish the same for you and Thomas. But you were ours first. You'll always have a place to come home to, here." Papa leaned in to graze her cheek.

Arista's vision blurred as her eyes filled with tears.

*No, no. None of that. I can't betray my harsh marine persona.*

Arista brushed a tear off his cheek. *You've never had me fooled with that, Papa, and I doubt you've fooled anyone in there either.*

*Ready, little one? 'Cause we can still duck out the back, if you'd rather.* His eyes glistened with the laughter crinkling his eyes. *Just say the word.*

*No, no chance. But thanks for asking. Let's go, Papa.*

He kissed the back of her hand, then placed her fingers in the crook of his arm. *As you wish.*

Arista stepped into the entry, and her breath caught. The room was completely ablaze with candles, high above her head, nestled by the windows, and surrounded in holly and magnolia branches. Beyond, next to the minister and Thomas, a full array of candles lit a candelabra. Ahead, Thomas waited for her, a broad smile growing on his face with each additional step she took. James, acting as best man, stood stoically by his son. After all they'd been through as a family, his father's gaze rested proudly on Thomas, with no words, James's face saying it all. No telepathy needed.

The warmth of Papa's presence left her as Thomas's hand covered hers. "Thomas?"

His gaze drank her in slowly, tracing her body from head to toe. "You're drop-dead gorgeous, love. Ready?"

She nodded, her gaze pinned to his. "Let's do this."

THOMAS DOWNED another glass of wine. How many had that been? He'd lost count hours ago. The snow piled up in drifts now, and he cast a worried glance at the remaining guests. Harry had taken Thomas's parents to town hours ago thankfully. Staying in town tonight, close to the train station hopefully, they'd be on their way still, in the morning. Even though his time with them had been cut short, Thomas had felt their love and support. His father standing up for Thomas at his wedding would be a memory he'd cherish for the rest of his life.

Scrubbing his hand down his face, Thomas watched Jack approach, concern creasing the man's forehead. "Yeah. I know what you're about to say, and I'm not even reading your thoughts."

"And I know what you're thinking. Believe me. I'd rather you not have to stay the night either. But it's dangerous out there. After Harry took your parents into town, he encouraged some of the guests who lived farther away to spend the night at his house. The ones who haven't left yet, I've invited to stay here. Hopefully tomorrow will bring some clearing. Until then, you and Arista need to stay put. Your getaway will still be there tomorrow or the next day."

"Jack...Jack. I agree. You can stop the sales pitch. We'll stay. It sounds...awesome."

A hearty laugh escaped Jack's mouth as he slapped Thomas hard on the shoulder, eyeing his empty wine glass. "Glad you're listening to reason, son."

"I haven't had *that* much to drink." Jack's eyebrows arched. "Jack, it's not that I'm ungrateful. This day has been wonderful, thanks to you and Whisterly. We'll never forget it."

"You're welcome. Happy we could have everyone here. Speaking of my lovely wife, she and Belle are out in my office, your guest suite for the night. I think you'll like what they've done with the place. Why don't you grab Arista and go take a look?"

"What? I'd assumed it would be maxed up with out-of-town guests."

Jack shook his head. "I've taken your bags out there. You're all set."

Thomas froze, racking his brain for any other feasible option. Right about now, a tent in the forest sounded pretty good.

"Well? Go on. Get outta here."

*Come here, love.*

Watching Arista glide toward him made Thomas's heart melt for her all over again.

Her smile fell, when he and Jack quieted at her approach. "What is it? What's wrong?"

"We're staying the night here," Thomas answered with a fake cheerfulness he couldn't hide.

"Oh." Arista's gaze batted from Thomas to Jack. She took Thomas's hand. "Makes sense, I guess." Arista pasted a smile on her face, leaning into his side. "We'll make the best of it."

"That's my girl." Jack kissed Arista on the forehead. "I'm going to check on accommodations for everyone else."

"Papa? Thanks for everything."

"You bet."

"Not how I pictured this night ending, love."

"The night is just beginning, Thomas," she whispered. "Now get me out of here."

Thomas blinked slow. "You won't have to tell me twice." Grasping her hand, they headed for the back door. Ahead, through the dark, snowy December night, a soft light beckoned from the office. "Wait. We forgot your coat...I'll go get it."

"No. I don't need it. It's a short walk, and besides, I've got you."

Thomas's mouth ticked up, and he drew her closer. The brick walkway had been recently shoveled by some kind soul. "Thank you, Jesus, for whoever did this," Thomas mumbled, bending his knees and scooping Arista into his arms, "but I'm still gonna carry you. Hold on tight."

Arista giggled. Fresh snow peppered her hair, face, and mouth, and Thomas couldn't stop himself from kissing the smile on her lips. Balanced in his arms, Arista turned the knob, opening up their room for the night. "Over our first threshold as husband and wife," Thomas announced, giving her another kiss before stepping fully into the room.

"Oh, my goodness." Arista slid from Thomas's arms. "Mother? Belle?"

"Sorry, honey, we're on the way out."

"It's beautiful." Arista spun in place, her mouth falling open.

She was spot-on. Poinsettias and sprigs of holly decorated the entire first floor, and off to the side, a tiny Christmas tree topped a table fully laden with wine, cheese, and fruit. A fire crackled in the stone fireplace, inviting flames licking away the chill in the room. "Thank you both."

"We had fun doing it. Belle is up to any challenge, I've found."

Belle curtsied, then hugged Thomas around the waist. "I got to stay up real late tonight, but I'm getting a little tired now." She yawned and headed for the door.

"Judging from your dry shoes, I guess Simon finished shoveling the walkway?" Whisterly asked.

Thomas and Arista shared a glance. "Uh, yeah. He did." Thomas leaned into Whisterly's embrace. "Please thank him for us."

"I will." Whisterly turned toward her daughter. "Goodnight, little one, beautiful bride."

Thomas watched their emotional embrace, imagining the thoughts the pair were sharing at that moment, and seconds later they were finally blissfully alone.

"I wanted tonight to be perfect for you, Arista."

"And it is. Just look around you."

Thomas shook his head and chuckled. "I have a bad habit sometimes of focusing on the wrong things." He reached out a hand and pulled Arista to him. "This is all really nice. It is... But I've got *perfect* right in front of me. Nothing else really matters." Thomas stroked Arista's cheek and brushed his lips with hers. Wrapping her in the folds of his arms, he molded her body to his. Their mouths met again as Thomas dug his fingers into her hair, pinning her in place.

Arista let off a soft moan, her fingertips sliding down Thomas's arm, then to his chest, raising chills on him having nothing to do with the cold. Her fingers worked the buttons on his shirt, and his hand traveled to her back. "Damn these buttons, Arista."

"You gonna let those tiny things get in our way?"

"Neither wild horses, dogs, witches"—he grinned against her mouth—"or warlocks could keep me away. So certainly not buttons. We've waited long enough."

Arista gave Thomas her back, allowing him better access, while she poured them both a drink. "How's it going back there?"

"I. Am. Done," he announced, a note of pride ringing through his voice. Her wedding gown cascaded down her shoulders and pooled at her feet. "More layers. Of course. I get it now. It's like an endurance test." Trailing light kisses down her neck, he murmured, "Turn around, love. Let me see you while I get rid of these last pieces of fabric between us."

Outside, the wind whistled through the trees, snatching Thomas's attention as she complied, swiveling, handing him his drink. At the same moment, something warm and fuzzy slithered against his leg. "Arista, what the hell is that?"

"Shadow!" Arista bent down to pick up the cat.

"Great."

"She must have followed Belle out here."

"Uh-huh." Thomas took a large swallow of wine. "Wasn't that cat the cause of this place going up in smoke?"

"Now that you mention it, I think so..."

Thomas grabbed Shadow from Arista's arms and headed for the door.

"What are you doing?"

"Taking her to the house."

Returning in under a minute, Thomas pushed through the door and stopped, stuck in place by the goddess in front of him. He swallowed hard, pushed his weight against the door, and twisted the lock. "God, Arista..." Thomas fought for a breath. "I think I'm having a heart attack."

"No more layers."

In the glow of fire and flickering candlelight, she waited for him by the fireplace, with not a stitch on. Thomas quickly shed the shirt hanging open on his shoulders, yanked his belt free, kicked off his shoes, and, hopping on one foot, tugged at his pant leg, falling in the process. "Gods, Thomas, we've gotten this far. Don't you dare hurt yourself."

He closed the distance between them and swept her up in his arms. "Not a chance." He sighed, pressing her body against his. A tiny gasp left her lips before Thomas's mouth collided with hers, and they sank to the blankets beneath them. He eased back, his thumb caressing her cheek. "You feel so good, love. It's like I'm in a dream—you're finally all mine."

"No more waiting."

Thomas shuddered and threaded his fingers with hers. "No. Not one more second," he gritted out.

## 24

"*T*here you are, Jack." Harry closed the distance to his friend. "I was hoping you hadn't turned in yet. After all, big day...long night...a storm to cap off the fun."

"Bed? I can't sleep. My house is filled with wedding guests, my daughter and son-in-law, who don't want to be here out in my office turned bridal suite, and we're in the middle of the first major snowstorm of the season." Jack poured himself a drink. "Join me?"

Harry held up his coffee cup. "Whisterly made a fresh pot not too long ago. When I started carting guests back and forth, I switched over. Seemed like the smart thing to do."

"Agreed. Me—I'm sticking to the hard stuff. Cheers." Jack took a large swallow. "Listen, Harry. Thanks again for tonight. I don't think we could have housed everybody here and given Arista and Thomas some privacy. Bad enough that their trip's been delayed."

"Happy to do it. More important, Maggie is happy to do it. I married up, no doubt about it."

Jack slapped Harry on the back. "You're both a godsend."

"And you have a married daughter. It's hard to comprehend.

Watching you and Arista walk down that aisle today had my stomach tied up in knots. Congrats again, brother."

Jack gave a humorless chuckle. "I had next to nothing to do with how she's turned out. Whisterly raised her. I haven't been actively in her life for long at all."

"Oh, but Jack, you *have* made a real difference. Let's see. Arista is born of the true love you share with Whisterly. You were instrumental in bringing her mother back to life, then mentored her husband, after bonding over shared experiences on Remeon. Furthermore, you dug deep and found a place in her life and in her heart by being the father she'd always wanted and needed. Have I left anything out?"

"Being here today, walking her down that aisle was everything, Harry—a dream come true to have a place in her life and Simon's."

Harry heard the love flow through Jack's tone as he spoke. "Both of your kids have come so far. Simon is like a different person altogether from when he arrived."

The typical confidence that threaded Jack's voice was absent as he answered. "I'm not getting my hopes up yet. Things could still go to hell, just like that." Jack snapped his fingers and threw back the rest of his drink. "I know that better than anyone else."

"Damn, Jack... Well, you and your kids impress me. At least I have a road map to follow. Huh?"

"Don't sell yourself short, Harry. You're the finest man I know." Jack dipped his chin and swallowed, his face straining to keep control. "I hate to break it to you. There's no road map. Worse—no manual. Just you and your child making your way. You'll do just fine." Jack continued, a hint of laughter in his eyes, "if you listen to Maggie."

"I fully intend to," Harry said through a grin. "This may not be the right time, with everything going on, but I brought your Christmas gift, thought maybe we could exchange before the holiday this year. You'll have Arista and Thomas back from their trip, Simon and probably Rae, along with Daniel and Belle as well, right? You and me aren't just you and me anymore."

"You got that right." Jack cleared his throat, failing to hide the emotion in his voice. "Belle, Thomas, and Arista will visit Elizabeth and James right after Christmas through the New Year. Afterward, Arista and Thomas have responsibilities to return to on Remeon. We'll see about Belle. We'd love to have her back. She understands Simon better than any of us. But to your question, sure, I put your gift under the tree yesterday. And strangely enough we have a few moments of quiet right now."

"Let's plan our own party for New Year's, Jack, you and me and whatever kids are around."

"Sounds good."

Harry handed Jack a beautifully wrapped gift with a tiny bell attached. "What the—"

"Yeah, my wrapping has gotten an upgrade. Bless my wife."

Jack tore through the paper, setting the bell aside. "Ah, *The Wayward Bus*. I've heard some mixed commentary on this, sparked my interest in it for sure. I take it you've read it?"

Harry nodded. "Yes, and I was enthralled, not by an engaging plot but the people and how well Steinbeck brought his characters to life. A little off-color in spots, but you're a people person, Jack. Innately you know what makes them tick. I think you'll enjoy it."

"Thanks, Harry. Can't wait to dig in."

Jack rummaged through the gifts under the tree, looking for Harry's. "Should be right on top... Here it is. Merry Christmas, Harry."

Harry held up the package, admiring the rich red paper, tied perfectly with a tartan bow. "I'd give you shit for Whisterly wrapping my gift, but I know it was you, Jack. Down to the last detail, I can tell."

"Truth." Jack busied himself tying the small bell to the tree while Harry ripped the book free.

"I've heard of this one. Kingsblood Royal... Quite controversial from what I understand."

"Yes, but timely, given what we fought for in the war. I think you'll find it interesting and disturbing. As it should be for everyone."

"Thanks, Jack. I look forward to it."

The two collided in a hug. "Don't think this gets you out of a gathering sometime during the holiday," Jack warned, releasing Harry from his embrace.

"I wouldn't dream of it, brother from another mother. New Year's. Remember?"

"Okay. I'll hold you to it then."

Harry emptied his coffee cup." Well, time for me to find my way back to home base, so you can get some shut-eye."

"I hate sending you off in the night with only coffee, after all you've done today, all your help."

"You're not, Jack. I'm a rich, rich man, and you're a large part of that." Harry waved his book in the air as thanks and watched Jack close his door on the snowy early morning. Howling winds layered the old snow with the new, creating a pristine landscape to sink his boots into.

Tucking his coat tighter against the cold, Harry shuddered, turned over the ignition, and headed for home. As the car slowly puttered, weaving a path through the ice and snow-covered twists and turns of the familiar road, a sigh of relief washed over him. *All safe and accounted for,* Harry muttered, knowing Jack would remember the frequently used assurance from their days of service together.

*And by God's grace we'll weather the night,* Jack replied.

How many nights had that been their only prayer, ass deep

in mud, ducking for cover, half frozen in a foxhole? Too many to count. That's for damn sure. Harry's tires sprayed the road with dirty snow and rock, pulling his concentration back to his ride. Suddenly he couldn't wait to get home to Maggie, baby Harry, and his houseful of displaced company. Today had been the best of days, full of love and celebration, and he wanted to revel in it still, for the only certainty—tomorrow would bring change.

ARISTA DOZED to the steady rhythm of the train, the radiant heat from the sun filling her with pleasing warmth. Thomas's hand closed around hers. "Not long now. Almost home, love."

"*Mmm.* It's been such a wonderful trip. I don't want it to end. I just need a few more minutes..."

"You said that to me last night, and you woke up for me then."

Arista blinked her eyes open, a smile spreading on her face, heat inching up her neck. "You're incorrigible."

Thomas kissed her softly. "Guilty as charged," he whispered against her mouth.

Their whirlwind honeymoon to the West Coast had lasted for seven glorious days, cut short by a two-day weather delay, but, other than that...perfection. Humans got this right, or maybe just her human. Disappearing, losing themselves in each other, had been luxurious and decadent, strange by the standards of her structured life on Remeon, necessitated by her role as council chair. Times like these...she definitely needed more often.

The breathtaking expanse of miles and miles of rocky beaches they'd walked, relaxing in the sun and sand, the acres of forests they'd explored, full of the magnificent regal trees which seemed to carry centuries-old stories within their rings, and the nights when they would surrender to each other. She had no words for the intensity with which humans loved each other and expressed emotion so completely. In Remeonite culture, what she and Thomas had didn't exist, except for Papa and Mother. Maybe it had long ago, before PR 251 had changed the landscape of their race. Maybe, going forward, they could find what they'd lost so long ago as a civilization torn apart in their struggle to survive.

Arista eased herself from Thomas's kiss, her finger drifting down his cheek. "Remember. You promised every year we'd return for a vacation here on Earth. I love surprises, so don't tell me where."

"Yes, ma'am." His eyes shone through a lopsided grin. "I'd love nothing better."

Arista straightened in her seat as they rolled into the train station. Papa would be picking them up, and thankfully today the weather appeared to be cooperating. When they disembarked, Papa was there, waiting for them.

He wrapped her in a hug. "We missed you, little one. How was your trip?"

"Wonderful. I loved every minute."

Papa smiled, reaching out a hand to Thomas. "Welcome home, son."

For Papa, of course, their home was here, in Provo. For Thomas and Arista, *home* was here and in Virginia on Thomas's family's farm and lastly on Remeon. It would take some getting used to.

"I'm glad to hear it," Papa said, returning his attention to Arista. "Let's get you all outta here. Whisterly's made lunch, and Daniel and Belle are beside themselves waiting for you both to return."

Strands of garland and wreaths adorned the storefronts, streetlamps lit early apparently for the happy shoppers clogging the streets—so much to do and see among these Earthlings. Intricately decorated Christmas trees caught Arista's eye as they wove in and out of the maze of people, working their way to the car. The revelers hurried in the chill, pristinely wrapped parcels tucked away underneath their arms. If Arista had her way, they'd linger a little longer.

"With Christmas less than a week away, Belle and Daniel are a bundle of energy," Jack continued. "Nothing slows them down. Even Simon can't keep up with them."

"What is that glorious aroma?"

"Roasted chestnuts," Thomas mouthed against her ear. "They're scrumptious." *Like you. We can come back into town later, love. Jack obviously wants to head home.*

*That would be agreeable.* "Aren't the decorations beautiful, Papa?"

"What?" Papa and Thomas wrestled the bags into the trunk of the car. "Oh, yes...yes." he agreed, slamming the trunk shut. "Would you like to look around some?"

"No. Don't worry about it. Thomas and I will come back today or tomorrow."

"I'm sorry. Something's distracting me." Papa gave her a sidelong glance as he pulled out onto the road and headed for home. "And I can't put my finger on it. Like I'm forgetting something important. I thought picking you up would put the nagging feeling to rest, but, you're here and fine, and it hasn't passed."

Arista met his gaze, surprised to find his eyes swimming with worry. His brows furrowed in an uncharacteristic frown, his concentration turned back to the road. Arista dipped into his thoughts, her way to let him know she was there with him in whatever *this* was. Papa squeezed her hand, and they drove on in the quiet of their subdued thoughts.

When they arrived at the house, Thomas carried their bags up to Arista's room. Feet hit the floor in another part of the house, rapidly picking up speed as they neared. "*Arrrisssttta...*" Daniel called, still not in view. "You're home!"

Arista sensed Papa's tension easing, just a little, as he arranged his mouth into a smile—a show for Daniel. When her mother came in close on Daniel's heels, and Arista slid into her thoughts, it was apparent—the unease wasn't forgetfulness, but something of a much higher significance.

The three of them shared a glance, bonded by an unusual fear, one that they couldn't name and hadn't experienced before. "Let's get Daniel some food. He's been waiting so long. Then, Arista, we'll contact the coven together."

Arista answered with a tight nod. "Okay. But where are Belle and Simon?"

"I'm not sure. They're masked to me."

Papa lifted his head. "What? How could that be?" He searched Whisterly's face, and she blinked back tears. "You two go on downstairs. I'll find them. Thomas can see Daniel gets something to eat."

Arista spun on her heels, Thomas at her back. "I sense it now too. The bond Simon and I had is active again, but it's changed, different somehow. I don't know what it means exactly though."

"Go, love. I'll take care of Daniel."

Silence hung in the air in the seconds it took for Papa to disappear and return, one shotgun slung over his shoulder, another in his arms. His expression darkened, as he paused, grazed Mother's cheek with a kiss and a whispered word. She squeezed Papa's hand and turned toward the basement.

HARRY JUMPED in his car and headed for Jack's. Whatever had his friend so messed up he couldn't communicate meant that Jack needed help. Shifting into fourth gear, Harry tightened his grip on the wheel, hugging the twists and turns in the road, then loosening up on the straight away. Dread coiled in his gut. He hadn't felt like this since the war.

Maggie squeezed his hand. They'd already agreed that she'd take Daniel home with her. When she'd asked about Belle, Harry had shaken his head, knowing intuitively that the young girl had an important part to play in what was unfolding here, now.

BELLE CROUCHED LOW, Simon in her view, the scene reminiscent of a few weeks ago when she'd encouraged him to confide in Whisterly and Jack. She tried again to reach Whisterly, but the strange crackling in the air must have blocked her attempts. Her gaze lifted, focusing on the odd disturbance, a magical presence, Belle was all but certain. The man who appeared like a giant hovered over Simon, his pain palpable as it thundered back through Belle from her connection to Simon.

The seer had surprised them on the way back to the house to meet Thomas and Arista. With the little time until they were both discovered, Simon had used his power to shield Belle, but in the process, the spell seemed to limit her own abilities as well. While watching and listening, Belle focused on what she could do.

Digging her fingers into the ground, she let her eyelids fall shut, summoning the essence and power from deep inside the Earth's core. Sparks of light peppered the air, surrounding her. They were here too now—the little people—working to free her, answering her call. The ground shook, roiling under her command.

She directed her gaze to Simon, where he appeared to be locked in a battle with the seer. A deep blue aura flashed, announcing Simon's attack. Spontaneously Belle's aura shone a vibrant yellow, joining with his.

She'd broken free.

Her fingers blurred, weaving him into the pulsing energy of the forest and solidifying him into the lives of those who dwelled here.

*Grandmother? Simon's blood oath, I feel it.*

*Go to him now, child. There's very little time.*

*What can we do?*

*Our power is with you, but Kix has gained the strength of his own coven as well. Over a period of time, weeks most likely, they have conjured a spell that we cannot reverse without intense study and a significant amount of time. We're working to repair the damage already done, though Simon appears to be doing the Seer's biding, against us, unaware of the destruction he's wreaking on himself. Stop him. Now. Whatever the cost. If you don't get to him, we can't save him. Not in this world. Not in the next.*

"Hurry, Arista. We must go." Murmuring a spell, their apparitions thrust forward, thrown into the midst of Simon, Belle, and Kix. The magical forces clashed in the sky as they approached.

"Mother, what can we do?"

"Quickly. Join our power with his. But first we must redirect it."

"That's it, Simon. Embrace it!" the Seer demanded. "You're finally using all that magical ability you were blessed with at birth."

Simon winced at the noise rising in his thoughts. This time

not only the Seer accessed him directly. The promise he'd made to his mother, sealed in blood magic, drew her to him, but also Belle, Arista, the coven, even Papa and Thomas. *Good. They would witness the final steps of Simon's success as he took the strides alone.*

"Remember the direction when we'd set out? Your independence?" The Seer's grin claimed his face. "Just one more word and you'll be free, a warlock, separate from the witches who pursue you as their own."

The air crackled, alive with magic as Simon sped his way through the grimoire, his hand motions gliding him backward, forward, searching for the incantations needed to finalize his path. What he and the Seer had begun, Simon would end today. He delved deep, accessing pieces of the great tome closed to him until just now. Almost there...

Power trembled at his fingertips, unfurling before him as never before. Magic thrummed, sending a quiver through his veins.

He uttered the words to conjure the spell, freeing energy to deal with the overabundance of telepathy fighting for control of his consciousness.

*Mother...*

*Simon, only together can we exist. Apart from our source, we're nothing. You sense it. Reach for it now, before it's too late.*

*No. This was wrong. All wrong.* Through the hazy murkiness of his thoughts, brilliance shone. Belle's light surrounded her, Mother, and Arista, their auras culminating into one blinding force. Lastly, the coven charged forth as Simon's essence poured out in a streaming flame, armed with the might of the generations of witches who'd come before him.

Simon stumbled, his breath catching in his throat. Coils of enchantment seized him, and he shivered, writhing under their force, as they cut at the source of Simon's magical essence. How could he have been so blind to the Seer's ultimate plan—to rob

Simon of his heritage, of him at his core. The aim of the plan evident only now at its fruition.

"My final gift to you, Simon. Now, because I sense our darkest end is upon both of us. You played well, right into my hands. But, before you wither away, go with the knowledge of what you truly are. Still are, despite your playtime among the humans."

A pain ruptured inside, searing a path through his entrails and up into his throat. Simon fell to his knees, gasping for breath. Memories assaulted him, their tiny barbs sinking into him all at once: The totality of Janus's repetitive abuse, Simon's rise to power, the hatred he spewed, the women he'd attacked, the people he'd crushed, killed along the way...for fun...for pleasure. All in the name of dominion. To gain their surrender or—just as easily—their death. He lifted his gaze. The Seer wrestled with Simon's cursed ball of light. The Seer wouldn't live. At least there was that.

Memories flickered in and out of Simon's vision, each one agonizing, as he watched how he'd become the man he was—a sick monster. The weight of his thoughts tore a path through his head, coming faster and faster. He groaned, cradling his head, bending over, then collapsing. At this pace he had no way to internalize all of them.

From different directions, Papa, Mother, and Arista rushed for him—such goodness amid his torment. No wonder his parents had shielded him from the animal he'd become. Across the distance, Papa's gaze met his, filled with so much grief and pain. Well, it would finally end. Nestled in Papa's oasis, Simon had found love, for a time, and at least he'd leave with that intact.

Mother's voice seeped into his thoughts. *Fight, Simon!*

Sweat poured down Simon's face, and pain consumed his ragged breaths, but the agony wore on. His magic...the enchantment...the grimoire... slowly they drifted from him, piece by piece, like leaves scattering in the wind.

The Seer's chuckle rattled through Simon's body. *You've torn yourself from the grimoire, Simon, a fate only accomplished by the coven or the warlock himself. The task took us weeks to assimilate, to culminate toward this end, but my guidance got you there. My revenge is almost complete. Your magical being no longer has a home. Swallow that down as you end your meager existence within the realms of chaos of the universe.*

*Gods... I deserve it. We almost made it Rae... And I'll never get to say I'm sorry.*

*Seems fitting, right, Simon? One wretched existence for another? Mine...yours...*

Small hands ran down the length of his arms and across his chest as the world shifted in slow motion. *Belle...* When Thomas's worried face appeared, Belle swayed the ground beneath them, sending her brother backward. *Belle, beautiful Belle. I'll miss you. You believed in me.*

*Hang on, Simon. I'm not done with you yet.*

Sparks of light littered the sky. As far as Simon could see, his vision filled with the little people. Belle worked at a furious pace, at something...her mouth moving and wet earth dribbling from between her fingertips. The ground rumbled beneath him once more as she smeared the mess on Simon's face, tore his shirt, and covered his chest also. Through it all, she chanted.

*This isn't so bad a way to go, Belle.* The lights drew nearer, the tiny voices breaking the barrier to his thoughts.

*I'm with you, Simon. You feel them?* Belle gazed deeply into Simon's eyes. *The little people are with you also.*

He nodded. *Belle...* But words left him speechless. As radiance overcame his torment, he met their light. *Where am I?*

Papa skidded to his knees, scooping up Simon. "Stay with us, son."

*Thank you... Papa... I never deserved... you... or Mother...*

Papa pressed a kiss to Simon's forehead, just before his eyelids drifted shut.

A tear slid down Belle's cheek. *We did it, Simon. They have you now.*

A final breath shuddered through him.

AN ICY MANIACAL hatred had transformed Kix's features. Whisterly's vision darkened as something slashed inside her, a ripping apart that felt like her insides had spilled free. She wasn't close enough... Shots rang out... She lurched forward... One, two, three... Then three more answered, fired off in quick succession. Harry charged toward Kix's toppled body while Jack cradled their son in his arms.

*Simon...*

"Arista, almost there."

"Mother...Mother!" Arista grabbed Whisterly and wheeled her about, coming face-to-face with her mother's tear-rimmed eyes. "He's gone."

Whisterly closed the distance to Jack; together on their knees, they bundled the limp mass of Simon's body between them.

Whisterly met Jack's eyes, dark raging storms of blue. "I've failed, baby," he gritted out, tears sliding down his cheeks, "worse than I've ever failed before, and he paid the price."

"No, Jack, I should have seen Kix's plan. But I missed it... Gods, how did I miss it?" she sobbed. Jack linked his consciousness to hers while Arista, Thomas, Belle, and Harry gathered around them and joined in the bond.

---

## 25

*J*ack made his way through the mass of coven members and up the basement stairs, Stephen and Belle close on his heels. "Jack, wait."

He sucked in a breath, attempting to rein in the emotion that had moved in, taking up residence in his soul, leaving him with little control in the haze of his thoughts. "Yes?"

"Would you like some company?" Stephen wouldn't meet his gaze.

*Stephen...* Jack needed to remember to call Thomas *Stephen* on Remeon. But simple stuff like that escaped him right now. Didn't seem important, even though he was here on planet. Jack should say something important and life defining. Offer a bit of wisdom or solace. Trouble was, he was fresh out.

The coven's recognition of Simon's life didn't touch on the person Simon truly was—who he'd become. Jack had gained no comfort whatsoever from the event. In fact, he had more anger than anything else, and his family didn't deserve that. "No. I'd prefer to be alone. Thanks for the offer though."

"Sure. I'll report back for duty until we leave for Earth

tomorrow. Arista and I, and Belle of course, would still like to be with you for Christmas. If you want."

"Christmas...oh. I'd almost forgotten. Sure," Jack responded absentmindedly. Dark thoughts sent him spiraling to places he'd thought he'd left behind for good. Whisterly and his children had brought him back from the edge of his madness, decades old. That sickness had eaten at him for so long he'd surrendered to its presence, until love had rescued him from the mess he'd mired himself into. Now he found himself haunted, pressed into that cage again.

"Well, Whisterly and Arista will be with the coven for a while longer." Stephen lowered his gaze. "I'm available anytime, if you need anything at all."

"Thanks, son," Jack said, forcing a warmth into his voice he didn't feel. "Go. Do what you need to do. Please." Jack turned and headed for the quiet of his quarters. Maybe he could rest until he and Whisterly met with Vinique later. *Rest...* Who was he kidding?

He hadn't truly slept since before Simon died. Wasn't sure he ever would again with the nightmares of his failure visiting him every night. Jack shuffled to their window, which spanned the length of the room and overlooked the passersby below.

A bright future awaited the people of Remeon. Much better than the decades that had come before, marred with sickness and ongoing conflict with the Night Dwellers. The differences today were nothing less than remarkable. Under Arista's and Vinique's recent leadership, the Night Dwellers had been reintegrated with the Day Watchers. Testing for PR 251 came first, then administration of the cure of course. But the process was proceeding well.

Generations of families lost to each other during the separation that had divided the society into the two factions were coming together again—in most cases a joyful reunion. Those directly under Simon's leadership, however, were imprisoned, some of them still awaiting trial, as it should be, until their actions could be evaluated through the process of the justice system.

A knock sounded. Jack growled low in his throat. What did he need to say to Stephen to get through to him? The door whooshed open. "Vinique?" Jack glanced at the appointment time on the wall. No, he wasn't late.

"Jack, may I come in?"

"Sure. Next to no company, my preference right now," he stung her with a glare; "I guess you'd be top of the list of who I'd like to see...sometime other than now." Despite himself, Jack couldn't help the smile lifting the edges of his mouth.

"Jack, I've missed your sarcasm and our talks."

"Me too," Jack admitted. Vinique was like a little sister to him. They'd weathered so many trials together. "What did I do to earn this extra visit? Our meeting with you isn't for a while yet."

"Can't I just come to see you because I'm worried about you?"

Jack's forehead folded into straight lines. "Certainly. Although I don't think that's the case. And, oddly, you've blocked your thoughts from me. So I'd wager this is a much bigger conversation we're about to have. Should Whisterly be here?"

Vinique shook her head. "May I?" she asked, gesturing toward the bar. Jack inclined his head. "I wanted to speak with you separately first. Momentarily you'll understand why. I talked with Whisterly before we left the company of the coven."

"Ah, I see. The divide-and-conquer maneuver. I know it well."

"Not exactly." Vinique offered Jack his glass, filled her own, and they both took a seat in the living room area.

Jack took a generous swallow. "Okay, spill it."

Vinique leaned in and squeezed his hand. "This might be difficult to hear."

"More difficult than the past few days? Hell, I hope not." Jack narrowed his eyes. "Is Whisterly okay? Is she not telling me something? Because if—"

"No—" A hint of a smile fell to her lips.

"How is this funny? You're tearing me up here."

"Jack, it's just that Whisterly had the same initial reaction. You two are perfect together. She's fine."

Jack shuddered out a breath. "Thank the Lord for that at least. Please, get on with it."

"Simon had a son."

Jack's eyes bulged.

"We found him when we began searching for homes for the abandoned children among the Night Dwellers. The commanders who reported to Simon, those who are still alive, are pretty tight-lipped about it all. As of yet, we haven't resorted to invasive telepathy on them. First, we'll exhaust other measures."

"How is he? And what of the mother?"

"The boy is an infant, a bit undernourished, but healthy otherwise. From what we've uncovered, it appears the mother died in childbirth. Apparently she wanted to have the baby in secrecy, to protect him from Simon. To give her child a better life, away from the leadership of the Night Dwellers."

"Sadly I completely understand."

"We've tested him. The boy is of Whisterly's bloodline. He'll have a future here, within the coven, if that's the route we choose... *You* choose."

Jack's gaze pinned her in place. "What exactly are you saying to me, Vinique?"

"Whisterly and you are the child's closest relatives. Next in line would be Arista, as his aunt. You could petition to raise him, and if granted, you could take him to Earth. I'm not sure what you've planned for you and Whisterly going forward, where you want to reside, or if a baby could fit into your future at all...just consider the possibility."

Jack's mind barreled ahead. He didn't need to consider. His answer was on the tip of his tongue, fighting to be set free. But he needed to talk with Whisterly. A baby...Simon's son... To have some part of him back... God, the wounds were so fresh. "I, uh, need to speak with Whisterly." A single tear escaped down his cheek. "But I won't turn my back on Simon's child."

"I understand. When we meet in a little while, I'll have the boy with me. That's why I wanted to speak to you both beforehand."

Jack nodded, already deep in thought, wrestling with the questions crowding his mind, when the door slid open. "Whisterly..." Pain etched the lines of her face. Jack wanted to erase every one. When she rushed toward him, he caught her in an embrace. Moving softly back and forth, Jack murmured, "Tell me now if you don't want this. I need to know before we see him." He leaned back, searching her eyes.

"With no doubts whatsoever, yes, I want him."

"God, I love you." Jack kissed Whisterly's forehead, before pressing his lips to hers. "Let's go meet our grandchild."

"You need to come and see us, Vinique. Soon." Jack and Whisterly gazed down at the little boy who already had their hearts wrapped up tight.

"As soon as your daughter returns to take over the helm, I'll plan a trip, set a date."

"I hear you, loud and clear," Arista cut in. "Stephen and I will return in a few weeks' time. Thanks for carrying the load in my absence."

Vinique canted her head. "I'm not complaining. I miss you. Your people miss you."

Arista kissed Vinique's cheek. "Understood."

Vinique flung her arms around Whisterly and Jack. "With the fierceness with which you love your children, this little guy better hold on with all his might."

"He's already got quite a grip." Jack freed his finger from the baby's fist and leaned into Vinique's hug.

"Did you decide on a name?"

Whisterly eyed Jack and gave a solemn nod. "His name is Samuel Henry Livingston," Jack answered, a note of pride ringing in his voice.

Belle leaned over the small bundle. "His eyes match yours, Mr. Jack."

"That's right, Belle, they do."

"Oh, and, Belle," Vinique added, "you better visit us often. Your training is still ongoing."

"I will. Just need to convince Ma and Pa first."

Their goodbyes said, the lot of them disappeared into the swirling winds as the vortex opened.

After spitting them back on Earth, the portal dissipated. Jack handed over the sleeping bundle to Whisterly. Gauging his son's distance, Jack prepared himself for the force of Daniel running at him full speed. The events of the past week had been tough on the boy.

One day soon, Daniel would accompany them to Remeon. Jack still wanted that experience for his son. But not yet. Not like this. The layers of Daniel's grief where Simon was concerned were just now being peeled away. The boy needed time.

"Lemme see... Lemme see him."

Jack scooped up Daniel and threw him on top of his shoulders. "How about from up high? How's this?" Daniel screeched his delight and howled even louder when Jack let him tumble into his arms. "Okay. Easy now. You gotta be careful. He's little, like Harrison."

Daniel peered at the tiny scrunched-up face, the baby's mouth busy sucking on his fist. "He looks hungry. We should feed him."

Jack's lip tipped up in a crooked smile. "Sounds about right. Just like you, always hungry."

"Uncle Harry said you named him after my dad."

"That's right—Samuel Henry—after two men I respected most in the world, except for Harry here of course. And we couldn't have two babies named Harry among us, now could we?" Jack made a face, prompting a cacophony of giggles from Daniel.

"I don't know," Daniel said. "That would be pretty funny."

Harry and Jack shook hands, then Harry yanked Jack closer. "You look like hell, man, you know that?"

"Yeah. I feel like it too."

"A baby. Simon's baby. This is big, Jack."

Jack's throat tightened. "The thing is, he's already worked his way into the core of me. Both of us. We already love him like he's our own."

Harry's answering grin wiped the tension from Jack's face. "Come on. Hand him over. That's it... Come on over to Uncle Harry. You and I have lots to talk about. Sammy, you and my Harry...you'll be best of friends. Grow up together and never leave each other."

Jack blinked back tears as Harry lightly bounced the baby in his arms.

"'Cause that's what best friends do. They're closer even than brothers. Like me and your old granddad," Harry choked out. "Don't worry. I'm an expert. I'll be here to teach you how."

"Harry, thank God you walked into my life that day on the train."

"Amen, brother," Harry whispered, settling Sammy back into Jack's arms.

"Wanna come over for opening gifts tomorrow?"

"Nah. Jack. You all need some space. I'll catch up with you in a day or two."

Jack slapped Harry on the back, his eyes misty, "Merry Christmas, Harry."

"Merry Christmas, Jack."

JACK HAD PROMISED Whisterly a Christmas she'd never forget. How could he ever top this, bringing home a baby the day before?

The morning had already been a blur; even so a peacefulness muffled the house. Jack rose early, filling her in on the mysteries of Santa Claus as Whisterly warmed a bottle for Sammy. "Shouldn't you have told me about this sooner? I feel like this is late. Very late. Now, on *the* day."

Jack kissed her, handed her his cup of coffee, and poured another. "I'll forgive that 'cause you're tired, it's Christmas, and I think I've gotten you addicted to coffee, *and* you haven't had your morning fix yet."

Whisterly took an eager sip. "How can I argue with a man who makes me coffee and pancakes?"

"Exactly. Don't."

"And syrup. Don't forget the syrup."

The day wore on in a hazy fog, a mixture of good food, festive decorations, perfectly selected gifts, and naps by the roaring fire with their newest addition. All this—threaded with the undercurrent of deep raw emotion brought to the surface with only a word or glance.

Whisterly had invited Rae to join them, but understandably, she'd declined. The poor girl was dealing with so much. Christmas, on top of the sudden loss of the man who she'd planned to marry one day. Add a baby to the mix that neither she nor Simon knew about, and that would make the day almost unbearable for the poor girl. Whisterly would keep trying. Simon gave his heart to Rae; she belonged here among his family.

Silence wove among them like a living being, beating and pulsing, competing with the crackle and pop of the fire as the flames reached their glowing fingers into the room. Simon's gifts to all them were the only packages still under the tree.

A smile crept up Daniel's face. "I'll hand out the rest of the gifts."

"And we'll take turns opening them," Jack added.

"Sure, Papa," Daniel agreed over his shoulder.

Simon and Daniel had spent quite a bit of time together, especially over the past few weeks, as Daniel had schooled Simon on the meaning of Christmas. Many late evenings found the two of them huddled together, deep in conversation over Jesus's birth or the veracity of an earthly Santa Claus.

"You first, Thomas," Daniel urged.

"Why me first?"

"'Cause I helped just a little on yours."

"Oh...okay." Thomas ripped the paper off the gift and stared in openmouthed shock. Turning the carving over in hands, he murmured, "It's an eagle."

Daniel bobbed his head. "Simon wouldn't settle for any other bird. He said only this one would do because it represents—"

"Freedom..." Thomas murmured.

"Right. So I helped him find one by the cliff, along the edge of the woods. We went back to the same spot each day for him to carve this, until he was done."

Thomas locked eyes with Jack, then dropped his misty gaze.

"You're next, Arista," Jack said.

Arista slowly tore the paper away from the small box and raised the lid. "It's a cross."

"Made of cedar. Simon came to me for help with cutting it from the wood. The rest of the finishing work was his. Want me to help you put it on?" Jack asked. Arista nodded; Jack latched the necklace around her neck.

"Smells divine. How about you next, Papa?"

"Sure."

Daniel shuffled the few remaining gifts and picked out his father's. Thomas shifted uneasily in his seat.

"A book of poetry by T.S. Eliot—" Jack murmured.

"I uh..." Thomas began, "Simon asked me what kind of poetry you might read. Hell, Jack. I didn't know. But I remembered my dad commenting on this guy. I was so shocked Simon asked me. I thought he was joking at first."

"Regardless, excellent choice. He's one of my favorites." Jack lifted the cover, read the handwritten note inside. *"Papa, For your love of words. Yours aren't lost on me."* Jack's voice wavered. *"Merry Christmas. Love, Simon."*

"Now you, Whisterly." Daniel passed the gift to her.

Whisterly held the item, closed her eyes, and sniffed. "I have an idea what it is." A knowing smile pursed her lips.

"Simon knew you had some problems adjusting to sleeping here on Earth. I worked with him on a potion—all via telepathy. He did all the work," Arista said.

"I can't wait to try it out."

"Just me and Belle left," Daniel said. "Here's yours, Belle."

Belle ripped into the present and held up a beautifully intricate carving. She beamed. "The little people of the forest."

"Simon said he'd seen them firsthand because of you and couldn't wait to get the image out of his head and into solid form. He spent hours trying to get all the details just right," Jack added.

"It's perfect."

"Now me," Daniel exclaimed, excitement and wonder warring on his face. He made quick work of the wrapping, then stared in awe. "I'm not sure what this is, but it looks really neat."

"Well, don't look at me, sport." Jack shrugged. Whisterly waved her hand. "It's an enchanted device. Simon used magic to store some Remeon bedtime stories on there. With the alternate endings included, there are over one hundred variations. All spoken in Simon's voice. All he had to do was speak a sample into it, and his voice was replicated throughout the collection. It is extraordinary. I want to hear one of the stories when you give it a go. We'll have Sammy listen too."

"Wow... Can we try it out tonight?"

"What do you think, Jack?"

"You bet, son." Jack scanned the room. "Seems to me Simon learned the meaning of Christmas in record time, coming to each of us for help with another. I'm amazed—a straight-up Christmas miracle in my opinion."

Belle wiggled her way in between Whisterly and Jack.

"What is it, honey?" Whisterly asked.

"Well, Simon can't go back to the coven, and that's bad, right?" Belle's eyebrows lifted in question.

"Among my kind, it is thought so, yes."

"He had a place to be. He wanted you both to know that."

Jack leaned in closer, a groove forming in his forehead. "Explain what you mean, Belle."

"He has a place among the light, with the little people."

Whisterly took Belle's hands. "Does that mean you can communicate with Simon?"

"Well, sorta. But it's more like a feeling." Belle tilted her chin. "Think of how you feel and what you smell after a spring rain cools the air or when a brisk breeze brushes over your skin. That's how it is most of the time. Words are more difficult to pick out..."

Jack's mouth snapped open as he and Whisterly shared a glance. "Can you teach us?" Whisterly asked.

"I'll try. But it's different for people who aren't like me...and Simon."

## 26

*C*hristmas came and went. Four days later, Arista, Thomas, and Belle traveled to visit Thomas's and Belle's parents, making Jack's house feel too empty...abandoned. With the loss of Simon still fresh and raw, Jack and Whisterly threw themselves into the constant busyness of caring for the baby. Nights were hard at first, but once awake, Jack could rock Sammy for hours, feeding him, then lulling him back to sleep. Some nights, awakened by his little brother, Daniel would come in, insisting that they weren't *doing it right*.

So they'd let him take over for a bit, and more times than not, both Sam and Daniel would be asleep ten minutes later. Occasionally Whisterly or Jack would wake to find Daniel asleep on the floor next to Sam's cradle, shivering from the cold. The boy rarely let Sam out of his sight, except for at night, when exhaustion mandated his attention.

Daniel dealt with Simon's death in small spurts. One day at a time. At first Daniel had been inconsolable, oscillating between sadness and anger, convinced that somehow Simon would find his way back to him. It didn't help that Simon's service was held on Remeon, without Daniel, so Jack requested a private ceremony at their church, just for family—and brothers from another mother—held three days after Christmas. Jack, Whisterly, Daniel, Thomas, Arista, Belle, Rae, Harry, and Maggie attended. If nothing else, the service helped to solidify for Daniel the fact that Simon was gone and wouldn't be returning.

Jack had thought so anyway, until his son told the pastor on the way out that his brother was special and he'd be coming back from the dead and that God could wait his turn for Simon.

Jack fought the insane laughter rising in his throat but lost that battle because, hell, it was true. People came back to life on Remeon. Jack's wife was living proof. But Simon's case wasn't the same, and Jack didn't quite know how to explain the difference to Daniel.

At the time, Daniel's outburst hadn't helped the situation much. The pastor's eyes had filled with concern, his gaze bouncing back and forth from Jack to Whisterly, like he wanted them to do something. Then came the look of pity in the man's eyes. The truth was, Daniel was working through his grief as best he could. Jack and Whisterly would be there for him with plenty of space and time to do so.

Rae had crumbled during the service. Jack and Whisterly tried to be there for her too. Where the hell were the girl's parents? Odd that they'd never met them. Simon had. Shouldn't they be here for their daughter?

Afterward, Rae had asked for distance, saying she needed time away to get over the loss of Simon, so she could find a way forward again.

"Anytime you need us, we're here," Whisterly had assured her. "We'd love to see you. But you decide when."

With tears in her eyes, Rae said she'd be in touch.

One day last week, Jack and Whisterly spotted Rae from a window in the kitchen. Rae had lingered at the edge of the forest, swaying back and forth. Maybe she'd sensed Simon's presence there? She didn't come to the house, and they didn't go to her. She needed to make peace and say goodbye in her own way.

In the cold chill of a January morning a week after New Year's, Jack fed Sammy and crawled back into bed, praying for a few more minutes of quiet before their day started.

"Jack, your feet are cold." Whisterly inched away from him.

"Not for long if I have my way."

"*Mmm,*" she murmured.

"Baby?"

"Just a few more minutes..."

Jack pulled her on top of him. "I need to ask you something."

She nodded against his chest.

"Will you go with me to the mine site? I want to take Daniel, Arista too, if she can disappear for the day with us."

Whisterly opened her eyes, still blurry with sleep. "Sure, later..."

Jack held her, while she drifted back to sleep, kissing her head as heavy even breaths took her under again. He smiled against her cheek, grateful to have her close. Running his fingers through Whisterly's hair, their hearts thudded in a singular rhythm, his thoughts easing back into hers. And in the calm that followed, he let his own eyelids sag shut. The day would come for them soon enough.

THEIR OLD STOMPING ground felt just the same. The mine was closed, boarded up, but the surrounding countryside hadn't changed much. The trees were taller though. Today a light snow fell, dusting the ground with a fluffy white coating. Jack picked his way to the tree—his and Sam's tree—the baby wrapped in a blanket snug in his arms. Daniel scurried to keep up; Arista and Whisterly trailed a few steps behind.

"That's where you used to work, Papa?" Arista asked.

"Yep. That's the place."

"Looks creepy," Daniel blurted out. "Can we go in and explore?"

"No, Daniel." Jack shook his head emphatically. "It's dangerous. One wrong move and you could fall to your death, son." Daniel swallowed hard and grabbed Jack's hand, his eyes trained on the old mine entrance, like it just might suck him in.

Whisterly threw out a blanket. "I know it's kind of chilly for a picnic, guys, but did you know Papa and Sam used to eat their lunches right here under this tree?"

"Wow, that sounds like a long time ago, Papa."

"True. A lifetime ago, son."

"Come on, Daniel." Whisterly held out her hand. "We'll take a quick look around before we eat. Arista, do you want to come too?"

"Sure," she answered, tossing a worried glance at Jack.

"Go. Sammy and I will be here, holding down the fort, keeping warm." Scooting down the tree trunk, Jack situated himself on the blanket, baby Sam sleeping soundly in his arms. Jack dragged in air and let it loose, his breath coming out in puffs of mist, hovering in the cold afternoon.

As his eyes closed, the years came tumbling back. Except this time, Sam came out of the mine and trudged up the hill to meet Jack, as they'd planned all those years ago before the world had blasted to hell.

"You look tired, Jack."

"Sam. I was hoping you'd come."

His lips broke into a smile. "This little guy here means I'm a great-grandpa. May I?"

Jack handed little Sammy to his much bigger namesake and waited for the pair to get comfortable.

Sunlight broke free from the snow clouds and glistened on Sam and Sammy, bathing their faces in warmth and light as he babbled nonsense to the baby.

"Now you're just showing off. Did you commission those beams just for us?"

"Hell, what fun is it if I can't share it with you two?"

"What if you could do it all over again, Sam? Would you? I've wished you back to life so many times I've lost count."

"I haven't. The number is 1,052. The latest one last night before you went to bed."

Jack barked a laugh. "Yeah, that sounds about right."

"Nope. No take backs. No do-overs. I accomplished exactly what I was supposed to during my time, even if it was cut short by human standards. And you are too."

Jack nodded, too full of emotion to speak.

"This little one, plus Daniel, Arista, Simon, and Thomas... through them—your legacy—your love is yielding results."

"Simon? I failed my son miserably from the beginning, Sam."

"No, Jack, you brought him love and welcomed him into a life he'd never known before. You'll see him again. Someday." A smile full of satisfaction stretched Sam's lips. "I'm proud to have had a small part in your life, son."

"Small? You're everything to me, Sam."

"And you're everything to Arista, Simon, Daniel, Sammy, Thomas, and Whisterly, along with so many others. I'm so proud of you. Now go. Finish the race, Jack."

Jack's gaze met Sam's and in their depths, experienced an outpouring love.

"Feel that? That's just a small sampling of what those kids feel for you, and Whisterly of course." Sam kissed the baby's forehead and passed him back to Jack. "Glad you came to me almost full grown. I wouldn't have known then what to do with one of these."

"You knew exactly what I needed, Sam."

"The world's not done with you yet, Start-Up." Sam kissed the top of Jack's head and straightened. "Look alive, son."

Time paused, steeling Jack in place, hugging him tight. Tears slid down his cheeks as he lifted his gaze and watched Sam saunter away. At the last second, before his form dissipated, Sam turned, winked, then faded into the whiteout of the newly fallen snow. A smile spread across Jack's face. "Figures you'd take the little bit of sun away with you."

*You've got your own burst of light heading your way Jack. Incoming...*

Jack wiped his face with one hand and held tight to Sam with the other. Daniel ran up the hill, struggling to keep his footing in the slippery snow. "Can we eat now? I'm starving."

Jack chuckled, and the heavy-handed ghost of his biological father's past, decades ingrained, shifted, then loosened its grip inside Jack's chest. He sucked in a deep breath. "Sure, sport. Here. Take Sammy for a minute."

Jack waited for Whisterly, his gaze fixed on the warm smile that graced her lips. He drew her into an embrace and kissed her, gentle and slow.

"What is it, Jack?"

Jack cupped her cheeks. "My father—I've finally kicked him outta my head for good."

"It's about time. You're nothing like him, from what you've told me of the man."

Relief rippled through him. "No. God help him, I'm not."

"Well, what's changed?"

Jack suppressed a smile. "Someone gave me a good swift kick in the ass—over the course of many years—and reminded me that the truth lives on in my family. I'm a slow learner. It finally hit home."

Whisterly leaned her forehead against his. "Thank the gods, Jack."

Arista topped the hill. "It's pretty here, Papa."

Jack reached out his hand and joined her. "In some ways, I guess. More so now with that wretched mine shut down."

"Hey, come on," Whisterly called out. "Let's eat, you guys. The soup in the thermos is still warm."

Jack grabbed Arista's hand. "Let's go, sweetheart, before Daniel eats everyone's lunch."

BELLE WANDERED into the forest on the outskirts of the farm, eager to have time alone after finishing her chores for the day. Intent on her task, deeper and deeper she trudged, the brisk walk warming her as the wind whipped through her hair, stray branches tugging at her coat along the way.

A familiar clearing spread wide before her. She dropped to a log and gathered handfuls of dirt, murmuring the words that would summon her companions to her—the little people. At once a spark ignited, and in minutes, their brilliant shimmer painted the space around her. She reveled in their twinkling glow, drinking in their light. Today would be the day, she hoped.

"Simon," she whispered to the wind. "Simon..."

Belle paused, closed her eyes, a breeze chilling her as Simon's presence washed through her. Twirling about, she giggled. Everywhere she felt him, smelled him, and when she blinked her eyes open, the bright lights had rearranged. She shrieked. Before her, they had formed one word.

*Belle.*

*Simon—we did it. And this is only the beginning!*

# EPILOGUE

November 1958

*T*he magical energy hissed, the force from the vortex forming, humming, and vibrating in the air. Jack held on tight to the two ten-year-olds—not a small feat—who knew better but were still prone to run through the opening the second a familiar face appeared. "Calm down, you two. They've only been gone a week." The portal winked shut, Jack's signal to turn the two natives loose, and, with laughter bubbling in his throat, Jack looked on while Sam and Harrison plowed into Daniel first, then Harry.

Harry... God, the years weighed on both of them, had taken a harsh toll in many respects. He and Harry had been to hell and back more times than Jack cared to count. But the signs of age showed more prominently on Harry, and he wasn't much older than Jack.

Small creases lined Harry eyes, crow's feet pronounced, his laugh lines more prominent, and Harry wore glasses to read now. Not that Jack paid that much attention to the matter... But Whisterly informed Jack that they both appeared about the age of thirty-five-year-olds here on Earth.

Evidently the witches' predictions had been correct. That nasty concoction he'd drunk during Whisterly's reintegration did provide some age-halting properties for Jack. To Jack, Harry appeared decidedly distinguished, settled, and happy. His friend had proudly earned every mark of distinction on his face.

A satisfied smile swept across Jack's face as he turned his attention to the reunion in progress. Daniel bent low to accept the boys' hugs and pointed the two toward Harry, close on Daniel's heels. Daniel, at nineteen, the embodiment of confidence, youth, and health.

And to hear Arista tell it, breaking hearts all over the compound. Jack pulled Daniel into a hug. "Welcome home, son." Harry threw out a hand to Jack, a boy clinging to both legs. "And to you too, Harry. As you can see, you've been missed."

"Ah...always fun to get away. Gave me some time to think about that offer we have on the table, and as a side bar, got to watch this kid of yours in action. Uh, Jack...kids are growing up so much smarter than we were. How's that possible?"

"Whoa now? What action?"

"You know there's someone special, Papa. Gia is her name. Remember?"

"Just don't go using the *L* word to pull her through the portal. Not yet."

Daniel raised a brow. "For someone who married at seventeen, I'm already a bit behind the eight ball, right?"

"Different times and unusual circumstances, son."

"Uh-huh. So I've heard. I'm in no hurry, like I've told you a million times before. But I do have a surprise for you, Papa."

The energy of the portal initiated again, anchored this time by Daniel.

Jack waited, praying that his son was true to his word and that Gia wasn't the one coming through right now.

"Vinique." *Thank God.*

Daniel grinned. *I heard that, Papa.*

"Jack, I hope you don't mind the impromptu visit. Your son here is so convincing. I mean, who can resist that face?"

"Not at all. Glad to see you." Jack looped an arm over her shoulder. "Not much has changed since the last time you visited, except for these two weeds."

"Arista and Thomas send their love."

"And my little princess? How is she?"

"Renia is adorable and has Thomas wrapped around her little finger."

"As it should be. I can hardly believe she's five already."

"She's going to be a force of steel one day. Thomas is training her in combat maneuvers, disguised as play of course, and Arista feeds her a steady diet of witchcraft. She's soaking it all up with ease."

"Can't say I'm surprised that my granddaughter is a genius."

"So is your grandson. Sammy is as powerful as Simon was. Maybe more so. We need to discuss when he'll spend a significant amount of time with us, Jack. It needs to be soon."

Jack dipped his head in silent acknowledgment. "I know. Talk to Whisterly while you're here. She's dragging her feet, and I understand why... She doesn't want the magical forces on Remeon to overpower him, even though Sammy has been in training all his life. But the boy is patient, strong, and kind. He'll be ready for immersion, when the time comes."

"I agree, Jack, but Whisterly needs to have faith in that too. By the way, Harry confided in me regarding the decision you both have to make."

"Yeah. I'd like your input."

"Good." Vinique leaned into Jack's ear. "Take it. Sounds like a wonderful opportunity. Perfect for both of you. Fits right in with your unique set of experience and skills."

"You think so?" Jack counted heads as they filed into the car. "Tight fit. Everyone squeeze."

"Yes, I do. They'll be extremely fortunate to have you both."

Jack eyed the back seat through the rearview mirror, unable to hide the smile creeping up his face.

"Harrison, son, you reek."

"Sammy hogged the shower this morning, after we went shooting. Not my fault, Dad."

"Come on now..."

The back seat jiggled with laughter. A hand fell to Jack's shoulder. *It's good to be home, Papa.*

*Missed you, son.*

"I guess Whisterly knows you're here, Vinique?"

"Of course, Jack. Do I really have to remind you that your mate knows all?"

"No... I've known since I was seventeen that I was hopelessly outsmarted. Nothing has changed over the years in that regard. But dense as I can be at times, I sense you're not telling me something."

Daniel chuckled in the back seat.

"*Shh*, back there," Vinique scolded. "I don't like having my hand forced by my nephew."

Jack raised an eyebrow. "Vinique..."

"Jack..." she mimicked, a hint of laughter in her voice.

"Who is he?"

"I'm obligated to officially tell my sister first, and I would have on my own timetable, if not for your inquisitive son."

"I see... Good work, Daniel."

"Thanks, Papa."

Jack squeezed Vinique's hand. "Does he make you happy? Is he good to you?"

"Very happy. So good, Jack."

Jack's lips broke into a smile. "Then I'm on board, little sis. I can't wait to hear more."

THE SOUNDS of laughter and conversation floated from the kitchen into the small study that extended off the den. Jack poured a whiskey for himself and Harry. "It's good to hear them all together again. A week seems like an eternity when Daniel's away." Jack raised his gaze to Harry. "You too of course."

"Missed you this trip, Jack."

"The boys and I kept busy. Whisterly is struggling with changes Sammy is going through. In her head, she's making up for Simon. I, for one, completely understand that destructive thought process." Jack sighed and took a large swallow of his drink. "Translation...I was needed here."

"Understandable."

"Well, shall we?"

"Sure. Let's talk."

"Business is booming. Five years ago, when you finally agreed to become a full partner, damn, I was thrilled. You know the story. Even with Daniel's help and the manual labor we hire, we can barely meet the demand. I want to continue that growth, Harry. This latest opportunity..." Jack shook his head and laughed. "I don't think I can pass it up. It's a dream in the making. But I'm not prepared to give up my lifelong dream either—our business. So lay it on me, man. What are your thoughts?"

"I'm blown away by the chance to work with NASA. The connection we've had with NACA over the years has paid off in grand style, Jack. Better than we'd ever imagined. So...what if we could do both?"

"I'm listening."

"Stay with me a minute here. We contract with NASA, become consultants, negotiate a retainer of sorts. Work with them on essential projects, moving in and out as needed. Keep them hungry for our services, so they'll come back for more, but always leave them satisfied, providing exactly what they need. That way we can call the shots. Meanwhile, most of our time could still be here, in the thick of the business, doing what we love. On a side note, we'll want to be selective about the projects we agree to, or we'll get buried and divorced fast."

Jack pressed his lips together. "We'd have to be in DC for meetings occasionally. No doubt about that."

"Easily arranged. One of us could plan to stay here, and from time to time, Daniel could handle the office a few days solo." Harry chuckled and slapped Jack on the back. "We've done a great job with him."

"Yeah. We have." Jack tipped back his drink and poured them both another. "Harry, damn...this could work. How many people can look back and say they helped their country get a man into outer space?"

Harry flashed a grin. "Well, I guess us, Jack."

"Let's call with our proposal. What do you say? Are you ready now?"

"Hell, yeah. It's worth a shot. What have we got to lose? First things first though. Let's run it by the bosses, Whisterly and Maggie."

BELLE HAD STRUGGLED with the decision for years, always determining that the best course of action was to keep quiet, after the initial conversation with Jack and Whisterly regarding communication with Simon. Was she hurting anyone by keeping the secret, more so than tearing up that healed wound?

Over time Belle had committed herself to developing more

meaningful communication with Simon, often to the exclusion of all else. What that said about her made her too uncomfortable to put much deeper thought into the matter, other than she'd continue down that path. How could she not? They were kindred beings now.

Ma and Pa had been her greatest source of strength—and Thomas. After seeing the toll of this secret shared with Thomas over time, that had been the final straw for Belle. Keeping this knowledge from Arista had ripped him up inside. So Belle would start with her sister-in-law and would work her way up to Whisterly and Jack.

Every year after harvest, Belle spent the fall with them—the Livingstons. From August to September they were all together. Daniel was like a second brother, and since his initiation into Remeon, when he'd turned thirteen, they could communicate telepathically. He'd never stopped idolizing Simon.

Words continued to fail her when she contemplated sharing her secret with someone who didn't understand the complexity of what Simon had become, what had really happened. The invitation that Simon had accepted in the forest the winter before his transformation had been binding. And, at the moment when Simon's body failed, his essence had lived on through the little people of the forest, whose existence was tied to the lifeblood pumping and renewing within the earth.

That same power had flowed through Belle for as long as she could remember. The odd reality of her abilities was too much for most people, so Belle didn't bother to explain. People just saw her as supersmart, intelligent, or skilled in odd ways. But Belle's unusual gifts came from those capable Fae beings, and one day she'd return home to the little people.

"You about ready, Belle?" Pa shifted in the rocker, turning his attention to his daughter as she cleared the door. She tipped her face up to his, giving him a warm smile, and reached for his hand. Pa insisted on walking her to the portal each time. His way of participating in her extraterrestrial adventures.

When she'd return, he'd eagerly soak up her latest adventures but vowed never to go to the "strange planet" himself. Thomas had been wearing down Pa recently, encouraging him to visit, with the hope that their parents would eventually acquiesce.

Since the birth of their granddaughter, Renia, Pa's tone had changed. A twinkle sparkled in his eyes when he spoke of her. Personally Belle predicted Pa would cave. Soon. Very soon. They settled into a slow pace, walking toward the portal.

"What is it, Belle?"

"What do I say to Arista, and eventually to Jack, Whisterly, and Daniel? I'm not sure I know how to do this."

"You tell them they've been granted a gift—a way to communicate again with Simon."

"They won't understand."

"I imagine not. Not at first. But, just like with us, you'll guide them, sweetheart, and they'll know him on a totally different level."

"I've kept this secret a long time. What if they don't want to?"

"Then it's their loss."

Belle bowed her head. "It's a precious gift, Pa."

"They'll feel that through you. Now go. Nobody else can do this but you, Belle."

She met her pa's gaze. "You remembered when I said those same words to you, and it's been so many years."

Pa nodded and whispered gruffly, "Think what would have happened if you'd not gone back that day to help Whisterly— or rather what *wouldn't* have happened."

Belle fell into his arms. "Thank you, Pa. See you soon."

An unsettled energy snapped to life, filling the air with its magical essence. The trees fought the intrusion with their haughty sway and jiggly dance but ceded to the invasive power, as they always did.

With a quick pivot, Belle waved and disappeared seconds before the vortex collapsed.

James stared into the emptiness, where the void had opened, and paced back and forth, stopping occasionally to toss a glance back to the spot, where Belle had crossed from one planet to the next.

Fifteen minutes later, his decision made, James hurried for home.

"Elizabeth?" James called from the door, out of breath from his run.

"What's the matter? Is Belle all right?" she asked in a flurry of words.

"Elizabeth," he said through a grin, sweeping her into his arms, "pack a bag—we're going to Remeon." Her mouth dropped open, and James leaned in and kissed the surprise off her face. "Not today." He grinned. "But soon. Damn, after all this time it feels good to say that."

JACK, Whisterly, and Daniel sat staring at each other, silently listening to the clock ticking the seconds away, linked in their own telepathic communication as they awaited Belle's arrival. Wringing her hands together, Whisterly sighed. Jack reached for her, stilling her movement. The waiting was awful—agreed. She lifted her gaze to his, speaking volumes without words or telepathy. Jack kissed her fingers. It had been almost ten years since Simon's death.

Ten long years...

Each year since then, Belle had returned right around harvest time. To visit. Catch up. She was family. But her homecoming would be different this time.

Daniel shot to his feet. "She's here!"

Jack disentangled himself and strode for the door ahead of her knock. "Belle." Her name eased from Jack's lips, taking with it the tension that coursed through him. "Finally." He folded her into a hug. "It's good to see you," Jack whispered against her ear. Belle pulled away, her eyes blurring with tears. "Come. Sit. Would you like a drink? Water? Coffee? Tea?"

"No. Nothing for me. Not now," she added, stepping into the foyer.

Jack led her into the den. "I wish you would have let me pick you up from the station."

"It's okay, Jack," Belle said through a small smile. "More than ever now, I value my time alone."

"Belle!" Whisterly and Daniel circled her in a group hug. "You must be tired from your trip. Have a seat?" Whisterly asked.

"No. I'd rather not." Belle took a step back. "I want you all to know I never intended to hide the information I had about Simon. I just didn't know how to explain, or what that commentary, if anything, would offer you, except perhaps additional sorrow. I did confide in Thomas because...well, because it was tearing me up inside."

"Belle." Whisterly took her hands in hers. "I'm sorry for your pain. I wish we could have helped you bear it in some way. We knew you had a connection, from what you'd mentioned after Simon was attacked. We assumed you'd tell us more when you were ready." Whisterly and Jack shared a glance. "Over the years we'd decided your relationship within the realm of the little people wasn't one we could share."

Belle wiped tears from her cheeks. "I wasn't sure you could either. But I've experimented with different connections— Simon and I have. Telepathy for one. Before him, my communion with the little people has always been magical...effortless. But I think I've found a way that might forge a bond among all of us." Belle swiped at her face once more as her shoulders shook. "Words are...difficult to formulate. You won't hear many —maybe none at all."

Jack swallowed hard. Words? He would have never imagined possibilities such as this. "Understood."

"Where's Sammy?" Belle asked.

Echoes of Sammy's footsteps abruptly ended as he poked his head into the room. "Here I am, Belle."

Belle crouched, addressing the boy. "Your daddy loves you. He told me so."

Jack nodded to his grandson, meeting his inquisitive gaze. Then Sammy tilted his head, studying Belle.

Jack and Whisterly hadn't kept secrets from Sammy regarding his father or Sammy's heritage as a warlock. In fact, the opposite was true. He spent his days immersed in the craft and everything Remeon. Whisterly saw to that. Soon, Sammy would spend larger and larger chunks of time on his home planet for in-depth training with Arista, Vinique, and the coven.

The boy was ready.

Disciplined, and strong of character, Sammy made Jack and Whisterly proud beyond words, but it was time. The magic within Remeon already called to him, pulsing through his veins like a drug. Earth couldn't offer the same training ground. The intrinsic forces weren't the same.

"Let's go." Belle led the small procession into the forest. When they arrived at the clearing where she had first introduced Simon to the little people, she hesitated, as if listening. "Here... They're here."

Like a starving man, bereft of food, barely able to contain himself, Jack rasped, "What do we do, Belle?"

"Connect your consciousnesses. All of you, with me. Try not to be alarmed when they come. Or when you feel their essence pass through you."

Jack gave Belle a startled glance and squeezed Whisterly's hand. Sammy wiggled his way through his grandparents and Daniel, until he reached Belle. "I'm ready. Show me."

"Indeed, you are."

The small pockets of light in the distance drew closer, brighter. Hundreds, maybe thousands, of tiny beings clad in brilliance surrounded them. There was no way to tell.

"Open your thoughts, your minds," Belle invited.

Closing his eyes, Jack held Whisterly in front of him, his arms crossed over her chest, when an unnatural rush of air whisked between them. Gulping a breath, Jack's skin prickled, while his son's spirit swept through him. Simon... Jack's eyes snapped open. He smelled his son, sensed the presence that was uniquely Simon.

*Pa...pa.*

The syllables came to Jack, slow and uneven. Tears stung his eyes. *My God... Son?*

Ahead, Sammy called out, "Father?" Pinpoints of sparkling light encircled the boy, and he giggled, darting among them.

Jack turned Whisterly around to face him, tugging her closer, wiping tears from his face. "Baby, I never thought anything could surpass telepathy. But this...What is this?"

Speechless, Whisterly leaned her forehead against Jack's and kissed him. "You're asking the wrong person." They both homed in on Sammy. "Go to him," she said, gifting Jack a smile.

Emotion rising in his throat, Jack made his way to Sammy and fell to one knee as the boy crashed into him. "Papa, it's Father."

"It is, son."

"The little people will teach me, Papa."

Jack's eyes held Belle's watery gaze. Then, nestling Sammy to his chest, Jack chuckled. "I have no doubt, son."

A soft joyful sound drifted on the breeze. *Laughter? Simon?* Jack's gaze slid to Belle's as her grin broadened, telling him all he needed to know. And in the twinkling brilliance, Jack joined in, his heart light and full.

## End of book

Hope you enjoyed reading *Remeon's Legacy*! Visit my website (www.jwgarrett.com) to join my newsletter list and keep up-to-date on all upcoming releases.

# ABOUT THE AUTHOR

J.W. Garrett is a multi-award winning author and has been writing in one form or another since she was a teenager. Her early love of the fantasy genre goes all the way back to elementary school when she read the Hobbit for the very first time, and she's been hooked ever since. She currently lives in Florida with her family where she writes speculative fiction from the sunny beaches of Jacksonville, but she'll always love the mountains of Virginia where she was born.

Her writings include novels for young and old alike, as well as short stories and poetry. When she's not hanging out with her characters, her favorite activities are reading, running and spending time with family.

You can visit the author and sign up for her newsletter at: www.jwgarrett.com

## DEAR READER

Thanks so much for reading! I had so much fun writing this final book in the Realms of Chaos series. I hope you enjoyed *Remeon's Legacy* and the journeys of all the characters in this last installment. They are your family now too.

I'd love to hear from you! Please consider leaving a book review at your favorite site, or feel free to drop me a note at my website at: www.jwgarrett.com.

Until next time,

J.W. Garrett